PRAISE F

MW00773594

Alternate Endings

"A complex story of a woman at a complex part of life—Bea's story is told with humor and care, and the romance Rosen crafts for her is gentle and tender and so satisfying."

—Kate Clayborn, *USA Today* bestselling author of *The Other Side of Disappearing*

"I adored Bea and Jack's second-chance love story. Their chemistry and banter are top shelf, Rosen's prose is witty and insightful, and the Irish setting is gloriously realized. I'll be the first one at the table for every story Rosen wants to tell."

—Emma Barry, author of *Chick Magnet*

"Ali writes the kind of characters I want to be friends with in real life and gives them the beautiful love stories they deserve. *Alternate Endings* is the perfect blend of sharp wit, delicious tension, and breathless romance that will have you yearning from the onset and thinking of it long after you've reached the end. A must read in 2024!"

—Tarah DeWitt, *USA Today* bestselling author of *Savor It*

Recipe for Second Chances

"As a reader and a writer, I am always over the moon when I find a new author with a refreshing, wonderful new voice. Such is the case with *Recipe for Second Chances*—I couldn't turn the pages fast enough. When I got to the last page, I felt sad that the story was over. I wanted more. To me, that is the mark of a really good writer."

—Fern Michaels, author of 153 (and counting) *New York Times* bestselling novels

"*Recipe for Second Chances* is the ultimate 'one who got away' romance—especially for lovers of lusty chemistry, glamorous locales, and decadent cuisine. A heartwarming, escapist treat!"

—Tia Williams, *New York Times* bestselling author of
Seven Days in June

"*Recipe for Second Chances* is a sweet, utterly charming romance that swept me away to the Italian countryside, and I never wanted to return! Full of lush settings and mouthwatering food, I absolutely loved every delicious morsel of this book."

—Lynn Painter, *New York Times* bestselling author of
Better Than the Movies

"This tender, sun-drenched tale of second chances and emotional growth unfolds as richly as ricotta—livened by the lemon tang of the past. *Recipe for Second Chances* will sweep readers away against a vivid backdrop of luscious food and heartwarming friendships."

—Jen Comfort, author of *Midnight Duet*

"Great banter, a sexy good-guy hero, and the kind of strong female friendships we all love to lean on—plus Italian truffles and chocolate cake. I'm in!"

—Elizabeth Bard, bestselling author of *Lunch in Paris* and
Picnic in Provence

Ali's Cookbooks

"I found this book to be a life preserver of the highest order."
—Andrew Zimmern, Emmy- and James Beard Award–winning TV
host, chef, and writer

"Ali Rosen is saving our dinner parties one dish at a time."
—Carla Hall, chef and television host

Unlikely Story

OTHER TITLES BY ALI ROSEN

Alternate Endings

Recipe for Second Chances

Cookbooks

Modern Freezer Meals

Bring It!

15 Minute Meals

ALI ROSEN

 Montlake

Text copyright © 2025 by Ali Rosen
All rights reserved.

No part of this book may be reproduced, or stored in a retrieval system, or transmitted in any form or by any means, electronic, mechanical, photocopying, recording, or otherwise, without express written permission of the publisher.

Published by Montlake, Seattle

www.apub.com

Amazon, the Amazon logo, and Montlake are trademarks of Amazon.com, Inc., or its affiliates.

ISBN-13: 9781662527920 (paperback)
ISBN-13: 9781662527937 (digital)

Cover design and illustration by Liz Casal

Printed in the United States of America

To Annie:
I hope letting George live on through this book gives you a smile—even if I respect that you'll watch a '90s action movie a thousand times before reading this novel.

Psychologically, I'm very confused . . . But
personally, I don't feel bad at all.
—*The Shop Around the Corner*

She had blue skin,
And so did he.
He kept it hid
And so did she.
They searched for blue
Their whole life through,
Then passed right by
And never knew.
—Shel Silverstein

CHAPTER 1

The one upside of being a therapist is that everyone around you always assumes you have it all figured out.

Except, of course, your own therapist.

If I was in front of a patient, my hands clasped and sitting up straight, they would know I'm listening, engaged, and ready to help them conquer their problems.

But I'm sitting in front of Ari, and she knows that today it's a tactic. It's a way for me to stay quiet. She sees my thumbs gently circling each other and clocks that it's a way for me to stay in motion unobtrusively.

"How was your holiday weekend?" I ask, hoping I can delay whatever Ari has for me on this Tuesday evening.

"It was fine," she says without pause. "Anything happen over yours that you want to discuss?"

Ari tilts her head and levels her most patient stare at me. When she's looking at me like this, she reminds me of my dog, George. Both are focused and unyielding, with wiry black hair sticking out without care. The only two creatures on earth who somehow see through my reserved facade.

Thank goodness one of them can't talk.

Although that doesn't help me right now, when I'm in front of the one who can.

"I had a barbecue with my parents and brother," I answer, avoiding getting to today's real topic. "And it was exactly as you'd imagine—my mom accidentally bought spicy sausages instead of hot dogs and left the ice cream out on the counter. So it wasn't exactly a raging success, but we had fun."

"I'm hoping that means you didn't take on the meal yourself," Ari says in her pointed way.

"Nope," I reply quickly, leaving out that I *did* have that impulse. I wanted to take over the way I would've when I was a kid, whenever my hapless parents inevitably wandered away: picking up the tongs and standing awkwardly at the smoky grill so that my brother wouldn't end up with only a bun for dinner. But Ari has taught me to use my ability to contain for my own good. So that wasn't this weekend's story, thankfully.

Instead I say, "My mom lit her illegal balcony grill; my dad cheered for her; she burned everything. And I just stood and watched."

Ari cracks a smile because she, of course, is well aware of my parents' ineptitude, so this back seat boundary drawing is considered a win. I know she'll let it go as long as it isn't hurting me.

I'm used to it at this point, so it rarely does.

"So. What's got you all sullen today, Nora?" she asks, changing the subject now that she's satisfied that my parents aren't today's problem, the dart she's been aiming finally able to be let go.

"I'm not sullen." I shrug. "I'm just tired."

"If you say so," she replies.

We sit like that for a few minutes. Ari is extremely capable of waiting me out.

In general, she's much more talkative than the typical therapist (certainly leaps and bounds more than I am). She's almost eighty and seems to have reached a stage of her life where she no longer cares to sit silently; she actually enjoys sharing an opinion more than most would. And that style works for me, I think because I'm the kind of person who needs the push. Since I never had pushy parents, Ari has actually been the perfect unsubtle bulldozer of a therapist for me.

But she can also go quiet when she wants to, and somehow because it's *her*, it's doubly effective.

Damn it.

I take a deep breath and think about my day. I think about the copyedits and the accompanying notes. I walked over here determined to finally tell Ari about J.

I like to believe that, in general, I've been a pretty honest patient. After all, what's the point of individual therapy if you're going to withhold?

In my work, with couples, there are all sorts of reasons for a patient to withhold. You may be reaching the inevitable end of a relationship, and you don't want it to hurt more; you may not *want* it to end, and you're withholding a secret that would upend everything; or you've grown so distant that the idea of withholding is simply second nature. But as an individual, it's just a waste of your own time to keep things from your therapist.

So I've shared my life with Ari. She knows everything about my bumbling family and my own need to prop everyone up. She knows how to encourage me to be less of an introvert. She's seen my inadequate relationships. She's even understanding of my codependence with George.

But I've never told her about J because it doesn't seem relevant to my real life. He's not in my *actual* life.

Except maybe, after today, I want him to be.

"I'm not sullen," I repeat, wondering if maybe saying it again will rev me up, an engine not quite turned on that's trying to get into gear.

"Why don't you start with the broad explanation and work your way up to whatever the actual feeling is?" Ari suggests, dart firmly in the bull's-eye now.

For most adults, when you don't talk about your feelings a lot, the vocabulary for it atrophies. When we're kids, we're taught to identify our emotions. We use color charts or characters or affirmations to help us go from useless blobs to fully formed people. We learn how to say

"I feel *blank* when you *blank*. I want *blank*." We work on expressing ourselves without throwing tantrums. But then as adults we get better at camouflage. We learn how to redirect so we don't have to always feel so deeply. We comport ourselves so we can live in a world of adult feelings and expectations.

As a therapist, I'm used to coaxing emotions out of others. It's my job to be able to identify the holes we've allowed to grow inside ourselves.

So I think I understand better than most how much of a crutch I've let J become. But there's something different about saying it out loud to Ari.

It's time to say it out loud, though.

"So you know the anonymous column I write?" I ask, starting small.

"Of course," Ari confirms, with a small snort, as though I should expect better than to even question whether she knows these basic parts of my life. "I read it every week. I love seeing how good you are at your job, even if no one else knows it's you."

"Well, that's not real therapy," I deflect. "An advice column hardly scratches the surface of being able to help someone."

"Nonsense," she says with a wave of her hand. "We all need impartiality. And sometimes we need anonymity too. You give people an answer in a way you couldn't if they actually knew who you were. We can sometimes, counterintuitively, be more personal as therapists when we don't have a real relationship. So I think it's a nice counterbalance to your regular work."

I can't pretend it doesn't warm me a bit to hear Ari's approval. My column for London's *Sunday Tribune* started out as a favor for my friend Celia, their features editor. I went to college in the UK, so we've known each other forever. Ask Eleonora was an idea she had after realizing that most British advice columns were much more acerbic than ours. She said she wanted one with "the earnestness that only an American could provide." I started it when I was right out of grad school and didn't really have enough patients of my own. I didn't expect it to become so popular that I'd still be doing it seven years later.

"Thank you," I reply sincerely. "So . . . ," I continue slowly, not sure I really want to keep talking. "I write it every week."

"Yes, I think that part is obvious." She gives me a mischievous smile and drums her fingers on her large wooden chair's armrest. She's not impatient, but she's certainly encouraging me to get to the point. I look up at the ceiling because I don't think I can say this out loud while she's looking at me with so much knowing.

"Okay, so I've had the same copyeditor all these years," I say. "And we don't actually know each other in real life. I mean, I don't even have his email because we do everything in the cloud—Google Docs in Google Drive, so everyone has access to the same files always. He just shows up as 'J. W.' But because we're always sort of writing to each other about my relationship advice, we've kind of become . . . friends."

I sneak a look back and see that the expression on her face is still as placid as a lake in winter. What I would've considered shocking information hasn't fazed her a bit.

"Why are you expecting me to have a reaction to that?" She verbalizes my own bubbling question for me.

"Isn't that weird?" I ask.

"Why would it be weird to have a friend?" she volleys back.

"It's not weird to have a friend. It's weird to have a virtual friend."

"Lots of people have virtual friends," she calmly points out. "My son is in his fifties, and I swear some of his closest friends are the men he goes on raids with."

"What?"

"Video games. Groups you do stuff with in multiplayer games. I have no idea what the appeal is. But he's always loved it." She shrugs, and the lack of judgment is so evident it's almost as simple as breathing. I've gotten pretty good at that myself with clients—after all, we see more than most people, so very little shocks therapists—but I don't always have the same energy for myself and my family.

"Okay, well . . . it's not a video game," I reply lamely.

"I was merely saying that friendship comes in many forms."

She pauses again, waiting for me to speak, even though I'm desperate for her to keep going.

"Right," I finally say, even though I'm not sure I actually agree.

"Why would you be against having a virtual friend?" she continues. "It seems to me like you might be able to express yourself better to someone you don't actually have to see or feel obligation to."

I cringe at how obvious I must be to her. Her point is one I think about a lot when it comes to J. I've never been able to decide whether it's a positive aspect or just another indication that I'm incapable of having fully honest relationships in real life.

"I'm not against it," I reply truthfully. "But it wasn't something I sought. It started from commentary on the columns, really. He would make his edits, but he'd also always leave a note at the end. It started with your average editor sort of stuff—a summation of what was missing, or encouragement if he thought everything was working really well. Eventually he started leaving his thoughts on the pieces too. Little things like agreeing with the difficulties of living with a partner, or expanding on his own story of a mortifying relationship event. I would always reply, because usually we would go back and forth at least once or twice anyway to answer questions in the edit. It felt like . . . it became a sort of ongoing conversation."

Ari takes that in, careful not to speak too quickly like she normally does. Ari understands I'm a bit skittish when I bring up a topic I'm nervous to talk about. I can sense her need to not spook me into waving off this subject like I do with so much else.

"So why are you telling me now, after seven years?" she pinpoints. "What made it suddenly relevant to your day-to-day life?"

I take another deep breath and fiddle with the sleeves of my linen blazer, the green one I love so much, from that vintage store down the street where I'm always overspending.

I'm avoiding, thinking about breathing and clothes, instead of processing what to say. Because I know this is the part where maybe I lose her. This is the part that I've been wondering about for the better part of a year and have always thought sounded completely insane in my own mind. And I can't believe I'm going to even try and say it out loud.

"I think . . . I think I'm in love with a man I've never met or even spoken to?"

CHAPTER 2

I watch as Ari takes this statement in.

She tries *so* hard to have no expression. I recognize the look because it's one I try to employ with my own patients, although usually less effectively. I'd find it amusing if it wasn't about me.

"Why did you phrase it as a question?" she finally asks, putting the onus back on me.

I blanch. "It should be a question, shouldn't it? Like . . . is that even possible? How ridiculous is it to even think you're in love with someone you don't know?"

"I don't think the word 'ridiculous' is particularly helpful here," Ari says kindly, so very unlike her normal demeanor.

I must really be a basket case for Ari to go soft on me.

I sigh and put my head in my hands. I try to breathe in and out slowly, the way I always tell my patients to. "I think I'm really lonely," I finally say, into my hands.

"Why do you think that?"

I look back up at her. "Isn't it obvious I'd have to be lonely to think I'm in love with a fake person?"

"He's hardly a fake person," she points out, needling me on a technicality.

"You know what I mean."

"I'm not sure I do." She leans in toward me, looking at me with new eyes, like when you pull up your couch cushion and discover you've been living with lint and popcorn kernels underneath you the whole time.

"I should know better," I sigh. "This is clearly some sort of projection that I've transferred onto an unavailable person so I don't have to face the actual loneliness in my life and lack of a real relationship."

She chuckles and looks at me the way you would a lost puppy. "Do you think being a therapist precludes you from having the same emotions everyone else does?"

"No," I counter. "But I should be able to see it more clearly and stop myself from being destructive."

"Maybe," she says, looking around like she's trying to decide something. "Maybe. But I'm not so sure we should expect that much of ourselves. If we could, every therapist you know wouldn't also be in therapy."

"Touché," I reply softly.

"Can I ask what happened today that made it necessary for you to tell me?"

I nod. And then I stand up and pace around the room. Her office is pretty sparse, so it certainly makes for good pacing. Two chairs, a lot of ferns, and a big rug are all she has. No knickknacks to distract or bookshelves to fill the space.

"I've been thinking about loneliness because that's what my column is about this week," I explain. I'm still pacing, and I don't look at Ari. Maybe this will be easier to explain if I'm in motion. "The person who wrote in asked about loneliness in relationships—if we can have a partner and still feel lonely. And if we *do* feel lonely in our relationship, is it necessarily the wrong one to be in. I got . . ." I pause. "I was a little personal in my response. Since I'm anonymous, I sometimes include details about myself because I think it can speak to the broader issue for more than just the person writing in."

"I like that about your writing," Ari says.

I appreciate the confidence, but I still don't look at her as I keep talking, the explanation easier if I keep up the momentum. "I admitted, in my response, that I've *always* felt lonely in every relationship I've been in. And it's been a major reason why I was always sure those relationships weren't right."

"Vulnerability is hard for you," Ari says, years of our therapy work condensed into a single sentence.

"Yes, but that's kind of the point. We don't need to get *everything* from one person, but a true partnership shouldn't ever feel lonely because you should naturally be yourself in it. Vulnerability is the antidote to loneliness. If you're feeling disconnected from your partner, there's some part of you that's holding back. So my advice was to either try to open up to the partner or—if that feels impossible—to let the relationship go."

"And then what happened with your copyeditor?" Ari's not going to let me get bogged down in explaining my column when I'm avoiding the point.

But I keep pacing and take a moment to consider my answer, because frankly I don't even know how to explain it to myself yet.

Even though Memorial Day was yesterday, since it's not a holiday in the UK, this week isn't different from a normal publishing schedule. I submit my column every Monday at the end of the day. Because of the time difference, I wake up to J's edits on Tuesday mornings, and I answer his questions before I leave for work. We write comments back and forth throughout the day to make sure we've resolved everything before submitting the column for publication. It's a rhythm now, our messages setting the cadence for my Tuesdays.

Maybe I also wake up on Tuesdays looking forward to seeing whatever he's going to say. And so that's how today started.

> I must say (if my opinion on these things matters), I think this is among your best. Maybe I'm biased because this one in particular really resonates for me. Truthfully, I think you blew my mind a bit by somehow articulating how my last relationship felt,

even though, until this moment, I hadn't even realised it. I bet a lot of people will see themselves in what you've said. And maybe it'll give them the strength to walk away when they should.

So . . . I've been pretty angry the last few months at my ex-girlfriend for leaving me. I've been stubbornly sticking with the script that she should've tried harder or should've let us both try harder. But reading what you wrote made me wonder if perhaps trying harder wouldn't have solved the core issue, that neither of us ever really let the other one in. And if we weren't going to do that after so much time together, well . . . it's probably better this way.

To be honest (as though I'm ever capable of anything else, ha), I've been thinking lately about how lonely I've felt since she left; but reading what you wrote made me realise that it's not recent—I was lonely *before* she left as well. I just hadn't allowed myself to realise it.

And I think you've made me believe there's a world where I should strive for more than that. So. If your goal is to help more than just the original writer, you've already succeeded this week, before even publishing. Thanks for that.

Enough of my sob stories. I don't know how I always get there! This is what advice column work has done to us! At any rate, let me know your thoughts on the tracked changes. I'm sorry that my editing always modifies your Americanisms, but I'm really

> saving you from yourself. "Band-Aids," by the way,
> wouldn't work even if we were publishing this in the
> US. "Band-Aid" is apparently a trademarked term.
> The generic equivalent in the US is "bandage," which
> sounds way worse than the generic British version
> of "plaster." Sorry if that hurts your American sensi-
> bilities, but at least it's a comfort you couldn't use
> "Band-Aid" either way.

I'd stared at his words for a long time. Not because this kind of tan-gent was particularly unusual—this many years in, the nature of writing to each other about a relationship column had certainly produced its fair share of personal intimacies—but because it was the first time he'd mentioned his relationship ending.

Over the years, we'd both been in and out of a few, and we'd fig-ured out pretty early on we were similar ages, so we were often at the same stage of trying to find a partner. But I knew this woman was the first he'd ever lived with, and it seemed more serious. I hadn't realized it was over.

And it startled me how much that fact was sitting with me.

I accepted all his edits in our tracked changes (at this point he knows my writing well enough that I almost never argue with a change). But as to writing back . . . it took me a while to think of what to pos-sibly say, my cursor blinking in the response box for far longer than it normally would.

> Maybe the first step to fixing loneliness is admitting
> you're lonely? Like alcoholics but with less interest-
> ing/destructive stories?
>
> No, in all seriousness, I'm glad admitting mine helps
> you even a little with yours. For whatever it's worth,

> you do deserve to strive for more. You absolutely deserve more than feeling lonely.

I typed and deleted a dozen different little quips to end with. He's always ending our notes that way. He can never leave a personal story as a personal story; he has to write in some joke about his copyediting, as though I wouldn't have already seen it in his tracked changes. I understand the impulse, though. That feeling of going out on a limb can be blunted by the extra cushion of wordsmithing.

But since he went out so far with his admission of loneliness, I left my own words without buffer.

I spent the next few hours with patients, but when I had my lunch break, I went back to see if he'd replied. And of course he had. He always did.

> Thanks for being a brilliant writer but also a brilliant friend (Can you be friends with the person you copy-edit? Or is that the height of lame? Like a primary school pen pal but nerdier. I'm not sorry, though!).
>
> I do have to say . . . I don't feel lonely when I'm writing to you.

That final sentence knocked the wind out of me. They were the words I'd known deep down for quite some time but never articulated. *I don't feel lonely when I'm writing to you.*

And it was the first time I'd let myself really wonder if it's possible to be in love with someone you've never met.

So, naturally, that impulse made me think I needed to talk to my therapist, stat.

I keep pacing, but I finally tell Ari the gist of the conversation. When I get to the end, I look over at her.

I'm surprised all my movement hasn't left a dent in her carpet. But she's still sitting calmly, watching me. That head tilt is back, her eyes moving over me like she's waiting to be sure I'm done.

"What's the problem, from your point of view?" she finally asks.

"The *problem*?" I scoff. "The problem is, I'm supposed to help people's relationships function, while I'm out here with the textbook definition of an unavailable crush. That's dysfunctional, to say the least."

"Why do you believe he's unavailable?"

I gawk at her. "*That's* the tactic you want to take?"

"Why wouldn't I?"

"Aren't you going to like . . . explore with me why I'm projecting onto a deliberately unattainable scenario?"

"I don't see it as projecting." She shrugs. "I think you *want* to believe it's unattainable because that's a safer option for you. You like safe options. It sounds like you want me to cosign your instinct to not explore this idea because it's a little out of the norm. But I'd rather explore *why not*."

"Why not what?"

"Why not find out?"

I sit back down and stare at her. This is absolutely not the direction I thought this conversation would go. She is, of course, absolutely correct that I wanted her to talk some sense into me, because surely it's not only the *safer* option but also the *only* option.

"It's not impossible for you to find out who he is," she continues undeterred, ignoring my silence. "It's not impossible for you to go to London and ask him out for a drink. It's not impossible for you to suggest a phone call or some other way to have a conversation offline. I'm wondering why *you* believe it's impossible. Why don't you stand up for yourself and take more responsibility for your own life? If you think you're in love with someone, don't you owe it to yourself to at least ask the question?"

I stand up and pace again. Ari doesn't say anything else. She's played her move, and I can tell she's fairly certain she has me in a checkmate anyway, no matter how long I try to think of a way out.

But as I pace around this sparse office, focused on the carpet, avoiding picking at my jacket again, my own words to J come back to me. *You absolutely deserve more than feeling lonely.* Why am I so quick to tell others to stand up for themselves but not myself?

"Okay," I say slowly.

"'Okay'?"

I'm amused by her surprise—she thought (or knew) her advice was right, but I don't think she expected me to agree with her without pushback. On the contrary, Ari is always encouraging me to be braver, and I'm always giving her excuses for why it's not practical right now.

But I can be braver. I need to be braver.

"Okay," I reiterate, as though I need to say it again to make it stick. "I'll really give that some thought."

And after everything today, I think I'm going to have to. Maybe it's time for me to stand up too.

CHAPTER 3

After meeting with Ari, I normally just walk down University Place until I reach my building. I'm lucky that she's only five minutes from me—as close as can be in a city as large as New York.

But today I need a longer walk. I need to breathe out that conversation.

I take a loop around Washington Square Park, walking the perimeter and watching the cornucopia of city life inside: lounging students, shrieking kids playing, smokers shooting the breeze, skateboarders practicing, tourists snapping photos in the shadow of the famous arch. There's pure early-summer bliss emanating from behind it as the sun starts to dip and the water of the giant fountain catches the light.

The conversation keeps replaying in my mind, no matter how hard I try to distract myself. It's one thing to decide you're in a rut and need to do something about it. It's another thing to know what actually *to* do.

For as easy as Ari made all her suggestions sound, they're not exactly easy for *me*. It's been hard enough in recent years to take her advice about my family and stop trying to contain my feelings through just the sheer will of ignoring. Actively knowing what I want and going after it has been Ari's yearslong project for me. But can she really expect me to apply that to a man I've never even met?

Happily, though, my train of thought is interrupted by one of my favorite sights as I walk back toward home. Three of my neighbors are standing in front of our building, chitchatting.

There's nothing inherently special about our building from the outside. It's ten stories tall and made of brick and concrete, and it was built at the turn of the twentieth century as a printing factory. In the seventies, a group of people bought the abandoned space and turned it into a co-op apartment building. If you can imagine the kind of people who wanted to live in Greenwich Village, amid the dueling crime and bohemia of that era, that's the majority of my now–senior citizen neighbors.

And because they were all friendly with each other, very few of them ever left; as a result, most of the original tenants (that are still alive) remain here. So I'm surrounded by either elderly badasses or young professionals like me, and there's no one in between.

I bought my little top-floor studio apartment from a woman who was an accomplished portraitist (she'd even had a retrospective at the Whitney in recent years) and who'd said she always loved the light that streamed in from the northern view. She was leaving in her nineties to finally move in with her "kids." To say she was a character would be an understatement. And the few people my age in the building all have similar stories to mine.

I've been here for five years now, and I can't imagine living anywhere other than my little slice of New York.

Meryl kneels on the sidewalk with her face up against Kwan's border collie, Lucy. Meryl's usual billowing skirt tiers out across the ground like a cupcake, and she's howling with laughter as Lucy licks her trademark small, circular purple glasses. Tom—Meryl's adoring husband—and Kwan are barely paying attention, because nothing about Meryl's behavior is out of place. As I get closer, I realize they're dissecting some minutiae from the semiannual neighborhood Build the Block meeting they always insist on going to.

". . . Maureen always wants to act like trash collection isn't a public safety concern, but when the bags aren't tied up, it can really wreak havoc," Tom is saying.

"And it's bad for the dogs!" Kwan points out.

"Absolutely right. Absolutely," Tom concurs, shaking his head with as much condemnation as you'd expect for a triple homicide.

"Hey, guys," I say, sidling up to the conversation. All three of them immediately smile and start talking at me at once. Meryl even stands up and brushes herself off so she can get right in my face, as she always seems partial to doing. She shushes Tom's and Kwan's hellos to get her own word in edgewise.

"Hi, sweetie. How's the cheaters, snoozefests, and soon-to-be divorcées?"

I purse my lips to stop myself from laughing. She always describes my clients with an ever-expanding disastrous vocabulary, as though anyone in marriage or relationship counseling is automatically a train wreck.

"Not everyone can find someone to be obsessed with for fifty years, ya know what I'm saying?" I tease.

She pooh-poohs me even as Tom looks at her with a playful smile. Whenever he watches her, he takes on the air of a young boy instead of a tall, silver-haired man in pressed pants and a button-down. He's still as striking today as I bet he was all those years ago when they worked together in a newsroom, where he was the big shot anchor and she was the wild production coordinator he fell for. I can see why her opposing whimsy must've been appealing. I never know with them whether I want to be envious or ask them to adopt me.

"I like this green on you," Meryl says, changing the topic completely, as is always her way, and rubbing her hands across my blazer in a tactile assessment of what I'm wearing. "You know if you want vintage things, I've got a whole storage unit filled to the brim with the eighties."

I smile, not wanting to admit that I'm too much of a coward to wear anything as flamboyant as what Meryl wears.

"You doing okay?" Kwan asks, ignoring Meryl and clearly picking up on something being off with me. Great, my insides must be showing on my outside again.

"I'm a little tired from the day," I admit, shifting to more generic pastures. "The Tuesday after a long weekend is always hard."

"Wouldn't know a Tuesday from a Saturday at this point." Meryl shrugs.

"You knew it was Memorial Day yesterday, because you were very gracefully pointing out all the many items that were on sale," Tom murmurs.

"Yes, but isn't it one of those holidays that falls on a specific date and not on a day of the week? Like Christmas or Veterans Day? *Memorial* Day? We're memorializing some specific day, right?"

"I think it's for veterans," Kwan points out.

"But there's already a Veterans Day?" She frowns dramatically and squeezes her eyes shut, like she's trying to solve a particularly hard math equation in her head.

"Is that different?" Kwan asks.

Tom sighs deeply, like he's disappointed in both of them. "Veterans Day is for all veterans. Memorial Day is for the veterans who died."

"But," Meryl points out, "on Memorial Day we barbecue and on Veterans Day we get all solemn? That doesn't seem right."

I can tell she's now trying to get a rise out of Tom, and he's clearly going to fall for it, because he's such a literal person who always falls right into Meryl's teasing.

And I figure that's my cue to leave, before this whole conversation devolves more than it already has. Tom, Meryl, and Kwan will probably still be out here in an hour when I come down to take George for a walk. Our building takes neighborly interest to a new level. And I can't say I mind it; there's a comfort to this weird little single-structure community amid a giant city.

"I'm gonna go make dinner and take George out. Kwan, let me know if you still need me to take Lucy on Saturday night. I'm happy to do it."

"Thanks, Nora," he says, rubbing my arm the way you would to a pet who's been particularly good. "Such a sweet girl you are."

"You're just buttering me up so I take your dog more," I tease, and his full-throated laugh makes me smile.

"Oh, and Nora," Tom says, stopping me before I can open the door. "Esther's unit was turned over to her grandson today. I know you're right above it, so I figured you'd want to know."

Well, that *is* news to me. Esther died a few months ago, but I haven't kept up with what's happening with the apartment below me. I really admired her, though—Esther was a cantankerous, tough broad. She was apparently one of the first female mathematics professors at NYU, and she remained tenured and teaching classes right up until she passed away.

"The family didn't sell the place?" I ask. Esther was British, and I knew vaguely that most of her family still lived in the UK, so I'd just assumed there'd soon be another thirtysomething singleton looking to buy her studio apartment.

"No, the grandson is moving in," Meryl cuts in excitedly. She loves a dose of gossip, so I imagine she's already pulled up his entire history and we'll know soon if he's gotten even a parking ticket. "He's apparently a writer, so I suppose he can live anywhere. Although I heard he was divorced or separated or something, so maybe he's fleeing the country."

"Heard from whom?" Tom asks, seemingly not expecting an answer, because he doesn't even bat an eye when Meryl cryptically waves him off.

"Well, thanks for the heads-up," I say as I put my key into the lock and open the door. They all say goodbye, and I'm bolstered as I get in the elevator. This day has felt both exhausting and inspiring, but my neighbors are always entertaining.

I get off the elevator at the tenth and top floor and open my apartment door to the impeccable sound of little feet racing across the wooden floor.

I sit down cross-legged and let George hop onto me, the familiarity of the scene calming down all the confusion from my day.

Maybe other people would think it doesn't count, but I know George understands me best—even without the ability to tell me in words. He knows me and I know him. He might be the mangiest-looking rescue dog around, and he might hate most people with an indifference that could haunt you, but he's *my* little, particular, mangy pup. He won't eat food that isn't a little wet; he'll pout when it's cold outside; he growls at pretty much anyone. But he suits me. He doesn't smile and jump around like an enthusiastic show monkey; he lets me brood when I need to; he doesn't seem to mind when I need to veg; he curls up on my lap when he senses I need affection, without fanfare or chatting. He gets me.

I rescued him after a solo trip I took following a breakup with a boring guy I'd stayed with too long. I went on the trip to try and reflect on what I was doing wrong, but the main takeaway was that I just really needed a dog. I strolled by a rescue event and saw so many cute puppies and boundlessly happy dogs getting attention, while George—this all-black, stocky dog with one white paw—was curled up in the corner, ignoring everyone.

Something about his disinterested nonchalance struck me as something I could use more of in my life. When I asked about him, the volunteer warned me that he was so irritable he was already on Prozac. I found it hilarious that a dog could take the same medication as humans while also feeling a bit defensive that someone would think anyone was lesser than for needing a bit of anxiety medication. But it made him feel even more right. I could protect him from the anxieties of the world, and he could teach me how to not give a shit about what others think. It seemed like kismet.

I brought him home that day, and we've been inseparable ever since. I'll often wake up to that one white paw resting on my arm, as though we've got each other no matter what.

And right now, as usual, I could probably take a little bit of George's attitude. If George were a person, he'd definitely stand up for himself. He'd go after what he wanted and accept nothing less.

And now I'm hoping to aim as high as my dog. Nice.

Yet no matter the day I've had, it's always a balm being back in my apartment. I don't think I'll ever stop appreciating the sanctity of having my own space. I spent my entire childhood sharing a room with my brother, even when I was in high school, all teenage angst to his middle school awkwardness. My parents never thought it was strange, even though it clearly was, so we both just muddled through it. And then it took graduating from college and grad school for me to finally have enough income to not have roommates. Being able to build a life where I get to introvert alone is one of the greatest advantages to aging.

But before I can try and focus on that sentiment instead of the ruins of my day, my reverie is broken by a loud banging right below me. George hops up and barks at the floor, as though that'll solve anything.

It stops for a moment before starting back up again. And then it falls into the same rhythm for at least ten minutes—banging, followed by seeming silence, only to resume once more.

Normally, I would just wait it out. So what if it's after hours and you're not supposed to do anything particularly noisy after 6:00 p.m.?

But watching George get more and more anxious makes me want to take action. He can't help but be confused and upset by this intrusion on his space. Maybe today I'm bolstered by my conversation with Ari. I feel the urge to ask for what I want instead of blithely waiting for the circumstance to change. Against all my normal judgment, I stand up and walk the one flight down until I'm standing in front of Esther's old apartment's door.

I knock. Softly at first and then, with a bit more determination, slightly harder.

But my burst of confidence is short lived when the door swings open and I see who's on the other side.

Because staring back is a face that I *know* is not happy to see me.

CHAPTER 4

"*You*," the face says, squinting at me as though he's trying to come to terms with my presence right outside his home.

I'm at a loss for words. This man, Eli Whitman, was sort of a client of mine because of his ex-girlfriend Sarah. I've only ever met either of them over Zoom. I usually insist on being in person, but Sarah was referred to me by a friend from college, so I didn't want to say no, even though she was in the UK. Sarah was so mortified to even be talking to a couples counselor that she thought the idea of someone on a different continent was actually a plus.

Our sessions started with just her, and they didn't last more than a few weeks. She was practically a textbook case—a calm, quiet woman in her midthirties who wanted to ignore all the relationship red flags because she was ready to settle down. But she was admittedly unhappy. They'd moved in together after dating for around two years, and instead of resolving cracks, it exacerbated them. She started therapy because, she said, she wanted to fix their problems. But my hunch from the start, once she started describing herself and him, was always that they were the wrong fit.

That hunch was easily confirmed once Eli joined a session. He was loud in all the ways she was quiet. Compelling, but bombastic. Without seemingly meaning to, he took all the air in the room. He rushed and spoke without thinking, which led to him getting worked up and saying things he probably didn't mean just because his defensive ego took over.

Ali Rosen

I'm someone whose entire life has been defined by retaining control in untenable situations; few things irk me like someone who has the privilege to react without thinking. So maybe it was my own biases (every therapist has them), but I found his inherent acceptance of his own intelligence and charm annoying, even if I should blame society for probably consistently pointing it out his entire life—the way it always goes with men.

I begrudgingly could see why Sarah found him attractive—he had that cocky, boyish thing that so many women like. Sarcasm combined with charisma is potent for some people. And she was reserved in all the ways he wasn't, so I can imagine a part of her thought having someone to take charge was appealing.

But it was never going to be enough—he's the kind of man who *thought* he was really in it, when in reality he only thought that because she'd been too afraid to verbalize all the ways the relationship wasn't working for her. He had no idea what was coming, because he'd taken charge like she'd wanted, and then realized too late it wasn't right for her.

She'd asked me to help her end it during a therapy session, because she was afraid that he would try to talk her out of it. Which he did. And when she didn't back down, he resorted to blaming me.

I get that sometimes that's easier when you've been blindsided. But I certainly didn't let him get away with his distraction tactic, and *that* didn't go over well either. I stood in the firing line for Sarah because it was best thing for her, my client, in that moment. But I got all the brunt of his shocked (and once again unthinking) reaction.

It was unpleasant at best. Thankfully, I haven't seen either of them or thought about them for months.

And now he's . . . my neighbor?

Shit.

Beyond that terrible ending, in general it's just strange having someone in front of you who you've only ever seen virtually. It's as though their textures become reality and you have to square this version with the one inside your head. His hair is a little darker and curlier than I remember. He's broader. Taller than I expected. The lines on his face more apparent. And . . . okay . . . he's more attractive in person somehow. Maybe he's one of those guys who doesn't photograph as typically handsome, but somehow in person it all works. I guess that's one thing I've underestimated about him.

But he's looking at *me* like I'm the least attractive thing on earth. I'm a slug, a combatant, a bad smell left to waft into the ether.

I need to keep this conversation in the neighbor category and *not* let it spiral.

"You're making . . . noise?" I finally say, and I cringe at how it comes out as a question.

I hate that I always do this. I soften; I shrink myself; I give in just to make things less unpleasant for everyone. And especially, in front of this man that I know resents me, my determination to stand up has been instantly replaced by my typical people-pleasing.

"*You*," he repeats, his British accent making him sound even more clipped, his expression now sitting somewhere in the center of a Venn diagram of stunned, annoyed, and intrigued. "You're Nora Fischer. You're my therapist."

So much for avoiding the topic.

"Well, not anymore, and not really very much." I'm saving myself with a technicality.

"Yes," he says, bemusement lining his tone, "because you basically told my girlfriend to kick me to the curb after a couple of Zoom calls."

He leans against the doorframe, taking me in now with more interest, and it's hard not to notice the way he moves. I hate that I'm making this comparison, but the way he casually leans and watches—in that effortless British cheeky-while-curmudgeonly way—reminds me a little bit of Jude Law from *The Holiday*. Except, apparently, *mean*.

"I did no such thing," I reply, still softer than I'd like, but attempting to find my voice again. Maybe I want to be agreeable most of the time, but nothing gives me more backbone than someone questioning my professionalism. "It's not my job to tell anyone anything. I'm there to help someone communicate their feelings more effectively and come to their own realizations about what they can work on."

His gaze narrows. "You don't like me."

"I don't have opinions about clients," I harrumph.

He points at me, his expression tipping into entertained. "You're human."

"So?"

"So. You have an opinion. Maybe you *think* you don't share it. But everyone has an opinion."

I hate that he's pinpointed one of the same things Ari was trying to make me hear earlier.

But I shuck the thought aside. "You're misplacing your anger at Sarah onto me," I say calmly, trying to keep the kind of professional tone I would have with any patient who was unhappy. "I'm sorry this is still unresolved for you, but getting angry at me isn't going to solve it."

For a moment he looks almost as shocked as if I'd slapped him. But then he comports his expression back to neutrality, that momentary realization wiped off as quickly as it came.

"What do you want?" he says, sidestepping my commentary entirely and attempting to get back the upper hand.

Oh right. The actual reason I'm here. I'm so shocked by seeing him in person I almost forgot.

"I live right above you," I say, now unsure again as to how to approach this bizarre turn of events.

"Congratulations?" There's that sarcasm, front and center. He can't help himself.

"You were being extremely loud."

"I know you're used to dinosaurs who never change anything, but I'm moving in. I'll be hanging stuff up. I'll replace appliances. I'm going to sand the floors. Sorry if those normal activities create a minor amount of noise in the noisiest city on earth."

He crosses his arms over his chest like a defiant toddler, as though he's particularly proud of his barbs, simmering in his confidence. I know I should be focused on how petulant he's being, but instead I find myself looking at those arms. Why am I *noticing* him so much?

I shake the sentiment away. "I didn't say you couldn't do anything to the apartment," I mutter, my voice a little shakier than I wish it was. "But this building has hours when you're allowed to do work, and we're well past them. You don't have to be so snippy."

"'Snippy'?" he says, his British cadence slipping to copy my American intonation, his mouth curling up in amusement.

"Yes, snippy." I'm bolstered, my reserve getting ever so slightly chipped away by his sarcasm. "I came downstairs to kindly ask you to do something pretty basic, which is keep construction-type noises to regular business hours. And you jumped on me!"

"If I jumped on you, you'd know it," he says with an impish smile, clearly trying to get a rise out of me. It makes the air crackle between us, charged without him even noticing.

I feel myself blush, but I'm not taking the bait. "You took out your frustrations with me as a professional rather than listening to your neighbor. One thing has nothing to do with the other."

"Oh, you think my opinion of therapist Nora can be bifurcated from my opinion of neighbor Nora?"

I close my eyes and rub my fingers along my temples, a nervous tic I have whenever I feel myself getting frustrated. "Think whatever you want. Just please keep the noise down. You're bothering my dog."

"Ohhhh," he says, the amusement now radiating out of him. "Well, if I'm bothering a dog, then my sincere apologies. I didn't realize noises hurt dogs only after business hours. I'll make sure to only bother your dog from nine to five."

"Seriously?" I exclaim. "You're mocking me now?"

"Glad your spidey therapist senses picked up on that."

"Just . . . listen, I'm nice, okay?" I finally plead, exhausted by J and Ari and now this unexpected emergence. "I keep to myself. I'm a good

27

neighbor. I've had a long day, and I just want some peace and quiet. Is that too much to ask for?"

I can see the way this unexpected admittance hits him. Part of my job is recognizing when someone softens, even when they don't want to. And I can tell he has, even if his defiant crossed-arms stance is still his default.

"I was just hanging up some pictures. I'll do it tomorrow," he mumbles.

"Thank you," I say.

I'm not so thrilled that this new plan for standing up for myself was usurped by what amounted to pathetic begging, but at least I'm getting somewhere. Maybe my normal tactics shouldn't all be so easily thrown aside.

"But just as an FYI," he says, before I can even breathe a sigh of relief, "I *am* going to be doing a fair amount of work during the days. And part of what my nan owned was a section of the roof. She never did anything with it, but I'm going to. I'm adding a sitting area and plants and connecting the gas line up there so I can have a barbecue."

I stare at him, all my optimism once again drained. I know exactly what part of the roof Esther owned—it's the part right above *me*.

No one in this building has ever cared one iota about developing the roof, even the common areas that we all own together. When the building was turned into a co-op, some members that put in more money were assigned little plots on the roof as well. But since everyone here wasn't exactly what you'd describe as outdoorsy, no one ever did anything with them. The elevator doesn't even go up there. You'd have to get off on the tenth floor right in front of my apartment and then walk up the stairs.

The prospect of which means that the noise he's making by hammering a few photos into the wall is nothing. His devil-may-care self could have parties on the roof at all hours, and they'll stumble in and out in front of my apartment and then turn on loud music right above my head. His construction could create leaks that I'd never know the source of. Even small noise above us could throw George off his already, admittedly, wonky equilibrium.

This whole plan is my nightmare. George being more uncomfortable in his already-tight skin is my most-specific particular nightmare.

"I don't think you're allowed to do that," I say quietly, not confident at all in what I'm saying but wishing desperately for it to be true.

But instead of clocking my nervousness, he snorts, almost seeming like he's enjoying the back-and-forth. "Oh, I'm allowed to. I have to place a flooring barrier between the actual roof and whatever I'm doing, but I have it all planned out. I just need the formality of getting it okayed by the board at their next monthly meeting, and then it's starting."

"The board isn't going to let you create an outdoor rager pad on the top of our building," I hear myself stutter, not even really sure of what I'm saying.

"An 'outdoor rager pad'?" The amusement radiates out of him, and I hate that it's at my expense.

"This is a quiet building," I point out, my own quietude reaffirming the point. "It's a co-op. We're all good neighbors. And they've known me for a long time now. They're not going to let you build something right on top of me without any oversight."

I hate the way he laughs like he knows something I don't. "Nora, my nan lived here for almost fifty years. I've been visiting her since I was born. They loved her, and they've known me forever. They're not going to block a perfectly legal minor construction project because it makes someone they've known a few years sad. I'm going to do exactly what I've carefully planned to do, and you don't get to stop me."

There's something about his overconfidence that bolsters me, as though he's nothing more than a schoolyard bully enjoying pulling at a small girl's pigtails. I think about everything Ari said to me today and my determination to not stay in the same patterns I've always been in. The normal Nora would let this assured man talk her out of taking action. But I'm not doing that today. I'm strong enough to push back. I stand up straighter.

"It's funny that you want to say you're so close to everyone, when I've never even seen you here a single time in the last five years. And Meryl, Tom, and Kwan had only *heard* about you when I spoke to them today, so I know that you're not exactly a frequent visitor. If you wanted to go about this as a nice person, I wouldn't mind. You're correct that you have a right to that space. But you're standing here mocking me, belittling me, and questioning my professionalism."

If he blanched at my explanation, it was only for a millisecond, because by the end he seems to be back in sparring mode. "And so what? Now you're going to fight me on it?"

"Maybe!" I say, wishing I could've come out with something stronger but still a little shocked by even my own hint of antagonism.

And before I can regret my uncharacteristic sort-of-declaration, I turn on my heel and walk straight out the door, into the stairwell.

CHAPTER 5

In the week since my run-in with Eli, I'm ashamed to say I've spent a large chunk of my free time reading the building bylaws and googling articles about co-op disputes. I've written and rewritten a letter to the board apprising them of Eli's plans, trying to explain why they're a bad idea. But I haven't had the gumption to send it.

My best friend, Dane, is an urban gardener (which in New York City mostly means she plants tiny gardens for people in brownstones with a "yard" and creates living plant walls for companies that want to look like they're ecofriendly while actually sucking up a ton of water), so I've pestered her a lot about every potential hazard that could come with rooftop gardens. Those notes have made it into various versions of my letter, but I keep deleting portions when it looks too petty. Maybe knowing about the specific growing mediums for rooftops and the percentage of perlite you should add to maintain a healthy roof makes me seem a bit over the top.

It also doesn't help that every time I ask Dane another question, she responds with some version of "calm the hell down."

I've thought about mentioning Eli to my neighbors every time I run into them, but I chicken out at each opportunity. It's as though my people-pleasing gene can't possibly be switched off in order to even attempt to pick a real fight.

When Kwan came to drop off Lucy on Saturday night, I didn't even bring it up then, even though he was in my apartment with his dog. We talked at length about the visit he was going to have with his daughter in Baltimore and had a long chat about whether we felt the strawberries at the farmers' market had reached peak yet (the mutual decision was "not quite"). But I couldn't think of a way to ask whether he'd heard any rumblings about renovations without sounding like I had another agenda. So I left it.

Ari reminded me in our session yesterday that I've *also* left another thing to fester. I walked in ready to complain about Eli and also nitpick something my brother had said, and instead she immediately asked me what I've decided about J. When I admitted I'd pretty much actively avoided thinking about it, I got a lovely little lecture about the need to put myself first and not bury hard things.

I know she's not wrong. But after that conversation, trying to go to sleep last night was like a master class in failure. Ari's words floated in my mind along with J's, like letters in a thick alphabet soup. After last week's column's heavy confessions, this week's led to much lighter conversation. A woman had asked a question about the ethics of having sex dreams about someone other than your spouse.

Is it weird that all of my dreams are mostly about obtaining food? J commented. Like, why do you think some people are having their kinky sex dreams and I'm over here having dreams where I keep running and running to try and get my mum's shepherd's pie?

I've never been the kind of therapist who bought into Freudian dream analysis I'm afraid, so I don't have much for you on that front, I responded. But I'd have to agree that my subconscious is also probably mostly concerned with food too. Although for me it would be the ultimate New York choice of a black and white cookie. Or a bagel. Impossible to decide between carbs.

All my other potential answers were too loaded to even consider: *If you're really good in bed, do you not have sex dreams?* Wishful thinking. *Maybe you're too sexually satisfied to have sex dreams?* Not what I want to even consider. *Do you ever dream about me and you just can't say that?* Too creepy to even think about writing.

So as a result, I'm tired today from spending a night tossing and turning. After a week of hyperfocus-avoiding by considering and failing at a plot against Eli, the reminder of J both in written words and in therapist nudging made it impossible to go to sleep. And now this morning, out walking George, I'm dragging.

The only thing that got me up—other than George's persistent whining and the necessity of seeing my first client at 9:00 a.m.—was the promise of the early-summer Wednesday farmers' market. I'm lucky to live near the city's oldest and largest, in Union Square. And I had to give those strawberries another whirl to see if half a week had made them even sweeter since I last talked to Kwan about them. And pick up some bread. And see if maybe there was rhubarb left too.

The desire to make a strawberry-rhubarb something was enough to get me moving. I threw on my favorite floral vintage romper and headed out the door with George. He trotted in front of me like a prince making his way through a crowd of loyal subjects. For such a cantankerous dog, he sure loves to parade in front of people. He'll give a low growl to any poor enthusiast who thinks he must be friendly because he's a small dog and try to pet him; but he certainly loves being outside and getting to see what's happening.

And the market is almost invigorating enough to make me forget the fuzziness in my brain. This early, stalls are still finishing setting up, beckoning with their bounty. Bright-green textured lettuces are set out against deep-purple curved eggplant. Cheesemongers are forming their displays next to bakers' stands. New York always feels at its most magical for me in the mornings, when it's coming alive with community.

As I'm wrapping up my purchases, my phone rings. I'm surprised to see it's my editor, Celia—she rarely calls me. We're kind of a well-oiled machine at this point, and after seven years it's extremely rare for her to have any commentary on my column.

"Hi, Celia," I say, popping my headphones into my ears while I balance my tote bags, now laden with food. "Nice to hear from you."

"I *loved* the column this week, Eleonora," she starts in. She's the only person who even occasionally calls me Eleonora, which is how she claimed she could keep the column anonymous despite using my legal first name. "'Sympathy for Sex Dreams' is a great headline. Her poor husband, though! I'm not sure if I'd love it if Charles was waking up thinking about someone else."

"Well, the subconscious does what the subconscious does," I reply, wondering where this is going.

"Damn right!" she says with a laugh, and I consider if maybe she's had some dreams of her own that she wouldn't readily admit to. "Anyway, love, it's so nice to hear your voice. How've you been?"

It's funny how she says that as though we regularly catch up. We've been acquaintances since college, and I appreciated her thinking of me for the column, but I doubt we'd have maintained a real friendship otherwise. She moved back to London and I moved back to the US right after we graduated, and we mostly kept in touch through mutual liking of each other's social media posts from time to time.

But after I finished grad school, she reached out with the idea for Ask Eleonora. Ever since I said yes, we've been in regular contact now through that, even though I've only seen her a handful of times when she's been in New York. I do like her, though—she's to the point and always has my back. She's the kind of person who never asks for a favor that she wouldn't give.

But because of that, and because most of our correspondence is over email, I know she's not just calling to hear how I've been.

"I'm good. It's been nice to have the days getting warmer," I reply, hoping the easiest way to get through pleasantries with any Brit is to mention the weather.

"Oh, lucky. It's still dreary in London, I'm afraid," she replies, true to form.

"Well, soon enough," I reply.

"Indeed," she agrees succinctly, making me grateful knowing the chitchat is over. "Anyway, I wanted to give you a ring because I have some fun news!"

"Oh yeah?" I fidget with the strap of my bag, wondering what the possible context for that could be.

"I have a new boss who's taking over Lifestyle, and she's actually dying to meet you. She loves the column. They're doing a little lunch reception for her in a couple months, once she gets her bearings, and I'd like you to fly in to see her. What do you think?"

I've stopped in the middle of the sidewalk. I mutter apologies to the person who was walking behind me and almost ran into me when I made the cardinal New York sin of interrupting the flow of pedestrian traffic.

I move to the side and lean against a wall. Is this kismet? Right when I tell Ari about J and when she's now telling me to *do something about it*, a rationale to be in London opens up right in front of me? What better reason could I have to ask J if we should meet? Maybe he'll even be at the reception?

"Nora?" Celia says, and I snap back to the call. Right. "I know you like being anonymous in your column, but this wouldn't be a public event or anything. It's not even seated, so if you didn't want to make it a thing with anyone else at the paper, it wouldn't have to be. I just know Donna—that's the new boss—thought it would be fun if you came."

"Oh, yeah, no, that sounds really fun," I quickly reply, not wanting my silence to make Celia think I'm ungrateful. "I'd have to figure out the timing, of course . . ."

There's a part of me that wants to blame work and busyness and say no to it so I don't have to actually face up to seeing J. Ari's right that I avoid hard things, and this is, most definitely, a version of a hard thing. If I go to London, I'll have no excuse not to reach out, and that thought terrifies me.

But I have to admit that without the J stuff, I would say yes in a second. Not because I need to go back to London so badly (although who would say no to that? I do miss the UK after having spent so much time there for college), but because if Celia's asking me for something, I should say yes. Doing the column has been such a bright spot for me. And I owe this to her if she wants me there.

"But of course I'll come," I say.

"Wonderful!" Celia exclaims, with a bit more glee in her voice.

"Great," I reply, a little dumbfounded at the implications of what I've just agreed to.

"Well, I won't keep you," Celia says, in her typically polite brush-off. "The event will be at the start of August, so we have a couple of months to make plans. I'll send you all the details over email, and we can coordinate from there."

We say our goodbyes, and I start walking back toward my apartment. I can feel my stomach twisting up, knowing what I'm going to have to do. What I *want* to do but otherwise would've found a multitude of reasons *not* to do.

I'm so in my head I barely hear a familiar smoking-scratched voice call out to me. "Nora, sweetheart!"

I turn around and see Meryl sitting at an outdoor table at the local coffee-and-bagel place. Today's skirt looks like a billowy quilt come to life, and her usual glasses sit on top of her head in favor of some rhinestone-encrusted cat-eye reading ones. Although I imagine she's not doing much reading if she's noticing her neighbors walking by.

"Hey, Meryl," I say with a smile.

She immediately puts her water cup on the ground for George (who would never touch water he deemed to be stale or used, but it's a nice thought) and pats the seat next to her. "I have an extra coffee to bring back to Tom, but I'm happy to throw him overboard and give it to you if you keep me company for a little." She grins slyly, and it's easy to imagine her as a small child wreaking havoc.

I've got a client in less than an hour, but the lure of coffee when I'm this tired is too strong. "Is ten minutes enough to scam Tom out of his coffee?"

She snorts with happiness. "Oh heck yeah."

I sit down and tie George to the table. He looks up nonplussed but then lies down to take a nap and ignore me. Meryl slides the coffee over, and I sigh with my first sip. I'm not sure why coffee wasn't my first move of the morning.

"Haven't seen your hot brother in a while," Meryl says casually, and I almost choke on my coffee. "What? He's got that gangly look I like."

I shake my head. "First I'm taking Tom's coffee; now I'm listening to his wife objectify other men?"

She shrugs. "I don't think your brother is leaving anyone for an old bag in her eighties."

"But if he would?" I tease.

"Then sayonara, Tom. At least for a night." She winks at me, and I pretend (and sort of not pretend) to gag.

"He's fine," I say casually. "I haven't seen him for a bit, because whenever he starts avoiding my parents, he avoids me too."

Meryl's mouth goes taut, as she clearly doesn't like my answer. "That entire family of yours takes you for granted," she says, pulling a hard candy from some fold in her skirt and popping it into her mouth.

I roll my eyes, because even though I do get pulled into Meryl's coffee vortex a fair amount, I don't exactly overshare when it comes to my family.

But maybe I'm hiding my weariness worse than I thought.

"They are who they are," I respond, my typical attempt to underplay.

"Please." She gives an exaggerated sigh and pats my hand. "Paying our super to go look at a leak in their sink because they didn't want to 'bother' theirs and then realizing it's because they tried to install an illegal garbage disposal themselves should not be on you."

I shouldn't be surprised that Vardan, our building super and all-around handyman, let that little tidbit slip to Meryl. I think he loves gossip just as much as she does, despite being a bearish-looking man who you'd never expect it from.

I give her a shrug, not really sure what to say. But that never deters her. "And what do you think about that Eli, huh?" she asks.

"What about him?" I reply cautiously, wary to get into this conversation with Meryl of all people.

"Well, I heard he wants to do something on the roof. It's funny that none of us ever thought about that before!"

I know if I ever had an opening to sway someone (and someone who might repeat their viewpoint to everyone else in the building), then this is it. But I need to pretend to be casual about it so I don't look as desperate as I feel internally.

"Oh yeah, I heard that too. It's a nice idea as long as he comes up with a really solid plan to not keep people awake at night or wreck any common spaces."

"Oh, I hadn't even thought of that!" she says, and I try to hide my smile. Maybe this will be easier than I thought.

"Yeah, I wonder if the roof is thick enough to cover noise for the people on the top floor if someone's walking around above them. Or like . . . since there's no trash or restroom up there, we wouldn't want people tramping dirty feet back and forth up the stairwell, since the elevator doesn't go there. Or plants! We wouldn't want to cause a leak watering plants."

I stop myself there, because I'm starting to get the sense that I'm ceasing to appear *casual* on this topic.

"Those are such good points. We should ask some of the board members what they think about it," Meryl says.

"Tom's on the board. Why don't you just ask him?"

"He never knows anything," she says, waving my question away, and I laugh.

It is true that our building's board sounds a lot more official than it is. We're supposed to rotate every year, but considering no one ever actually wants to do it, a lot of the same people keep getting roped back in. Kwan has been the treasurer apparently for ten years now, because he worked in finance before he retired and he's the only person willing to even pretend to care about the building's budget. Tom is the sort of do-gooder that keeps getting persuaded to stay on out of fealty to his neighbors. I did it one year and found myself bored to tears by our building management company's frequent agenda items about tax statutes and building codes. I think most of the people who end up serving feel the same way and are doing it out of obligation. Kwan is a noble exception. Our building president, Hearn, seems to relish his little fiefdom and is probably half the reason why every meeting goes on too long. But while I think he's pretty universally disliked by everyone in the building, no one wants to challenge him because no one wants to actually take on the required work.

"Well, I'm sure Eli means well," I say, lamely attempting to be nice even while I'm trying to sabotage someone. "But yeah, we should all stay on top of the implications." I look at my phone and catch the time. "I've gotta go. Thanks for the coffee."

"Anytime, gorgeous." She blows me a kiss, and I start walking back home to drop George off before heading to my office.

And that's the beauty of starting my day. Whatever problems I have with J or Eli or my family, I'm well trained to leave them at my door and focus on my patients. My own life will have to take a back seat.

CHAPTER 6

"Why do you think it is that you've put more effort into plotting against your neighbor than in making a plan for how to reach out to a person you have romantic interest in?"

I look up at the clock to try and avoid Ari's words. We still have five minutes left in our session, and I'm not sure which situation I'm hoping for more—if it ends quickly, then that means I'll have to face Friday night Shabbat dinner at my parents' sooner. But if it drags on, then I might have to actually deal with more of my own crap.

Unfortunately for me, I don't get to decide the pace of time, so I'm stuck with everything.

"Can't I do both?" I finally ask.

"You could, yes." She leaves the rest of the sentence—*but you're not*—unsaid.

I pick at my fingernails so I still don't have to look at Ari. "I haven't found a natural way to tell him I'm going to London." I know it's a weak excuse, but it's kind of the truth. "It's sort of a hard thing to slip into a conversation that's usually about an advice column."

"Let's set a goal, all right?" she steers, ignoring my protestations completely. She always does this when she knows I'm waffling. I'm a task-oriented person, and I hate leaving a dangling thread. If she turns this into an assignment, she knows I'll do it. I'm surprised she didn't pull this tactic in the last few weeks, but maybe she felt I needed a minute to let the idea settle. After all, with J, it's an addition, not just an obligation. Turning J into a real person when my life is already pretty great and stable is a potential complication that a part of me feels I don't need.

Yet what Ari's saying is small enough that it doesn't feel like it's going to upend anything.

"Okay . . . ," I finally say, cautiously.

"Next Tuesday, when you get your edits back, mention your trip. You can also hedge by asking for his advice about where to go when you're in town, and then just say, 'Oh, and wouldn't it be nice to grab a drink too!' That way you mitigate the fear of rejection for yourself."

"Therapist and dating coach now, huh?" I joke, avoiding again.

Ari leans forward in her chair and clasps her hands together. "It's understandable that this is making you nervous. You're used to your role as the rooted center, and taking a chance on someone is very much outside your comfort zone. But just because you exist among bigger risk-takers doesn't mean you can't take smaller risks for yourself too."

I know this is pointed not just at J but at all parts of my life. Most of our session today, before this conversation, has actually focused on my family. At Ari's insistence last week, I finally got my brother to stop evading my calls, and he agreed to come to family dinner tonight. I need to have an unpleasant conversation with my parents, and he owes me enough to be there for it. I've taken the lead on corralling our parents most of our life, but I'm tired of doing it alone. Ari helped me articulate that, and now she's prepped me for what I need to do this evening.

Thank god for Ari and her inability to not share her opinion, because I always need it. And today I apparently need it across all dimensions, because she's done double duty with my family *and* J.

"All right," I say quietly. "I'll mention it on Tuesday when I get back his edits."

"You owe it to yourself."

She sits back and watches me, as though by never letting her eyes drift off me, she's making a point that I've been avoiding looking at her.

"I'm scared to lose this one easy, happy thing I have," I admit.

"I know," she says kindly. "But having something halfway also isn't fulfilling. So don't keep yourself in a holding pattern."

With Ari's advice rumbling below the surface, I rush from my session back to my apartment to grab George, and then I hop onto the bus heading east to my parents' apartment. They're lucky they bought their space thirty years ago, when everything downtown was cheaper. Although, in some ways, that dumb luck is part of why they keep acting the way they do.

I should be happy that they seem to scrape by without consequences, but it's always one step from the edge. They're like the Cat in the Hat, bumbling around having fun trying to balance insane things, and I'm that fish in the bowl just waiting to be dropped.

I enter their apartment with a knock and a shout hello. The smell of delivery Chinese food is wafting my way and relaxes my hackles. At least there's *one* advantage to our untraditional Friday night Shabbat dinner.

"Oh, honey, hi!" my mom shouts from the kitchen.

I walk over and give her a hug, setting down the black-and-white cookies I made last night. My mom squeals—whether at the cookies or my presence, we'll never know—and she envelops me, her warm, zaftig figure pressed against me for longer than necessary, her wild, curly hair tickling my nose.

This is the part that makes my relationship with my parents so hard. They're loving. All their intentions are good. So it makes my frustration with the rest of their behavior tinged with guilt.

"Hi, Mom," I murmur, gently extricating myself from the squeeze. "Food is already here, I see?"

"Your dad was worried they'd take a long time with the duck."

"Even though they never do."

"Well, there was that one time . . ."

"When he didn't even order duck," I remind her.

"Well, it's here now." She waves the entire conversation off.

She grabs some plates and takes them to the table. I follow with cutlery, and we lay everything out together, busying our hands.

At our presence, my parents' two large dogs start circling us with excitement. "Hey, Waldos," I say, reaching down to give both pit bull mixes a pat. One is tan and black while the other is a blueish gray, but yes, both are named Waldo. My parents thought it was easier because "then they both feel loved whenever we call for them." I think it's more that they never get sick of saying "Where's Waldo?" and then cracking themselves up, as though it's a joke they've never said before.

George trots away the minute the Waldos arrive, and I don't really blame him. He can hold his own, but they're bumbling, and it's not worth it for him to stay near their increasingly speedy tails.

"Whatcha reading lately?" my mom asks. This is our safest subject. I got my love of reading from her, and even while other topics remain fraught, we can always find common ground with books.

"I'm reading this series about a female detective after World War One. There's like fifteen books, so it's been nice to just keep reading."

"Are you sure it isn't World War Two?" she asks, abandoning table setting and now on the floor with one of the Waldos.

"Nope," I say, trying to not let her airiness irk me this soon after arrival. "I've read four books already, so I'm pretty sure when it's set."

"Huh," she says, standing up. "I must be thinking of something else. How's the endings?"

She winks at me, and I hate when she does this playful dismissal of my reading habits. Yes, I do skim the last chapter of a book before reading it. I don't like the stress of not knowing. But ever since she found out a few years ago, she's loved to tease me about it, despite my asking her about twenty times to stop.

"They're good," I reply. I want to say, once again, that the journey is still there even if you know it turns out okay. But I also don't want to get into this again with her. "What are you reading?" I ask, switching gears onto her, a surefire tactic to change the subject.

"Oh my *goodness*." Her eyes light up as though I've just asked her the most exciting question on earth. "I discovered this new writer, and I think you're going to *love* her. Her name is Glennon Doyle."

"Is the book . . . *Untamed*?" I ask, trying to keep my voice flat.

"Yes!" she says. I don't need to mention that that book has sold millions of copies. "It's very powerful. Important stuff about breaking free of society's expectations."

I look around this kooky room, stuffed from floor to ceiling with bookshelves and bric-a-brac, walls covered in nude abstract paintings, deflated beanbags lining the floor, and a chandelier made of clock sculptures. *No one* could be confused about whether my mother was living a life constrained to society's expectations.

"I'll have to give it a look," I say, hoping that will save me from a lecture about embracing my true self or whatever else is probably coming to me.

"You really should. It's very powerful," she repeats as she wanders away. I sigh and go grab the glassware to finish the table. "Nathan!" I hear her shout at my dad from another room. "Where's the treats for the Waldos?"

"Tina? Did I hear Nora's here?"

He's shouting from the bathroom, and lord knows why they couldn't have this conversation once he finishes.

"Yeah, she just got here!" she shouts back. "But the treats?"

"Oh, I think I put them on the bookshelf."

"Good thinking!" she says, inexplicably. *Good thinking?*

I never know whether to believe that my parents were made for each other or that two such similarly harebrained people never should've been allowed to partner up. I know I'm lucky to have parents who still love each other (and perhaps show that a little more openly than I need sometimes). But I also remain shocked that they haven't imploded on themselves at this point.

But maybe that's just because we've always been so different. I've always taken life seriously and gravitated toward others who do too.

I preferred puzzles to make-believe as a kid. My parents loved me for who I was, but I'm not sure any of us ever truly understood each other, even from a young age.

My dad comes out of the bathroom and gives me a suffocating squeeze. He's a brawny man, tall and totally bald and always, no matter the weather, wearing a flannel shirt. I sometimes think he doesn't realize his own strength when he hugs so tight.

"You look too skinny," he says, eyeing me up and down.

"We don't say things like that to people anymore," I point out.

"You therapists and your sensitive language," he laughs, and I resist the urge to tell him that it's not just therapists who want people to stop commenting on women's bodies. But again, intentions. So I let it go. "Do you know if your mom got the duck?" he asks, wandering off to the kitchen.

"Yeah," I say, hoping that my assumption is true.

I hear the door open, and turn around to see my brother, Ike, stride in. Yes, my mother's name is Tina, and yes, she named her son Ike. She oscillates between saying she named him that to be "funny and subversive" while simultaneously claiming that she "just liked the name, who would've known." So that is what it is.

"I'm here," he says, heading straight to the bar and pouring himself a bourbon. He gives me a pointed look, and I try to give him my most understanding smile back.

Ike and I both eschewed our parents' creative career paths—I went into therapy and Ike became an accountant—so I like to think that at some point soon we'll be on equal footing as responsible adults. But no matter how much time goes by, we never seem to shed the little brother / big sister dynamic.

He's five years younger, and for the majority of our childhood, I was the surrogate parent, the de facto babysitter. Both my parents worked in advertising before retiring—my mom as an art director and my dad as a graphic designer—so they always made work excuses for why they needed to go to parties or shows or wherever. They were generally present and loving parents, but if I didn't want a dinner thrown together from leftovers of wilted lettuce and stale taco shells, it was on me to make it happen. It *all* fell to me to make normalcy happen for Ike. My pencil sharpener did double duty as I marked up two sets of homework; I had to drag my mom into a kid-clothing store when Ike's pants were looking too short; I held out my arms as his little feet slapped against the slippery pool deck to make sure he didn't fall in prematurely while he attempted cannonballs without real adult supervision.

So now, even though we're both fully fledged grown-ups, there's still this expectation from all three of them that I'm handling things. The residual emotional exhaustion of that is something I've never quite been able to shake.

And Ike doesn't see it, because he's never had to. When I nudge him toward coresponsibility, he sits back and lets me take the lead. Those are our entrenched roles, and at this point it doesn't seem like it'll ever change.

He's been feigning busyness for weeks to get out of having this conversation. And because he's him and I'm me, it worked for a while. I completely understand his urge to take a break from our parents. But I couldn't hold off any longer.

My parents come in and coo over Ike, like he's a long-lost baby bird. They practically pinch his cheeks, they're so excited to see him. He hugs them both and acts as though his absence was entirely obligatory, and they eat up the excuses. It's sweet if you ignore that it's masking his suffocation and avoidance.

"Well, the food's hot, Fischers," my dad says to everyone, as though we're some kind of unit. "So let's sit and eat." He grabs the take-out bags from the counter and spreads them out on the table. It's been long enough that I'd probably describe the contents as lukewarm rather than hot, but I know it'll all taste good.

We go along for a while in a sea of simplicity, everyone talking over everyone else so no one has to actually engage. *This beef and broccoli is always so good. Did you see the Rangers score? What summer travel do you have coming up?* Ike is always a superior buffer. They lower their guard around me, for whatever reason, but with Ike they like to behave a little better. It's almost as though they know he can distance himself when he wants to in a way I never could (or would).

I wish I could be annoyed at him for it, but mostly I'm simply jealous of his ability to set better boundaries and the positive results that yields for him. I'm fighting the low-key buzz of sensory overload, and he's just eating some duck.

The Waldos sit under the table, hoping for whatever scraps will inevitably fall from my mother's clumsy fork. George has been napping, elevated on a beanbag chair, for the entire evening, deliberately safeguarding himself from potential interlopers. As always, I wish I could be more like George.

But when it's clear dinner is over, I know I have to bring up the topic I'm dreading.

"I had my annual chat with my financial adviser," I start. I can see Ike tense a bit, but thankfully my parents don't clock it. They're oblivious. Which I guess is why we have this problem in the first place. "And as you know, my financial adviser also does your planning as well," I say, hoping that they might start to realize this conversation is going to be about them.

"Right," my mom says, "that's so nice of her."

She smiles at me, and I want to roll my eyes but I don't. It's not *nice* that my financial adviser does it. I pay my financial adviser to do it, because ever since my parents retired early for no discernible reason, I've been justifiably worried about their finances. And my parents, who have no sense of propriety or embarrassment—which I suppose for this at least is good—thought it was a great idea at the time.

"Right," I repeat, taking a deep breath. "So she's concerned. Again."

At that, my parents look at each other. I wish the look was of the *uh-oh* variety, but I can tell what's passing between them. It's their *oh, Nora, always worrying* little commiseration. That annoys me enough to barrel ahead.

"As you know," I repeat, "she tracks your spending and what you have in savings. She's been a little concerned generally since you retired, as she's mentioned, but she wanted to talk to me on this particular call specifically about a few large purchases you recently made. She said you made some rash stock market investments that immediately tanked and that you also spent ten thousand dollars on something from a place called PetWorld?"

At that I see the light bulbs finally light up. "My tank!" my mother exclaims happily. I shoot her a confused look, but I don't have time to ask before my dad starts talking.

"I admit the stock thing was a little foolish," he says. "I've been enjoying talking to some folks on this website—it's called Reddit, and it's really wonderful." I can see my brother roll his eyes from the other side of the table, and I have to look away so I don't laugh. "I started going on there because your mother and I got very into that show *Outlander*, and I wanted some people to talk to about it. Did you know there's communities to talk about just about anything? I'm now in subreddits on ancestry, and sous videing and the East Village, and of course my *Outlander* friends. Anyway, I somehow got into a group looking at stock recommendations, and I thought they knew what they were talking about, the way people seem to know everything about *Outlander*."

I try to nod along in the hopes that if I say nothing, this wild yet entirely predictable story (which is roughly what I imagined it would be when my adviser said a large chunk of money was lost in the span of a few days on E*TRADE) will end. And true to form, when I say nothing, he doesn't continue. But then my mom butts in.

"You do have to come see the fish tank, though," she says, making me relieved that at least the word "tank" refers to a fish tank and not some inexplicable weaponry, because I wouldn't put anything past her. "I just felt like our room needed more movement, and Shelley said she and Dave got a fish tank and it was actually very sexy and soothing."

Ike puts his head in his hands. I wonder if it's frustration or the need to never hear his mother refer to anything as "sexy and soothing" again.

"It's four hundred gallons!" my mom continues gleefully, as though the size is the best part.

"Okay, well, respectfully," I say, wishing that chastising your parents about money could ever stay in the realm of respectfulness, "you guys don't have the funds to make large purchases like that and stay financially afloat for the duration of your lives."

"No one knows how long they're going to live, honey," my mom points out, as though I'm a toddler learning about death for the first time.

"Of course not," I reply, taking a deep breath and trying to not give in to my greater impulse to flee the room. "But that's why a financial adviser is helpful. They're there to make assessments about what you have and how to plan."

"I know that's a comfort to you," my mom says, as though this is all a fantasy and I've got some crystals and dream catchers to help me divine the future.

"She recommends," I plow on, ignoring the commentary, "that at this point you put the majority of your money into an annuity. I already have you in long-term care insurance, which is automatically withdrawn from your account, so that covers you if anything catastrophic happens. But the annuity would cover that as well as give you a monthly income to live on."

"Income is good!" my dad says, and I can tell he has no idea what I'm talking about.

"So we just give them our money and they give it back to us?" my mom questions. At least someone is listening.

"Yes, it's a way to have a guaranteed income for your lifetime. That way you can't spend it all. The way you're sort of doing . . . now."

Everyone is silent for a moment. I look over at my brother and see he's carefully looking through everyone so he doesn't have to make eye contact with anyone. He's such a coward when it comes to anything like this. He and I agreed that we needed to convince our parents to do something to keep them more financially stable. They've never been in debt, so obviously they've had some sense of what's in the bank. I'm hoping if there's a limit, they might actually adhere to it.

"How much of a dent could a fish tank really make?" my mother says, waving everything away the way she does when she wants to minimize.

"Mom, you spent ten thousand dollars on a four-hundred-gallon fish tank. That's absurd, even for you," my brother finally says. "In your financial bracket, with your low expenses and your mortgage paid off, you should be spending that amount over two months, not one day in a pet store."

I knew the accountant in him would be bursting to speak eventually, even if he always takes too long to join in. But I wish it didn't have to come out so harshly. I guess I wanted backup, though, and beggars can't be choosers.

"I'll do whatever you want, Nora," my mother says, ignoring Ike and turning to me. Maybe the bad-cop thing is good for me, because if she can feel smug for giving Ike the cold shoulder, then perhaps I can get her to agree with this more quickly. "You always take care of everything, and I'm so happy to let you."

She leans over and touches my cheek. I know she meant her words as a compliment, yet I can't help but have them land with a thud in the pit of my stomach. She has no idea how much extra time this setup is going to add to my life, even if she wants to maintain an unwarranted belief that this is all no big deal. Annoyance creeps and winds its way around my center, but I have to push the feeling aside. I need to close this out.

"Okay, great, so I'll bring the paperwork to dinner next week," I mention, shrugging off any other commentary I might want to inject.

"Lovely!" my mom says. She's clearly ready to move on, petting one of the Waldos under the table, and he's now begging for scraps and not-so-discreetly getting them from her. "Who's up for pie? I bought it with my own hands!"

My dad snorts at her terrible and overused joke, and my mom hops up to go grab dessert. I'm relieved the conversation is over, even if the topic isn't really resolved. I don't *want* to be the person haranguing my parents over fish tanks and online-forum idiocy. But I'm not sure what the other option is. At least getting their finances under control will take them off my back a little bit. This is what kids do for their parents.

I'm going to keep telling myself that anyway. And eat a piece of pie while I'm at it.

CHAPTER 7

One day I'll get you to admit defeat on extra hyphens in so many of your words. I'm trying to not be too amused by the fact that your error this week was thinking "overdoing" was "over-doing," since adding in that hyphen was really overdoing it.

Too cheesy? Sorry, can't help it. Grammar nerd. And I definitely can't relate to this week's column because I don't think I could ever get a tattoo. Not that I wouldn't want something permanent for someone I loved. But I'm fairly certain I absolutely could not pull it off. Someone who recently referred to themselves as a grammar nerd probably isn't going to look cool with whatever word-related tattoo they choose (see now that, by the way, is a great use of a hyphen). But now, thanks to your column, I have another reason to feel happy I never got a tattoo, because I wouldn't want to make a new partner uncomfortable. I think your advice was solid—after all, we don't burn every photo of an ex once we break up, but we would respectfully take the photo off our bedside table. Permanence is a choice every single day. Just

> because stasis is the path of least resistance doesn't mean it's the right choice.
>
> Anyway, well done on this one. (By the way, word-nerd alert that I just can't resist: "Well-done" actually does get hyphenated if it's a compound adjective, like describing a well-done steak, but otherwise it stays as two separate words. You're welcome).

Well, if I'd wanted a kick in the pants, he couldn't have said anything more obvious. Reminding me that stasis isn't the right choice just because it's easy is probably the clearest blinking light of a sign anyone could write.

I usually look forward to Tuesday mornings, but because of my chat with Ari a few days ago, I woke up with an uncharacteristic trepidation, knowing the time had run out on my promise to her about telling J about London. While it's easy enough to say something while sitting in a room with your therapist, it's quite another to take action when you know that action is waiting for you on your laptop.

I'd buried my head under the pillow for a full five minutes when my alarm went off. But ever the dutiful Nora, I pulled myself up, dragged my laptop over, and was once again instantly floored by the prescience of what J had taken the time to write me.

And I know it's time to take a leap for myself.

I take a deep breath, and write a response.

> I think if you got a tattoo it would have to be the words "Grammar Nerd" in some very simple sans serif font. You heard it here first.
>
> On another note, I'm coming to London in August when they're having that reception for the new boss. I don't know if this is weird but . . . do you want to

> grab coffee or something? If you're too busy I totally
> get it.

I close out the document and stand up from my bed. That document, that *note*, feels like a ticking time bomb. I could erase my response now, quickly, if I really wanted to. But once he looks at it, it's over. I can't unsay it.

But I need to say it. I have to keep reminding myself to take action over this one piece of my life, even if it's scary.

I quickly shut my laptop and make myself step away from it, knowing that if I'm close enough to erase my response, I probably will. I practically haul myself into the shower so I don't change my mind. I take my time, as though if I stay away, then maybe it's not real. I finish my morning routine without looking at my laptop—clothes on (a secondhand marigold shirt with shoulder pads that I *think* I can pull off), toast eaten, hair brushed, my minimal daily makeup on.

It's only when I'm ready to go that I stare at it. I *do* usually take a look before I leave, since often J will have responded to me as quickly as he gets the notice that there's been a change to the document.

I open the laptop again, gingerly, as though it might explode. And there, staring back at me, is a phone number. And another note:

> I'd really like that actually. This is my number—shoot
> me a text on WhatsApp, and then we can coordinate
> without having to use a technology that feels like
> waiting for a carrier pigeon.

I'm a little shocked it was that easy. I save his number on autopilot, only getting briefly stuck at trying to remember how to type the plus sign for the +44 to indicate his British number. After, I stand there for a moment, waiting for something to change or perhaps for a monster to jump out of the closet and say *Just kidding!* But I shove that notion aside and go to work.

My phone is burning a hole in my pocket the entire day. I'm listening to my patients, but I'm also wondering what on earth to say to J. Can I simply text him now? Say hello and talk about a trip to London that's almost two months away? Will we run out of things to say? Was he just being polite?

At around three, I decide that this obsession is insane, and I need to stop letting myself spiral. I convince myself to dive in before I can change my mind, so I type something out quickly and hit Send.

Hey, it's Eleonora. Now you have my number too.

I look at the green bubble, with its unread check mark. I read and reread it and immediately regret it. First of all, ugh, *Eleonora*. I couldn't just have said, *Hey, it's Nora from the column*? Second . . . my first text was *Now you have my number too*? As though he needs it? And when he said to shoot him a text to coordinate, did he actually mean, like, *months* from now, when I'm actually in London? And not expecting a random text from a person who he has a professional relationship with and isn't even potentially seeing for quite some time? Why did I send that? If I unsent it, would he see it?

My next client walks in, and in a fit of panic, I just . . . turn off my phone. Almost like if I can't see it, then it isn't there.

I'm reminded of the first time I ever told a boy I liked him. I can still picture it with crystal clear mortification to this day. I was walking out of the library with my friend Ian, and out of the blue I said, "I think I sort of like you." He stood there for all of one second, obviously taking that minuscule time to consider what I'd said. But before he could react, I bolted. I fully bolted from the entire situation and then basically avoided him for months. It was the most fourteen-year-old-with-a-crush move I could've possibly made. But in the moment, I just had to get out of there.

I hate that I have the same feeling today. I said the words out loud, and now I have to run away from them.

I'd tell a patient that it's okay, understandable even, to feel nervous around emotions so delicate. Romantic interest isn't always reciprocated, and it would be foolish not to worry on some level that by starting a conversation, you might eventually be rejected in the future. Especially in a situation as unusual as this one, where I've never even laid eyes on him.

But I'm harsher on myself than I am on any patient. I should know better. I should be able to handle myself better.

But I'm only human. So my phone stays off all day.

"You just texted him and then *turned your phone off.*" Dane shakes her head at me and leans over the pool table to shoot her shot. She sinks the first ball into the pocket without even looking away from me. Show-off. "That's the wimpiest thing I've ever heard and not a good reason at *all* for you not responding to *my* texts all day," she says. "Give me your phone."

"What? No?"

"It's late anyway in London. You can write him back, and he won't even see it until the morning," she suggests.

But I smugly take the out. "Yeah, but that means it's *too* late over there. It would be rude at this point to text and potentially wake him up."

Dane gives me a look that only a best friend could get away with. Disbelief mixed with pity.

"What?" I say, hand on my hip, like that'll give me more stature.

"I've spent years hearing you wax on about the interesting perspectives of your copyeditor. Your therapist finally gets you to admit you've got a raging hard-on for an invisible man, but now you're spooked?"

"I'm not 'spooked,'" I counter.

"Well, you shouldn't be," she flicks back. "I said 'invisible man,' not 'a ghost.'" She ignores my groan and takes another shot. "Actually, scratch that, because *you're* the ghost. You basically made the man give you his number, you texted, and now you're ghosting *him*!"

She laughs and goes back to focusing on pool. I don't have any quick retort, so I stay silent; I just sit back and drink my beer while I watch her practice.

Even when she's lightly teasing me, I'm at ease in her presence. Dane makes me feel comfortable because she never requires anything of me. Like tonight, while she's practicing at Amsterdam Billiards before her rec league starts for the evening, I can simply hang out, say nothing if I want, and we can both be exactly who we are, but together. I'm always the quiet, even-keeled sidekick with everyone in my life, but with Dane that role feels like a privilege.

She lives, inexplicably, in black combat boots and cardigans, and she's always topped with an Indiana Pacers baseball cap. She's from New York but started wearing the hat when she was a kid, because her dad was a huge Knicks fan and she loved trolling him with their most bitter rival at the time. The rivalry is functionally irrelevant now, but it's become so much of a staple for her that I can barely remember a moment when she wasn't wearing it.

I think she wears all the exterior armor so she can claim to be antisocial. But then again, maybe it's actually less that and more just decisiveness—after all, she sure wormed her way into my life and stayed put. Even though from the outside we seem different, our personalities were instantly simpatico. I take my reserve and use it to listen, keep out of the fray. Dane's version of being reserved is not giving a shit what anyone thinks and just living her life without talking to too many people (she prefers plants, anyway, which is why she chose to channel her talents into urban gardening as a profession).

Neither of us are the life of any party, but we'd always choose being alone together anyway. We both have steel spines, but I use mine to keep order and she uses hers as a warning. She wears her combat boots, and I wear my obsessive retro finds—like tonight's white tank top with a billowing seventies bowling shirt that I changed into post-work that I keep waiting for Dane to notice.

"I'll never understand how you can come here and not play," Dane finally says, after she's easily sunk every ball and decides to rerack and start again.

"I don't have the coordination to hit a ball with another ball and make it go where I want it to."

"Dude, it's just practice. It's muscle memory, not rocket science," she points out.

"Says the woman so obsessed she carries around her own pool cues," I laugh.

"Well, that's just common sense," she mutters seriously, leaning back over the table to break the rack and play against herself once again. After a few minutes of practice, she looks back at me. "You need a hobby."

"I have hobbies," I whine, not wanting her to go all best-friend-protective on me like she always seems to do.

"You have so few hobbies you're hanging out with me at my hobby before the actual fun part of the hobby even starts."

I take a large swig of my beer, as though it's an act of defiance. "Oh please, once the league people show up, you're so in the zone you don't talk to anyone. That's fun for you, but not exactly when I want to come hang out with you."

"Right, and when they show up, you inevitably leave to go home," she points out.

"You know with small talk I always just end up sharing random facts and embarrassing you," I say. I want to add that she knows I'm awkward around random people. When I'm at work, I have a task; that social anxiety around new people doesn't come out when there's a purpose to the interaction. Without a direction I have a hard time. But I don't want to get into all of that tonight.

"I'm not saying you can't leave. You do you." She shoots me a look, and I know she means it. Dane never judges me even while she's razzing me. She grabs her own neglected beer and takes a sip. "But I'm just saying that when you *do* leave, that's when a hobby would be nice."

"I shop."

"Browsing vintage stores isn't an actual hobby. It's just an expensive distraction."

"All hobbies are expensive distractions. Mine just clothes me *and* is good for the environment," I retort.

"Yeah, you're a real Captain Planet," she scoffs.

"I read," I continue, ignoring her. "Reading is a hobby."

"Reading is not a hobby."

I scoff back, mortally offended by this comment. I know she's riling me up for her own amusement, but I'm honor-bound to take the bait. "Reading is the ultimate hobby! I'm Captain Planet *and Reading Rainbow*! Reading makes you empathetic to other human experience. It takes you to other worlds! It teaches you about other places, careers, people, regions, cultures. *Your* hobby takes you to the same place every single time. *My* hobby changes every single night."

"So you admit, Captain Rainbow, you're at home reading in bed every single night." She smirks, knowing she got me game, set, match.

I can't help but laugh and playfully shove her as the smirk grows wider.

"I'm also baking," I point out, handing her the neatly wrapped strawberry-rhubarb cornbread I made with all my wares from the market. The smirk turns into a goofy grin, and I know I'm getting out of this conversation.

She particularly loves this tart-sweet combo, and every year she starts texting me about it the minute the strawberries begin popping up at the market. There's nothing like making something seasonal that seems like a hard-won prize every single year, when warm weather finally takes root. They live in the moment, unable to respond to our spoiled anything-at-anytime lifestyle. And the fluffy nuttiness of the bread combined with the zing of two flavors that meld seamlessly is something I've perfected over the years.

She rips open my aluminum foil–and–plastic wrap container swiftly, shoving a crumbly piece of bread into her mouth. The sigh that emanates from her whole body fills me with a deep satisfaction. Dane gives me so much that being able to wordlessly give her something back is one of the reasons I love baking so much.

The fact that I only have one person who I'd actually consider a close friend isn't really a result of being shy, the way some people assume I am, since I come across quite obviously as reserved. I think it's more an introversion that would rather go deep. I'd rather have one person who really knows me and understands me than try to spread that out across people. I like my job, and I enjoy untangling other people's problems in a rational and focused way, but I don't necessarily want to do that with multiple people whose personal lives I'm more invested in. Being with Dane always feels easy, and that's a powerful thing.

But of course, it also means that she never forgets anything, since we're both kind of only invested in each other's lives.

"What's happening with grandma-privilege boy?" she asks suddenly. Her mouth is still full of cornbread, but she's clearly unable to stop the thought once she's had it. I snort at her description of Eli.

"Weirdly nothing, actually." I frown. "If I haven't heard anything about it for two weeks, I should assume maybe he decided to not go after me, right?"

That same disbelief-pity look beams back at me. "You're joking, right?" It's hard to take her seriously when she's stuffed her mouth so full.

"No?"

"Men like that don't just slink off when they're challenged. I'd be *more* scared that he's gone silent."

"'More scared'?" I whisper, trying to ignore the dread pooling across my insides at the thought. I break off a corner of Dane's cornbread to try and wash the fear down with carbs.

"*Hey*," she says, pulling the cornbread back toward her. She's the most generous person I know, except when it comes to sharing my baked goods. But then she turns back to the conversation at hand. "Yeah. The kind of man who can be pissed at his *therapist* instead of himself when his girlfriend leaves him is not having some kind of self-reflection about whether he should pick a fight with a neighbor, you know what I mean?"

I sneer a little bit at the thought. "Yeah, probably," I admit.

"And, as I've said to you before, he has all the actual legal rights to the space. So even if he's going about it kind of in a dickish way, you don't actually have any leg to stand on."

"Thanks, Dane," I reply sarcastically. "Super helpful."

"Honesty *is* helpful," she says while I try not to be too obvious about my desire to sulk. "You should definitely still try to stop it since, yeah, having people come in and out of your hallway at all hours of the night is annoying. I don't blame you for trying. But I'm just saying, he absolutely has not given up. He's clearly got something up his sleeve if he went silent. Don't pretend like this is all going away simply because you want it to."

"A girl can dream," I grumble.

"A girl can dream, but a girl should also be prepared. *When* he makes his plans known, send them to me. I can flag anything that doesn't look kosher, from the soundproofing of his flooring materials to the drainage for his plants. And if he doesn't have that level of detail, you can call him out on that too."

"I thought you said I have no leg to stand on?" I remind her with a small grin, touched by her commitment to my lost cause.

"Oh you don't, but let's still make it as onerous and lengthy for him as possible. He doesn't get to be mad at you for literally doing your job! Men with egos like that need to dance a little bit before they can get exactly what they want."

She winks at me and takes a last bite of cornbread. Then she's up and reracking, and I'm perfectly content for my hobby tonight to be watching my favorite friend prepare herself for her own battle of her weekly pool rec league. We both have to have hobbies, after all.

CHAPTER 8

I wake up the next day from George wandering onto my head. Sometimes when he wants to be extra moody, he just plops right onto me, as though my head is merely an extension of the pillow and it's his for the taking. It's not exactly feasible to keep sleeping when there's a twelve-pound, breathing, furry object on your face.

I slide him off me and sit up. My phone is sitting on my bedside table, still totally dark and looming. It's like it's silently waiting for me to get a grip and turn it back on.

I have to admit I've kind of enjoyed a day without anyone having the ability to call me. When I got home last night, it was too tempting not to plug it in while still leaving it off.

But I can't keep avoiding. I turn my phone on and wait as it boots up. I open WhatsApp first and see that right there waiting for me is a message from J.

J: Hello! So you do exist outside a file on my computer!

The message was sent right after mine, at 3:03 p.m. yesterday. I see there's another one after that, though, at 4:23 p.m.

J: Obviously you exist. I just meant . . . well, I was going to say it was nice to be able to say hello on a day other than Tuesday, but it's still Tuesday, so ignore me.

Then below that, at 6:52 p.m.

J: (You know, you don't follow my suggestions as astutely when they're grammar notes.)

I'm trying to hold in the smile that's slowly drawing across my face, but I can't help it. This delightfully dorky man is just as *himself* over text as he is on the column edits. It's like turning something from a 2D drawing on a page to a digital animation. There's more flesh and bone to his words here, constrained less by immediacy.

Except I think about how nervous I'd been to text him and wonder . . . is it possible he was nervous to text me too? If I'd texted him and then seen no response all day, I'd probably also have texted little quips (and then probably regretted them later). I get a little surge thinking that maybe I'm not so on my own here. Maybe Ari was right, and I needed to trust my gut and reach out.

And I definitely should not leave him hanging anymore.

Nora: If my phone was off all day at work, and then I forgot to turn it back on, and now it's Wednesday morning—does that count as enough time of ignoring you?

Oh so you were following my suggestions? he writes back immediately.

I purse my lips, trying to ignore my relief that he didn't keep me hanging the way I obviously left him.

Nora: Promise just a busy day and then an evening out with my best friend that went too late! And sorry for texting you when it's clearly already the middle of the workday in your time zone—but I didn't want you to actually think I was ignoring you after berating you into giving me your phone number so I could steal all your best London recommendations.

Maybe I'm hedging; maybe I'm trying to create a little bit of plausible deniability. But I can't help it. I'm out on a limb, and I want to stay close enough to the trunk that I don't crack the branch.

The therapist in me doesn't want to interrupt my own peace by adding a man into my mental load. The cynical part of me is insecure about whether I'm delusional to even consider that he could be.

But I have to ignore all those thoughts. After all, there's already instantly something that feels so *right* and comforting about being able to text with J.

Texting timing doesn't matter, he says simply. Followed a few seconds later by The editor in me wants to point out that it's not stealing if it's given willingly.

We never stop working I see, I respond.

J: Grammar never sleeps.

Okay, maybe I've changed my mind. Your tattoo shouldn't be Grammar Nerd. It should be Grammar Never Sleeps. But in some old timey cursive font, I type as I slump onto my couch with a grin.

J: Or, a movie title. *Grammar Never Sleeps: A Biopic of a Terribly Boring Editor.*

I snort a laugh. We go back and forth like that for half an hour, little jokes and quips that lead into some genuine advice about where I should go in London, ranking locations based on their nerdiness (with positive nerdiness being anything literary, and historical nerdiness being less appealing to him). After a while I look at the clock and realize I need to get up for work.

Well, I don't want to make you feel like you have to put your day on hold to keep giving me advice—although I'm even more excited about this trip than I already was. But now I have a whole list of things to do! I hesitate, wondering if I should say the one thing I'm really thinking.

But something about this ease has spurred me, and I don't want to keep hiding. I'm glad I have your number now.

J: I'm glad too.

I look at the words for a few moments, the simplicity of those declarations. It's warming, as though breaking through that weekly writing barrier has given me something new, to be carefully cherished. But then I see him typing again and wonder what's coming next.

J: Maybe it's the nature of your column, but I've always felt like I could talk to you in a way I can't with other people. Is that a weird thing to say?

And there it is. The truth that's always sat between us, written out in bare honesty by this person I don't even know and yet who apparently feels as I do—that we actually know each other better than most of the people physically in our lives. It's as though he's taken the honesty we've always had in writing and given permission for it to exist in this new medium too. So I know he deserves for me to go out on that tightrope with him.

Nora: It's not a weird thing at all. I sort of feel exactly the same way. I'm glad we can chat like this now.

His answer back is rapid. Me too.

And because I don't want to keep bothering him while he's working—or maybe that's just my excuse to get my own bearings—I answer: I hope you can get some work done after all my rambling. Thanks for chatting. Hope you have a great day.

J: Anytime. Don't be a stranger.

As if that were even possible.

I close WhatsApp to try and get a handle on what's ahead of me today. I open my email, expecting nothing of importance, but staring me in the face is an unwanted and extremely annoying email from our board president.

From: Board President Hearn

To: Co-Op Everyone List

Subject: Roof Usage

Hi everyone! The Board is meeting later this week to approve renovation plans submitted by our new tenant Eli Whitman. Normally the board would handle this without input, but since part of his plans include updates to his designated roof plot, he very kindly mentioned that others might wish to see the documents he's submitting, since it will abut the common areas of the roof. We're planning to amend the building's house rules to take into consideration timing for the roof (Eli thoughtfully suggested no one on the roof between 11pm and 7am and I see no reason not to implement this). If anyone has any other thoughts or questions for Eli, he says he's going to host some neighbor drinks and snacks next Tuesday at 6pm on the roof to show everyone his plans and introduce himself to those who haven't met him. We're delighted to welcome him and hope you'll join us for some neighborly fun!

Shit, shit, shit. He did exactly what Dane thought he would do. He's been plotting, and he set all his pieces in place before I even took out my board, in the hope the game would be canceled. And now he's cosplaying as the friendly neighbor and buying them booze and snacks so everyone likes him. Damn, he probably doesn't even realize how much this crowd of people is easily swayed by a cheese board and cheap wine. Our annual building meeting is always just a bunch of people drinking and stuffing their faces while they pretend to listen to whatever inconsequential board updates they have for us.

Living in a co-op is like having the inmates run the asylum. We're all just hoping someone else takes care of everything enough that the building doesn't go up in flames.

I forward the email immediately to Dane. You were right. Look through these plans, will ya?

I pull up my unsent drafted email to the board, now looking *entirely* petty with its phrases like "according to Bylaw Article 3 Section 8 of the House Rules." I obviously can't send this now. He's got friendly outreach to neighbors, and all I have is grumbly annoyance at not wanting things to change. And while that desire for stasis might actually have worked in another context (especially with the lovable elderly curmudgeons I'm surrounded by), the fact that he's won over Hearn—the prickliest blowhard of them all, who no one ever wants to argue with because they just would have to listen to him longer—means my work is cut out for me.

George walks across the bed and quietly barks at me, his indication that he's suffered through inane giggling and texting and now angry email forwarding and he is done with my bullshit this morning.

He's right, though—not only is there no use trying to delay George once he's got his mind on a walk, but I need to get moving if I'm going to have enough time to not be rushed before my first client.

I throw on a red-and-white shift dress I got at a secondhand store in Paris last summer, which always makes me irrationally happy. I think I need it today to lean into the sunny *I'm texting with J!* vibes I want and not the *Eli is trying to ruin my life* cloud that's threatening to rain all over everything.

I shove some of the extra cornbread into my mouth (first rule of baking: never forget to make extra), grab George's leash, and throw on my sandals.

And with that, I'm ready to start the day on a new note.

CHAPTER 9

But of course, that wishful thinking has to be dashed almost immediately.

When I get down the elevator and open the outside door, I can't believe who I'm standing in front of. Kwan and another neighbor, Gladys, are happily chatting and laughing with Eli. Gladys is looking at him like he's a slice of cake she's ready to devour. And to be fair, it's jarring to see him this happy and easygoing. I got an image of him from our therapy sessions as a combatant, all downturned expressions and blocked-off posture. When someone is that defensive, they naturally look less attractive.

But standing here now, he's got more of a glimmer of warmth to him. He still has that bombast, but when he's in control, it seems less forceful. He's reeling them in, and they're more than happy to let him take the lead and regale them with whatever sucking up he's doing to get them on his side. He's got that stupid British fashion sense that looks effortless yet casual, and I mildly hate him for it.

Kwan sees me and smiles. "Hi, Nora! Have you met Eli yet?"

He's looking so expectant and friendly that I have to plaster a sanguine expression on my face so he doesn't think I'm a rude troll. Maybe that's what I've actually become in this scenario—my apartment is like the troll's lair under the bridge, and I'm just waiting to attack. But obviously I'm not going to show that side of myself to Kwan.

"I have," I say, reaching out to pet Lucy as she sidles away from Kwan and up to me. George allows it because Lucy is the only dog he seems to deem as acceptable to have a relationship with. Maybe she's stayed with us enough that he's over it. Or maybe he likes that Lucy doesn't try to make him play. She's a stoic dog and matches pretty well with his irritated small-man energy. "Nice to see you again, Eli," I say with a sweetness laced only with the tiniest tinge of prickle.

By the look on his face, I can tell I'm not fooling him. "Oh, I'm *so* happy to run into you, Nora!" If I was pretend sweet, he's now nausea-saccharine, the false enthusiasm clearly for my benefit since he already knows it'll annoy me.

He turns to Kwan and Gladys. "Nora was so helpful when I moved in. She prepared me with the lay of the land with regard to renovation bylaws and building timing. I'm so grateful she gave me a heads-up so I could be sure to come to the board totally prepared."

He turns to give me a subtle look that is both smug and entertained, as though his eyes are saying, *Game on.*

I'm surprised that instead of annoyance, heat snakes through me. His undertone is unexpected, like he's waging a secret war only for me. As though I'm a worthy opponent. I don't know why it's a little bit thrilling. Everyone who actually knows me sees me as the person who fixes things, and there's something strange about the idea that to him, I'm someone who's trying to knock things down. To Eli I'm a storm, a crash, a hurricane—so different from everyone else's concrete foundation. And I'm not sure what's possessing me to want to live up to this alternate role of adversary.

"I do know all the bylaws quite well," I say, hoping my bullshit will sound authoritative and a little mysterious. "There's so many specificities to keep in mind. I wouldn't want someone to start pouring money into a renovation that would get extra attention from all the various government entities and permitting places that have to approve them. Being from another country means you're probably not aware of everything that happens here."

There's a little flash of worry that crosses his expression, and it makes me internally triumphant. If my goal has to be to minimize whatever he's going to inevitably do, then the best way to get him to pare back is to cause him to do it preemptively out of concern. And I do have one actual trick up my sleeve.

"But I'm glad you had Hearn send out the full plans, because my best friend is an urban landscaper, so she's going to look everything over and make sure there's no holes in what you're planning."

I can see that my deliberateness throws him off. I don't think he expected me to have taken it that far already. "That's so helpful, Nora," he says slowly. "Thank you for looking out for the whole building."

"Anytime," I reply, trying to subsume the laughter that I'm holding in. He's so easy to rile up. It's probably why he couldn't handle therapy. Being open to therapy requires some amount of humility; it requires some self-awareness that's open to change. But he's a bowling lane with the bumpers put up. There's no option for him but to hit the rails and go straight ahead.

"Nora seems like such a great addition to the building," Eli says with an undercurrent of steel in his voice, now changing tactics. I'm not sure I like where he's going. "Gladys," he says, turning to our neighbor who's still just as enthralled with him. "Could you imagine we'd all have ended up here when I was hanging out in your apartment as a little kid decades ago? I'm so lucky to have been around here for so long, and it's so nice to see new people taking to it as well."

I watch as Gladys completely falls for this trip down memory lane, and it douses the flame of victory I'd allowed to grow inside me over the course of this conversation.

"Oh yes, it's so nice to have you back, Eli," Gladys says warmly, petting his arm like he's a lamb she would rather coo over. "Esther would be so happy. She loved how many summers you spent living here as a child with her."

Well, that's news to me. I didn't realize he *lived* here as a kid. Even if he hasn't visited much as an adult, that would endear him to anyone. *Shoot.*

And Gladys keeps going. "I just miss Esther so much. She and I used to walk almost every morning together. She got me out of my house and never let me slow down. I really feel so incredibly lost without her."

"I bet Eli would love to walk with you," I blurt out, not sure if now I'm taking it too far, because I can see the surprise lining his expression. But he quickly recovers.

"You know, Gladys, I would love that. And I bet Nora would, too, since—look—she has a dog and probably already walks every morning. We've all got you covered."

He pats her on the shoulder, and she beams, his physical reciprocation melting her like sun on an ice cream cone.

Every time I think I've got him one-upped, he swoops back in again. There really is no way to decline, especially when I started it.

"Great point, Eli," I finally say begrudgingly, knowing that George is *not* going to take kindly to a chatty companion on his morning walks. "We should definitely do some walks together, Gladys."

"So kind of you, dear," she says, clearly touched, and now I feel bad for unwittingly dragging her into this immature feud subtext our conversation is having. "I never think to ask because you always keep so much to yourself. It would be lovely to spend some time together."

That gets a genuine grin out of Eli, as though he's won the war of being closer to our neighbors. I want to shout out *I HELP KWAN WITH HIS DOG!* But I know there's no way to bring that up without making our poor, unwitting conversationmates wonder where this chat went off the rails.

I have to get out of this. I have work and a dog to walk. I can't spend my whole morning letting Eli get under my skin.

"I'm going for a quick walk right now, if you want to join?" I say to Gladys, hoping maybe I can kill two birds with one stone.

"Oh, you're so sweet," she says. "But I don't want to impose. You're so busy, and I'd just slow you down."

I feel a bit guilty for only really offering out of a desire to get something in return. I know New Yorkers don't necessarily befriend every neighbor (and how could they?), but I don't want to be using an old lady's sadness over her departed friend as a way to simply make a point.

"Maybe I need to slow down," I say truthfully. "Come on, show me the route you used to take with Esther. My first client isn't until nine; I have plenty of time."

Her eyes light up in assent, and I'm genuinely glad. Maybe pettiness can have some positive side effects after all. I loop my arm in hers and resist the urge to look back at Eli to see what he thinks of this development as we set off.

Half an hour later, I'm buzzing with the kind of joy you only get from those serendipitous New York moments. A stroll with Gladys was actually a pure delight. We spent our walk talking about music mostly. I never realized that Gladys had worked for a big record label when she was younger. We talked about streaming versus physical music, and she gave me some great tips for deep cuts of artists I enjoy that are actually digitized now.

When I get back to my apartment, I take George's leash off but pause in the doorway. I have to admit, after that walk, I don't want to keep going like this with Eli. I don't want to be the kind of person who invites my neighbor along in order to poke at someone else. This isn't me. I can respectfully question what's happening to my roof without turning it into a war.

I walk down the stairs and knock on Eli's door. It swings open, and I can see his surprise at me standing in front of him. But his surprise is nothing on mine, because he's only wearing a towel and his hair is wet and slicked back, beads of water dripping down like he's in one of those elaborate shampoo commercials (that are really only one step above porn, if we're being honest). I wouldn't have pegged him for looking so *good* half-naked.

I want to be an adult and not look . . . but I can't not look.

"Ah lovely, if it isn't the saboteur," he says, schooling his face into his typical smirk.

I wonder if he senses that he's thrown me off. Because yeah, I'm thrown off.

"Why aren't you dressed?" I blurt out.

"I'm in my own apartment," he says, as though I'm the one misunderstanding things.

"Yeah, but why wouldn't you at least ask who's at your door before you answer it without clothes on?" I throw back.

Just then the elevator dings, and a delivery guy gets out and hands over a paper bag with TOMPKINS SQUARE BAGELS written on the side. Eli pulls out the single bagel, laden with cream cheese, and holds it up to my face as though it's evidence.

But all it does is make me more exasperated. "You paid for delivery for a single bagel?"

"Welcome to New York," he says, feigning the worst New York accent I've ever heard. Brits really do make the worst American imitators.

"You were *just* outside," I point out.

"Good of you to keep tabs on me, but I didn't feel like walking over there and waiting in the line. I happen to believe my time is valuable. So I enjoyed one of the perks of living in a thriving American metropolis consumed with capitalism and ordered myself a single bagel."

It's hard for someone to look so pleased with himself when he's holding up a towel around his waist, but he's managing.

I remember why I'm there, though, and try to snap back into my desired professionalism/neighborliness that I want to redirect us to. "Well, great for you, or . . . something," I say, leading with ineloquence, apparently. That smirk along with . . . everything else . . . is really disrupting my focus. I can pull myself together, though—I deal with people's emotional states on a daily basis. I can handle this guy. "But I just wanted to say, I think we got off on the wrong foot. Taking the walk with Gladys was actually really great, and I truly don't want to have any acrimony in the building. I obviously care about what happens here, but it doesn't have to be antagonistic. I don't *want* it to be antagonistic."

I might have spit a lot of words out, but I'm happy with the sentiment. I'm expecting his response to be equally contrite. But based on the deepening of his smirk, I can immediately tell that my hope was way off base. He's eyeing me, the look so heated it almost shimmers, and I hate that when he stares at me, it's as though he can see right through me.

"So you're going to tell your landscaper friend to not comb through my proposal anymore?"

"Well . . ." I pause, surprised, not knowing how to respond to that. "No, I'm not saying I'm not going to do basic diligence—"

"Which the building is already doing. So *extra* diligence," he points out.

"Yeah, but—"

"And, am I right in assuming you actually *have* looked into every possible building rule and government entity that could delay me?"

"I'm not saying I'm going to use any of that—"

"*And* this is all after you realize I actually know a lot of people in the building quite well?"

"Okay, but—"

"And I'm supposed to think you're here because you've had a change of heart after walking with Gladys and now suddenly you don't still think I'm an arrogant blowhard whose girlfriend was right to leave him? All that is now completely moot?"

I tap my foot, not sure if it's nervousness, contrition, or irritation propelling the movement. "If you'd let me get a word in edgewise," I finally get out, "I understand why you might be wary, but I'm not a person who starts fights with people. I'm the opposite of that. I don't know why I let you get me so riled up the other week or this morning, but I don't like it. It's not who I am. So this is my olive branch. Can you just *take it*?"

"Your capitulation?" he says with a laugh.

"My *olive branch*!" I repeat, getting more frustrated by the second.

How does this man bring this out in me? With anyone else I can contain myself. I have so many agitating people in my life—look at my damn family and all their constant nonsense—but I think maybe because with him it's purposeful, it's harder to reel it in. Most people in my life who have a lot of emotional needs and boundary issues aren't *trying* to be that way. They just are who they are, and I'm the person they expect to catch them. But he's antagonizing me on purpose. And enjoying it.

And apparently considering me. He's watching me now, like he's trying to answer a question without having to ask.

Then he leans over until his mouth is against my ear. It throws me off having him this close. That unexpected effect he's had on me ever since I saw him in person isn't going away. I can't explain it, and I resent that he knocks me so off balance. But it's undeniable that heat pools through me at the proximity. The bare chest and the towel aren't helping.

"I wouldn't have expected you to cave so easily," he whispers in my ear, amusement laced into every note. "I thought you were a stronger adversary than that."

I step back, trying to clear the tension he's wound in me—that sensation of never quite being able to brush his gaze away—and trying to summon my usual clearheaded self. "This isn't a game," I say, and internally cringe at how much I sound like a boring schoolteacher keeping the kids in line. But at his delighted laugh, I can't help but double down. "It's not funny!"

"It's a *little* funny," he snorts.

"This is my life," I say forcefully, letting the defensiveness that's been snaking its way to the forefront finally burst out. I never let it, but apparently I'm full of surprises today. "You're so entitled. You come here, to another country, with some apartment you *inherited*, and want to act like this isn't other people's actual homes. This isn't some foray into cosplaying as a New Yorker. I live here. I have a job *that I'm good at* where I help people with their emotional complexities, and I deserve to have this home that I've worked hard for. I've carved out this one peaceful space for myself, and you're taking glee in trying to ruin it. You're *selfish*."

The outburst lands on him and spreads, as though he's taken in every word slowly, and with each morsel the amusement slips away.

"Well, I'm glad we've decided to stay professional," he says with a sad coldness I'm not sure I was prepared for.

"This isn't a professional context," I say weakly, while I simultaneously can't help wondering if maybe going so far as to call him selfish was more than I should've said out loud.

But I can see him steeling himself again. So much of my work is noticing people's masks when they raise and lower them, even when they don't want people to see. Eli's more obvious than most, even when he's trying hard.

"Well then," he says, standing up even taller. "I'm going to just continue my glee-filled cosplaying at New York life now, with my bagel and my privileged inherited apartment. Any other olive branches you want to yell at me?"

"Not anymore," I say, all my good intentions having long since vanished.

"Great. Enjoy reading the proposal. Hope your friend finds some minutiae for us to argue over again. Maybe you can come yell at me about it at the roof party next Tuesday?"

He's baiting me, expecting I'll say I won't come. I can't tell which outcome he's hoping for, though.

"Oh, I'll absolutely be there," I spit.

I turn around and storm away once again, all my plans for a peaceful restart having been summarily torched to the ground.

CHAPTER 10

"Imagine there was no 'should'—what would actually work for you?"

I can see the wheels turning for Shauna, taking my unexpected question in, even as her wife, Cassie, blinks back at me, unsure.

I've found that most often in couples therapy, there's one pusher and one watcher. Usually one person insisted on coming, then made the appointment, then is the one with a lot of thoughts and feelings that they spill out in the first half dozen sessions or so. Often the other person is just as off kilter, but doesn't (or can't yet) articulate it.

That's how it's been with Cassie and Shauna. They're empty nesters, and Cassie's the one who insisted on starting therapy. She'd shared right from the first session how Shauna didn't help around the house; Shauna didn't give affection; Shauna spent too much time on her phone; Shauna didn't want to retire even though she and Cassie had agreed on it.

Shauna acknowledged every time that she should do more, pay attention more, give more. But she didn't know how.

And that's how today started too. It's my last session of the day, so everyone's already exhausted, and right off the bat, as usual, Cassie barreled in with "Shauna should've been on the call with me last night because then she'd know all the details instead of me having to relay them."

Maybe it's Ari rubbing off on me (although that's a little frightening) or maybe it's all my frustration with Eli nagging at me (something

I haven't been able to get off my mind), but instead of starting as we normally do, I think everyone needs a reset.

So I ask. I ask her to imagine there is no "should."

At first Shauna's a foal on unsteady legs, not quite trusting the question to carry her through. "Cassie's not being unreasonable . . . ," she says quietly. "I did tell her I would do that . . ."

"If Cassie wasn't speaking first," I prod, "what would you *want?* Not what you *should* do. But if you *could.* If you could do what you want, what would it be?"

I can see the moment the thought takes a leap. Cassie's not ready for it, but I am. After weeks of sessions, that one question is going to make it all tumble out.

And it really, really does.

Shauna turns and faces Cassie. "I don't care if the house has flowers or if we decorate for holidays—so why should I have to do it? I *never* was affectionate—why should I have to be all of a sudden now that the kids aren't there to give that to you? I'm relishing the quiet of the kids out of the house—why are you taking that personally? I don't want to retire—why do I have to?" She turns back to me. "It's not personal. It's not aimed at hurting Cassie. It's just me."

It's like watching Dorothy walking into Technicolor Oz. We just had to reveal the possibilities. The permission to chip away at "woulds" and "shoulds" has made space for "could."

After that tumble, inevitably, there's a lot of crying. A fair amount of hugging. And for once, Cassie doing the listening. The whole rest of the session is a doozy. Shauna's words are messy and unprepared and rapid fire, and there's a lot to parse. But it's undeniably a breakthrough.

Now, I'm still a realist. I don't think Cassie's going to instantly stop all the nagging. I don't think Shauna is suddenly going to stop ever tuning out. But it feels like real progress.

A reminder that we all can benefit from listening.

I walk out with that duality I often feel at the end of a workday—elated and drained. It's counterintuitive after sitting all day and mostly listening to people talking, and yet I frequently leave my office as wound up and jazzed up as if I'd spent the day running on a hamster wheel. But I think silence can sometimes be our most active space. We often talk without thinking, but real listening takes work. It's active in a way I'm not when I'm physically moving but mentally spaced out in a song or a daydream. It's exhausting but deeply satisfying.

That's what my job is—little sweeps at the pebbles in our way, until one day, hopefully, the path is clear enough that we can walk without stumbling. That's what today's session with Cassie and Shauna really felt like.

And in this moment, I realize what I want most is to text J about it.

I've been hesitating to reach out to him again over the last few days after that first burst of texts. While he said not to be a stranger, I didn't want to overstep. I was *scared* to overstep. I talked myself out of so many potential texts, overthinking whether it was something he'd find interesting or whether it would be too much. I didn't want to push on the fragile newness of it all.

But I need to stop doubting my gut instinct. And I don't want to doubt that he meant what he said, because he's never given me any reason to. I picture my own voice saying back to me, *Imagine there is no "should."*

And so I take out my phone.

Nora: Do you ever finish editing something and step back and think "wow, I did a great job there"?

J: If I answer "yes," does that make me conceited?

Nora: No! I ask because I'm feeling happy with how things went with some clients today, and I wondered if that same feeling translates to your job. So if you're conceited then I guess I am too.

J: Nah, I know you're not conceited, just based on your writing. You're like the person who would actually help out in an exit row in a plane emergency and somehow still stay calm about it.

Nora: I think the very definition of being in the exit row is that you agree to help out.

J: See! You saying that is exactly what I mean. Just because someone agrees doesn't mean they actually do it.

J: Come on, don't you think most exit-row people are just looking for the legroom, and then when the plane actually goes into the ocean, they'll be the first ones jumping out?

Nora: I've never even considered that as a possibility.

J: You're never going to be able to look at people on a plane the same again.

J: Sorry? (Not sorry?)

I'm grinning at my phone, but I'm jarred back to reality (and realize I should probably not walk and text at the same time) when I hear a voice call my name.

"Nora! Share the joke, please."

I look up and see Kwan laughing at my walking/texting/grinning while sitting at a table outside the coffee shop around the corner from our building. Lucy is curled up at his feet, as though she's a small cat and not a forty-something-pound dog. He's got a drink that looks like it's more whipped cream than coffee, and a deck of cards is dealt out in front of him, along with some poker chips. There are also cards waiting in front of the empty chair across from him, so whoever was there seems to have gotten up.

"Do you think people in an exit row would actually help in an emergency, or are they just there for the legroom?" I ask him, hoping to get another opinion.

"I think it's given to frequent fliers as a perk, so I'm not guessing anyone is factoring in helping out," he says definitively. He laughs again at the scowl that's overtaken my face, and it takes him a few seconds to realize I was serious. "What, you were expecting everyone to be as nice as you?"

"Oh, she really is the nicest!" I hear behind me, just as two hands sharply come down onto my shoulders.

I swivel my head and see Eli, grinning mischievously behind me. *This* is who Kwan is playing cards with? Come *on*. He's just desperate to wriggle his way into everyone's good graces.

"Hi, Eli," I say, attempting to take all exasperation out of my voice and probably failing miserably. I take a step back, because—loath as I am to admit it—his nearness jars me, especially since the image of him in his towel is now unhelpfully flashing through my mind. His physicality always seems to throw me off, and I hate that I now have an even more arresting image to accompany it.

But Eli clearly doesn't notice, because he sits back down in his chair, across from Kwan, and pulls up his cards again. "Ready for me to beat you handily?" he asks, ignoring me and restarting the game.

Kwan looks back up. "I was having a bad day," he explains, while he and Eli throw in chips and turn over cards without saying another word to each other. It seems like they're playing some version of poker. I can see Eli's whole hand since I'm standing behind him, and I fight the urge to whisper what he's holding to Kwan.

But once the chips are in, Kwan looks up at me again. "My daughter was going to come up this weekend, but now she's too busy."

"Oh, I'm sorry," I say genuinely. As a widower who lives alone, Kwan is always counting the days until he can go to Baltimore to see his only child or excited for her to come visit. "It's hard when plans fall through like that."

He nods while throwing in another chip and laying down a card. "I ran into Eli as I was coming out to walk Lucy. Perceptive kid." He raises his eyebrows at Eli, who shrugs the impending compliment off by staring at his cards even more intently. "He said he wanted someone to play poker with, but I think he could tell I was a bit bummed."

"You're underestimating my desire to take your money," Eli drolls.

"I wouldn't bet against Kwan, though," I say, wanting to defend him. "He plays pool with my best friend a lot, and those two are ruthless together."

"Yeah," Kwan chimes in, "I could hustle you in pool much better than cards."

"Well, thank goodness we're playing cards," Eli says with a smirk. I can't help but notice this smirk is a friendlier version than the one he gives to me, more mischief and less irritation embedded in it.

Kwan puts his cards down with a smug look at his hand, which includes three jacks. "Not 'thank goodness' for you!" he says, breaking into a belly laugh that shakes the table. The glee is glowing from his face. For being such a softie sweetheart, Kwan really is a treacherous competitor. I've seen him with Dane at the pool hall, and you'd think they were in a blood feud based on how seriously they both take it.

My eyes flick to Eli's cards, and I realize he actually has Kwan beat—three queens. But before I can even make a noise, Eli folds.

"You got me," he says, miming disappointment.

I'm frozen watching Eli. Kwan notices nothing as he merrily gathers up all the chips while Eli quietly shuffles the deck again. He's not hamming it up, but he's not hyping Kwan's win either. Did he not see his own cards?

Not possible.

He let Kwan win. Subtly. Without fanfare. I would've expected any moves to win over the neighbors would be overt—hammering in his memories of his grandmother or buying people's affection with treats. Letting them think they won a game of cards would fit right into that tactic.

But I can't help but admit that this isn't that; this isn't about winning over or scoring points. This is a dollop of kindness.

It's strange to realize this abrasive man has a tender spot.

It's hidden under all those layers of confidence and surety, but it's impossible not to see now that he's accidentally shown his hand both literally and figuratively.

Before I can delve into the pit that *that* thought has created in my stomach, my phone buzzes. I look down, hoping to see another text from J, but instead it's a text from my mother.

Tina: Emergency!!! I need you to call me!

With any other person, I'd immediately scramble to pick up my phone, but with my mother I know it's probably nothing, so I can take a second to say goodbye. I lean down and first pet Lucy, who looks up at me contentedly.

"I'm off home," I say to Kwan. "If you need anything this weekend, I'm around. Hope your streak continues."

I look over at Eli to see if his expression betrays anything, but he's clearly good enough at poker to not let on that anything's amiss.

Kwan pats my arm. "You're sweet, Nora. Maybe Lucy and I will come for a walk with you and George on Saturday or Sunday."

"That'd be fun," I say with a smile. I turn to Eli. "See you later," I mumble.

"Looking forward to seeing you on the roof on Tuesday," he says pointedly with that smirk he seems to reserve only for me, erasing whatever momentary goodwill I'd begrudgingly let seep in.

I can feel my jaw tighten, and I take a deep breath. "Wouldn't miss it."

I walk away before I can say anything I might regret.

It's annoying to have accidentally witnessed his little act that borders on altruism. Even though I know everyone is more than their surface—my work couldn't possibly let me forget it—sometimes it's easier to view someone through the single dimension you want to keep them tethered to.

But before that thought can worm its way in, my phone rings.

"Nora!" my mom says, breathless. "I think my new fish tank is broken, and I'm afraid all my fish are going to die."

I pop my headphones into my ears so I can take out my keys as I approach my building. "Why do you think it's broken?" I ask, knowing the simplest question will probably turn into the most complicated when it comes to my mother.

"It's making some gurgling noise," she replies. "And one of the Waldos keeps *staring at it.*"

"Tan-and-black Waldo?" I ask.

"Yeah!" she says with amazement, as though picking out the most likely fish starer is a magical ability.

"He likes to watch stuff," I mention. "I wouldn't read anything into it."

I open my own door to George standing there, like a gremlin who knows exactly when I'm going to be home. It would startle me if it wasn't so frequent. I reach down to give him a pet.

"I just can tell something's wrong. The fish are anxious. Waldo's anxious. I need you to come look at it."

"Waldo is fine," I say, and George tilts his head at the name, like an accusation because I shouldn't be speaking any other dog's name in his presence. "And I don't think fish can get anxious?"

"What about the gurgling?"

"Is there a manual of some kind for the tank?" I ask. "A YouTube video you can watch? A help desk phone number?"

"Oh, that's an excellent idea," she says spacily, as though calling her daughter is the first line of defense for fish tanks and any other solutions are a brilliant but unknowable alchemy.

"I'm sure there's a warranty," I add.

"Oh, you know I don't save paperwork," she says with an air of disdain.

"Thankfully most things are digital at this point."

"I appreciate you finding it. You're the best, Nora."

"I—" I'm about to say no but cut myself off before I even get started. What's the point? It'll be faster to just look up the damn thing for her rather than having her call me fifteen times about it. "Send me a text with the make and model of the tank, and I'll try to find the manuals online."

"Where would the make and model be?"

"On the back of the tank?" I guess, now apparently fully pulled into this nonsense. I grab George a little green treat, and he seems to forgive me for mentioning Waldo.

"I'll find it and send it to you," she replies.

"Great. And don't forget to look over that paperwork before Shabbat dinner, okay?" If I have her on the phone, might as well remind her.

"Oh, can you print it out again?" she replies, distracted now by, I imagine, her ridiculous, theoretically faulty fish tank.

"I left it on your desk in a manila folder," I remind her. "It should be right there."

"I think your dad was organizing," she says. "Anyway, gotta run because I think Waldo wants to go out. I'll send you a photo of the fish tank later, okay?"

"Okay," I sigh. At least maybe if she gets distracted by Waldo, she'll forget about this fish tank.

"Bye, love!" she says and hangs up before I can even respond.

I think about Cassie and Shauna and resign myself to adding a note to my to-do list to print out the bank forms again. I have to remind myself that getting my parents in a better financial position is just clearing the path. She's not going to change, but I can get us all to a better place. I've *got* to get us there.

My phone dings again, and I expect to see photos of the fish tank, but instead it's the most wonderful opposite of that.

J: By the way, I attempted to google stats on exit-row help, because I can't help myself.

J: Unfortunately there's nothing concrete, but I did find an article from the *Journal of Air Law and Commerce* (which, yes, is a real thing that I bet only extremely cool people read), and it's called "Taking Exit Row Seating Seriously," and it's all about why we shouldn't let exit rows become a perk. And I think it's right up your alley hahaha.

J: However I did stumble across my new favorite statistic, which is that almost half of all men believe they could land a plane in an emergency (vs. 20% of women), and that's the most wild, unearned bravado I've ever heard. So the journey was worth it.

I smile, grateful that at least *this* attempt to make a path is turning out even more delightful than I could have expected.

Chapter 11

As the days roll along into mid-June, even with this strange Eli roof mess looming, it's hard not to feel good. The sun is shining, the strawberries are actually starting to hit their peak in the market, and after that initial trickle, I'm finding myself texting with J pretty much every day.

There's something sort of delightful to texting about everything and nothing. He asks about my work, I ask about his edits, but mostly we're just texting about topics that have nothing to do with anything personal: The chocolate chip tahini cookie recipe I love from this magazine where I accidentally doubled the sugar the other day. The family-friendly movie he rewatched for the first time in thirty years and realized he was now older than the parents in it. The small elderly man on my subway car who started belting out Rod Stewart's "Da Ya Think I'm Sexy" very loudly at seven in the morning before most people had had their coffee.

Somehow, in the span of a week, texting with J has become an integral part of my day. Usually the only person I text with is Dane, and she's not exactly the most effusive—it's basically a lot of updates about the pool league and photos of plants and flowers. Or I get the occasional stream of consciousness from my mother.

But I've never shared my fleeting observations so casually. Or had someone share theirs with me.

So a couple days ago I walked past this little shop that had a kit for making a ship in a bottle, he texted me earlier today.

J: And I don't know what impulse made me buy it, but I did. And every minute I'm doing it now, I'm thinking "this is extremely tedious" and yet somehow I can't stop thinking about it? I get home, and I'm like, "I need to glue this tiny thing onto another tiny thing." Is this how people realise they've gone insane? Am I preemptively turning into a retired person without being retired? Can you please explain, in your professional opinion, the psychological implications of obsessing over a tiny ship?

I write back in between patients. I'm gonna go with thalassophobia—fear of open water.

Ah, perfect, he responds immediately. I knew I'd come to the right shrink. Is that the most bizarre phobia you can think of?

No therapist would categorize any phobia as bizarre, I point out, my need to avoid mental health stigmas stronger than my need to joke. But I think my favorite is triskaidekaphobia.

J: Fear of poems with three lines?

I shoot back a question mark, and he responds, tristichs.

That's the dorkiest word-nerd thing you've said yet, I type back while laughing. But no. Triskaidekaphobia is fear of the number 13.

J: I think open water has more potential to harm than the number 13.

Nora: I don't think phobias are meant to necessarily be rooted in rationality.

J: Now you're just getting technical.

Every time we text, I can't help but grin. Can you have banter over text? It sure feels like it. I put my phone away hastily as my next clients come in. But the conversation stays on my mind.

You must have a favorite word, I ask a few hours later, letting my next question practically type itself between clients.

Defenestration, he writes back immediately. I send another question mark.

J: It's a word that means to throw someone out a window. I just think it's so bizarrely specific. Like, in the English language we don't have a word, for example, for your sibling's in-laws, but we have a word about specifically throwing someone out a window?

Nora: That is an amazingly specific word.

Nora: What are some words other languages have that we don't?

I don't get to see if he answers, though, because the rest of my day is completely back to back. And for some reason, every single client seems to be having a particularly rough week. When I finally get out of work later, I stand in the waning sunshine for a few minutes. I'd booked an emergency session with a client who needed it over lunch, and there's something sterile about being in an office for hours on end without any break.

But I let the noise and humidity envelop and calm me as I walk home. I know for a lot of people that might seem counterintuitive, but the energy of New York actually centers me. It's always there, humming in the background, the symphony of constant motion, the steady backdrop to my life. I might be a fairly quiet person to others, but I feed off the bustle around me.

I get home and grab George to take him for a walk around the block. I'm excited for the prospect of blobbing out on my couch for the evening, so maybe I move a little faster than usual. After I enter the building's elevator, a hand stops the door from closing, and Kwan steps in.

"Hey! Are you going to head up to Eli's little neighbor roof shindig?"

Oh shit. I'd forgotten about that. Was that tonight?

I suppose I could beg off. After all, I'm not in the mood to spar with Eli. And I hear my phone ding, the little WhatsApp notification sounding.

"I'm probably just going to call it a night," I say, my mind now unable to think of anything other than the phone in my pocket.

"Ah, come on. You said you'd go," he reminds me. "Just come up with me now for one drink. You'll be glad you did!" he nudges.

The elevator stops on my floor, and we both get out. Right, everyone is going to be directly on top of me anyway. I can actually hear the soft tones of some music coming from above.

And *this* is why I need to make sure I'm represented there. I sigh, and Kwan lights up when he sees he's won.

I open my door and let George back in. He turns around and stares at me when he realizes I'm not coming in with him.

"I'll just be gone a couple minutes, Georgie," I say, kneeling down to give him a pet that he begrudgingly accepts, like I'm wasting his time. I leave my phone on the counter without looking at it so I don't fixate while I'm upstairs.

Kwan and I walk up the steps and push open the heavy metal door that leads onto the roof.

The scene is unexpected—I'm not sure I've ever even been up here, but it's actually an enchanting view. The buildings in this area are pretty low compared to the rest of the city, so it's a straight shot above Union Square, and far behind it are the bright lights of the Empire State Building. Water tanks dot the sky around us, and I take in the view of all our neighboring buildings' roofs from above.

Ours isn't anything really to write home about at the moment. It's just paved, with our own water tower looming over us in the middle of the building. But Eli has gone all out with his attempts to showcase what it could be like up here. Classic British rock tunes blare from a little speaker, creating an air of revelry. He's dragged up a bunch of chairs and placed out a long folding table, which he's covered with a red-and-white checkered tablecloth and lined with various drinks and snacks. He's laid out what looks like a large swath of fake grass. He has a small grill sizzling with hot dogs, with a cooler stuffed full of beer and seltzer next to it. I'm not thrilled to see Gladys laughing with our board president, Hearn, over a game that appears to be cornhole.

It's convivial, despite the slapdash impermanence of the decorations. And with this hazy summer day, even the weather seems to be screaming out for a casual rooftop party.

I see Eli in a small crowd of neighbors. It's strange watching him before he's clocked me. In our few interactions, he's always been combative and on edge. But with everyone else, all that expressive energy is attuned in a different direction, the way it was with Kwan the other day playing poker. He's animated, gesticulating at every point made as though he's the conductor of the orchestra.

I don't want to admit it, but I'm jealous of his effortless cool. He's always carrying it with him, whether he's antagonizing or entertaining. It's like he was born with a chip on his shoulder that makes him both assertive yet charming. He's got Tom and Meryl, along with two other neighbors from the third floor, debating something until they're all doubled over laughing.

When they stop and Tom has wandered off to look for a drink, Eli absentmindedly pulls out his phone and looks at it, displeased, and then—of course, because it's my luck—he clocks my arrival.

He saunters over, looking like a cat on his way to get the cream, eyes narrowing in on me with amusement.

"Well, well, well," he says. "Come to break the party up? Find any loopholes about permanent imprisonment if someone drinks a lager on the building roof?"

I scowl. "Your exaggerations aren't helping anything."

His laugh is full throated, and I can't help but once again *notice* him. I brushed it off more easily when he was sitting down playing poker with Kwan, but as he stands across from me, that potency is revived. I keep forgetting about it—it's as though when I imagine him, he's a regular (very annoying) guy, but when he's in front of me, he's this live wire of tangibility.

If I'm being honest, maybe "forgetting" isn't the right word—I've tried to *actively* not think about him, since otherwise our previous towel-clad encounter would, inexplicably, live on in a loop in my head. After seeing him like that, I find it frustratingly hard not to notice the way his T-shirt sits across his chest. It's baffling why I can't shake whatever it is that sits between us.

But luckily whenever he opens his mouth, the strangeness of our proximity dissipates. "Do you want to take a megaphone out and tell everyone to stop?" he teases, clearly enjoying berating me. "I bet that'd endear you to them. Maybe you could suggest everyone goes back downstairs quietly in a single-file queue?"

"You've made your point," I grumble. "Besides, Kwan dragged me up here."

"Sinister, isn't it?" he says, sweeping his arm across the scene. "Look at all this *fun*. Hearn brought up a *delightful* American game I'd never heard of called 'cornhole,' and I imagine it's probably puncturing the roof as we speak."

I roll my eyes. "Cornhole isn't the problem."

"I'm the problem?" he says, baiting me.

"You certainly are *a* problem," I retort, and he laughs again. Maybe it's the fuzziness of a few beers, but he's watching me more intently than I've ever noticed before. It's like he's cataloging me and taking mental notes. Now I'm the one who feels exposed.

"Are you going to try for another pretend truce?" he pushes.

"It wasn't *pretend*," I say, folding my arms and wishing I could somehow extricate myself from this situation. "I genuinely don't want to fight with you. But I also think it's fair to say I could hear the music from my apartment. It doesn't mean you *can't* play music up here, but it just means I wish you would take note of what things will affect the apartments below and take that into consideration."

"You're the only person who assumed I wasn't," he lobs back.

Is he a lawyer? He should be a lawyer. He's always at the ready with a quip.

"Well, be that as it may, I'm here now."

"I can see that," he says, and the look he gives me up and down makes me blush.

I can never tell if this pseudo-flirtatious thing he does with me is an attempt to throw me off. He obviously doesn't like me, based on all his belligerence, which seems aimed only in my direction. But whether he throws in those kinds of innuendo to make me step back or just because he enjoys it is impossible to say. After all, I don't really know him. And on top of that, the strange kindness toward Kwan last week also refuses to stop buzzing in my periphery, like a gnat you can't quite swat away.

The song changes, and I can hear the early strums of War's "Why Can't We Be Friends?" come over the speaker. I see Eli's eyes light up and immediately know where he's going to take this.

"*No*," I say preemptively.

There's that laugh again. Head thrown back, endless amusement, cheeky desire. He grabs my hand. "Oh yes indeed, neighbor," he says with a chuckle. "Everyone, let's dance!" he shouts at the gathered crowd, and everyone whoops and joins right in. I shouldn't have expected anything better of my neighbors. They're all a bunch of old hippies.

He starts to put his other hand around my waist but stops and catches my eye. I'm not expecting to see that the look there isn't antagonistic. It's asking permission, his eyebrows raised in a question, as though behind his bravado lies the kind of man who's conscientious.

The kind of man who lets a disappointed neighbor win at cards without being obvious. The kind of man who isn't going to put his hands on a woman, even in a friendly-dancing kind of way, without her permission. That hidden Eli, the one I've caught glimpses of but never seen outright, needles me forward. I'm surprised by it.

So surprised that, against all my other judgment, I find myself giving him just the slightest nod.

He takes the win and swings me around until I'm unable to not start smiling at the absurdity of the scene. Gladys and another elderly neighbor are twirling together, while Tom leads Meryl in a much more formal box step of some kind. Kwan, Hearn, and a few other neighbors stand on the side, clapping and dancing. I'm a little worried that one of them—a petite woman in her eighties named Aretha, who, according to old "glory days" photos she consistently insists on showing me, has had the same bob haircut for the last fifty years—is going to dislocate her shoulder with how much she's shaking her arms above her head.

They're all cheering Eli on. It's impossible not to note the affection in some of their voices and let myself give in to it.

"Give her a proper dip," Kwan shouts, and I can see from the impish grin that takes over Eli's face that I'm in trouble.

But before I can object, he's already swooped me down, and the sensation is unnerving. I'm dipped so far I'm practically upside down, but his hand is across my back, steady and unyielding. There's no fear of falling, but the way he's holding me is making my heart race. He pulls me back up and wraps his arm around me more tightly, the jaunty beat of the song keeping us in a ridiculous pace but swathed with gaiety.

I'm out of breath and laughing with more abandon than I could've expected from a slapdash rooftop soiree. I keep expecting to hear myself tell him to stop, but that would be a version of me that hasn't apparently lost the ability to speak. This version—this one that Eli's spinning with ease—is evidently letting go and succumbing to whatever this night is turning into.

"You know Esther would've *insisted* on more than one dip!" I hear Aretha shout, and I see the wistful look that passes Eli's face at the mention of his grandmother. I guess Meryl, Tom, and Kwan *weren't* the best sources of information, since I see a few other neighbors nod along at the memories of their friend Esther, clearly inextricably linked to this man who I saw as a newfangled interloper.

Before I can even look back at him, he's succumbed to the crowd and dipped me down again, even lower this time, to the delight and whoops of everyone around us.

I look up, and I'm surprised by how much my heart pangs at the boyish joy on his face. He's had me physically on guard since the minute we met in person, but there's something vulnerable and intimate that's especially jarring in this moment.

I keep wanting to stick to my dislike of him—I've seen glimmers of good, but those are fleeting. The largest pieces of him are wildly unpleasant. Those overt slices that I saw in therapy, and then almost everything I saw after, confirmed my initial judgment of a person too self-satisfied to give leeway to anyone else.

And yet.

The music is swirling, asking, *Why can't we be friends?* and those nagging inklings, that poker face, make me see him differently for a moment. Could I have seen only the worst sides of him? Did I only see him in a (woefully ineffective) defensive crouch on the verge of losing his girlfriend? Did I later see him hiding complex grief from the loss of a beloved grandmother?

He's watching me now too—back arched, cheeks flushed, hair wild and tumbling toward the ground—and I wonder if he's having the same thoughts about me. I wonder if his impression of me as the dour executioner of his relationship and as the busybody neighbor is the only slice *he's* gotten. Our eyes are locked and asking the same questions.

There's something so tactile about dancing, as though the speed of my pulse is coursing into him, and whatever our eyes are seeing is combined with whatever we're feeling, too, as though my insides have turned to liquid without my permission.

He lifts me back up to applause—I'm not sure when it even began. His hand slowly leaves my back, and I can feel its absence almost as strong as when it was holding me up against gravity.

I clear my throat, trying to figure out how to break this eye contact that's unmooring me.

He pulls out his phone from his pocket, a nervous habit that showcases only an empty screen.

"Somewhere you need to be other than your own party?" I ask.

I'm not sure I like the sharpness embedded in my tone. Do I always sound like this when I'm talking to him?

He seems distracted for a moment but then shakes his head. "No, um . . . no, sorry."

"Oh . . ." I'm not used to him being flustered, and it's rubbing off on me. "Okay, well. I've gotta get back. George, probably," I stammer. I see his brow furrow. "My dog. George. He's the anxious one from the banging. He's probably wondering where I am. Thanks for inviting me."

"I invited everyone," he says, but the same bite isn't there. A little smile emerges, as though he's waiting for my retort.

"Well, at least if you guys keep dancing, I can let you know how the sound is from downstairs. You know, for when you're paving and soundproofing. So you can know what the baseline is."

He doesn't say anything else. He's making me *nervous* now. All that swinging and dipping and twirling around has gotten my head screwed on backward all of a sudden.

"Okay, bye," I finally say, turning around before I can see his reaction and pushing open the big metal door to take me down the stairs.

What *was* that? What kind of pathetic, jittery stumbler did I just become? From a *dip*? A hand on my hip?

It makes me worry that I'm imagining whatever I think is happening with J, because *clearly* I'm so starved for affection or romance or something that I'm inventing wordplay dalliances and letting a man who hates me get me flustered from a turn around a rooftop pretend dance floor.

I close my door and stand behind it, breathing out deeply. I notice my phone sitting on the counter.

I immediately go to it and open WhatsApp, instantly distracted by the thought of an answer from J. I haven't looked at my phone since I asked him about words other languages have that we don't.

He responded a little while ago—probably right when I heard the ding from my phone in my pocket after I'd run into Kwan.

> J: Oooooh. Well, "schadenfreude" is such a good word in German that we've basically adopted it into English (Enjoying someone else's misfortune). I also have always loved the word "tartle"— it's esoteric and Scottish and describes when someone hesitates in an introduction because they've forgotten the other person's name.

I lean over and pet George as I respond with one hand, happy to be in this much less confusing conversation.

> Nora: Been there. How would you use it in a sentence?

> J: Like . . . "I experienced a moment of tartle when introducing a new client to my most forgettable colleague." Or . . . "I hoped my neighbour didn't notice my tartle, since I've met him at least ten times."

> Nora: We wouldn't want our neighbor to defenestrate us.

> J: Ha! Exactly.

I go through the motions of getting ready for the night and climb into bed. George hops in with me, and it's all extremely cozy. This is so much better as an evening plan than whatever else is still going on upstairs. It's louder than I wish it was, though, and I find myself irritated at Eli all over again.

Nora: Although now that you mention it, defenestrating (is that the right usage?) some of my neighbors sounds appealing.

J: Uh oh, neighbour trouble?

Nora: Sort of. Just one pushy person who's probably winning over the rest.

J: If you've got pushy neighbours, you've got to stand up to them. Never show weakness when it comes to where you live. You've got to make them think you'll never give in, and that way you can actually find the compromise.

It's amazing how J always sees me. I don't think I've ever really admitted to him that I worry that I'm a pushover, but even without that overt description, he still gets where I'm coming from.

Nora: I have to admit that's kind of what I need to hear.

J: You can do it. You give everyone else so much insight into their lives; you're allowed to take a little back for yourself.

Nora: Sometimes I feel like I'm so much better at giving people advice than taking it myself.

Nora: So I appreciate having you cheer me on and hype me up.

J: We shall fight with growing confidence and growing strength. Never surrender!

Nora: Are you . . . quoting Churchill at me?

J: Probably paraphrasing more than quoting, but sure.

I can't help but chuckle. He's such a linguistic dork, and it's exceptionally endearing.

Nora: Well, thank you. Anyway, I know it's super late over there so I don't want to keep you up.

J: Totally fine. It's always nice to hear from you.

Nora: You too. Goodnight.

CHAPTER 12

A week later, I wake up on Tuesday morning with a hangover that I immediately resent.

My mother "stopped in" last night with two of her friends around 9:00 p.m. Supposedly they were going out for drinks in the neighborhood and they just happened to be walking by my place. So I somehow—despite probably knowing better—agreed to a quick hello and letting them up for a glass of wine for everyone.

Two hours later, every subtle hint at bedtime had been completely ignored and three bottles of my wine had been consumed. And I wasn't going to suffer that experience without a drink. But as a result I had significantly more than I normally would, especially for a Monday night.

So today my apartment is in shambles, along with my head, and I now have to drag myself up and get ready for work.

At least I know I get to hear from J.

Even with all the texting, J hasn't stopped leaving me notes in the comments of my articles on Tuesday mornings. For all our discussions of our daily lives, I still enjoy getting his thoughts on various relationship issues. Although now instead of just having notes in the article, we can also text about it after.

I get up, sit at my desk, and pull open my computer. This week's column is about a woman who's been with her partner for eight years, and he hasn't proposed yet despite her saying it's important to her. While

J's notes start with his usual grammar comments, I'm a bit floored as I continue reading.

> I always marvel at your sensitivity amidst direct-ness. I'm not sure I could've been as rational with this woman. It's as clear as day to anyone that this person should leave their partner—I don't know why, but it makes me think of that scene in *Love Actually* where the mother is explaining making the octopus costume to Hugh Grant and she says very firmly something like, "eight's a lot of legs, David." All I can picture now is this letter writer saying "eight's a lot of years, David." (Sorry for the *Love Actually* tangent, and I really hope you aren't one of those people who've decided it's actually the worst, since I still love it, inexplicable plot and all . . .). ANYWAY. As I was saying. You somehow manage to avoid judging her on her long-term bad choice while also nudging her toward freedom and self-respect. I hope your advice resonates with a lot of people in ruts.
>
> People say actions speak louder than words, but as a person who finds words often having more impact than actions, I think using the right ones can have a profound impact on someone's life.

I don't know what's happening to me—maybe it's the hangover or lack of sleep or straight-up patheticness—but I can feel a tear rolling down my cheek. It's so uncharacteristic that I lift up my hand to feel it and know that it's real.

I *never* cry. Not at movies, not at frustration about my family, not when work turns personal. I'm just not someone who is incapable of controlling my emotions.

And yet.

This sentiment J has sent across the ocean . . . it touches me in a way I can't explain. Much like his comments about standing up to my neighbors the other night, the way he always sees my intentions, just through words, is uncanny. He takes the edge away with a joke or an aside, but he cuts through every time. His notion that words can speak louder than actions has never felt truer. Not because of me, but because of *him*. His words lately echo not just across my whole week, but throughout my days.

And maybe it makes me feel a little brave again.

So instead of writing back in the notes, I just text him directly.

Nora: Love Actually makes me happy and I reject all logical breakdowns of the plot (mostly because they are technically correct, but incorrect in that I still love it).

J: Thank goodness. I don't know if we could stay friends if you were a true hater of cinema's most delightfully deranged romance-adjacent holiday masterpiece.

Nora: I wouldn't dream of it.

Nora: But seriously, thank you for your kind words. I might say the same about yours to me—they often do speak louder than any of the actions of the people I see in person. I appreciate the encouragement you always give.

J: I'm really glad.

J: I feel like you're always giving me free therapy advice, so anytime I can just give one small smidgeon of that back, I feel grateful.

J: Need any terrible therapy today? I promise I'm unlicensed but extremely in your corner.

I laugh and wipe the last tear away. I take a deep breath to try and get my headache to go away. The thought of last night irritates me and spurs me to actually take him up on his offer.

Nora: You joke, but my mother and her friends came over last night uninvited, drank me out of house and home, left a mess, and caused me a particularly unwelcome hangover today.

J: So my advice the other day to take some things back for yourself really was taken into consideration, eh?

Nora: I know you're teasing, but I did appreciate that.

Nora: It's harder with parents.

J: Considering how many columns I've commented on with whiny things about my own parents over the last seven years, you already know you won't get an argument on that from me.

Nora: Not whiny. Just normal I suppose. Everyone has tough positions with their parents.

J: Yeah, but you shouldn't let your mum take advantage of you. It's okay to say no. And if you ever need a bit of strength before doing so, just text me and I'll remind you.

Nora: Thank you. I actually really appreciate that.

J: Anytime.

J: Actually, I know exactly what you should say to your mother. You should stand up and say, "I fear this has become a relationship where you take exactly what you want and casually ignore all the things that really matter."

J: (to Britain)

Nora: First Churchill, and now you're quoting the fictional Prime Minister Hugh Grant from Love Actually?

J: Paraphrasing. Quoting is entirely nerdier. Paraphrasing is much more casual.

J: And look, it's not my fault that your presidents don't really have any quotable oration and even our fictional ones give us a lot of inspiring stuff to work with.

Nora: I think when I'm in London I'm going to bring you a few books about American Presidents. It seems that your education system has failed you on that one.

J: I look forward to it.

The thought of seeing him in person makes my stomach lurch with some mix of fear and excitement. But before I can dwell on that too fully, George is giving me a growl to get me moving. So I shake it all off and get up, trying to find my swishiest skirt to give me armor against the headache-infused day ahead.

And it is indeed a long day. I have a full roster of clients and then a session with Ari, where she also doesn't let me off the hook for indulging my mother. I tell her what J said, and she agrees wholeheartedly. But then she also makes me discuss how I'm feeling about the impending trip, and that all just makes the nerves come back again.

My day finally starts to feel like I'm going to be able to relax as I'm walking home from Ari's office. My phone pings, and I pull it out, hoping it's a response from J, but instead, it's from Dane. **Want to join me at pool tonight? I need to distract Arbus and he always chokes when you're around.**

I roll my eyes.

Nora: What a nice invitation that makes me feel so loved and appreciated.

Dane: I'm saying I appreciate your presence.

Nora: Because I theoretically ruin someone else's game.

Dane: Right? And what could possibly be more imperative to my appreciation than helping me crush others at pool?

I get home and set my purse on the counter, shaking my head. How can I explain to Dane that there's absolutely 1,000 percent no chance of me leaving my home this evening?

But before I can write her back and let her down gently, I notice that George hasn't run up to greet me, and I start looking around. I know he can be a moody little worm sometimes, but he's *always* at the ready when I get home.

And then I hear it. It's a hammering that might actually *be* a hammer? Pounding over and over, coming through the ceiling like it's right on top of us.

Shit. It probably *is* right on top of us.

I go into my room and crouch to see under the bed. George is lying on the floor, looking exceptionally irritated on the surface but with a shaky layer of distress underneath. The pounding stops, and I coax him out.

"Sorry, sweet boy," I say, patting him and pulling him onto the bed so he's at least comfortable. His Prozac helps with his anxiety generally, but when something is disturbing his peace, I know it's particularly triggering. He normally projects such a tough exterior that whenever he's like this, it breaks my heart a little. I rub his back to try and give him something grounded and familiar to soothe him. "I'm sure that was just the worst of it."

But no sooner is the sentence out of my mouth than the pounding begins again. George crawls onto my lap and curls into a ball so tight I wonder if he's suddenly become spring-loaded.

I know exactly who's responsible for this, and it's making me all the more irritated. With George still glued to my lap, I gingerly reach into my pocket to get my phone and text Dane back.

Nora: I'm trying to be the bigger person with Eli, but if he's literally hammering something on the roof I'm allowed to be pissed about that, right?

Dane: Actually?

Nora: Yeah, and I came in and George was under the bed and very keyed up, so it's obviously not like a quick thing that just began. It keeps starting and stopping and George is a mess.

Dane: Fuck that guy.

Nora: It's too bad you're so reserved. I wish you'd just tell me how you feel.

Dane: You joke, but if I was there I'd go up with a hammer of my own and tell him to knock it off before I knock *him* off.

Nora: Normally I'd say that was extreme, but when it comes to Eli, I'm pretty sure he'd only respond to direct calls to violence.

Dane: So go tell him off.

The pounding stops for a brief moment, and I have a wave of relief, but then almost immediately it starts again. I figure I'll give it a minute before doing anything rash. I set my phone down to charge next to my bed. I tidy up and keep checking in on George, trying to calm him with soothing words. I'm about to pull out the ingredients for dinner when the hammering gets louder.

That's it. Eli can't play some game where he jovially spins me around one day and then expects carte blanche to jackhammer on top of my head.

I need to take J's advice and stand up for myself.

I storm upstairs.

"Eli!" I shout, bounding through the door onto the roof. In my rising annoyance, I fling it from its propped-open position so hard that it bounces off the wall and slams shut. "You can't just hammer random shit on the roof at all hours. You've been driving my dog insane, clearly for quite some time, and now you're driving *me* insane by hammering so hard that I can hear every single movement inside my house."

He's looked up from his position on his knees, his white T-shirt sweaty as he nails together what looks like flower beds or some other wooden structure intended for potting plants. He's staring at me, a look of horror and embarrassment crossing his face. I take a step back, wondering if maybe I went too far. Was he confused about the noise he was making? Does he not even realize how loud it is when he does that stuff?

But I could never have anticipated what he says next.

"Nora, I don't have my keys on me. The door was propped. You just locked us out."

CHAPTER 13

"What do you mean?" I ask, hoping that he's just messing with me. Although from the worried expression on his face, it doesn't seem likely.

"I mean, the door always locks when it's closed. You can't have a building where someone could climb onto the roof and then get inside."

"I wasn't suggesting that—"

"Right, so you closed it. It's locked."

He's staring at me now, almost daring me to understand the predicament we're in. And I'm going to start by refusing to believe him.

"Call Tom or Meryl. They're always home at night," I suggest, trying not to panic. "They'll just come open the door."

"You call them," he says, a note of irritation in his voice finally overshadowing his fear.

"I, uh . . ." I think about my phone happily charging on my nightstand. "No, you."

He stares at me, eyes narrowing. I shift uncomfortably at his focus. I can practically guess the next words out of his mouth.

"I didn't bring my phone upstairs with me." My mouth falls open. This is *bad*. This is extremely bad. "Please tell me you didn't just storm up here without your phone or keys to yell at me about making some noise at like seven at night and now you've locked us both out."

"Well, why don't *you* have *your* phone or keys?" I ask, trying to divert.

He stands up and walks toward me. I find myself backing into the door. With his muddy jeans and sweaty shirt, he looks like a dreamy dirtbag from an eighties music video. And I have no idea why that's the thought bursting into my mind, when in actuality I'm faced with a man who looks like he wants to murder me.

"I'm building a planter," he says. "I didn't bring anything with me because I didn't want my stuff to get dirty. It didn't occur to me that anyone would come up here and slam the door shut."

"Well, what if you had an emergency?" I counter, delaying the moment when we've run out of blame and have to actually contend with the situation.

He puts his hands on his hips. "Yes, obviously now I'm wishing I'd made some different choices."

We stand, staring at each other, my heavy breathing from running up the stairs finally starting to calm, even if my pulse is now racing for a different reason. How long are we going to be up here? No one else comes to the roof for anything. What's going to happen to George?

Oh my god, George.

He's going to have a meltdown over my disappearance. He'll be all alone and, yes, okay, I always have food sitting out for him, because he's the pickiest dog on earth and likes to graze like the weirdo that he is, but I didn't even take him out tonight! He's not going to understand what's happening. He's going to think I abandoned him. At some point he's going to start barking and never stop, and no one is going to realize my door is unlocked, and no one else has my key except our super, Vardan, and he doesn't even live in our building, and now it's too late for anyone to even call him since he's already gone home for the day, and—

Eli grabs my shoulders, and it shocks me out of the panic I'm spiraling into.

"Don't go there," he says quietly, his face close enough to mine now that I can make out the flecks of honey in his otherwise brown eyes.

"Go where?" I ask suspiciously.

"Panicking."

"I'm not panicking," I lie.

"What's got you the most worried?" he says, in an oddly calm voice. His hands are still gripping my shoulders, and I have to admit it's helping a little.

"My dog," I admit. "He was already freaking out"—I stop myself from saying *because of your hammering*, because it strikes me as extremely unhelpful in this particular moment—"and I haven't even taken him out tonight, so he's going to be uncomfortable and confused."

"He'll be okay, though," he says, much more soothing and matter of fact than I would've expected from him. It reminds me of his deft handling of Kwan through poker; he's showing a sliver of kindness without being patronizing or even acknowledging that he's helping.

It's strange to see this side of him again, and even stranger that it's in my direction. I'm sort of surprised he hasn't continued berating me. As much as I'll probably never admit it, this situation is obviously my doing, even if I didn't mean to get us into it. I'm never this rash; something about Eli *makes* me rash. But it's still my fault that I stormed up here without any keys or phone and then slammed the door in my worked-up state.

"He's going to be so scared," I say quietly.

"I know," he sighs. "But he's not going to starve, and the worst thing that'll happen is you'll have to clean up a bit of mess whenever you get home."

I don't love that phrase—"whenever you get home." At some point *someone* will come searching for us, right?

"Did you tell anyone you were on the way to shout at me?" he asks, verbalizing my own thoughts but with a touch of amusement in his voice.

It hits me. "Yes! I told my best friend, Dane," I cheer. "Or, well, *she* suggested I come shout at you, actually," I emphasize, as though another person encouraging me somehow lessens my own crime.

"The urban landscaper?"

"Yes." I'm shocked he remembers that.

"So if you don't respond, do you think she'll come find you?"

At that my heart sinks. "Well . . ." I shift on my heels, sheepish because I know what the answer is. "I suppose, at some point she'll find it weird. But she has pool tonight, and if I don't answer her, she's probably just going to go to practice and not really give it another thought. Sometimes, if I don't want to go out, I avoid texting her back. So she's probably just going to think that's what's happening."

He nods, taking it in. He keeps nodding well past the point where he should've understood, but I guess this situation warrants quite a bit of acceptance.

After what feels like an eternity, he turns around. Does he have a plan of action? Maybe he knows how to get us off the roof without keys? Maybe he was just messing with me and is now going to call someone?

But all those hopes are dashed when he unceremoniously plops to the ground and leans up against the planter he was building.

"What are you doing?" I ask.

"I'm sitting."

"Yes, I can see that, but *why* are you sitting? What are we going to do?"

The sun is starting to set, and the light makes him look unfairly angular, almost ethereal, up against the backdrop of steel and brick New York City buildings behind him. But it also showcases how weary he looks. He's got a smear of dirt across his face, and his hair is tousled. Instead of that sort of badass look I encountered when I first stormed in, he now just seems contemplative. There's so much expression written across his face that, in combination with the light, I find myself thinking that his profile is bursting to be photographed. There's so much life in this image in front of me. Frustration, defeat, acceptance, physicality, dirt, golden hour light, messy curls, and a shirt that sits just so while being crumpled enough to display how hard he was working.

I need to stop staring at him, so I do the only logical thing. I slump down next to him, trying to be careful with my previously-a-great-idea swishy skirt that now I'm realizing I'll probably have to sleep in.

"I'm sorry I closed the door," I say, because I am.

"It's not your fault," he murmurs, and my head whips toward him, incredulous that he'd let me off the hook so easily. He sees my stunned expression, and a small smile lightens his face. "Well, it *is* your fault, but there was no way you could've meant to do *that*. It was an honest mistake, and bad luck that we're the only two people on the planet who can go anywhere without our phones."

I chuckle, because it really is that. Truly bad luck.

"Are you worried?" I ask.

He nods. "I'm not worried about me, but yeah . . . I have . . . cats."

At that my eyes widen. "You? Have cats?"

"They were my nan's," he explains quickly, as though he's confessing something. I don't say anything else, because as a dog person, I never know what to say about cats. Cats are fine alone, right? Don't they prefer that? Does it really matter if he's gone? But he continues. "They're mine now, and I sort of . . . dote on them. So I'm a little worried that they'll get flummoxed if I don't come home."

I don't want that to melt some small corner of my heart, but it does. I can't help but let an image of this bombastic, overt, know-it-all man softening around little animals run across my mind.

"What kind of cats?" I ask, before I can stop myself. The need for the visual is too great.

He hesitates, but then relents. "They aren't like a specific breed or anything. My nan adopted them, and she never put much stock into thinking any animals were more special than any others." I think about my little mangy mutt of a George and couldn't agree more. "But they're both sort of . . . I don't know . . . white and floofy?"

"'Floofy'?" I choke out, trying not to laugh.

"Well, yeah. Their hair makes them look three times larger than they actually are. It sticks out straight, as though they've been electrocuted. So I don't know how else you would describe it. 'Floofy' is colloquial enough to make sense."

"You live with two porcelain-colored giant shedding maniac cats?" I ask, trying to mentally wrap my mind around this updated image of his home.

"I never said they were maniacs," he responds with a roll of his eyes. But he's not denying the rest either.

"That's surprising," I say.

He fixes me with one of his smirks. "Why?"

I purse my lips in thought. I can't say the sort of gross patriarchal thought that's floating through my mind. He's too *masculine* for cats. For *floofy cats*. But maybe, on second thought, it makes sense. "I guess I could see that," I finally say. "Cats are sort of prickly and arrogant."

He bursts out a laugh, and I'm surprised that he seems to enjoy the roasting.

"And as a dog person, you are . . . ," he leads.

"Oh, well, dogs are devoted," I say without hesitation. "They give of themselves. Dogs have no judgment. Dogs are the best."

"Right, the *dogs* themselves might be the best, but maybe that means the people who own them are insecure, praise-hungry clingers."

I snort out a laugh. Nicely played.

"What are your cats' names?" I ask, trying to picture them. And from the embarrassment that crosses his expression, I'm particularly delighted to have asked.

"Paws and Whiskers," he says, and now my laugh is even louder. "What?"

"Those are the kinds of names a toddler would come up with."

"I think you're going to feel *really* bad when you learn that my sister's kids named the cats."

"Actually?" I ask, unsure.

He pauses. "I have no idea, to be honest," he says and slumps a little more. "But it would make a better story, right? It's not inconceivable, since my sister does have two little kids."

I roll my eyes back at him and he smiles. It's funny how much his face changes, depending on the angle and expression. He's not classically handsome—it's why I never gave it much thought over video. Well, that and obviously the fact that he was sort of my patient. But in person he's dynamic. He's megawatt. And that smile seeps into whoever it's directed at. It's that masculine energy again, which is so much of what I dislike about him from afar. But up close it's captivating.

And it makes it even more obvious when the smile goes away.

"I didn't talk to my nan as much in recent years as I used to," he says quietly, surprising me with the subject shift and his sudden morose candor. I guess being stuck with an indefinite stretch in front of you makes you immediately let go of airs. "I spent every summer with her as a kid. We had kind of the same brain, only hers was more mathematical and mine was more linguistic. So we were very bonded. And I think my mum thought it would be nice for me to get out occasionally, away from London and everything. But lately, I didn't call her as much, because I've just been so damn busy. I still would've said we were close. When we talked, it was like nothing had changed. But I took her presence for granted, and I really regret it."

The sun is starting to set even more now, and he looks out into the sky, pink hues shifting the light.

"I didn't mean . . ." I pause, not sure what I want to say, because I know I didn't intend to make him feel like this. But he waves it off.

"It just got me thinking, when you asked why those were the cats' names. It's the kind of thing I would've known years ago. I'd probably have been the one to name them, to be honest. I've been thinking about that a lot lately."

"Well," I say slowly, "it must be a constant reminder, living in her apartment." It hadn't really dawned on me how much that must be weighing on him every day to be in her space.

"We have so many memories there," he says, tousling his hair like a nervous habit. "It's a lot, but in a good way. I'm surrounded by her, and I think I needed to be for a bit. But it's also why I want to change some things. I can't just stew in it all. She wanted me to have the flat, so I need to honor that."

"Did you want to move here?" I ask, suddenly curious.

I realize I don't really know much about his job or his circum-stances. It was never really relevant to therapy, so I don't have that context. His work wasn't a sore spot in his and Sarah's relationship, and she never brought it up.

He sighs, the question lingering in the air. I don't know how we got so heavy so fast from a conversation about cats. Maybe—fortunately or unfortunately—the therapist thing makes people get to the core of their stuff more quickly.

But then he turns and gives me a wry smile. "Well, for some reason my girlfriend broke up with me"—he chuckles—"and I was crashing at my sister's house, so the opportunity to move to a place of my own was very appealing."

I walked right into that one.

"I didn't—"

"I shouldn't have yelled at you when I saw you," he says, cutting me off. I can feel my eyebrows rising, the surprise of that admission strange in the air. He rubs his hands down his face and takes a deep breath. "I was still pretty mad about the whole thing."

"And now you're not?"

He turns his head straight toward the skyline again, watching the clouds move and darken as he takes the question in.

"This month here has been sort of cathartic," he finally admits. "Clearing out Nan's things and resetting has sort of made me . . . able to put the past in the past, I suppose. I obviously knew rationally you didn't cause Sarah to break up with me. But it was just easier to believe that for a while."

He's still not looking at me, but I can tell there's something palpable about letting that go for him. It's almost as though his shoulders relax with the admission.

"I can understand that," I say honestly. The therapist in me wants to ask so many more questions, but I stop myself. He's not my patient anymore—and really, he barely ever was. It was so short, and I talked to

Sarah so much more than him anyway. I'd rather stick to trying to find a way to coexist as neighbors. "So do you think you'll stay here? Or go back to London?" I ask, trying to switch gears a bit.

"Just making conversation or trying to get rid of me?" he retorts.

I shake my head. "You're impossible."

At that he grins, as though he's enjoying baiting me. "I'm not sure, actually," he replies, answering my original question. "I can work remotely, so it doesn't really matter where I am. I could see myself going back to London—it'll always feel like home, and my family's there. But I really like it here. I'm not sure I understand everything about America or New York, but for now it's suiting me."

"What don't you understand?"

"Like . . . I've always known your health care system is shite, but I didn't realize that eyes and teeth aren't included," he says, and I now have no idea where he's going with this, but I find I want to go down the rabbit hole with him. "Who decided that? Who designed a system that was like, right, hearts and bums and ears are all under this one plan. But if you want them to make sure your teeth don't fall out, that's dental insurance. And if you want to not be blind, that's a separate vision insurance. Why?"

I'm trying not to laugh at him, but it's such a good point that it's almost ridiculous. "I never thought of it that way," I concede. "But you left out the brain. It's even worse for mental health insurance—I get to deal with that all day long."

"I'll never understand it," he says, tossing his arms up, both of us finally succumbing to laughing over the factual absurdity of what he's saying but also, perhaps, our entire current situation.

I look around and notice it's almost dark. My stomach growls a bit, and it makes me nervous. I look over at Eli, and he's watching me with concern.

"Someone will come for us eventually," he says, accurately guessing my mood shift.

"Not tonight, though," I admit, despite not wanting to stare into the truth of the situation.

"Probably not," he concurs softly.

"What are we going to do?"

"Twenty questions? Thumb wars?" He considers. "I don't know— just whatever we can to pass the time and not go completely nuts while we overanalyze how long it's going to be until someone looks for us."

"Thumb wars?" I ask.

At my incredulity, he turns and comes to sit right in front of me.

Why does he take every single thing as a challenge?

He holds out his hand, thumb up, waiting for me to join. There's self-satisfaction written all across his expression. If I don't participate, then he wins by default by psyching me out. If I play, I'm a chump who's given in. It's lose-lose for me, and he knows it.

But there's nothing else to do on this ridiculous roof, so I might as well succumb to the madness.

I take his hand, watch it curve around mine, and immediately realize this was a bad idea.

I'm not sure I needed to know the texture of his grip. I'm not sure I needed to know how warm his hand is, even as the steamy weather has cooled off around us. I'm not sure I needed to know the ways my fingers feel small inside his.

Whatever visceral reaction I've been having to Eli since the moment we met, it's compounded by having these physical revelations. I want to shed them like a skin and burn them out of my mind, because for everything I dislike about this man, I'm going to have to stop kidding myself and admit that I'm undeniably attracted to him. It doesn't have any bearing on anything for a multitude of reasons—former patient, agitating neighbor, his entire personality—but it's still floating there, palpable and irrefutable, even if all rationality would say it shouldn't be so. My body inexplicably wakes up around Eli, and it ignores that that fact is a major inconvenience.

I realize I've been staring at our hands intertwined for too long and look up. His eyes are on me, unreadable. I'm finding it sort of hard to breathe.

"Ready?" he asks, and I huff incredulously. He has no idea what I'm ready for in this moment.

But he's oblivious as he starts moving his thumb and saying words I haven't heard since I was probably in middle school. "One, two, three, four, I declare a thumb war."

I move my thumb side to side along his, and I can't help but giggle. This is ridiculous.

And of course, because I'm not taking it seriously—and admittedly distracted—he smushes my thumb almost instantly.

"Aha!" he says, throwing his hands into the air, as though the victory is for something other than two bored people locked on a roof.

I'm grateful for the loss of his hand on mine, though, because I need to get whatever thoughts are running through my brain to exit. Immediately.

"So that was a really great activity for passing thirty seconds of time," I say dryly, hoping to put an end to any consideration of another round.

He laughs and shakes his head. "Okay, yeah. We can probably do better than thumb wars," he admits. "Truth or dare?" he asks, eyes widening as though he's had a really brilliant, unique idea.

"What are you, stuck at the age of seven?" I ask.

"Just someone who was stuck on a lot of long car trips with my little sister as a kid and hasn't had a need for entertainment without audio, books, or television for quite a long time," he points out.

I stand up, maybe to get a better lay of the land, but mostly to shake off whatever's lingering after touching him. I need to tamp down the firestorm that's exploded across my insides.

I look across the mostly empty roof, the expansive skyline of New York City stretching out in front of us but so unreachable. We really are in a closed circuit here. There's the water tower and some air-conditioning equipment, but otherwise it's just us, Eli's in-progress planters, and a locked door.

I sigh, the movement having allowed me to pull myself back together, and sit back down—although this time a little farther from Eli to keep some physical distance between us. "I don't think any dares are doable in a place with nothing around us."

"Okay then, truth," he says, clearly not the type to be put off by wrinkles forming in every single plan. "Tell me an embarrassing thing."

"You first," I say automatically, as though my default with this man is distrust.

"I really like my food burned to a crisp," he responds without hesitation. "Like, if you give me a piece of meat fully charred, I'm so happy. And I'll eat a vegetable that's been cooked to within an inch of its life."

"That's not *embarrassing*," I remark.

"It is when a rare steak is placed in front of me."

I roll my eyes. "All food?" I ask.

"Not junk food or dessert," he says. "I love to bake, so obviously you don't want to burn any of that."

"You love to *bake*?"

The idea of this man in an apron dusted with flour seems anathema to his wiry, tough exterior. *I'm* a baker. I'm an introvert who loves to be alone with books and recipes and snacks. Not this guy.

But apparently I've gotten another thing wrong about him.

"Oh yeah," he says, clearly enjoying upending my expectations. "I was totally the gawky little kid with that kind of pudding-bowl haircut who would sit on the counter and lick the spoon while my nan was baking for me. I was a super-picky eater, but I loved cookie dough and cupcakes and really any baked good. And it's what my nan did with all her free time, so I got used to watching her and then eventually she taught me too."

"Huh," I say, trying to imagine it. Trying to picture brash Eli as a small child nestled in with a middle-aged Esther, chocolate frosting getting scooped out of a bowl. The edges of young Eli are fuzzy but there.

Yet there's one part I *cannot* picture. "It's so strange to me, thinking about Esther as maternal," I say, almost to myself. "She was always so stern. Mathematics professor has always made sense to me, but doting grandma baker is blowing my mind."

His expression softens as I talk about her. Even with her being described as stern, he seems to love the memory.

"She was definitely no nonsense," he remembers. "And she wasn't exactly maternal; you're right about that. But we sort of fit together. It was *easy* for me to be with Nan. We understood each other, and we didn't require a lot of energy from one another. We liked a lot of the same stuff, and we had the same sort of logical way of approaching things. So she brought that into baking, too, and it really worked for my style as well."

I can't help but think it's like the opposite of my family. Eli and Esther were hexagonal pegs in a world of round and square holes, but they went together. Whereas my brother and I are those normal rounds and squares, but my parents are pterodactyl shaped, completely off the board of anything you can imagine. I wonder if my parents ever wished they had kids who saw the world the way they did. What a comfort it must be to be a unique entity who happens to be related to a similar unique entity.

"Okay, now it's your turn," he says, breaking my thoughts.

"None of those were particularly embarrassing," I point out. "More like fun facts."

He smirks. "Okay then. Your turn for some fun facts."

I feel sort of boring, because I don't have an instant answer to that query. There's nothing about me that I would say automatically stands out. I try *not* to stand out. The only person who seems to make me go off the deep end of normal behavior is Eli.

But that's not something I want to admit.

He doesn't let it go, though. "How about—what if I asked your landscaper friend? What would she say?"

"Dane?" I think. There's a million things Dane would love to embarrass me with. "She also mocks my baking, even though she's probably the largest consumer of its spoils," I say with a smile. "She does like to knock the way I read, though," I admit.

"How can someone mock the way you read?"

"I always read the end first," I admit.

At that he stands up, incredulous. Dramatic. Typical. "You can't be serious!"

"Just like the last couple of pages." I cross my arms across my chest, armor against his disbelief.

"The whole *point* is to wonder how it ends. That's a crime. That should be officially entered as a criminal act. You can't *read the ending* before you even start!"

He's pacing a little, and now I'm sort of enjoying how much this boring fact about myself has flummoxed him.

"It's comforting!" I explain with a shrug. "You can get into the story and the details without all the anxiety of not knowing what's ahead."

"That's life, Nora. No one gets to know what's ahead." He crouches down until he's in front of me, and I'm once again rattled by his nearness. "That's the *fun* of it."

CHAPTER 14

Apparently, starting with embarrassments can open up an entire world of conversation.

As a therapist I get handed people's deepest secrets all the time. But the mundane fragments of life can often be the most illuminating.

Up on a roof with nothing to do and nowhere to go, we allow our conversation to wind around, plucking small pieces from each other's tapestry. It's a way to pass the time, but in doing so we're weaving something new—and the more we talk, the further away I can push that earlier sensation of being physically on guard around Eli.

Instead, sitting dutifully distant, we hand over small irrelevant intimacies, like how when he's alone, he'll order a particular cider called Strongbow that he loved as a teenager, but he would now get ruthlessly mocked by any fellow Brit, who would see it as a ridiculous watered-down drink. Or how his mother made him take ballet class as a kid and how he stuck with it until he was eight. How he broke his left arm as a teenager and had to wear his watch on his right wrist, but then he got used to it, so now it's the only way he can wear a watch.

And I tell him how I got George because of the trip after my breakup, and he howls with laughter that my big takeaway was deciding I wanted an old cranky dog. Or how as a kid I never realized it was weird that my brother would eat all the cream from inside the Oreos before handing them to me. Or the fact that I still know a song—that names every country in the world—from a random cartoon VHS I had as a kid, and it's the song I sing to myself whenever I get nervous. He makes me do a demonstration, and I love how much the absurdity of it delights him.

"Do you get nervous a lot?" he asks, once he's made me sing this ridiculous song three separate times. "I would think at this point you'd be unshakable, having to listen to so much of people's lives. It's like, most people are told to imagine everyone in their underwear, but you sort of get the verbal version of that from your patients every single day."

I consider it. "It's not the same when it's about you, though."

He nods but still seems skeptical. "I just think you get to know people so much more than most of the other people in their lives."

"Yeah, but they don't know *me*," I reply.

I can see that land.

"Is that . . ." He pauses, as though we're teetering on some precipice of conversation. We've shared a lot in however many hours have gone by since we got locked up here. Our drawbridges have been lowered from their usual battle-ready position. We're hungry, tired, and uncomfortable. That's certainly made for a feeling of being in something together. But we haven't really gone too deep yet. And I'm not sure whether I'm wishing that he would.

But, as with anything with Eli, he doesn't wait on a precipice for long. He just jumps. "Is that lonely?"

I blow out the breath I'm holding in. It's a heavy question. "I do wonder sometimes if holding everyone else's problems makes me less likely to discuss my own. Or rather, have space with others to even want to talk about myself."

"And them? Like if your friends complain about their lives to you, do you feel like you're at work?"

"I don't have that many friends," I admit before I can stop myself. It's strange how easily that honest assessment simply slipped out. "I operate better with just one best friend. I talk to Dane a lot, and maybe that's why we get along—we're both sort of inherently unable to abide personal complication. She's the most straightforward person I know."

"But does that mean she never asks you about yourself?"

I consider that. I talk to Dane about my day as it goes along, and she's not afraid to call me out. But we don't exactly delve into my hopes and dreams. I can't help but think about J and wonder how he's become the one person in my life that actually probes deeper.

"She does, although we don't get into it a lot. But I feel totally supported by her. And I have another friend lately that I can get into weightier things with more," I admit. "Having two people seems almost extravagant." I laugh softly.

"I have one friend like that," he says, stirring to readjust his position. Sitting on the ground for hours on end is not going to feel great tomorrow, but there really isn't another option. "I feel less lonely when I can talk to her."

"You feel lonely?" I ask, surprised.

It's not that I don't know that the way someone presents themselves often hides something underneath. That's sort of psychology 101. Yet maybe with Eli, it's been easier to place him in a box and believe the extroverted man wasn't introspective enough to pinpoint his own loneliness.

But it's clear from how he shifts uncomfortably that maybe this conversation has scratched too close to the surface.

"Sorry," I say. "Therapist habit to pry."

It's not a totally honest statement. I'm actually pretty good at separating work from life. But I don't want to admit that I'm curious more than anything.

He just shakes his head, though. "No, it's okay. I mean . . . what else have we got to do, right?" He chuckles.

"Right," I say, one of many reminders that the last few hours haven't been a choice, but that we're stuck here with nothing but conversation to keep us away from wondering how long we'll be trapped.

"I thought about that a lot when Sarah and I broke up," he says, not looking at me again, as though the admittance can't be said straight on. "I thought being in a relationship meant someone knew me, and so

I was terrified to lose that. But after she left, I didn't really miss *her* so much as having someone pottering around the flat. And then I'd chat to this friend of mine, and I realized I'd always told her a thousand times more than I ever told Sarah. I felt less lonely talking to a friend than I had through my entire relationship." He puts his head in his hands and blows out all the air from his lungs. "Christ, that's a sad-sack thing to say," he mumbles. "I think being stuck on a roof is making me morose."

I hate that in describing his life in a real way, he's programmed to believe it's pathetic. I know a lot of men feel that way, but it's heart-breaking to see. This live wire, this ball of charisma, this surety can hide so much. I've always felt it's more natural for lonely people to be introverts. But maybe that's just because I am one. Extroverts can be seeking that connection even more and desperately hanging on to whatever comes along.

It shouldn't be surprising that either of us has turned morose—we're stuck on a roof with no end in sight, and as time goes on, the lack of food and water feels more and more dismal. But for all that baggage in front of us, it's strange that I don't feel more scared. His presence has, shockingly, brought comfort instead of panic. And as surprised as I am that he's unexpectedly wormed his way in, that admission of his sadness shifts something even more and makes me want to fix whatever small things I can control in this moment. And perhaps that means letting down my guard a little bit too.

After the thumb war, I've kept a safe distance all night. But I push past the nervous invisible fence I've set up for myself and scoot over. The ingrained need to soothe him in this moment is overriding the physical trepidation I get when he's close. I rest my head on his shoulder. I can feel the surprise in his posture at the movement, but then he relaxes.

And instead of it making me feel on edge again, I find that now it's easy to sink into him, easy to fit next to him. It's natural in a way I would never have expected. And after hours of leaning against brick walls and planters, there's something especially reassuring about warm humanity.

"It's not a sad-sack thing," I say quietly. "I think it's lucky to even have one friend who you feel actually knows you. Loneliness exists in so many relationships—more than you would imagine. I don't think being in a relationship is a barometer for that. Some people are naturally lonelier than others, some people haven't found someone they can be themselves with, and others just are going through a phase where they feel disconnected. But I'd lean into the relationships and friendships that do feel real—even if it isn't necessarily the person you would've expected it to be, if it's bringing you some peace, I wouldn't question it."

I imagine what J would say, if this was one of my columns. He's really become that person for me, the one who I can tell anything to. It occurs to me that he might've texted tonight and is wondering why I haven't texted back. I hate that whatever tentative move we've made toward reality is potentially being questioned by my inadvertent silence.

But the worry over J is interrupted by the very real sigh of the person whose shoulder I'm currently resting on.

"Thank you," he says quietly. "I hate that we got stuck up here, but I'm glad at least that maybe now we can be . . . friends?"

"I'd like that," I whisper back.

Because at this point, after the hours of being up here, it's actually true.

"Okay, this is both funny as hell and deeply sad for your backs."

I hear Dane's voice, and I'm confused. But then I open my eyes, and suddenly it all comes back to me. The roof. The door. The night spent talking.

There's a crick in my neck that feels like the worst kind of punishment. I must've fallen asleep resting my head on Eli's shoulder, and he in turn tilted his onto mine. I don't know how we slept like that, or when we even fell asleep, but at least I'm comforted by the fact that there probably wouldn't have been any better option.

I lift my head and stretch, pulling my arms up and trying to get my body to stop screaming. I feel Eli shift next to me, and I wish he weren't so close that I can catch the dreamy scent of sleep wafting off him. I can still feel the warmth of his shoulder pressed on my cheek.

I know we said we'd be friends now, but ugh, I can't keep lusting after this man. I'm glad he opened up, and I'm glad I saw a different side to him. But I need to shake the inconvenient attraction, because this isn't a place where my mind needs to go or ever *could* go.

"This must be the famous Dane," I hear him croak beside me.

Dane looks exceptionally pleased that her reputation precedes her. She's standing over both of us, her Pacers hat backward and her Doc Martens unlaced, as though she ran over here in a rush.

"Yeah, sorry it took me this long to put two and two together," she says, with her typical casual air that implies she's not really that sorry. "I figured you were just avoiding coming out, since, you know, that's something you often try to do, especially on a weekday."

"Fair," I mumble, mildly hating being called out so effectively.

"But then I texted you this morning, and you didn't answer, and that felt like a red flag. And then I *called*, and you didn't answer, which is not something you ever do." I like the grateful look she sends me. It's true what I said to Eli—I feel seen by Dane, even if we don't often delve into words. If Dane calls, I always pick up, and vice versa. So I can imagine she was probably alarmed a bit by my silence. "You weren't in your apartment, but your phone was. And the last thing you said to me was that you were going up to the roof, so . . ." She waves her arms out, like *Here we are,* and I imagine the scene in front of her looks fairly absurd. Two pathetic grown-ups who got themselves locked out. "I'm glad to see that my fear of a potential murder didn't come to fruition."

Eli chuckles next to me, and I'm grateful he finds Dane amusing rather than too much. A lot of people think Dane is a lot, and it's usually a good barometer for me disliking someone.

"I considered it," he says slyly. "But too obvious once I was caught."

"Yeah, you wouldn't beat that rap," Dane concurs. "And probably not great for your amusement at riling this one up if she wasn't around to torture."

I scoff, because what a *ridiculous* theory. But looking over at Eli, he's gone a bit red. *Has* he been riling me up more than he would have otherwise because he finds it amusing? Surely that's a stretch.

"Well, I think after a night of starvation and forced proximity, there's a détente anyway," he says, turning to look at me. "Wouldn't you say?"

"Yes," I admit. "I certainly agree we got off on the wrong foot, to say the least."

He laughs as he stands up and stretches again. A small sliver of his stomach shows as his shirt lifts, and I immediately move to look back at Dane, as though staring at Eli's body is going to burn me. She lifts an eyebrow, because she catches every damn thing. *Great.*

He holds out a hand to help me up, and when I put mine in his, I can't help but be reminded of every second of the thumb war last night. I thought I'd effectively tamped down whatever touching him had done to me, but apparently I needed to keep *not* touching him in order to shake it off.

He pulls me up, and it takes a second to feel normal after sitting so long. One leg is asleep, and the other is cramped. I'm definitely ready to get down from this roof, even if the morning light off the buildings and the glow behind the water towers dotted across the skyline make for a beautiful view.

"You okay?" he asks, and I nod, even as I hop around and twist to try and get my body back to some semblance of normalcy.

We all walk downstairs, and I immediately fling open my door to an ecstatic George. For a moody little gremlin, he's all love right now, his tiny stub of a tail wagging so hard the entire back half of his body is in motion. I flop to the ground, and he jumps into my lap, licking my face like it's his job, leaving no inch dry.

"I'm so sorry, George," I choke out, trying to pet him and squeeze him as much as I can even as he jumps and wiggles with excitement. "I'm so, so sorry. I didn't mean to leave you. You know I'd never leave you alone on purpose. It was so stupid of me. I'm so sorry."

Dane pushes past me, shaking her head like she's disappointed in my maudlin display. She starts getting eggs out of the fridge and puts a pan on the stove, prioritizing getting me some food after a long night of unintentional fasting.

When George has practically licked me clean, I lift him so I can stand up as well. I look behind me and see Eli is still there, watching the scene unfold.

"Do you think Paws and Whiskers will launch themselves at you when they see you?" I ask as I try to wipe all the dog drool from my face.

"Not a cat's style." He shrugs, a small grin blooming.

There's something strange sitting between us. Not necessarily bad, but different. We've been through a weird thing together, and now we're on the other side, but perhaps not quite used to the idea yet that it's over. He looks like he has something to say, but doesn't. We watch each other, a pause in the air, something left unsaid even after *so much* was said. So many small things were shared; in the light of day it seems like they added up to something large.

"See you around then," I say, unsure of what to do now. "I hope you don't have any other neighborly escapades that lock you out."

"I don't know." He furrows his brow like he's lost in thought. "Gladys might have some shenanigans up her sleeve."

"Oh yeah, she's a real party animal," I snort.

"I know you're taking the piss, but back in the day she and my nan were probably the coolest cats around."

"'Coolest cats'?" I say with a laugh. "You really have been hanging out with octogenarians too much."

But Dane's voice cuts through the moment. "Nora, stop flirting and come eat something before you pass out!"

I can feel my face heat up. Goddamn it, Dane. Why does she have to make any interaction as awkward as humanly possible for me. *And was I flirting? Shit. Does he think I'm . . . flirting?*

He puts a hand on my shoulder and shakes his head with a small smile on his lips, a wordless commiseration that acknowledges my friend is razzing me. I appreciate him letting my embarrassment go unsaid.

"I'll see you soon, Nora," he says with a squeeze. "Thanks for the lovely if unintentional evening."

And with that, he turns around and opens the door to the stairwell. Leaving me to round on a smirking Dane and give her the hell she's expecting.

CHAPTER 15

"That was *extremely* awkward," I say, trying to fix her with my most stern stare even as she ignores me and sets an omelet on the table.

"Being up on your roof all night with a dude you can't decide if you want to murder or bone? Yeah, that must've been hard."

She grabs a fork, pours a glass of water, and then sticks them both next to my plate, eyeing me and then the chair. She sits down and watches me until I give in and sit across from her.

If she is trying to use melted cheese as a distraction tactic, it's working. At some point the hunger had started to feel normal, but shoving that first bite of hot pillowy eggs and velvety molten bliss into my mouth makes me even more ravenous. Dane watches as I inhale the entire omelet without saying a word and then wash it down with the full water glass.

"Hungry?" she jokes.

"I didn't quite realize how hungry," I admit in between bites. "I didn't have dinner before I got locked upstairs last night."

Dane leans in to look at me closer, like she's inspecting me for something. "So you didn't bone him?"

"Stop saying 'bone,'" I retort, the seriousness a little diminished by my mouth being full of toast.

"Yeah, I guess the roof, with no cushioning or like . . . wipes . . . would be a subpar experience," she snorts.

I fix her with another look, and she just chuckles.

"This wasn't like a choice I had," I emphasize. "It was a shitty situation, and we made the best of it."

"Well, not *the best*," Dane counters, still laughing under her breath.

I rub my hand down my face, not sure if I can take her mockery. It would be funnier if I wasn't feeling the remnants of being so inconveniently attracted to him. But perhaps it's a little bit like Stockholm syndrome, and none of that will seem real in the light of a normal day.

"Look, maybe he's not as bad as I originally thought," I admit, and I hate how smug Dane now looks. "But no, I am not interested in him. He's still not the kind of person I would hang out with on purpose. And he's sort of a former patient, so even the thought is on the border of ethical. Please just drop it," I sigh.

Dane holds up both hands in surrender. It's one thing I love about her—she calls things like she sees them but never belabors a point, especially when it's clearly bothering me. She gets up and sticks two more pieces of bread in the toaster and starts busying herself with making a cup of tea. She's mothering me, but I sort of like it after the night I've had.

I hear my phone chirp and remember it's been sitting there abandoned all night. I stand up to go retrieve it. There are a lot of messages on it—Dane's increasingly bewildered reaction to my nonresponse; my mother reminding me I'm supposed to take her to the farmers' market before work today because "I'm not sure how to pick the right tomato. How do you know if it's good or if it's mealy?"; a previous Tinder date who I'm probably going to ghost. And there, the newest message, is from J.

J: Are you a gym person?

I have no idea where this is going, but I'm mostly glad he didn't text me last night when I couldn't respond. Sorry to say I'm not, I write back.

I stare at the screen, watching the little dots that indicate he's writing something back, anticipating with a slight giddiness I can't pinpoint.

J: Oh don't be sorry. I just wanted to make sure, because I'm definitely NOT a gym person but I didn't want to do that awkward thing where I berate gym people and then you tell me you run a 10k every morning or bench press before breakfast.

Nora: I'm not only not running a 10k before breakfast, but I don't even have a concept for how far that is.

J: To be fair, it was the bench pressing that was before breakfast.

Nora: Ah, okay. Well in that case, definitely that person. Does it count if I'm only bench pressing a small irritated dog?

J: Absolutely. That's one dog more than I'm doing every day.

J: . . . I realise it sounds really bad to say I'm doing a dog every day.

J: This is what I get for trying to be clever and for typing before I think—implying that I'm attracted to canines. Well done, me.

I cackle, and Dane shoots me a look. I wave her off and go back to my phone, unable to stop grinning.

Nora: I would point out that we've gotten off track of the original question, but that seems obvious at this point.

J: Yes, I'd say so.

J: Right. Gyms. Before I was so mortifyingly embarrassed by my own words, I was *going* to ask if you thought I could still mock gym people even if my back has started to feel fifty years older whenever I sleep even mildly funny?

Nora: I think a key tenet of mocking people is being a little self-loathing, so I say mock away?

J: I knew you were the right conspirator on this.

"Are you . . . giggling?" I hear Dane ask from the other room.

I wander back in as she sets down my perfectly buttered toast along with a steaming cup of tea. I nestle back into my chair and take a bite, slower now that I'm not completely famished.

"I'm texting with J," I explain, as though that should cover everything. I look up and see she's watching me with a soft smile. "What?" I ask.

She shrugs and sits back across from me, leaning over the table as though she's trying to detail the lines of my expression. "It's cute. You like him."

"Yes . . . ," I say, feeling my face heat up a bit at the observation. "I think we've covered that, though."

"Yeah, but . . . it's real now. It's not just like you projecting on someone's writing."

I understand why she feels that way. I'm too embarrassed to try and verbalize that it's *always* felt real. And I'm not sure how I even would explain it—texting seems more immediate, more real, as she pointed out. But the substance and weight of our conversations haven't deepened. They're just more instantaneous. Texting has been easy because talking to J has always been easy. This is simply a new, faster medium.

"So now what?" she continues.

I take another large bite of toast to give myself a moment to answer. "Well, we agreed we'd meet up when I'm in London."

"And when's that going to be?" she asks.

I frown. "Oh, well, we haven't like set a particular time yet or anything. He'll be going to the event for the new boss, too, but we've just generally said we'd have coffee or something as well when I'm in town."

"Don't you want a more concrete plan?" she asks.

I squirm in my seat. In all our texting, I haven't actually brought up the original point of getting his number again since we started. "It's still like a month away." I shrug.

"So you're just going to keep texting this dude every day but then wing it when it comes to actually seeing him in person?"

"I'm seeing him in person either way at the event," I remind her.

"But you don't even know what he looks like, so you could see him but not *see him* unless you actually make a plan," she lobs back.

I know she sees that small piece of me that's still hesitant. Meeting J in person is going to have an effect on me, even if it doesn't on him. And that potential for unwanted friction is making me tentative. After all, I've been fine—my life is good. Is it worth potentially blowing up my serenity for a man? A man who may not even want me?

But the *possibility* of it being worth it—that little piece in the back of my brain that says it doesn't hurt to hope your life could dial up from a nine to a full-on ten—makes me know I'm not actually backing out now.

"I'll make a plan," I say firmly, as much to myself as to her.

My phone rings, and I look down. My mother is video calling me. Wonderful. But unavoidable.

I swipe to answer, and she immediately starts talking when her face pops up on the screen. "What time do you want to go to the market? I don't want to leave it to too late, or you'll be with patients and all the good tomatoes will already be gone."

"I'm sorry I didn't text earlier; I was—"

"Don't worry about it, just want to make my schedule for the day!" she says breezily.

I want to believe she's being nice, but I can't help the prickle of annoyance that she doesn't even consider asking *How are you?* before launching into her own queries. If someone who is usually prompt didn't text me back for a whole night, I'd at least have a cursory wonder if everything was okay.

But my mom has never had that mother's intuition that allows her to consider her children's well-being outside of her own. If I said to her, *Mom, I was stuck on the roof all night,* she would absolutely overreact and make a big fuss, but it wouldn't occur to her to even ask after me. She assumes I'm always fine; it's a comfort to her to believe I'm always fine.

"I should be ready in half an hour or so, if you want to start making your way over here. Nothing opens until eight a.m. anyway," I finally say. "I'm going to hop in the shower quickly, but otherwise I'm good to go. And George needs to go out too." He looks up at me, grateful for the acknowledgment.

"Great, great, great," she says, blowing me a kiss. "I'll text you when I'm close. Bring some treats for Waldo."

At that she hangs up.

"Your mother is a piece of work," Dane mumbles, grabbing my plate and walking it over to the dishwasher.

George is now standing, a little silent entreaty to get moving. And since I don't want to dwell on whatever kind of piece of work my mother is, I take that as my sign to follow George's implicit instructions and start getting ready.

Somehow, even after a strange night, I'm able to pull my day back in order. I jump into the shower and let the scalding-hot water rinse off whatever remnants of the evening are pervading my skin. It's a reset.

When I'm dry and dressed, I come out to a patient George. I worry that he thinks I left him on purpose, and this is his way of showing me he can be more of a team player. Even though most people would be happy with a dog that waits nicely, I don't like this unsure version of him. But I'm hoping after a day or two of normalcy, he'll go back to believing he's king of the home.

Dane has cleaned up everything, and I give her a wordless hug. She reciprocates with a kiss on the cheek, and I know that's all we'll ever have to say about this. I'll never have to mention my inadvertent locking out if I don't want to. And for that, and many other reasons, I'm forever grateful to have Dane in my life.

I head out at eight, once I can see my mother's location approaching mine. Her phone is dead half the time, so it's not always an accurate way to time her, but whenever she's remembered to charge it, it's easier than trying to get ahold of her. It took some coaxing to get her to turn on her location sharing—she claimed she wanted to be "off the grid"—but I eventually got her to accept the basic fact that if she's going to have a smartphone, the phone is tracking her whereabouts whether or not she's allowing me to see it, and eventually she relented.

Our trip to the market is easier than I feared it might be. It's still early enough that the large Wednesday market isn't overrun, my mom brought the more low-key Waldo, and she doesn't debate me about which tomatoes to get. We wander over to my favorite stand, Eckerton Hill, and she proceeds to ask the twentysomething college-student employee more questions about soil than I think he was prepared to answer. You'd think she was a country dweller or an agricultural biologist and not a neurotic New Yorker who gets freaked out when she sees a moth.

And thankfully, out in the light of day, George is trotting along, head held high in his normal state. He's ignoring every dog, including Waldo, and barking at leaves he finds offensive. It might not seem normal for most dogs, but it's blissfully normal for George. I let myself worry slightly less that I've given him irreparable trust issues.

Armed with three different types of tomatoes and new knowledge to spout about cucamelons (*Did you know about these, Nora? Surely you couldn't if you hadn't brought them over to me*), my mom waves goodbye half an hour later. I have enough time to drop George off and give him an extra cuddle before heading off to work.

My clients today are mercifully straightforward. It's as though the universe has recognized I had enough nonsense last night and need to not have anything too dramatic to deal with.

I get home and spend the night cooking and baking. There's something essential for my nerves about the manual step by step of a recipe. I make shepherd's pie, because I've been thinking of it ever since J mentioned it, despite it being totally unseasonable. And it's definitely the right move because a warm, creamy, meaty, stew-like concoction is essential to setting me back in a centered place. And as I scoop out the dough for black-and-white cookies, I imagine handing them to neighbors and clients tomorrow and seeing the small smiles that cookies inevitably bring out in anyone.

It's calm. After a night of the unexpected—unexpected scenarios, unexpected people, unexpected revelations—I need a night where nothing happens and everything is easy. It's as though I started with my scalding shower and ended with cooking to fully put the strangeness of last night behind me.

But when I get into bed later that night and pull out the new book I purchased yesterday, my hand hovers. I want to skip to the last few pages like I always do, just to be safe in the knowledge that I know it'll all end okay. But I hate that Eli's voice is now in my head. *That's life, Nora. No one gets to know what's ahead.*

It's certainly true of Eli. My judgments of him were all . . . off base.

Or maybe that's not fair to me. They were based on a context. And that context is often our reality when we meet someone—we're not free when we're introduced to a new person. We're slotting them into some role—employee, friend, first date, man in therapy who doesn't want to be there. We see someone a certain way based on how they're projecting themselves onto that role. It's so rare when we just get to be wholly *ourselves.*

And maybe that's why the texting with J feels so uninhibited. It feels freer than any other relationship in my life right now.

I *don't* know what's ahead. It's frightening. But I'm proud of myself. I'm taking the leap without knowing the ending. I'm putting myself out there with J, and it feels worth it. I'm doing it my own way—slowly. Carefully. But I'm not avoiding it anymore. I'm not hiding behind a document.

It's so annoying that I once again hear Eli's voice from earlier. *That's the fun of it.*

CHAPTER 16

Coming home from a Friday family dinner always leaves me feeling a bit wiped out.

The way my parents talk is a sensory overload. They talk past each other, over each other, interrupt and correct, all while going a mile a minute and never seeming to take a breath.

Tonight's topics ranged from whether they should turn the butterflies in the Bronx Zoo butterfly house into art once they die (because apparently my mom spent a *long* time speaking to an artist who preserves butterflies and believes that there's a missed opportunity for the zoo, and she's now looking into who she can contact) to the intricacies of whether my dad can fix a clogged pipe by pulling up *just a little bit* of grout from the tile. There wasn't a point explaining to my dad that he'd probably end up having to retile his entire bathroom floor if he started this particular DIY project. In the same way, there wasn't a point explaining to my mother that the Bronx Zoo probably already has a plan in place for their butterflies.

And this was *after* a session with Ari where she wanted to, once again, talk to me about setting more boundaries with my parents. So I walked in already on edge.

My brother had conveniently begged off, with some excuse about working late (because accountants are known to be particularly busy in early July . . .). So it was just me, absorbing all my parents' energy, like overwatered soil in a pot with nowhere to spread all the excess.

I wish I could be more like Ike and leave my parents to themselves when I'm not in the mood. But I think that's a little brother prerogative. I don't have it in me to skip Shabbat dinner with them. That's not my role.

I'd once again brought the documents for my parents to sign—documents that would move most of their assets into the annuity. My dad signed it without looking at it, which wasn't exactly what I was hoping for. My mom flitted around ignoring it all night. As I got ready to leave, I decided to try asking her about it one more time.

"Can you please read through everything this week?" I plead. "If you want to talk to Tracey—"

"Who?" my dad asks, and I sigh.

"The financial planner."

"Oh, right, right." He's listening even if my mom isn't.

"If you want more information, just schedule a call with Tracey," I say pointedly to my mom.

"You know I find all of this financial stuff so boring." She rolls her eyes conspiratorially, as though she's sharing a secret between two friends.

"I know," I reply. "That's why I'm trying to make it as easy as possible."

"You're such a doll," my mom coos, kissing my cheeks about twenty times and leaving me with the distinct impression that she's going to feed the papers to one of the Waldos before actually reading them.

I resign myself to having to have this conversation again next week and say my goodbyes.

I make my way home and then trudge into my apartment, carrying a heavy package of what I assume is the dog food I ordered. The evening has exhausted me, so I immediately slump happily onto my couch. George nestles himself into my lap, and I grab my latest half-read book off the table (yes, with the basics of the ending already known. I eventually caved. I am who I am.). I pull a blanket over me and open WhatsApp, because I have a few missed texts from J, sent while I was at dinner.

J: I know this is seasonally nonsensical, and I don't even celebrate, but please hear me out.

J: Why are there so many birds in the "Twelve Days of Christmas"? Everyone sings this song like it's totally normal, but we're talking about some psycho showing up to their partner's house every day with increasingly larger live animals. On the first day it's like, "Aw, a partridge and tree I can plant in my yard. How nice!" Second day you're like, "Oh cool, turtle doves can go with the partridge." But after the french hens and calling birds, you're going to wonder what's up. The fear is mitigated by the golden rings, and maybe you think, "Okay, this makes much more sense for Christmas." But then the next day the person shows up with GEESE!? Then it aggressively gets larger with swans. Why is this person not stopped?!

Then I see he wrote again, after an hour went by with no reply.

J: Sorry. This is what working from home does to someone's brain.

I'm laughing as I start typing back.

Nora: You forget I talk to people about their innermost thoughts all day long. A long but logical dissection of the bird jump-scares of Twelve Days of Christmas is nowhere close to the weirdest thing I've heard all day.

Nora: And actually, yeah, it's kind of amazing how many songs we sing along to with no thought to the words we're saying.

The little dots pop up, an immediate indication that he's typing and stopping. I look at the clock. It's past two in the morning in London, and I wonder what's keeping him up so late.

J: You don't think it's totally normal to sing "I am the walrus"?

I snort a laugh. He's such a British stereotype—of course he'd go straight from Christmas carols to the Beatles.

Nora: Well if we want to get philosophical about the Beatles, I really think starting with Yellow Submarine has to be the best place.

J: I should look up who wrote "Twelve Days of Christmas"— maybe they also turned to LSD for more abstract lyrics.

Nora: It's an excellent theory.

Nora: Anyway, I'm sorry I texted you back so late, but I clearly couldn't let those musings go without a response. Hope I'm not keeping you up. Better let you get back to dreaming of a house full of geese and swans.

George hops off me and goes to smell the package I've brought in. He looks over at me and gives me a small bark, like I'm not moving fast enough for him.

"All right, big man," I say, pulling myself off the couch with a groan. I walk over and open the package so George will stop bothering me. Maybe he doesn't need to confirm visually that it's his food, but I'm guessing he won't stop smelling the box and trying to get my attention until I put the food away.

However, when I pull the bag out, I'm frustrated to realize they've sent me the wrong thing—it's not his typical dog food but the same brand's cat food. They must've mixed up the packaging.

I hop onto the app to try and initiate a return. They agree to send me a new bag, but when I ask for a return label I'm informed the food is too heavy to make it worth sending back.

So, what, I'm just supposed to throw away a perfectly good bag of food?

I try to think of who I know who has a cat. And of course, the obvious answer sticks out right in front of me: Eli.

In the week and a half since our roof debacle, I haven't seen him. It's not unusual—our building does only have one elevator, but I'm not exactly constantly going in and out. And while I realize I actually still have no idea what Eli does for work beyond Tom vaguely saying he's a writer, he doesn't seem to be on a nine-to-five routine the way I and a few other people in the building are. And without a dog, he's also not on that particular schedule either.

But since we left things off on a positive note, there's no reason to not bring him some cat food, right? Maybe that would be nice, actually.

I grab the bag and walk down the stairs. When I get in front of his door, I knock and then wait. I hear some shuffling inside, but it's slow and muted.

When the door finally opens, it's clear what's taken him so long. Eli looks terrible. His nose is red and raw from a cold. His hair is mussed and looks pressed to the side, as though he's haphazardly slept on it. His face, usually so smooth, is covered in patchy stubble. He's swaddled in the coziest-looking sweater, hood up, as though it's a barrier to the outside world.

"Are you . . . okay?" I ask, trying to not be completely obvious that I think he's looking worse for wear.

"Hey, Nora," he says, a little confusion in his scratchy voice, but mostly tiredness. "Oh yeah, I'm fine. What's up?"

I give him another look up and down. "You're clearly not fine." I hold up the bag of cat food. "I accidentally got shipped this cat food, so I thought I'd bring it to you—"

"Oh thanks—"

"But seriously, what's happening to you?"

He reaches out for the cat food, as though that's going to solve everything, but I hold it back. Maybe it's not nice to offer something and then withhold it, but I'm getting the sense that if I don't insist on an answer, he's just going to crawl back into his man cave and let illness overtake him.

"It's just a cold," he says, his voice so depleted that it comes out almost like a sad sigh rather than a statement.

"It looks like a lot more than a cold," I respond, the biggest understatement ever. "Do you have any medicine, at least? Have you been to see a doctor?"

I can't help it; I reach out to feel his forehead. He leans into the touch, as though it's the most soothing comfort he can find. I would feel sorry for him except that I'm more alarmed by how much he's burning up.

"Have you taken anything for your fever?"

"It's just a cold," he repeats. "I've been on my laptop doing work all day; I'm fine." I can't help but roll my eyes. I've seen a lot of men with the opposite reaction to man flu—usually a lot of whining over a fever that barely breaks ninety-nine degrees. But this is stubbornness of a different kind.

"You can't just say you're not sick and have it be so."

"Well, I got a lot done today, so I'll sleep it off and be better tomorrow," he says with effort.

"You should've been asleep already if you're feeling this sick," I respond.

"Well . . ." At this he looks away from me and shuffles a bit, like a little boy caught in a fib. "I tried earlier, but it's been hard to get comfortable," he admits. "It was easier to just try and focus on work instead. But I'll fall asleep eventually. This isn't a big deal."

I'm not even sure he believes himself with that tale. He can't go on like this.

"I'm coming in," I say, mind made up.

I push past him and set the cat food on the counter. His apartment is a bit of a mess, and I somehow get the immediate impression this is not the way this space typically looks. The bookshelves and desk are organized and methodical—I'd guess that's the regular state of affairs. But the sink and countertop have abandoned mugs and half-eaten plates of toast strewed around. The lights are all dim, and every cabinet seems to be in some version of ajar. The couch is covered in cushions and blankets, but his laptop and phone are sitting open, as though the evidence of technology at hand might drown out the rest of the mess surrounding him.

Two cats wander into the room, and I can't help but smile when I see them. There really *is* no way to describe them other than "floofy." They look as though two delicate, dainty white kittens got their paws stuck in an electrical socket, and it immediately made them puff out. I reach down to give them a pet, and one of them leans into my hand the way Eli did earlier when I touched his forehead.

I turn around to see Eli staring at me, unsure. I can't tell if he desperately wants me to get out or if he's one step from begging me to stay. I imagine it's some mental tug-of-war over both.

I walk into his bathroom and open the cabinets. Totally bare except a spare toothbrush and a few travel soaps.

"Do you have any cold medicine?" I ask, turning around to him again.

"It's the middle of summer," he grumbles. "When I moved here, I didn't think I'd need anything."

"Well, you know the whole catching-a-cold-in-the-cold thing is not how a virus works, right?"

"Yes," he pouts.

"Okay. Good, because you *are* sick. You need to hydrate and take some cold medicine and probably . . . shower?"

I feel bad saying it, but I bet it would make him feel better. He looks like he's been sleeping in the same clothes for days.

He's silent for a minute, and I wonder if I've pushed it a little too far. But then he speaks again, with his voice now so small and his eyes on the ground. "I don't want to shower, because then when I get out, it'll be really cold."

He seems so in pain that I take hold of his wrist just to give him some indication that I hear him. It's hard to watch someone being this fragile and stubborn simultaneously. It kicks something into gear for me.

"You need to shower," I insist. "You'll feel better, and you're already up. Come on—I'll turn on the heater in the bathroom and put a lot of towels in there and fresh clothes, and it'll be hard, but it'll really help. And then we'll get you into bed, and I'll go get you medicine, okay?"

"Okay," he says quietly, nodding slightly, as though he wants to say yes but it hurts too much to move. To be honest, I'm surprised that he's immediately acquiescing. "Thank you for that."

"No problem," I reply, swiftly getting into gear now.

I turn on the shower and the heater in the bathroom. I open the linen closet (thankfully Esther's old apartment has the same exact layout as mine) and grab two big towels, then find a new shirt and shorts in his drawers. I carefully guide him into the bathroom and look around.

"Do you need help in here?" I ask tentatively, not sure if I'm *way* overstepping by now discussing what is essentially his undressing. But he's looking so out of sorts that I can't help but worry he might not be able to get his sweater over his head.

He shakes his head softly. "I've got it, I think."

I nod and close the door. I can hear him slowly moving, and I step away, not wanting to eavesdrop.

I look into his room and see his sheets are a mess—sweaty and disheveled. I go into caretaking autopilot, stripping the bed and placing fresh sheets on top. I pick up a knocked-over box of tissues and tidy up around the room. I fill a large glass of water and place it on a coaster on his bedside table. I light a candle to try and make the atmosphere more soothing than stale. Then I put the dishes in the dishwasher and wipe the counters.

Paws and Whiskers watch as I go, heads pinging back and forth as they follow my movements.

He comes out of the bathroom a few minutes later, already looking a little better. I can see the relief written all over his tired expression. He walks into the bedroom and stands in the doorway, looking at his tidied room and newly made bed.

"You did all this?" he asks, turning toward me and fixing me with a confused stare.

"Yup," I say, brushing past him, not wanting to make a thing out of any of it. "I'm running out to get you medicine. Are you allergic to anything?" He shakes his head. "Okay then, lie down. Leave your phone and computer in the other room so they don't tempt you to try and be productive again, and I'll be right back."

Chapter 17

I walk out without a glance back. I go upstairs to stop by my apartment for my wallet. George hops up, so I clip his leash on, and we walk outside.

I'm not really sure what exactly has gotten into me. Maybe it's my ingrained professional need to help when I see someone who really needs it.

But as I hear George snorting at me as he trots along, I get the sense that even he knows I'm fooling myself.

I might've avoided Eli for the past week and a half, but it doesn't mean I can forget whatever shifted between us on the roof. He's more human to me now, more precious after I've gotten an inadvertent inside vantage point. And maybe sharing loneliness is the most tethering admission someone could make to me.

I get into the drugstore and grab whatever seems useful—cold medicine, zinc (Dane swears by it, and she swears by very little), cough drops, a thermometer, and rapid strep tests, just in case. I pause at the VapoRub and then decide against it when the thought of rubbing anything on Eli makes my heart rate speed up unnecessarily.

Ridiculous. *Not* the thoughts I need to be having.

I check out and head back to our building, dropping off George before heading downstairs to Eli's apartment. I knock and make my way in.

I see his laptop and phone are still abandoned right where he left them by the couch, so I'm glad he took at least one piece of advice.

One of the cats is sitting by the door, almost as though she's been waiting for my return. I pause, trying to gauge what her goal is. But instead of protecting her domain, she rubs herself across my leg. I guess that's a seal of approval from a cat, if there ever was one.

The other cat is on the bed with Eli, who's left the door open and is curled up, with his head on the pillow and everything else under the covers. He normally seems perpetually in motion—moving, talking, filled with expression and verve—so this quiet makes him seem almost like an entirely different person. He's a cat without its claws. I'm hesitant to disturb the scene.

But he sees me lurking and shifts himself to sit up.

"I was wondering if I'd dreamt you," he murmurs, I think not quite realizing what he's saying. I try to shake it off.

"Nope, your friendly neighborhood shower forcer and medication pusher isn't a fever dream, I'm afraid," I joke, pulling a chair from the corner of his room to sit down next to the bed.

The cat that was by the door has wandered in and hopped onto the bed, too, so now Eli is framed by little furballs on either side.

His stare on me is disquieting. I fidget and pull up the bag of all my drugstore purchases. "Start with this," I say, unwrapping the cold medicine and handing it over to him.

He dutifully takes it and downs it with some of the water I left by his bedside. I pull out the rapid strep test and prep it. "Let's swab this, too, because if you have strep, it's actually an easy solution to get antibiotics. If it's a virus, it'll just be a lot of hydration, cold medicine, and waiting for it to pass."

He nods and takes the swab, going through my prescribed motions without hesitation. I swirl it around and set it aside to give it time. I hand over the thermometer.

"Why does it matter?" he says. At my confused look, he continues. "I just mean . . . I get that I'm ill. I'm not pretending anymore that I'm not. I just don't see what I gain from knowing *how* ill."

"Well, if you're over a certain temperature, that becomes more of a medical issue."

"Do you think it's that bad?" he asks, his uncertainty making it clear he's feeling even worse than his particularly rumpled state already suggests.

"I think knowledge is power," I say, as kindly as I can, while I hand over the thermometer.

He sticks it in his ear without complaint, and we wait for the beep.

"I have no idea what Fahrenheit temperatures mean," he says, handing the thermometer back over. I look at the display and try not to let the shock show on my face. His temperature is at 103.4, which is sort of on the cusp of where I'd want to take someone to the hospital. But even after spouting my *knowledge is power* mumbo jumbo, I'm not sure he needs *that* information.

"It means you're sick, but I'm guessing you'll live," I reply with what I hope is a comforting smile. He blows out a sigh and crumples back onto his pillow.

I pull the strep test back over and see, unsurprisingly, that it's positive.

"Well, we have a winner," I say, turning the test so he can see it.

"What do I do?" he asks, unsure.

I pull out my phone. "We're going to input your information and schedule a telehealth doctor's visit," I say, typing as I'm talking. "Since we have the rapid test, they can prescribe you antibiotics without seeing you in person, and you can start taking them ASAP. I know it seems worse than a virus, but this means it'll actually be gone faster."

I put us in the queue and then get started on the forms. "What's your middle name?"

"Eli."

"Not your first name," I say, hoping I can get him to focus long enough to do this before conking out.

"No, Eli is my middle name," he replies. I stare at him. "What?"

"Okay, so what's your first name?"

He purses his lips. "It's Jarvis," he says begrudgingly.

My eyes go wide, but I keep my mouth shut. I'm not going to ask him what it's like having a name most associated with a robot. But maybe since he goes by Eli, he didn't like the name *before* it became an Avengers accessory.

"All right," I enunciate, ignoring my natural urge to rib him. I type in his address (since I obviously know that) and estimate his height and weight. "Do you have insurance?"

"Not for my body, eyes, or even teeth yet, I'm afraid," he says, and I quirk a small smile, thinking of his strong opinions on the roof.

"Well, it's not a big deal. These telehealth things are usually like fifty bucks anyway. And I'm sure your antibiotic can be a generic, so that won't be bad either."

"Okay," he says. "Thank you. I guess I really did need a friendly neighborhood shower forcer and medication pusher."

The sincerity is etched into the exhaustion on his face. I'm imagining him fighting this all day—sending emails and texts, trying to get work done, and feeling so frustrated to not be able to muscle past it. He's used to gunning through life on his own, even when he's had people around him. I can obviously relate to that. The permission to stop and rest is probably not something he gives himself often.

"No problem," I whisper.

I type in the rest of the information and wait for our turn. He snuggles back onto the pillow and closes his eyes. His hair is a curly mess, and I have an urge to push it back, to soothe him again with something physical. I wonder if he'd purr like the cats, leaning back into my touch the way he did earlier.

But the reverie is interrupted by the chiming of my phone.

"Hello, Mr. Whitman," a friendly voice says. I hold up the phone so it's facing him and he doesn't have to expend the effort, although he does sit up, as though he can't quite bring himself to be so informal in front of a doctor. "I'm Dr. Banks. I see in your notes that you took a rapid strep test and it came back positive."

I hand him the test, and he holds it up to show her. "Yes, I've been feverish all day but trying to ignore it. Obviously that wasn't going so well."

She chuckles, clearly not surprised by that course of action. "What's your fever now?" she asks.

"I took some medicine, so I'm hoping it's a bit down, but when I took my temperature before, it was . . . I'm sorry, this feels so silly to say, but 103.4? Fahrenheit?"

"Well, that's not silly, Mr. Whitman; it's actually quite a bit higher than we'd expect."

"Oh, I just meant . . . in Celsius you'd be dead with that . . . never mind," he says, the effort to explain clearly more than it's worth. "What do you mean 'higher than we'd expect'?" he asks nervously, suddenly realizing what she said.

"It's not at a level where we'd be concerned, so don't be alarmed," she says in a soothing voice. "I just meant we normally see those fever spikes in small children, not grown men."

He grumbles something inaudible, and I have to stifle a laugh at his annoyance at the comparison.

"It probably means you were overdoing it and this is your body's way of fighting back. I'm glad you finally took some time out for yourself," she says, and I see him wince. I know that feeling too—the understanding that you haven't put yourself first, and the way it eventually creeps up on you.

"So what do I do now?" he asks, skirting past it.

"I'm going to prescribe you some antibiotics. You've got your pharmacy info already in, so I'll send it over right away. That should knock it all out, and you should start feeling better in a day or two. If you're not, then you'll want to go see a doctor in person. But that would be very unlikely. Strep, once it's diagnosed, is usually pretty easy to get rid of."

"Thanks very much, Dr. Banks," he says, and with a few more basic instructions, she lets him go.

He shifts toward me once the phone is off, moving with effort to sit up taller, as though buoyed by the knowledge that there's a plan ahead.

"I don't know how to thank you," he says sincerely.

I can feel my face heating up, along with the rising urge to minimize. "Just think of it as though we're even now. I ruined one night by locking you up on a roof but fixed another one by inappropriately barging in and shoving a doctor in your face."

I try to smile and make it into a joke. But he reaches out and tenderly takes hold of my wrist.

The sensation of his thumb sliding across my pulse point makes every part of me flush, as though the touch has transferred the heat from his body to mine. There's something in the simplicity of the movement that makes it all the more affecting. This isn't a thumb-war grip; it's affection and gratitude. It's softness, something that seems so hard won when it's coming from Eli.

I lift my eyes from where his hand is touching me and see him staring back at me.

"You're decisive," he says, and I'm not sure exactly why that's what's stuck out to him, but I do know he means it as a compliment.

"It's in my nature to try and fix people's problems," I say with a shrug, once again downplaying, trying to ignore the heat crawling its way up to my cheeks.

"Most people don't," he says, watching me, his gaze burrowing past the defenses I'm throwing up.

But before the heat of the moment engulfs me, he gingerly removes his hand from my wrist and sinks back into his pillows. As though he knows a little distance is necessary.

He's silent for a moment while he looks down at his hands. Then he speaks so softly I almost don't hear him at first. "When you went to the store," he says, "I was thinking how, if you hadn't happened to come by, I probably would've just suffered alone, carrying on and pretending like everything was fine. And even if someone else had come and asked if I was okay, I would've begged them off and underplayed it."

"Whereas I just barged in," I scoff, the heat still not quite gone from my face.

But he shakes his head and looks back up, straight into my eyes. "You know how to handle me," he says, an unanswered question written into his expression that I already know he's not going to ask. "I don't know why, but you seem to always be one step ahead of me in a way no one else is. I didn't like it as a quality in a therapist," he says with a chuckle, and I can't stop a sheepish grin from showing on my face. "But I like it like this."

That tactile sympathy I've been feeling for him all day, the urge to push his hair back, to have his thumb graze over my wrist, to give comfort in a solidified way, feels especially present now. I reach out and squeeze his forearm, still so hot to the touch. "I'm glad I could help," I say honestly.

But I stand up, before the moment can get any more charged.

"I'm going to go pick up your antibiotics, okay?" I say, moving the chair back and putting some space between us.

"I just hope you know how much I appreciate it," he says, not fully allowing the previous conversation to drop without notice.

I nod, and walk back out.

It doesn't get quite so heavy again.

With antibiotics in his system, the cold medicine bringing his fever down, and sleep clearly imminent, I leave him alone for the rest of the evening, with my phone number scribbled on a Post-it in case he needs something.

The next morning I bring homemade chicken broth and some of that strawberry-rhubarb cornbread.

"You saved my life, and now you're bringing me soup and baked goods?" he asks after opening the door, already looking worlds healthier than he did yesterday.

"Don't be so dramatic," I say with a sigh. He grins, takes the food containers out of my hands, and beckons me inside. "You seem a lot better today?" I venture.

He starts heating up the broth and then turns back to me. "I've gotta say—if my opinion on these things matters—antibiotics are pretty great."

I shake my head, trying to tamp down my smile as I sit down at his kitchen table. "Is that a matter of opinion?"

"With the craziness of the world today? You never know what counts as facts anymore," he says, grabbing the broth out of the microwave and sitting across from me.

"I think we're all pretty universally in agreement on antibiotics."

"You'd hope," he retorts, then lifts the bowl to take a sip straight out of it. He closes his eyes and murmurs, "This is so good, Nora."

"You're just dehydrated and hungry after being sick."

He sets the bowl down and leans forward, catching my eyes. "You're really bad at taking a compliment," he says, the challenge inherent.

But I'm not going to bite. Probably because, as I'm learning with Eli, he usually only dishes it out when he's mostly right.

"Fine," I counter. "Thank you."

I like how when he grins, one side of his mouth curves up more, making his little displays of joy slightly goofier and more open. I like how he seems to have more of them in store now that he's feeling better.

"Do you need anything else?" I ask, changing the subject.

"No, I'm good," he says sincerely. "I really do feel a lot better today. I think I'm just going to take the doctor's orders and stay inside, watch a movie, and take it easy today."

"Is that what Dr. Banks said?" I ask.

He chuckles. "I meant *you*. I'm taking your prescription of staying off my laptop and accepting my convalescence very seriously."

"Good."

He's night and day from where he was yesterday, but he definitely needs to not push it.

"What exciting Saturday plans do you have today?" he asks, picking at a piece of the cornbread now that he's drained the soup.

"No plans," I say. "Although I did *pretend* to be extremely busy, because my mother has been texting me nonstop for recipes without nightshades, since she now believes they're the source of all her inflammation."

He lifts an eyebrow, the skepticism written all over his face. "Does she have a lot of inflammation?"

"Not anything identifiable by anyone other than herself," I say, in an attempt to be diplomatic.

"And what are you supposed to do about it?" he asks, taking progressively larger bites of the cornbread to the point where his voice is a little muffled. At least this time it's from carbs and not a sore throat.

"What am I ever supposed to do about any of it?" I say with a roll of my eyes. "She decides something, upends her life, insists on everyone else upending theirs, and will probably forget about it by next week. She's concerned because tomatoes are a nightshade, and I've entered my summer 'eat tomatoes on everything' stage."

"Ah, a very important season."

"In my house, absolutely," I laugh.

"Well, if you're avoiding your mum, why don't you stay in and watch a movie with me?" he asks, standing up and clearing his plate. "Maybe then I can scam some more of that absurdly good cornbread out of you." I pull more out of my bag, and I love seeing the Pavlovian way his eyes light up. "You had that in there the whole time!"

"I didn't know you'd like it that much!" I explain. "Dane loves it, too, so I packed some for her. But I can make more; I always do."

He comes over and slowly picks up the extra cornbread, like he's carrying an especially fragile important object.

"Okay, since I'm stealing your friend's cornbread, you *have* to let me at least give you an out for your mother. I can't take all this debt I owe you now."

I stand up. "I told you—I got you locked on a roof, so now we're even."

He shakes his head solemnly as he walks over to the couch and flops onto it, grabbing the remote as he goes. "That was yesterday. Now on top of saving my life, you've given me the American marvel that is cornbread."

"Stop saying I saved your life," I reiterate, and sit down with slightly less gusto than he's showing in his movements.

He hands me the remote. "I propose you pick the film—any film you want—since you saved my life." He smirks at that, clearly pleased to be continually riling me up.

"So I keep you company instead of watching a movie in the comfort of my own home, and this is supposedly a favor to me?"

He tosses a blanket my way and snuggles under one that he's laid on top of himself.

"Exactly. Doesn't this friendship work great?"

Chapter 18

And so somehow, with that, we've actually become neighbor friends. After one movie turned into two, he asked what time I walk George usually. He liked the idea of getting a walk in every morning before work—he says he spends too much time sitting at home in front of a screen—so now for the last two weeks, he's been waiting outside when I leave the building. No fanfare, just a morning walk and talk to get the day started. Sometimes Gladys joins us, too, although she usually prefers weekends, when we can walk a bit later, since she says her "bones are creaky if it's too early."

The first day, he said his only rule was that we had to talk about anything but work, since it was the sole time for the next eight hours he'd get to think about anything else. I wholeheartedly agreed—as someone who only writes one thing a week and finds *that* daunting, I can only imagine how important it must be for full-time writers to clear their heads before the day starts. And since I really shouldn't talk about patients, the idea of ignoring the day ahead for a little bit is actually freeing. We talk about articles or books we've read; we discuss the latest happenings with George, Paws, and Whiskers; we share what things we've noticed changing in the neighborhood; we debate the best versions of every baked good you can find in New York. The morning-walk chats are everything and nothing, like a staple steamy cup of morning coffee to get the day started.

Even after just a couple weeks, it seems like those mornings are inevitable.

I wonder now if maybe we've been slowly shifting toward each other from the start. First circling as combatants in a petty building war, then as comrades in the battle against a sleepless night on a roof, until finally the vulnerability of seeing someone at their sickest shed the last pretenses.

When I bring this up to Ari, she asks me how it relates to J, and I balk.

"It doesn't in any way relate to J."

"I don't know," Ari says, leaning forward and eyeing me in that way she does when she's clearly not sure I have a grasp on my own life. "You haven't felt particularly strongly about any men—even the ones you were dating, frankly—for so many years. And now you have two that you're opening up to more. I think it's absolutely wonderful, because you so often close yourself off so as not to be a burden to others. But I just find it interesting that it's happening simultaneously."

I squirm at the thought. I know there've been small moments with Eli that have felt charged. But J is who I'm interested in. And conflating them in any way is just confusing. They're like two separate earbuds; if they were attached somehow—wired headphones at the bottom of my bag—I'm afraid they'd become tangled. I don't need tangled.

"J and Eli are in no way even in the same ballpark."

"How so?" she asks, clearly ready to dismiss me out of hand, even if she's pretending like she's asking an innocuous question.

"Eli would never even factor into a *romantic* discussion."

"Why not?" She's really not going to let me off the hook.

"Okay, it's an objective fact that Eli is attractive; I'm not disputing that," I admit, and Ari snorts as though I've stated the most obvious thing. I'm ignoring it and barreling on. "But he is fully, completely in the friend column." I try to say this definitively to end the conversation, but Ari's not biting.

"Why?" Ari lobs back, like we're in a tennis match and I keep thinking I'm ending the point while she easily gets it back over the net.

"Well, let's start with even *thinking* about him in a sexual way is unethical," I point out. I'm a little stunned when Ari dramatically rolls her eyes at me. She looks like an exasperated teenager instead of the elderly put-together doyenne she normally presents as. *"What?"* I huff.

"First of all, no one can help thinking anything sexual about anyone," she says, and I'm going to have to table the immediate curiosity about Ari's sex life that *that* comment sets off. "But come on, he was barely a patient to begin with. You had a few calls with his girlfriend and then maybe two or three with him, where he never really said anything, and then she promptly broke up with him after also being the person who initiated and paid for the sessions. Ethical rules are about patients you have deep knowledge of so it can't be used against them in a relationship setting. This isn't that."

"I cannot believe this is a hill you'd want to die on," I mumble incredulously. I know Ari's a little looser than most therapists—especially of her generation—but that's a *particularly* loose take.

But she's not even listening as she continues on. "He's also not your patient anymore; you know him in a completely different context now, and you have an entirely different friend relationship that has nothing to do with your past professional interactions. So let's cut the pretense that your avoidance of your attraction to this man has to do with some ethical boundary."

"Okay, sure, let's set that aside, even if I'm not sure I agree," I say, giving in to her logic, since there's no point in actually arguing with Ari; instead, my only tactic is to change the direction. "But beyond being neighbors—which is another reason that anything beyond friendship is a bad idea—knowing about his last relationship and just, you know, *knowing him*, I have no desire to get into *anything* with him. Absolutely not."

"Okay." Ari shrugs, suddenly letting it go much more easily than I would have imagined. "Like I said, I'm just happy to see you opening up to people."

"Yeah, me too," I admit, still not sure why she's suddenly accepted my answer.

She changes the subject back to my family and lets this particular thread go for the rest of our session.

But later, I find myself thinking about everything she said.

I can't pretend I haven't gotten closer to Eli; I can't say that at this point he isn't a real person in my life that I now tell some things to. And it's confusing to suddenly go from having very few people I let into my life to having two new yet constant presences.

But I brush it off. As Ari says—it's a *good* thing. Maybe it just means that I'm growing.

I do wonder if we've maybe taken it a step too far, though, when I find myself the following Sunday, the last day of July, on the West Side Highway with a rented bike, a borrowed helmet, and encouragement from the one person I would've sworn I'd never trust for anything.

"Don't I get training wheels for this?" I ask Eli, the long path ahead of me looking especially daunting. To my right is the Jersey skyline, rising up across the small waves of the Hudson River. In front is the glistening far-off Freedom Tower, improbably touching the clouds. But we're not getting anywhere near it today—I'm not sure I can make it ten feet ahead, let alone the two miles it would take to get all the way downtown.

"You're too old for that," he says as he adjusts my seat.

"Why is it about age and not skill level?"

"Because you can balance more effectively now than you could when you were five or six," he retorts, now checking the gears, as though the state of the bike is going to be my largest obstacle.

"I think you're overestimating my athleticism."

At that he looks up and gives me a cheeky grin. "I didn't say you needed to be athletic to do this, don't worry."

I'm not quite sure how exactly we got here. The twists and turns of conversation have apparently failed me. How did bike riding even come up? I may have admitted that, because my parents are the kind of parents they are, I never learned how to ride a bike. It was like one of those essential childhood things that they simply forgot about and skipped over. Living in New York without a yard and with ample subway and walking access, it just wasn't something that was necessary. And I never pushed.

But Eli pushes. In fact, I think Eli is now going to *literally* have to push. He talked up the ease of renting one of the city's perennial Citi Bikes, dotted around in any location we could want to start biking. He extolled the delight of Hudson River Park and its easy, wide bike paths for miles along the water's edge of Manhattan. He pointed out the freedom I would have if I knew how to use a bike in the city. He's so convincing. So adamant. So insistent.

So here I am, supposedly ready for action. I've got on my bike shorts and my favorite, billowy button-down with a front tie. I felt like maybe if I dressed as a casual, easygoing bike-riding gal, I could be one.

"Okay, so first things first, I just want you to hold your legs up, and I'm going to push you. Do you ever see kids on those balance bikes? That's good for spatial awareness and gross motor skills and helps you get used to the concept of a bike."

"'Spatial awareness'?" I say, dubious.

"I don't know—it worked for my niece, okay?"

"Your niece who is currently like six years old?" I ask, now doubting the steadfast nature of this plan.

He's trying to stand taller, as though if he puffs out his frame, it'll give him authority. For a decently tall guy, he really sometimes projects small-man energy.

"Well, why would it be any different?" he counters.

"Okay," I give in, knowing there's no use in arguing with him.

I swing my leg over the bike, and I can see him almost tell me *Good job*, but then he stops himself. *Good.* At least he has the minor self-awareness to know he shouldn't patronize me right now.

"Okay, lift your legs up, and I'm going to push."

I do as he says, and the whole thing is hilariously awkward. We look like a drunk circus act. It's blessedly early enough that the bike lanes aren't crowded. But people who actually know what they're doing go around us while watching what we're doing with bemused looks.

"Do you feel like you understand the balance?" he says after a while, huffing a little bit from the effort of pushing me and keeping me upright.

"I think we just have to try and fail," I reply, and he shoots me a disappointed look, as though my doubt is somehow more personally about his teaching abilities than my lack of bike skill.

I get back up and put one foot on a pedal.

"Okay." He claps his hands together like he's trying to hype me up. "So you're going to push your right foot forward and down to get the pedaling started, and then you should focus more on the staying upright than the pedaling. But don't forget to pedal or you'll lose speed and fall. And if you get—"

"Eli, this isn't helping."

"Got it," he says, and he grips my back. I sit up straighter from the contact. I don't think I could be any more casual, with my hair in a messy braid and my billowy boxy shirt, but every time he touches me, it's as though he's pulling a match too slowly across its striking surface—not quite enough pressure to light the fire but certainly enough to cause smoke.

"I'm going to start pedaling," I say, as though if I get moving, I can push the thought from my mind.

"I'm going to hold on for the first few tries," he says, and I nod, wanting more than anything to just pedal away and get the feel of his fingers out of my consciousness.

I push with my foot, pressing down on the pedal, and with shaky legs I start going forward. I know Eli's holding me upright. I know if he lets go, I'll almost certainly fall. But we're really moving. I'm pedaling slowly, and he's going alongside me. I'm (sort of) riding a bike.

Well, I'm riding a bike until he lets go, clearly as an attempt to let me continue on my own effectively, but it has the opposite effect.

Without him holding me steady, I careen off to the side and land on a patch of weeds and wildflowers, sharp and solid and unforgiving.

"Oh my god, Nora, are you okay?" he says, running up to stand over me, assessing my injuries. I wish I could say it's just embarrassment, but I look down at my leg and see I'm all scratched up.

"I fell," I mumble, and I can see from the look he's giving me that not only is *that* obvious but I'm also really straddling the line between tragic, pathetic mess and deeply hilarious sideshow.

He's trying so hard not to laugh, but his face looks like he's holding in a sneeze—it's a contortion of attempting to look concerned while being extremely close to laughter. It reminds me of cast members on *SNL* when they know they *shouldn't* break, but the more they think about it, the harder it becomes.

And the effort he's making to not laugh in my face makes *me* laugh. I'm on the ground with the bike still on top of me, splayed out, my legs a tapestry of cuts. But now that the laughter has been unleashed, I'm doubled over, tears forming, my gut straining from the force of it. And when I start, there's no stopping Eli from joining in. His laughter is a dam exploding, everything he was holding in bursting out until we're both left gasping and giggling.

"I'm sorry," he says, trying to breathe through it. "But you just look so . . ."

I wave him off, still laughing and trying to not let it turn into hiccups. "I know I look pathetic," I admit. "I don't think anyone could've expected I'd have flamed out that dramatically on my first attempt."

He wipes tears out of his eyes. "Listen, when you go for something, at least you go all the way. You gave it your all."

I move to stand up, and he holds out his hand. He pulls me up and surreptitiously looks me over, probably to ensure I'm not *actually* injured.

"I think we can agree we gave it a good try and I should call it a day, yeah?"

He winces, the dirt and angry scratches across my legs more apparent now that I'm standing up. "I think that would be fair," he says, pulling up the bike now. We walk off the bike path and onto the promenade that goes along the river. We walk in silence for a minute until he finds a dock for the bike and returns it, ready for a rider that might actually know what they're doing.

"I'm sorry I let go," he finally says, now that our absurdist laughter has regressed back into normalcy and we've both caught our breath.

"Oh please," I say, waving him off. "It was the right technique, just the wrong student."

"We can try again some other day?" he asks, but I know from the question in his voice that even he realizes I'm probably a lost cause, or at least a lost cause to learning while balancing the city around me.

I dramatically indicate my legs. "I think we can let this one go for now," I admit. I try to brush off some of the dirt, but it doesn't really do much. I go to straighten my shirt and realize something. "Oh shit, I think one of the buttons came off."

I pull it out further so I can see. It's a vintage shirt I got at one of my favorite stores in Alphabet City. It's meant to button down and then tie into a bow at the bottom, but the tie has come undone and the button above it has popped off from the force of my fall.

I frown. It's annoying because I can't replace it—the buttons are a specific pearled tint and too large to not notice when one is different from the others.

"Let's go and search for it," he says without hesitation.

We walk back toward the area where we were, but it's hard now to tell where exactly I fell. Every part of the path is the same—paved, with a thicket of bramble on either side to separate it from the other areas. We halfheartedly search through for a few minutes, but it's clear the button is lost. And my leg is kind of hurting now, and I want to go home. So much for the outfit making me more of a serious bike rider. Everything's backfired today.

"It's okay," I say, trying to be breezier externally than I feel inside. "Come on, let's get some ice cream and congratulate ourselves on the attempt."

He nods, clearly not going to argue with me when I'm so banged up. "Sounds like a good plan to me."

Chapter 19

We walk back home (maybe I hobble a little bit, let's be honest), and I reject the many ice cream trucks he points out in favor of holding out for something better. We stop into one of my favorite spots, Pamina Dolci e Gelato, and have a long debate over flavors, with him ultimately being excessively boring and ordering vanilla (and refusing to say *fior di latte* on principle, even though I promised him it would sound better in a British accent than any of the American ones surrounding him). I attempt to embarrass him by fully Americanizing *nocciola* and *fragola*, but he deliberately ignores it.

We lazily stroll with our cones as we head east, winding through the tree-lined streets with majestic brownstones as we make our way through the West Village and into Greenwich Village. Maybe part of the strolling is that I slow down as we go along, my attempts to forget about my leg not really working the more I walk.

"Sorry that I'm a slow mess today," I say.

"Well, usually we have George, so I've never been on a really speedy walk with you either way," he points out. "And as for a mess, you're conveniently forgetting that you took care of me when I had strep, so I'd say you're still worlds better than I was." He takes the last bite of his cone, and it's extremely distracting. "We've certainly seen each other at our least attractive." He chuckles as we approach our building.

I want to ask, *Why would that matter?* and it's on the tip of my tongue, the question hanging in front of me, exacerbating the niggling desire to know if he sometimes finds me attractive the way I often inadvertently do with him.

But leaning up against my building, typing away and engrossed in her phone, is my mother. She's wearing some lime-green spandex walking gear, even as her wild hair looks much too untamed for any sporting outing. She's got Waldo (the blueish-gray one) on a leash that she's holding so precariously I want to reach out and wrap it more tightly around her wrist. She doesn't notice as we walk up, but I'm sure she has to be here for me. Although I guess with my parents, it's safest to never be sure of anything.

"Mom?" I ask, and she looks up.

I can see Eli's eyes flick toward me, surprised and putting the pieces together. On our long night on the roof, I had some not-so-flattering things to say about my mother. Maybe it was the frustration of being trapped or maybe it was that particular way that Eli makes me incapable of obfuscating. But I appreciate the concern already embedded in his expression.

"Oh, honey, hi!" she says, pushing herself off the wall and coming to give me a hug, apparently oblivious to my disheveled state. I wonder if she doesn't see it or if perhaps she's so used to being in her own states that it doesn't seem unusual. Waldo gives my leg a lick, clearly the only one of this duo who's going to notice that I'm bleeding.

"I was going for a walk and wanted to bring you something." She holds out a large wooden sign with FISCHER ISLAND painted on it. "See, it's funny because in Florida there's a Fisher Island, but it's our last name instead."

"I got that, yes," I say drolly, wondering why this is an item she's bringing to me.

"Suzy gave it to me; I think maybe she made it? I don't know what she was thinking. But anyway, it's cute, right?"

I keep staring at it. It's confusing on so many levels. It's a joke that isn't funny and is too specific to really even make sense (none of us have been to Fisher Island, and it's not famous enough to really make an actual joke out of). It's painted on some kind of driftwood, so it seems more appropriate to a house *in* Florida than an apartment in New York. And most importantly: Why would *I* want this random decor instead of my mother, the recipient of the "gift"?

"It's very cute," I lie. "But I'm not sure what I would do with it."

"Oh, you could stick it on your wall somewhere," she breezes.

"My walls are pretty well decorated at this point," I say, trying to figure out how to politely wriggle out of this situation. "And besides, if Suzy made it for you, don't you want to keep it for yourself?"

"Oh, you know I have a thing about text on the wall." She shrugs, as though that's an obvious, normal proclivity I should remember. "It's a little too 'Live, Laugh, Love' for me."

"But not for Nora?" I hear a voice say next to me.

In the surprise over this inane discussion with my mother, I forgot Eli was standing beside me. And apparently she didn't notice, either, because her head whips toward his voice, suddenly *very* interested and seemingly amused at the rude man in my company.

"Oooh, hello," she says. "You're a sharp one."

"You're handing your daughter a piece of *art*"—he says the word like it's dirty, and I have to stifle a laugh—"that you yourself don't like. That would make anyone sharp."

I've forgotten how acerbic he can be when he's bothered and self-righteous. It's as though I've peeled away those layers and forgotten about them in the subsequent weeks. But that version of Eli—that therapy-evading, renovation-provoking, know-it-all combatant—is still him, even if he's softened around me. He always lingers above the surface before anyone can get below.

But of course, my mother being my mother, she just laughs. She enjoys being the windup toy that confounds and annoys.

"I never said I don't like it," she teases.

"You don't, though," he replies quickly, not letting her off the hook.

I watch, enraptured. I never call my mom out on anything. It's not worth it. Normally all I want is for whatever line of questioning she has to end. But in this instance I have to admit I'm enjoying watching it play out.

"You can like something and not think it's your style," she counters.

"That's just a nice way to say you don't like something."

"Oh, you're a doll!" she says, doing one of her favorite conversation tactics of completely ignoring what someone has just said and instead giving them a vague compliment to distract them. "I don't think we've been introduced." She sticks out her hand. "I'm Tina."

"I'm Eli. I'm Nora's neighbor," he explains.

"Well, very neighborly of you to look out for my daughter."

He grumbles something under his breath, and I have to step in before he fully turns back into the pissy version of himself I've mostly expunged from my life. "Mom, thank you, but I don't think I have space for it," I say, trying to steer the conversation back to what I need to share.

"Oh," she says, deflating. "But I walked it all the way over here! And that was especially hard with Waldo."

"Do you want me to hang on to it and then I'll bring it back whenever I'm next at your apartment?" I ask, noticing that Waldo is looking sort of desperate to get a real walk in. My mother can sucker me in fairly easily, but add in a dog, and I'm a goner.

She claps her hands together. "Oh that would be great, thanks, love. And then you can also see how it looks in your apartment, in case you change your mind."

"She's not changing her mind," Eli says under his breath.

"Oh, you Brits always take life so seriously," my mother says, waving him off.

"Like someone who can't deal with 'Live, Laugh, Love' signs?" he retorts.

And at that I grab his arm and unlock the door.

"Okay, Mom, well, don't let me keep you!" I say, grabbing the sign in question and trying to make this whole interaction end. "I'll see you at dinner next Friday, okay?"

"Yes! Just don't bring any tomatoes; I'm still avoiding nightshades," she says.

I wave as I pull Eli in, then shove him onto the elevator.

I stare at him, and he stares right back. He doesn't press the button for his floor, so I guess he's coming up to mine. When the elevator opens, I walk out and open my door. George pops up from his perch on his bed, his black shaggy hair in need of a cut. I reach down and pet him, still ignoring Eli even as he walks into my apartment and sits down at the table.

"Why do you let her do that to you?" he finally lets out, articulating what I know he's been itching to say.

"If I answer that, will you answer why you always seem so primed for a fight?" I put my hands on my hips, defiant and unwilling to give in that easily to his passive judgment.

"Sure," he says with a wicked smile, clearly thinking he's won whatever fishing expedition he's on.

I sigh, caught now in having to try and explain *my mother*. I turn on the kettle to keep my hands busy and then start pulling out tea bags and teacups.

"It's easier," I finally say, hoping that's enough.

"Bullshit."

I pour the tea, bring the cups over, and sit down across from him. I like the way my dainty painted mug looks in his large hands.

"It is, though," I say. "She makes everything so complicated. It's like, she could be walking in a straight line from point A to point B and somehow break her foot, cause a car accident, knock over an unwitting bicyclist, and shatter a planter. So when she starts *anything*, it's easier to just go along with it as much as possible and push back only as far as needed to get where I need to be."

"Yeah, but you *didn't* get what you need," he counters.

I take a long sip of my tea. "But I did. I don't care about sticking this thing in my closet for a week. I *need* to not have her questioning why it isn't hung up. I *need* for her to not tell Suzy to come over and look at her art in my apartment. I *need* to not give an opening to the idea that my apartment is open for decoration. So I did that but also didn't drag it into some giant thing."

"That's exhausting," he says, blowing on his cup as though he can get the frustration out through that small action.

I'm surprised that's his response. I always expect him to needle me more, but maybe when it matters, he knows that sometimes a person just needs to be seen. "It is," I concur.

He seems satisfied by that admission. So I attempt to change the subject. "Okay, your turn."

"Oh, I'll blame my parents, too, for all my detriments," he says with a grin. When he sees that's not enough, he tries again. "My father is a barrister, so I was raised to be primed for a fight?"

The question at the end makes it quite clear that that isn't the whole answer. I fix him with a look, and he smiles sheepishly, knowing he's not getting away with anything.

"There's a version of you that isn't like that," I prod, and he puckers his lips in thought, taking the sentiment in.

"I am like that," he says, tilting his head, considering.

"I don't think so," I challenge. "You are *sometimes*. You were like that in therapy, on your guard. You were like that when we met in person, when you wanted to challenge me. But I think when you're comfortable, it's not you at all. You're open and fun and not this spiky person you start out as with everyone."

He lifts his tea and blows on it again, even though by now it's probably cool enough. But I think he wants the excuse to not say anything for a moment. He's trying to have a poker face, but the fact that he isn't capable of that—except while playing actual poker with Kwan, apparently—is one of the best things about him. He looks caught; he looks like he's considering an idea he's never considered before.

It's easy for me to stay silent and watch as the concept plays out and settles into his mind. Part of being a therapist is knowing when to go quiet and let thoughts marinate.

And finally, he sets the tea down. "I don't know why I have that shell . . . I mean, I wasn't completely off base when I said it was probably about my father. But you're right that it wasn't just his job. It's sort of who he is. My father always made me live on my toes. But not in a kooky way like your mother. His version of it is that he's naturally combative. And I just . . . well, I guess I mirrored it. Or used it to deflect and keep my mother and sister away from it."

"That's hard," I say softly, wanting to give him the validation he so kindly offered to me earlier.

He lifts his shoulder, like it's no big deal, but his body language can't outrun the expression on his face. "I guess you have to be spiky if you're the only one standing at the front line."

"I like seeing what's below the spikes," I say and reach out to pat his hand. He doesn't look at me, only at that simple movement.

"Thanks for the tea," he says, abruptly standing up, a physical closing of the conversation. "Sorry I conned you into an activity that got you scraped up."

I look down at my legs, having forgotten completely.

"Oh shit," I say, realizing only in that moment that I'm actually now bleeding.

At my expression, Eli immediately kneels down to take a look. He lifts up my leg, and the way he's holding it is like it's something fragile. It's just a small cut, but it must have come open more while we were walking.

Whatever dull sting I'd been feeling from the cuts is erased by the total awareness of where his hands are. I can't breathe while they move up and down my leg, like he's mapping me, taking stock of every scrape and of every curve. An electric current shivers through me at the way his hands brush me, and I wonder if the goose bumps that burst across my skin are making my internal thoughts obvious now.

"We have to clean this up," he says, standing again, the absence of his touch now glaring.

He walks into my bathroom and roots around for a minute, noise clanging and helping to break me from whatever was happening a moment ago.

But it's short lived, because soon he's kneeling in front of me again. He props up my leg on his knee and assesses, taking it as seriously as a surgeon would in an emergency. He pours hydrogen peroxide on a cotton ball and carefully blots it against me. I hiss, and he grips my leg, as though he's trying to help me through the pain. And then he blows on my skin, right where it's stinging. I know he's simply trying to help, and maybe this is just my recent dry spell, but I swear it's somehow the most erotic thing anyone has ever done to me.

The shiver goes beyond my legs and reaches my thighs. I'm bacon in a pan, not realizing when I started sizzling because the heat's only gradually been turned up, but now it's fully on high.

Our breathing is the only sound between us. In and out, a metronome of consistency belying what's happening for me under the surface. I wish I could see below *his* surface. I wish I could poke inside and see his very simple assessment of a friend's injury so it could maybe tamp down whatever nonsense is living inside me right now. Every time I'm convinced that by being friends, this unrequited attraction will go away, I have to have some palpable reminder that it's still there.

He'd probably be mortified if he knew. I've never met a man so insistent on using the word "friends."

And I think he *needs* a friend. He started over in a whole new country, and the only person he'd had here was the one person who died and left him the apartment he moved into. Maybe he thought the place of childhood peace could be a reset.

But that attraction always seems to hum for me, no matter how much I willfully ignore it. And right now, it's inescapable, and incredibly inconvenient. His grip on my leg is like a fire, creeping up and burning as it goes. I want to pull away, but I worry it would make it even more obvious.

He's still looking only at my leg. His gaze doesn't travel up. He bites his bottom lip in thought, and it just makes everything happening inside me worse.

But it's then that I suddenly realize . . . he's feeling it too.

I've been so concerned with my own reactions that I haven't noticed *him*. The inability to meet my eyes. The furrow in his eyebrows. The way his jaw muscles have tensed. I thought my inconvenient gravitation was one sided, but the way he's shifted makes me suddenly *aware*.

Have I purposely missed it? Has this always been sitting between us and not just singularly in my mind?

Maybe I've deliberately not noticed it because my life is already too confusing and I've been adamant about the former-patient line. The specter of going to London and seeing J has taken up all the romantic headspace that I'm capable of. And this definitely isn't romantic. This isn't the weird spun fairy tale of true love I've woven for myself with J and remain terrified of. This is a version of desire I'm not used to.

And with his eyes deliberately not meeting mine, I can't gauge how to get out of it. I want to laugh with him like we usually do and say, *Hey, isn't this funny?* I want to brush it off; I want to have him look at me and make me realize, *Oh, actually, you misinterpreted.*

But I also want. I want, I want, I want. I'm at a boil, and I don't know what to do with myself.

But thankfully, before I implode, he suddenly lets go and stands up. He douses the fire with distance. And a rigid stance I'm not used to.

He clears his throat. "Sorry again," he says, and I know he means it about the cuts, but I also wonder if he means the prolonged holding of my leg. "Thanks for the tea."

"You already said that," I point out, unable to move, the high of the moment only starting to dissipate slowly.

"Right, I did, that's true." He nods. And then grimaces. How did we both get so *awkward* so fast. "Okay, well, next time a regular walk. George would like that better anyway."

I notice George staring at both of us. His expression is a version of *Don't bring me into your nonsense, please.* Which is fair enough. I don't want to be in this conversation either.

"That sounds great," I say, so breezy, so casual, so ignoring that my entire body was tingling a few moments ago from him blowing on my boo-boos like a pathetic, lusty, completely bewildered person.

He runs his hands through his hair, tousling his curls and not helping my situation at all. "Okay. Great. That's great. I'll see you soon, Nora," he bumbles.

And within a moment he's out the door, like a cartoon character who leaves so fast there's a hole in the wall.

And I'm left with some cuts and scrapes along with an equally inconvenient feeling of total confusion.

CHAPTER 20

I like now how sometimes when I check my phone after work on Tuesdays, I get even more of J's thoughts on the column. Instead of containing everything to our document, it's now a continuing conversation throughout the day.

Although I wasn't quite prepared for this many texts to be waiting for me when I left the office, all sent a few hours ago.

> J: I've been thinking all day about this week's column. It's left a kind of gloomy cloud hanging over my week, if I must be honest (although to be fair, I was already primed to be gloomy this week for other reasons).

> J: I keep thinking about the guy who wrote in, and his feeling of just never being the one picked. I get how it would sort of eat away at him. I guess it makes me wonder if I've consciously tried to put myself in a position where no one would *have* to pick me.

> J: But of course, then if you try to have any intimate relationship— even one where you think you're the person more in control— that can always be upended. There's no way to guarantee you'll be picked, unless you only allow a life where you don't enter the game at all.

J: But then, as always with your writing, your advice to him upended my viewpoint. There's power in not viewing it as "being picked," and more about being compatible for the right person. And so I guess the fear is in deciding who that is and choosing wisely.

J: Anyway, that's a somber text to send, sorry. It was just on my mind. Your columns are always so insightful, so I can't be blamed for thinking about them beyond just editing! And also your fault for allowing these discussions to now exist outside the confines of our edits.

There was a break in texting, and then ten minutes after that group was another.

J: Blimey, just re-read that, and it sounds like a man saying "You asked for it," so please forgive me as I go crawl into a hole and consider deleting my number. This is why YOU are the writer and I am but a grammarian and editor. My words are all in there, but they seem to be much more jumbled when I try and write them out.

I smile at the rambling nature of his stream of consciousness. I used to only get the typed and curated version of J. Now, with texting, it feels even more honest and less polished.

I like it, even if I don't love whenever he doubts himself.

I think your words are pretty great, I reply, wanting to give him encouragement after all that.

Nora: They're a gift I'm grateful to be on the receiving end of.

I start to put my phone away as I approach my building, but I don't look up soon enough and run straight into Eli, who was also apparently too engrossed in his phone to see me coming.

"Shit, Nora, I'm so sorry!" He grips my shoulders to steady both of us. It achieves the main outcome of not having either of us falling down, but having his strong hands holding me again instantly reminds me of those same hands on my legs, and I inhale a sharp breath.

I think the memory comes back to him, too, because he immediately takes a step back.

That frisson with Eli has been looming over me for the past two days. Mostly because, after the mental gymnastics of convincing myself that I made it all up, he's skipped the walks with George the last two mornings, texting me some vague bullshit about busy days.

I suspect what he really wanted was a moment away from me. I sort of can't blame him—nothing happened, and yet that palpability felt loaded.

But since I don't *want* anything to happen, maybe it's for the best that we're running into each other so I can nip in the bud whatever awkwardness exists.

"It's okay, no harm done," I say with a smile, finally looking him in the eye. Although now, looking at him more directly, I can see how distracted and unlike himself he seems. He's dressed up in a suit—something I've *never* seen him wear—yet his hair looks like he's been pulling at it from every direction. "Where are you going?"

"I have this thing for my nan." He's fidgeting, so unlike his usual bravado. "I had to run back here because I forgot something."

"What *thing* for your nan?" I ask softly, curious but also wondering if I'm wading into something sensitive.

"Her department got a plaque made for outside of her old office, so they're unveiling it and then having a little drink after. I'd promised to bring some photos she had in her flat, but then I went over there without them, so I'm just popping back for a minute."

"Do you . . ." I don't want to overstep, but seeing him frazzled like this inexplicably unmoors me. "Do you have anyone with you?"

His eyes finally lift up to catch mine. "No."

The silence hangs between us. "Do you want a friend?" I can see the shades of relief with just the question, so I nudge a little more. "I can come with you. Just give me five minutes to walk George around the block, and then I'd be happy to come so you have someone you know there."

He doesn't answer right away. He bites at the inside of his cheek, ruminating on something. "Do you have something else you're supposed to be doing tonight?"

"Nope." I shake my head.

"Promise?"

I breathe out an exasperated sigh. "Why would I lie about that?"

"Because I get the sense other people always come first for you. I don't want you deprioritizing yourself for me too."

My eyes widen in surprise. His offhand assessment makes me feel practically naked. How does he always seem to *see* everything? But I clear my throat and shake the sentiment off.

"That's nice to ask, but I really was just going to hang out at home tonight. If you'd rather not face a horde of mathematics professors alone, it's no trouble for me."

He chuckles at the image, and I can see him let go of his concerns. "Okay. Let's meet back outside in five then."

I'm glad from the moment I arrive that I came with Eli. This event is a *crush* of people. This isn't a small little plaque hanging—this is over a hundred people milling around a room, drinking cheap wine out of plastic cups and vying to tell Eli every story about his grandmother that they can remember. We linked arms to walk over, and when we arrived, I tried to slip my arm out from his, but he held it like a security blanket.

It's fascinating to hear about this woman that Eli's described, but through so many other people's lenses, paint added in innumerable colors onto a pencil sketch. Mostly I'm watching his face. There's surprise in each anecdote he hears. Her former students all describe

Esther as tough, but every one of them then shares a story of some kindness behind the austerity. They all thought it was just them breaking through, but soon everyone is laughing at how much empathy lay behind that rigid, brilliant presence.

Three separate men introduce themselves over the course of the event and say they dated Esther at various times. Each interaction seemingly blows Eli's mind. I try not to laugh, but it's amusing seeing him turn over the fact of his grandmother as a woman with a potential sex life across her many decades.

And it seems as though every member of the mathematics faculty (and a smattering of others from different departments) has a story of Esther's competitive spirit, work ethic, and powerhouse mind. They all loved her, feared her, and admired her simultaneously.

Eli listens with fervor to every person who comes to talk to him. He seems to pocket each story, as though every additional insight is a gift. "I never knew she had a phase of going to the opera a lot," he whispers to me. And later, "It's hard for me to imagine her on a beach vacation" or "I wouldn't have thought she'd have had the time to take over someone's teaching load in the middle of a semester. That must've been exhausting, even if it was the right thing to do under the circumstances."

When someone tries to lead him away to go see the plaque, I start to untangle my arm from his, wanting to give him a moment alone with it. But he shakes his head ever so slightly and just pulls me closer, tracing a finger along my elbow, as though he needs the reassurance that I'm still there.

I try to not let my mind drink in the feel of his touch as much as it wants to.

But he loosens his grip as we come closer to the plaque, and I listen to the head of the department tell him all about it. He finally lets go when they insist on him giving a small speech, and all eyes turn to him with the clinking of glasses.

"I'm so grateful to be here as you honor my nan," he says, slipping back into the wiry confidence he's so good at, shielding the emotion that's been building in him all night from coming too far out. "She was a brilliant, accomplished woman. My family and I watched as she was feted with accolades her entire career, and I know that her work will be the thing she's remembered most for. She always considered it her greatest achievement. But it's all the small things I didn't know about her that you've shared today—your kind words and stories—that for me build on top of the mosaic of who she was and what she actually accomplished. Thank you for these new shades and sides to a woman I loved so much."

He stops talking, and the room is silent for only a moment before applause breaks out. And then the department head is leading a toast, and a few more speeches come after.

Once everything has wrapped up and as we walk home, the sky now inky against the light of the streetlamps, Eli doesn't say much. He's lost in his own thoughts, in all the new information he's added as scaffolding onto this woman, who he'd previously thought was done being built in his mind. I don't press him, and I relish the silence after so much talk.

When we reach our building, he takes out his keys and opens the door. "Thanks for coming with me."

We step onto the elevator. "Happy to. It was fun to get to hear all those stories about Esther."

"She was one of a kind, that's for sure." Her absence is written across his voice. "There's so much I never knew about her."

"No one knows everything about anyone," I remark, trying to banish some of that sadness from his expression as much as I can. "We're all the sum of all the many, many people who've loved and loathed us, and everything in between. That can't possibly be quantified."

He huffs out a laugh. "Thank you."

I nod, not needing him to say anything else. He puts his hand on my elbow again and traces where his hand lay earlier in the night, the movement making my body suddenly spark in a way it wasn't when he was holding me earlier for stability.

The door opens, breaking the moment, and I realize he forgot to push his button, so we've ended up on my floor. I step out, the loss of his hand leaving an invisible mark. I hold the door open for a beat, not quite sure what to say now. He's watching me again, drinking me in, in that way he does that always makes me feel somehow excited and nervous at the same time, like a liquid slowly seeping into me that I can't brush away.

"See you for a walk with George tomorrow morning," he says finally, and I'm grateful: grateful that he's going to stop avoiding me, but also grateful for a way out of this moment. Every time he gets too close, those lines delineating "friend" seem to get thinner and thinner. And I don't need anything else confusing me.

"See you in the morning," I say, taking my hand off the elevator door and watching as it closes.

CHAPTER 21

Nora: I can't believe this trip is coming up so soon. Are you looking forward to the party? Or do you do stuff with colleagues all the time so this isn't as big of a deal to you as it is for me? I've never met anyone!

J: I used to see people more, so yeah, this will be a good event.

Nora: Oh like, you used to go into the office more? Pre-Covid and all that?

J: Yeah.

Nora: I wish I could work from home.

J: Yes, no, that's true. I'm grateful I can work from wherever.

Nora: It's nice to have control over your schedule. Mine is so dictated by appointments and client consistency.

J: You have real people to deal with, and I just have people's words.

Nora: good point!

Nora: So *would* you like to grab coffee while I'm there? I totally understand if you're too busy.

J: No not at all!

J: I mean, no to being too busy. Not no to coffee.

J: Yes to coffee.

J: I'd really like that.

J: Can we decide on the time the day before? Just have to figure out my schedule for next week.

Nora: Oh sure, of course. I'm just going to the party and doing some sightseeing, so I can meet whenever.

J: Great. That's really great. We'll definitely do that.

The trip to London is less than a week away, so the prospect of seeing J has been looming, and my texts with J have been more normal and yet more abnormal. I know most people wouldn't think of topics like the intricacies of being picked as normal, but that's the part with him I'm used to. The logistics piece is a foreign object, a tool I'm clumsy with when I wield it.

This was the only time I've brought it up, and maybe I'm interpreting him as skittish because *I'm* skittish. But his whole response just feels odd. It's as though I'm on the precipice of an important moment, and his reply is too vague to even get a grip on.

I should just try not to think about it. It's going to be whatever it's going to be, but I can't stop myself from the extremely cringeworthy mental exercise of imagining every multiverse of scenarios, from extremely awkward to happily ever after. Neither is reducing the pressure I'm putting on myself.

And that jumpy feeling also hasn't been helped by things with Eli. Whatever is sitting between us has me more on edge than ever before, even if he *has* shown up for our last few walks and managed to act excessively normal, much to my relief. But still.

I've got two hovering, imminent knocks at my door, and they both only get louder as time goes on.

So a nice quiet evening with my best friend was supposed to help with that.

Too bad Dane dragged me to her pool hall, and now both Kwan and Tom are standing giddily next to me. Apparently this is how my Sunday night is going to go. My best friend mostly ignoring me, and my elderly neighbors trying to peer pressure me into practicing a sport I'm indifferent to.

And . . . is that our building president?

"Who invited Hearn?" I ask Kwan as I see Hearn waving to all of us.

Tom gives me a small shove. "Don't be unkind," he says, and I stop myself from pointing out that he's sounding more and more like Mr. Rogers every day in his retirement.

I take a large sip of my beer as Hearn walks over. "Well, look at this trio!" he says, ignoring Dane because, frankly, she's not exactly hanging out with us anymore while she gets in some solitary practice. "We should do a building party here sometime!"

"Oh that would be fun when it's cold outside," Tom encourages.

"I loved that little mixer Eli had," Hearn says. "He's such a good boy, isn't he? Esther would be so proud."

I wish I could ignore how much it tugs on my heartstrings to hear someone say the one thing about Esther that I know Eli would want to hear. Even if it's coming in a patronizing way from Hearn. But Tom and Kwan are nodding along, so maybe that consensus would be the best thing of all.

"*And* it's so nice how he's scaled back his roof plans a little bit. He said he talked to a landscaper and didn't want to cause any potential drainage issues with his planters, so he readjusted without us even having to ask." Well, *that* part stuns me. Eli changed his roof plans? But before I can ask anything, Hearn changes the subject. "Anyway, I'm meeting up with my team."

"Your team?" I ask, not having quite noticed before that he's wearing a shirt with a logo that has two pool cues crossing.

"Oh yeah, big invitational coming up soon. We've gotta crush everyone."

I try to school my surprised expression. I wouldn't have pegged Hearn for having any friends or hobbies beyond nitpicking at our building.

Dane walks over, and suddenly Hearn's face turns serious. "*Dane*," he says, with mock formality.

"Your honor," she says with the same competitive bite, tipping her baseball cap in his direction.

At that, Hearn walks away, and I turn to Dane, bewildered by the whole exchange.

"He's a retired judge. And his team is our biggest competition," she shrugs.

"*Hearn* is good at pool?"

"Not as good as me," she says, swiping my beer and taking a large chug. With a wink she wanders back over to the table next to us and reracks. Kwan joins her while Tom and I stand and watch.

"So what's going on with your stranger?" Dane asks, never taking her eye off the balls.

"Oooh, what stranger?" Tom asks, looking delighted.

"It's nothing—" I start to say, but Dane cuts me off.

"She's in love with a dude she's never met," she explains, as though I'm not standing right here. "He edits an advice column that she writes. At first it was love notes in the margin, and now it's a full-scale texting relationship."

"I'm not sure I'd call texting a relationship," Kwan says, taking his time making his next shot after Dane's went flawlessly.

"I think that's very romantic," Tom interjects.

"Thanks for the extra-special glimpse into your insights about my life," I grumble, not loving all this attention suddenly on me, even if I know Dane's doing it to try and move me forward through sheer will. "It's not a big deal."

"Well, it's relevant!" Dane says to me and then turns back to Kwan and Tom. "She's going to London for work in a few days, and they're going to meet up for the first time."

"If I didn't know any better," Kwan says, trying to rile Dane up now that she's clearly beating him, "I'd say you're going soft and gooey."

"I'm not gooey; I'm just Team Nora," she responds matter-of-factly, and I can't help but feel a little fuzzy inside. But Dane clocks my reaction and rolls her eyes.

"I know you didn't necessarily want to bring this up with us," Tom says in a statement so obvious that it probably didn't need to be articulated, "but I am curious. Do you really think you can know someone without meeting them? Is this generational?"

"Definitely not all of us," Dane mutters.

I finish my beer and try to think of how to explain something that seems so unfathomable.

"I know him," I finally say. "I don't know a lot of the surface things. I don't know what color his eyes are or even what he looks like, that's true. But I think you can fall in love with a person through words. I think in some ways, that's more powerful than all the other external things."

"But if he walked in here right now," Kwan points out, "he'd still be a stranger."

"Yes, but he's a sort of intimate stranger," Tom says, and I give his arm a squeeze of thanks. Tom is so straightlaced and by the book, but I like to think being married to a free spirit like Meryl has made him perennially open minded.

"I think that's a good way to describe it." I pick at the label on my beer bottle, considering. "There's so much I don't know about him, so in those ways he *is* a stranger. I don't know his contours. But I know his mind. So I don't know how to explain it, but I just feel in my gut that this person is my person."

"Are you nervous, then?" Tom asks. "For your meeting?"

I laugh. "Uh, yeah," I scoff. "What if he's different in person? What if he doesn't like me? There's a million what-ifs that are all just as realistic as the next."

"But I think when you know, you know," Tom says, giving me a reassuring pat on my hands. I smile, imagining whatever Meryl is up to tonight—probably getting into trouble but still speaking about Tom just as lovingly.

"How do you know he's not married or like . . . a troll?" Kwan interjects, still skeptical.

He's been a widower for the better part of twenty years, so I imagine that's hardened him. I wonder if Kwan and Tom—men of the same generation—started with the same level of optimism, and then their disparate experiences moved them into opposite mindsets. Evidence will change us, after all.

"He's not married," I say, brushing the thought away. "I write a therapy advice column, so we talk about relationship stuff pretty openly. I've been writing it for years, and we've always sort of written notes to each other. So when we were both in relationships, at various times, that came up in the conversations. He broke up with a girlfriend a little while ago. It's kind of the thing that made me start to admit to myself I might even have these feelings—that his breakup made me feel a certain way."

"And you suspect he feels the same?" Tom asks.

I hesitate, thinking about all our texting lately. "Intimate stranger" really is a perfect way to describe it. The freedom to be intimate with someone you don't know, who you've realized understands you better than some of your closest people, has been a gift. And I know *that's* been the same for him, because he doesn't hesitate to point it out. But romantic feelings? "I have no idea, honestly," I admit. "We are close; there's no doubt about that to me. But it feels so absurd to claim romantic feelings for a person you don't know that I sort of hesitate to imagine he could feel the same way."

"Well, I hope it goes the way you want it to," Tom says.

"Just for the record, I do, too, even if I'm an old grump," Kwan concurs, wincing as Dane handily beats him.

"Obviously me too," Dane says, before flagging the waitress and ordering another round of drinks. As Kwan reracks again, she turns back to me. "So what's this thing with Eli?"

At that I nearly spit out my drink. "There's no *thing*."

"Eli from the building?" Tom asks, and now I can feel the color of my face deepening a shade.

"Nothing is happening with Eli from our building," I say to him just as Dane interjects, "They hang out all the time, and he goes with her on her dog walks."

At that Kwan perks up. "I thought he was a cat person!" Man, nothing like a small building to spread useless gossip.

"He *is* a cat person," I say in a sad tone, knowing that Kwan, as a fellow dog person, will feel my pain.

"But then that just means he likes spending time with you," Tom points out.

"Yes, absolutely," Kwan agrees. "No cat person willingly goes on walks with a dog. It's diametrically opposed to their entire viewpoint on animals. And no offense, but it really must be about you, because if a cat person was going to pick a dog to hang out with, it wouldn't be George."

Dane chokes a little on her beer from that assessment, and Tom thwacks her on the back to help her.

"*Hey*," I say, morally obligated to stick up for my beloved but strange dog.

"George aside," Tom says kindly, "what gives?"

Being a couple beers in makes me feel looser. I guess there's no harm talking this out, even if Kwan and Tom are unlikely romantic-advice givers.

"I don't know," I sigh. "I mean . . . look, I guess I'm attracted to him. He's a good-looking guy."

"Ah *HA*!" Dane says, triumph in her gait as she takes the break shot.

"But it doesn't matter," I say, waving it off.

I want to point out that Eli was sort of a patient, but no one knows that other than Dane, and I'm definitely not allowed to share that information with people who know him. But even without that fact (and even without everything Ari said the other day staring me in the face), there's so much more to it than just the increasingly less relevant former-sort-of-patient thing.

"Why wouldn't it matter?" Tom asks. His curiosity is clearly piqued—I wonder if living with Meryl makes him more interested in gossip or if he'd always been and Meryl just seems like the more likely busybody.

"It doesn't matter because it's physical," I say, brushing it off. Although, the sense of selling Eli short rears its head, and I know I need to clarify. "It's not that I don't like him as a person . . . I actually like him a lot more than I thought I would. But he's too guarded and emotionally unavailable. I get pieces of him, but he's hidden behind a wall."

"And with your writer man, it's different," Tom says, understanding.

"Exactly." I'm grateful he's seeing the difference. "I don't know how to explain it other than . . . we're both free. I'm free to be me."

"What are you, Marlo Thomas now?" Dane says.

I snort. "It's insane. I know it's insane. But I can say anything to J, and he to me."

"So even though you want to get it on with Eli, you're not in that headspace since you're about to meet this other man?" Kwan summarizes.

"*Get. It. On?*" Dane laughs. "Kwan, come on, I know you're a geezer, but that's a lot even for you."

"I'm trying to think of a polite way to describe whatever casual mores your set has." He pockets the ball he was aiming for and gleefully turns to smirk at Dane.

"You'll figure it out," Tom says, patting me again to the point where I'm starting to feel like a puppy whose owner wants them to feel like it's okay that they've made everything a mess. "Just follow your heart."

"And not your loins," Kwan snickers.

"'Loins'? Now you're just fucking with me," Dane says.

Kwan shrugs, clearly enjoying getting Dane agitated. Maybe there's something to it, since he's ahead in this game.

"Nothing is happening with Eli," I say. "I know what I want. Just dealing with what's ahead when I go to London is enough drama for me. Eli is my friend, and you don't have to read anything else into it."

The waitress comes back and hands us all new beers. I take mine and lean up against the wall, my stomach churning and probably not in need of more alcohol, but that's what it's going to get.

It's confusing, conflating Eli and J like this. I should be entirely focused on seeing J in just a few days. Why does it stir something up in me every time I think about Eli? How can I feel this strongly about two different people?

It's all swimming and swirling in my mind, and I wish I wasn't heading into this trip feeling so confused. I shouldn't *be* confused. I know what's real with J. Eli is a friend who acts irrationally, for both good and bad—creating this mess about the roof and then apparently paring it back is just the perfect example. What's he playing at?

But as I take another sip of my beer, I refocus on my friends. I'm here to have a relaxing evening, and in a few days I'm going to meet J. That's what I'm focusing on.

That's what I *should* be focusing on.

CHAPTER 22

When I get back to my apartment around midnight, after Dane has thoroughly whipped Kwan in several games of pool, I notice a piece of paper taped to my door.

> I have a surprise for you! Come by my place whenever you're back (Doesn't matter how late).
> —Eli

Well, there go my attempts to ignore Eli and focus on everything else.

The walks *have* been normal since the biking incident and the plaque-evening weirdness. We've slotted back into our morning George routine, and there's nothing tension-filled about an early stroll with a cranky dog.

But I haven't gone to his apartment in a while. There's something so much closer about being alone inside. Outside, in the thrum of the city, we're two data points in a larger system. Inside, in apartments and apparently elevators, is where I get into trouble with him. Inside is where I get confused. And as we discussed—perhaps a little *too* much this evening—I don't need any confusion.

But I can't ignore a note like that. Not only would that seem weird but also I'm not immune to the promise of a surprise.

I walk downstairs and knock on the door. After a few short moments, it opens with vigor. Eli looks deliciously excited, like a kid in a candy store.

"Okay, you'll never guess what I have," he says, pulling me inside and looking giddier by the minute.

"A problem with illicit substances?"

He admonishes me with a look. "*No.* I'm just excited."

My lips curl into a smile. "I can see that." But as much as I'm intrigued by his uncharacteristic delight, something on the table is distracting me. "Are those black-and-white cookies?"

"Oh." He turns, like he's remembering something almost as exciting. "Yes, I made these." He grabs one and hands it over to me. They're not warm anymore, but the icing hasn't hardened, as though he just made them and then left them to set.

"You made black-and-white cookies?" I ask.

"Well, I liked yours, and I keep thinking if I do more New York things, it'll feel more like home." He shrugs, watching as I take a bite.

"These are really good," I say, trying to enunciate with my mouth full. He's talked about his baking, but I've never actually tasted anything he's made. I'm surprised by how fluffy and perfect they are. "Did your grandmother make these with you when you were a kid?"

"Oh yeah," he says with a grin. "When Nan moved here, she started out making biscuits and shortbreads and everything British. But then I think, as she put it, she wanted to date some New Yorker, so she got really good at black and whites. Eventually she said it made her feel like a New Yorker herself, so she didn't miss the old stuff."

"Are you missing home?" I ask, knowing that isn't why he asked me here but wondering it all the same.

"I'm . . ." He pauses, the lightness dimming for just a moment. But then he shakes it off. "It's fine. Anyway, I *did* want to give you a cookie. But I actually have something better for you."

"Something could be better than cookies?" I ask as he pops away to go grab something from his room.

"Oh yes!" he says, practically running back and holding out his hand. And there, laid flat in the middle, his palm curved to keep it safe, is my button.

It's the button I lost on the bike ride and assumed was gone. It's twinkling in the light, looking like a shining star against his skin.

"You found my button?" I ask in disbelief.

I know I can see it right in front of me, and I know it's unique enough that it can't be anything else, but it seems so illogical.

"I . . . yeah," he says with a shrug, tipping his hand into mine so the button falls softly onto me.

"But it was lost."

"Well, it was always there," he says quietly. I hold it nearer to my face, as though seeing it up close will make it all make more sense. "I shouldn't have let go while you were biking."

I snap my head back to him, my eyes questioning. "So what'd you do? Go inch by inch through all those thickets to try and find a single button?"

His brow furrows, and I wish I could take the sentence back— because it seems like that's *exactly* what he did. And he's interpreting my words as incredulity, not the sincerity that I meant. I can't wrap my head around it. He did this? For me?

"I just thought I'd be able to find it," he says, shrugging again, like he can shrug off the weight of my stare. "I thought you'd be excited."

My hand darts out to his shoulder, desperate to correct whatever thought is now burrowing. "I *am* excited. It's from one of my favorite shirts," I explain. "I just can't believe you did this for me."

"Is that so hard to believe?"

"Not *you*," I emphasize. I'm backtracking once again and trying to fix what I know I'm saying incorrectly in my stunned state. "I just can't believe *anyone* would do this. For me. For anyone. It's a huge pain. It's methodical. It's a lot of work!"

"Not a *lot* of work," he mumbles.

"No, Eli, it is," I say, my voice cracking a bit. "I'm really touched. You must've had to sift through a lot of uncomfortable brush, all while leaning over and . . ." As I'm imagining it, it seems about as painstaking as painstaking could be. I look back down at the button, so simple but so irreplaceable, now back in my possession. "I just really appreciate it."

"It's not a big deal," he says.

He looks embarrassed now, and I don't get it. *He's* the one who put the note on my door. He's the one who went through all the effort.

"I don't get how you were so excited to show this to me and now you're acting like it's nothing," I say. "It's so cool that you did this. I'm really speechless."

He rubs the back of his neck and looks away, the way he always does when he wants to avoid. "I don't know, I didn't mean to make it such a big deal," he finally says. "Like, now that you say it like that, I'm a little embarrassed."

"You're *embarrassed*?"

"Yeah, it's kind of overboard," he says, flipping whatever switch he's able to use whenever he wants to get his casual nature back. It's amazing how he can do that. It's such a skill to be able to pour ice over your emotions. Knowing him now, I find it sort of remarkable to watch the subtle difference when he shakes off his sincerity and puts the bravado back on.

"It's not overboard," I counter, not wanting to let him diminish. "It's really kind."

"Well, I thought you'd like it. And you do. So do you want another cookie? Or a cup of tea?"

He turns away from me and goes back to the table to get the plate of black and whites again, then he turns on his tea kettle. I don't move, just watch him as he flits around and tries to burn off his own nervous energy.

"You like to say that I can't take a compliment," I point out. "But look at yourself—this reaction is weird even for you."

He turns back and looks at me, staring so sharply into my eyes it almost makes me take a step back. I can't read him. He's watching me but doesn't say anything. He's holding something in, and I don't know what it is, the air filling with that heaviness that sometimes threatens to permeate the easygoing nature of our friendship. It's hard not to wonder why he's had such a sudden turn. Why would he do something so out of the way and nice for me and then in a flash want to minimize it?

And I can't pretend, when I see these rare pieces of him—the vulnerable, joyous, kind pieces—that I don't feel like there's something more between us. I can't pretend like I don't see all the ways he's beautiful when he lets his doors open a crack.

And for some reason, right now, with this button held tight in my fist, I'm suddenly desperate to see more of it.

"Hearn said you minimized your plans for the roof," I venture, knowing I'm playing with fire. I can't help but wonder how much our friendship has needled at him the way it's started to needle at me. I'm confused, and I have so many more confusing things looming, but in this moment I'm incapable of not pulling at the thread. Maybe it's the way he's looking at me. Maybe it's that button. But I need to know.

He doesn't answer immediately. He's watching me, gauging. He purses his lips, and it's distracting.

"I talked to Dane," he finally says.

"You talked to *Dane*?" I ask, mind whirring. She wasn't with us when Hearn mentioned Eli's changes, but surely if Dane had talked to him, she would've mentioned it.

"I asked her not to tell you," he says, immediately able to see where my mind is wandering. "I didn't want you to think I was looking for credit. I genuinely just wanted to do the right thing, and since I knew she'd already been looking at my plans—because of you—" At that he smirks, and I'm almost relieved to get that openness back instead of the weight of whatever's sitting between us. I'm relieved to see that familiar one side of his grin curl up more than the other. "So I just asked her what she thought I should do to keep everything as unobtrusive as possible."

"You did that for me."

It's not a question anymore. All these things, these seemingly small but actually huge things, they're for me. I squeeze the button tighter in my hand—the button he went searching for on a fool's mission. For me.

"Yeah, I did it for you," he admits quietly.

"Why?" I ask.

He rubs a hand over his face, like he's still searching for the answer. Like maybe he knows the answer but doesn't want to quite admit it yet, even to himself. And maybe so he doesn't have to look at me anymore while he responds.

There's too much distance between us, and I can feel myself unconsciously walking over to him. My heart's beating faster, and everything else that's usually taking up space in my mind has dissipated. There's only Eli and me, only this question hanging in the air. There's only his breath and mine.

"You do things for everyone else," he finally says, as though that's a reason and not just the basic facts of my life.

"Trust me, I know that," I chuckle. "But why did *you* do all of this for me?"

I'm standing in front of him now, in between the table and the counter, bracketed by his kettle on one side—now boiling and whistling at us—and the black-and-white cookies on the other. I move the kettle off the hot burner, and silence once again fills the room.

He sighs, and I can see it's an effort for him. He did all these things on impulse, because that's how he moves through the world. He wanted to find the button, so he just went for it. He probably threw on some long pants so he wouldn't get scratched and set off for the West Side Highway without considering why. He probably ran into Dane in the elevator and asked her, *Hey, what would you do if you were me?* He didn't mean to be so thoughtful.

But he was thoughtful.

And now I'm asking him to consider why.

I think I know why.

And instead of finding that scary anymore, I now find that it feels inevitable. For once I'm not thinking about J. I'm not thinking about what comes next. It's only me and Eli and the way he's not looking at me, like if he does, he'll have to admit it too.

"Why, Eli?" I say, my voice quiet even amid the silence.

He fidgets. He picks at the side of a cookie and eats it. He drums his fingers on the table. He's deciding.

And I wait him out. I need to hear him say whatever he's thinking, and I'm going to let him cycle through all his discomfort to get there, to get back to the open part of himself that I like so much but that is so often hard for him to let others see.

But finally he sighs and looks back up at me again.

"When someone does something nice for you, you always seem surprised," he says, his eyes on me a challenge now.

"I *am* surprised," I admit.

"I wish you weren't," he says softly. He takes a step closer to me, and now I'm the one who can't look right at him. I'm watching the way his hand glides over the top of his kitchen chair, the way it holds on, the way it smooths across. "I wish the people in your life did more nice things for you."

"I'm fine," I say, still looking away, now nervous at what I've started. Nervous that I poked so much that I made that inevitability happen.

But he gently places a finger under my chin and tilts my face up so I can see him again.

"I know you're fine. But I can't help how much I like seeing you smile."

His eyes scan my face, impatient and longing, as though he wants to come closer but hasn't quite decided. He lingers, watching me, unsure. He opens his mouth to say something and then closes it. Opens it again and then thinks better of it. He swallows, and his Adam's apple bobs nervously. He's blushing a tinge so gorgeous I want to reach out and trace it.

And *I* can't help but smile at the sight of his honest indecision.

"See, *that*," he says, removing his finger from under my chin and drawing it across my lips, slowly, reverently. "That smile. It does something to me."

"I can see that," I say, my body tilting unconsciously toward his, drawn in by watching this composed man succumb to trepidation, a long rope tightening around my heart.

His thumb sits on my bottom lip, and he watches, mesmerized but still unmoving.

"Are you going to kiss me?" I breathe out, so keyed up now that I can't stop myself from saying it.

"Don't you think it's a bad idea?" he says, his eyes still on my mouth.

"Probably," I agree, even though I can't stop drinking in the way he's looking at me. The way he seems to be holding himself back.

"We live in the same building. You used to kind of be my therapist." It's a quiet relief knowing that he's also thought about it; that he's batted around all these same complications and studied every nook and cranny of what-ifs. It's the opposite of rashness, of impetuous desire, of a spur-of-the-moment bodily want. He's turned it over in his head too. But he still went to find my button. "Wouldn't that make things complicated?" he finally breathes.

I nod. "Definitely."

"So tell me to stop," he says with a groan.

But I already know I can't.

"I don't think I want to," I whisper.

He closes his eyes and takes a deep breath, centering himself. I wonder if he's going to be the smart one. I wonder if he's going to take all those excellent points he just made and let them convince him to take a step back.

But the opposite happens.

CHAPTER 23

He wraps his arm around my waist and pulls me to him, kissing me with so much recklessness I gasp. He pulls back at the sound, his hesitation from earlier coming back into full force.

"No, keep going," I murmur, and he crashes back into me.

I'm consumed with want. It's as though all that chemistry that's been slowly bubbling between us has finally erupted in a stream of lava after weeks of lingering below, pressurized and then gradually causing the surface to fissure, breaking in an instant.

He tastes like the sugar of a cookie, sweet and delectable, and I can't quite get enough. He pushes me up against the kitchen counter and lifts me from below until I'm sitting, his hands still under me, gripping like he's never letting go. My hands are in his hair, pulling off his shirt, scraping across his back—going everywhere they can get. But his are the opposite. Even as we kiss like there's no tomorrow, his hands move up slowly, softly. He runs them along my side, delicately against my collarbone, and back up to my lips to touch where he traced them before.

I'm burning everywhere as he keeps up the dichotomy—the fevered kisses and the gentle touches. I feel starved—like I never get to take what I want, and suddenly I'm being allowed. Against better judgment, against what would be prudent, against what would be responsible. I want it all.

He squeezes the inside of my thigh tightly, and I can't stop the moan that escapes my throat. He pulls away from our kiss to watch, and I can feel the heat rising in my cheeks again. The way he's looking at me is hazy and has the same level of need I can feel in myself. It's intoxicating to be looked at like that.

He brings his mouth to my throat and kisses, slowly. "I want that sound again," he purrs against my skin. His teeth scrape down my neck, and he gets his wish.

He undoes the top button of my shirt. "If I rip off one of these buttons right now, will you be impressed if I find it?"

I'm so turned on I can't help but lean my head back and close my eyes as a small laugh huffs out of me. "I think I'll just be impressed if you can get them undone, because I couldn't do anything requiring dexterity right now."

"Hmm, a challenge," he says, and I can imagine his crooked smile from the tone of his voice. He undoes each button, torturously and leisurely, planting a kiss on the bare skin he uncovers with each. With every intake of breath he coaxes out of me, I can feel his grin against my body, like he's taking each button as a victory and savoring it. Until he's kneeling on the floor in front of me, the last button undone, and I tilt myself back to sitting and look down, because I want to see the expression on his face.

"You're so beautiful," he says, almost in disbelief, and his reverence makes my heart skip a beat. I'm not sure why it's affecting me so much to feel so *lusted* over. But maybe that attention is what Eli has always done to me, like he sees pieces of me that no one else does. All his charisma and surety beam right into me. Even when we were at odds, it was powerful—being an adversary instead of always the solver; a rule breaker instead of a person who toes the line; surprising and seductive instead of dependable.

His hand smooths across my thigh, and I shiver. His eyes drink in the movement, and he kisses me in the spot right where his hand was. Then he stands up, tall and imposing now, gently removing my undone shirt and sliding it off my shoulders. He comes closer, bracketing me in, his mouth next to my ear.

"I need to admit something," he hums quietly.

"You're secretly married to the cats?"

He snorts out a laugh. And it makes me want to keep going.

I continue. "The accent is a ruse to pick up women?"

"I wish I'd known Americans were that easily won over years ago," he muses.

"You didn't actually bake the cookies?"

"A sacrilege. I would never."

"Esther's still alive but faked her own death for the insurance money?"

I adore the mischievous smile that bursts out of him at that thought, as though nothing would be more delightful. "I wish," he says with a sigh.

"Okay, I give up," I declare, now hungry to know what secrets he's holding.

"I think about you too much," he finally says, planting a kiss behind my earlobe and making me shiver even more. "Even when I was mad at you, I wanted you."

We're so close, his hands on either side of me on the counter, his words a whisper, since his mouth is still next to my ear. And since I can feel him even without seeing him, it makes me want to admit things too.

"You threw me off the first time we met in person," I concede. "I didn't understand how I could be so attracted to someone I disliked so strongly."

He barks out a laugh and puts his forehead to my shoulder, wrapping one arm around me to steady himself from the amusement of my own admittance.

"Yeah, I felt that way too," he says with a sigh.

"So why did you keep antagonizing me?" I ask.

He pulls back, and I can see the glee written all over his face. "I was having too much fun goading you."

I close my eyes and shake my head, trying not to laugh at what should've been so obvious. But he holds my chin and stops me from moving. When I open my eyes, he's watching me intently again. "But only until I was having more fun just getting to be your friend."

"Is that what we are?" I ask, unsure, wondering how much I've inadvertently let this antagonizer turn into a confidant.

He rests his forehead on mine, breathing me in, eyes closed and peaceful. I can't tell if he's considering the question or simply letting the obviousness of it pass by.

But then he starts talking again, quietly. "I think I told you about my one friend who I can tell everything to."

I nod, moving us together, surprised that in the midst of all this, he's suddenly getting serious. But I'm curious to know where he's going with it.

"In the last few weeks, going on walks with you and hanging out . . . you make me feel that way too. Like I can be myself. It's just . . . I feel freer when I'm with you. Does that sound crazy?"

"No," I admit, thinking that, as much as I haven't wanted to see it, he's done the same for me.

I know I don't owe J anything, but the realization makes me feel a little disloyal, since it's almost the same exact language I used just tonight to describe *him*. How can I have felt unconnected to anyone for so many years, and now there are these dueling, different presences in my life, both somehow emerging at the same time?

But before I can question it, before I can let that confusion nestle its way in, Eli's mouth is on mine again, and I can't think about anything else. It's immediately frantic, as though his words have removed the last burden from his mind, and now instinct is the only thing taking over.

He grabs my thigh and pulls one leg around his waist. Then the other, until I'm completely wrapped around him, and he's got his hands under me again, lifting me up while I grip, unable to do anything but press myself into him, harder, needier, a tangle of limbs and mouths, the urge to get closer pulsing through me.

He walks away from the counter with me in his arms, and I hang on, the feel of him holding me so effortlessly only making me want him more. He kicks open his bedroom door and collapses both of us onto his bed, the weight of him on top of me a welcome tranquilizer to any other thoughts.

His hands go to the waistband of my skirt. "Is this okay?" he asks, featherlight touches skimming across my stomach, the promise of more making heat pool to my center.

"Yes," I hiss, taking over and pulling my skirt down before he can ask again.

He sits up, drinking me in, watching me breathe, tracing the line from my bra to my underwear and hesitating, like he's about to open a shaken-up soda can.

But I can't think any more about whatever will come next. I can't question whether this is a huge mistake or an inevitability we've been careening toward ever since I first knocked on his door. I can't wonder about J or my feelings or what it all *means*.

I just need him. He's heart pounding, warm skin, tousled hair, hazy eyes, and tangible touch in front of me, and I don't want to think about anything else but me and him and the way our bodies fit together.

So for the rest of the night that's what we do. He holds me and whispers in my ear, and we move together like we were always meant to be doing this.

I'm not going to pretend like I haven't had a lot of great sex in my life—I'm not the kind of person who goes back twice for mediocrity. But there's an irrefutable ease with Eli that I've never experienced before, and I find myself surprised by the emotion coursing through me because of it; surprised by how I'm able to let go in ways I never really knew I could before; surprised by how much he reflects me back—tender in all the places I want him to be, rough when I need it, playful instead of guarded. Point to counterpoint. Give and take.

The closer we are, the more it feels inescapable, undeniable. Like we've finally allowed our minds to catch up to what our bodies knew from the moment we saw each other: that it was always going to be this good and in sync and *hot*. It's so damn hot.

And when we're sweaty and spent and knotted up in each other and the twist of bedsheets, when his arm comes around me and pulls my body flush against his, I know I'm going to let sleep overtake me.

CHAPTER 24

I wake up with sunlight in my face and a cat hoarding most of my pillow. It only takes me a moment to realize where I am, and then the whole night comes flooding back. My lips are raw and my body aches, but I stretch in contentment. My mind isn't yet up to speed, although I'm awake enough to know that I probably should relish the *not* thinking yet.

I look over at Eli sleeping. It's adorable seeing him so peaceful instead of in his normal whirl. And he's got one arm lazily lying on me, and the other is . . . oh my god, he's actually holding hands (paws?) with one of the cats. I don't know whether to giggle or melt. It might be the cutest, most wholesome way I've ever woken up with a man. How does that even happen? Adorable.

But I feel creepy staring and watching him while he sleeps, so I turn to look around the room. I saw it when he was sick, but obviously not from this vantage point. His bed is pretty low, so it's like getting an inside view of the feet of his dresser or the bottom of his bookshelf. He has two little ships in bottles sitting on the bottom shelf.

Huh. I've never seen that before. Some déjà vu tingles, and I try to remember where I heard about someone making those.

And then I remember. J.

J told me he'd taken it up as a hobby.

Thinking about J propels me with nervous energy, and I don't like it, so I carefully extricate myself from bed, find my underwear from where it was unceremoniously tossed onto the floor, and pad over to the bathroom to pee. I just need to ignore this sensation. Whatever feeling is niggling is irrational. And I need to get up anyway. I can't leave George for this long.

But I don't want Eli to think I ran away. Maybe I'll leave him a note about George, and then I can always come back when I'm done. Does he *want* me to come back?

I wander into the kitchen to grab my shirt, crumpled like a material remnant of the previous night. I hear a phone beep twice and go to the counter to grab it.

It takes me a minute to realize, in my still-sleepy mental state, that it isn't my phone. But by then I've already seen the message that popped up.

> Celia: Looking forward to our Monday chat later today—do you mind if we push by an hour? Also—remind me that I have a couple notes on Ask Eleonora as well as the Sanders OpEd.

I nimbly put the phone down onto the counter, like it's scorching and it's burned me. I sit on the stool, pull my shirt on, and start numbly buttoning it up.

I look again just to make sure I haven't misread.

What the hell? What would Eli have to do with Ask Eleonora? Is that Celia like . . . my Celia? What does Eli . . . do?

I know Eli is a writer or journalist of some kind. But since that first walk, where we agreed not to talk about work, we've just had so much else to discuss. It never seemed odd that we didn't talk about our jobs with each other. It didn't seem relevant. Obviously he knows I'm a therapist, since I *was* his sort-of-therapist for a brief moment.

But I never told him about my column—and why would I have? No one in my life really knows about it except for Celia, Ari, and Dane. I'm used to not talking about it.

Why haven't I asked him more about his work? We've talked about the day-to-day of working from home, the unease of sitting in front of a screen alone. But I never really bothered to say, *Hey, Eli, who do you actually write for?*

Is it possible that Eli writes for the *Sunday Tribune*? Is it possible . . . is it possible he does something with Celia? Is it possible he has some oversight over Ask Eleonora? Is it possible . . .

Is it *possible*?

What the actual hell.

I stand up and start pacing, my dreamy state now replaced by some form of adrenaline and panic. I need to get the facts straight in my mind to try and make sense of everything: No one works on the column except Celia and J. I know Celia's boss gives the okay to everything once it's done, but she doesn't edit, and I guess the layout people handle it once it's ready to go online and in the paper. But it's not looked over and commented on by anyone else. If Celia is asking Eli about it, what else could that mean? Maybe he's on an editorial board of some kind? After all, his name is Eli. His name doesn't start with a J, so he can't be *my* J.

Except.

Except . . .

Eli is my middle name.

Jarvis Eli.

Holy fuck.

Moving on autopilot, I go to grab my phone from where it was tossed onto the counter last night. With shaking hands I pick it up. I open WhatsApp and type a message to J.

Nora: How was your weekend?

I hit Send and watch with horror as Eli's phone lights up.

Eleonora: How was your weekend?

No.

This doesn't make any sense.

J lives in London. J isn't brash. J isn't like *Eli*. He's sensitive and open. He's accessible; he's the very opposite, with all the walls Eli puts up.

How can Eli be J? I *know* him. I know *both of them*. They aren't the same.

And then . . . if J is Eli . . . why didn't J tell me he'd moved to New York?

That thought causes everything to go cold.

I'd spent so much time wondering if J felt the same way as I did, as if we had some unmatched ability to speak honestly with each other. But if that were true, how could he just conveniently leave out that he'd moved to the city where I live?

I think I told you about my one friend who I can tell everything to, he said. *You make me feel that way too.*

Is that me? But then he *didn't* tell me everything.

One open version and one closed. One standing in front of me and one obscuring where he was.

The freedom to be ourselves is a conundrum. The roles we play define how we present ourselves, and the pieces we can obfuscate either make us more or less likely to give a full picture in any particular context.

What *is* the full picture? Would *anyone* get the full picture?

I know I said to Ari a couple months ago, when I admitted my feelings for J to her, that it was ridiculous to imagine loving someone based on only correspondence, but I hadn't actually considered how right I was—how much could be *left out*.

How much *has* been left out.

My head is pounding. It's too much to process. I'm confused and unable to get a mental grip, and I need to get out of here.

I scribble out a note on the counter: *Had to go walk George.*

I pause, not knowing how to sign off. Should I say, *I'll come back*? Should I say, *I'll text you later*? Say, *Hey, funny story, did you know we've actually been writing to each other for years and now we just had sex and I was feeling sort of guilty because I thought I was in love with this other guy but that other guy was you and so . . .*

Wait. No.

I'm in love with Eli?

Is that the conclusion I have to draw from this?

I'm not *in love* with Eli. I'm attracted to Eli, obviously. I *like* Eli. But Eli isn't J.

Eli *is* J.

Crap.

I don't write anything else on the note. I walk out the door and go back upstairs to the safety of my apartment.

Chapter 25

Dane flings her door open.

"Someone better be dying for you to be knocking so fucking—Oh. Nora?"

Dane is in a T-shirt and boxers. Her stick-straight black hair is mussed, and I have to admit I'm not used to seeing it without a Pacers hat perched on top. She peers around me, as though someone else must've been the one doing the loud knocking on her door, but when she doesn't see anyone else, she looks at me, bewildered.

I guess I'm not the banging-on-the-door-at-seven-in-the-morning-on-a-Monday type usually. And because Dane works for herself and is project based, she rarely gets up this early, so I must've roused her.

She rubs her eyes and pulls me inside.

"Nora, what the hell? And . . . George?"

I almost forgot I'd dragged George over with me. He gives Dane a curt snort and then wanders into the apartment. George has never accepted Dane, and since Dane isn't one to beg, they've always remained sort of cold to each other. Unlike with most people George doesn't like, though, he never barks at Dane. I think she's too dominant a personality for him to even attempt it. So he stays content just eyeing her with disdain. But I don't think I've ever forced George into Dane's apartment. Clearly I'm not in my best mental state.

"He needed a walk," I say, waving the presence of her canine frenemy away as though that sentence explains everything.

Dane's watching me, unsure of how to react to this completely out-of-character version of Nora, but after a moment she decides to go to the cabinet to turn on the coffee maker. Caffeine is absolutely needed for this conversation.

"Did you bring anything to eat?" she asks, scrounging through to see what she has.

"I sort of just ran over here," I point out.

Her eyebrows furrow, like she's still waking up and trying to make sense of me bursting into her apartment unannounced and without any baked goods. Highly unusual. I guess I can wait for her to get her bearings.

Mostly because I have no idea what to say. My feet took me here on autopilot, and I still don't have my *own* bearings, so I'm happy to wait until we have coffee.

And apparently . . . veggie straws and peanut butter?

"What the hell is this," I ask when she unceremoniously puts a plate down in front of me.

"Don't knock my snacks, okay," she says, wandering back over to the coffee maker to grab our cups. "I'm hungover from drinking with *you*, and it's way too early to cohesively think about something to eat."

"Most people are awake by this time on a Monday," I rationalize, like my uncharacteristic appearance can be chalked up to plausible formality.

She clunks a cup of coffee in front of me on the table and sits down, indicating I should do the same. "You look like shit, too, by the way. It's not just me. So out with it. Whatever you've got on your mind seems like it's a lot."

I take a sip of the coffee and try to think of how to put this. But there's no way to sugarcoat anything, so instead I blurt out, "Eli is J."

She does a spit take. Like an honest-to-god, coffee-spurting-out-of-her-mouth-right-onto-the-table spit take.

"I'm sorry . . . what?"

"Eli. *Is.* J," I repeat, as though maybe the problem is she just didn't hear me. As though maybe I need to say it again for myself so I'll hear it and believe it.

"Back up," she says, grabbing a towel to wipe off the table and herself. "When you left the pool hall last night, you were going back to your apartment. What could have possibly transpired in the last"—she looks at her phone to see the time and grimaces—"seven hours to have allowed you to come to that theory."

"It's not a theory," I say quietly.

She stares at me for a minute.

"Oh my god, you *slept with Eli*, last night," she says, her mouth now curving into a grin, like a kid who's just discovered a secret candy store.

"That's not what—"

"You don't look like shit—you look like you had sex! You're wearing the same clothes. Your lips look like you had filler, which maybe is a good look for you, who's to say. Your hair is the definition of 'bed head.'"

"I could've just woken up," I point out.

"Okay, none of that actually matters, because you have a hickey on your neck," she chuckles, and my hand flies up, as though covering it will make it go away.

"Wrong side," she says, indicating I should move my hand, and I dutifully move it from left to right, because that's clearly going to do something.

"Okay, yes, I slept with Eli," I sigh, putting my head in my hands.

"I knew the lady was protesting too much," she laughs. "You literally had a conversation with us about knowing what you wanted and how nothing was happening with Eli, and then you went straight home and jumped him?"

"That is *not* what happened," I say sternly, sitting up and trying to ignore her amusement.

"Obviously that's not what happened, because you would never do that." I don't know why, but the assessment stings a little. "So what *did* happen?"

"First of all, *you* talked to him about the roof! Without telling me!"

She holds up her hands. "Guilty as charged. So what? He asked me not to tell you because he didn't want you to feel like he was doing it to get into your good graces, which I thought was kind of a rad way to deal with it. The dude has integrity."

I snort, and she raises an eyebrow.

"Unless for some reason he did something that would make us believe he has *no* integrity and we have to murder him?"

I shake my head.

"Good," she says, that momentary defensive hackle lowered. "So okay, he did a nice thing. That's not a reason to jump him."

"I didn't *jump him*," I sigh.

"All right. You very calmly realized you like him. As was obvious to anyone else with eyeballs. So what happened, other than his chivalry about the roof?"

I roll my eyes at her description, and she just smirks, enjoying needling me.

But I have bigger fish to fry today than trying to get Dane to take me seriously. I explain the note to her. The button. The tension. And then, yeah, the kissing and everything else.

"Was it good?" she asks, and I love that on *this* she's sincere. Dane could rib me a thousand different ways, but when it comes to my happiness (and sex), she's not going to accept anything less for me.

I can feel my cheeks burn, and Dane nods, getting the answer she needed. I can't even begin to contemplate *how* good it was, because that'll start another whole spiral.

"So excuse my ignorance, but what's the leap from the obvious liking of Eli to deciding that because you like both Eli and J, that they must be the same person."

"Well, that's the crazy thing," I say quickly. "See, to me, they're two different people. They're not alike at all. I would *never* have assumed that just because I was attracted to Eli, that he was somehow the same as J."

"That's selling Eli a little short," Dane says with a frown.

"No." I shake my head. "They're just *different*. I do like Eli. I do. But with J, we're on the same wavelength, always. It's effortlessly open." I pause, thinking about last night. Thinking about that heat, that ethereal feeling of total synchronicity, and it stops me in my verbal tracks. But I shake it off, reminding myself that that's not the same as actual verbal emotional openness. "Eli is like an onion that he forces everyone to peel bare-handed. He doesn't let people in; he isn't free with his feelings."

"Maybe he is," she says, but I shake my head again, determined to make her understand, because I need this to make sense.

"We talk all the time. We walk George, and we hang out. He's shared some personal things, but they feel few and far between. He's not introspective or sensitive the way J is."

"Well, he *is*, since he apparently *is* J," Dane notes. "But maybe in person he doesn't feel he can be the same way. You've seen particular sides to him, Nora; that doesn't mean he doesn't have others."

I put my head in my hands again and let out another heavy sigh, unable to keep up this mental jujitsu. There's no point arguing with her when of course she's right.

"Celia texted him," I explain.

"Your column editor?"

"Yeah." I nod. "I was discombobulated this morning—"

"By the great sex."

I shoot her a look, and she snorts at the look on my face. I deliberately ignore her.

"It was early and I was getting my bearings and I heard a phone beep and I thought it was mine. She texted him about a call but also about Ask Eleonora. No one else other than J would be talking to Celia about it that casually. So on a hunch, I texted him. I texted J, and it came up on Eli's phone."

"Doesn't Eli have your number, though?" she asks, confused.

I shake my head. "With J, we've always texted on WhatsApp, because he gave me his British number. Eli gave me his American number. So hilariously I must be in his phone twice—as Nora in his regular contacts and as Eleonora in WhatsApp. When he added my number into his regular phone, the WhatsApp contact wouldn't have changed."

"That's . . . huh," Dane says, considering, taking another sip of coffee. "But you've been talking to J for weeks about meeting up in London. If he lives in New York, why didn't he just say that?"

"I don't know," I reply slowly, that particular question already buzzing. "I'm so confused by having to reorient my entire mind around J *being* Eli that that part is making everything seem so much more complicated. Like J isn't who I thought he was—not just because he's a particularly damaged and difficult real man I already know, but because the J I knew wouldn't *lie*. He might not share everything, but it's just so out of the spirit of our conversations to pretend to be in London when he wasn't. It's like I really don't know him at all."

"But again, maybe you know one side of him. Or now, I guess two sides," she says, squinting at the mental gymnastics of putting these two personalities into one person. *Welcome to my morning.*

But she's not done with me yet. "You have to have known all along you weren't seeing *everything* with J?"

I put my forehead onto the table. This is all too much. *Have* I known that all along? Or did I actually believe that J was a living, breathing embodiment of only what he told me in his messages?

How could I have believed that, really? He wasn't claiming to be some perfectly evolved man. On the contrary, he was openly, constantly admitting to his failings in his own life and finding solace in having one person he could actually say things to. I should've known he was a person who wasn't forthright in his everyday life.

Especially since I'm exactly the same.

I'm one version of myself to acquaintances, a less inhibited version with my closest friends, and another slightly different version with my family. Are any of those versions of me *untrue*? Or are they just different shades of the same thing, some holding more honesty than others?

I can't help but smile thinking of Esther's plaque unveiling and all the versions of her that collided together in that single moment, stunning the one person who thought he knew her best. We're all made up of so many sides, tiny jewels sparkling at different angles.

But maybe that's why this is all the more confusing. With J, it seemed like he saw more of me, because I felt like I could speak without hedging. And he'd implied he felt the same.

So why did he hedge on the one thing that could have brought us together sooner?

"Isn't this good news?" Dane says, interrupting my spiral. "Like . . . the guy you have a crush on and just had great sex with is actually the same man you suspected you're in love with? What am I missing that makes this bad?"

I lift my head up and stare at her. I don't quite know how to answer that. It's natural for me to be *surprised*, but why am I feeling so much *dread*?

As though she can read the confusion, Dane puts her hand out and covers mine. "For a person who reads the last chapter first, I get that going out on a limb with J was already hard. There's a lot of unknown here. And now it's palpable. He's a real person."

"He was always a real person," I grumble, taking another necessary sip of coffee.

"But this is different. Someone you're writing to, you can write and rewrite what you want to say. Someone you write to, they aren't standing in front of you telling you what to do or forcing you to make any choices. In words, we can be honest, but we can also be measured. Reality is messier than that. And Eli is the *opposite* of measured," she chuckles, and I scowl, not loving how much amusement she's still deriving even when she's switched into supportive mode. "So I get why this is scary, Nora, I really do. I get that you had to take on the emotional labor of your dingbat parents from a young age, and the idea of adding anyone else into your equation who needs something from you is hard. And not to mention, the fear of rejection is scary."

My mouth falls open at the succinct diagnosis Dane has given me. Damn, I always thought I liked Dane in part because she's *not* a therapist, but maybe I've underestimated her.

She's still not done with me. "But you have to tell him. This is a good thing. It's harder and it's not the fairy tale, but it's also better."

"I know," I say quietly. I close my eyes and rub my temples, trying to stave off the headache I can feel pulsing below the surface.

But Dane isn't going to give me an inch. She stands up, like she's ending the conversation for me. "So go talk to him, yeah? You talk about feelings for a goddamned living."

"Other people's feelings."

She stares at me, disappointed but not surprised. And then she grabs my arm and hoists me up. "Nobody said love was easy," she laughs, then pushes me out the door.

CHAPTER 26

I walk back, my head still spinning, but with every step I feel myself getting stronger. I can do this. I can be brave. I can let the story play out, even when I don't know how it'll end.

But when the elevator opens, I come out to see Eli already standing in front of my door.

"Hi," I say tentatively, as he turns around at the noise, startled.

"Oh, hi." He pauses, looking me over, like he's letting his expression be determined by mine. It's a shyness I never thought I'd see on Eli.

But I guess there's a lot I didn't realize about Eli.

"I'm, um . . . I was just dropping George off, and then I was . . ." I fiddle with my keys, nervous at his nervousness. "I was going to come back and, um . . ."

"I saw your note," he says, saving me from my inept bumbling.

"Great. That's great."

We both stand there, waiting. It's not uncomfortable the way I might expect it to be when you see someone you've slept with in the light of day. But we're both unsure.

"I, uh . . . you were gone a long time. With George," he says. "So I figured I'd see if you'd come back to your apartment but not back downstairs."

Ohhhh.

"No, no, I took a long walk. I wouldn't just . . ." I rub a hand over my face. This is all coming out wrong. We're like two bumbling teenagers, each trying not to say the wrong thing when standing in front of their crush. And I'm suddenly woefully aware of how haphazard I look. I didn't even brush my hair, and I haven't changed my clothes since last night. I look like I freaked out and took my dog on an hour-long walk after waking up in his bed. Which is technically true, but not for the reasons he's probably thinking.

But then he kindly saves me from myself by reaching out and grabbing my wrist. "Nora," he says with affection.

I half sigh, half chuckle. "I know, sorry. I'm not trying to be awkward. This is just me." I give him a sheepish look, because at least that much is the truth. "Do you want to come in?"

He nods. "Yeah, actually. I need to tell you something."

At that my heart drops. Does he know? Has he always known? Oh my *god*, what if he already knew and didn't say anything?

No, that's not possible, because then why would he have my number in his phone under two different names?

But oh shit, then what could he need to tell me? Does he regret last night? Is he going to say *Sorry for the mistake* before I've even had a chance to tell him that I'm Eleonora?

"It's nothing bad," he says with a small laugh, clearly in response to the total blanking out that must be registering on my face. "I mean, it's not good, but it's not about . . . not about last night or anything."

"Oh, okay," I say, now fumbling to get the door open while George stares up at me like he regrets having me as an owner.

I push the door open, and George trots away in a huff, clearly ready to get away from me after my walk-detour to Dane's and then my total meltdown now.

"Do you want a coffee?" I ask, not ready to look at Eli while I don't have my bearings.

"I have to go back to London," he says, and I turn around sharply at the words. Thank goodness I don't already have coffee yet, or I might've done a repeat of Dane's spit take. "I was actually, funny enough, going later this week . . . I hadn't told you, because it hadn't come up. And . . . right, sorry, anyway, I need to go today, though."

"Um, okay?" I reply, not really sure what the right response is to him; this unsure version of Eli is throwing me completely off.

"My mum just called, and she's in hospital with, apparently, a broken hip. She fell this morning, a few hours ago her time, and luckily she was able to call an ambulance, but they're about to do surgery, so I need to hop on the next flight I can get."

"I'm so sorry," I say, hating that I feel relieved over an old lady breaking bones instead of all the scenarios I had playing in my mind. "So, um . . ." I stop, not really knowing what to say. "What does that . . ."

But he sees the helpless expression on my face and comes to me, putting a hand gently on my hip. "Sorry, I'm really bad at this," he says.

I snort, because the thought that *he's* failing when I'm internally combusting over information that might make his mind also explode is laughable.

"No, no, you're not," I say, putting my hands on his shoulders, like maybe if we can both hold on to each other, we can get past whatever this tentativeness is. "See . . . the thing is, Eli . . ."

Bad timing be damned, I just need to tell him everything. I want to get it off my chest. But he—like the bulldozer man I know—interrupts me.

"Listen, you don't have to let me down gently, or whatever you're about to do," he says, and I can see him start to pull away mentally before even his body does.

"No, that's not what—"

"I get it. I came on way too strong last night. I said a lot of things, and I probably scared you. I totally understand why you felt like this morning you had to escape."

"I didn't—"

"I mean, you already knew I was inept because of Sarah, and maybe it's weird that you got a front-row seat to *that* implosion, but I guess also it gives you sort of a better idea of why I'm so bad at this—"

"*Stop*," I finally cut in, and he looks surprised, like he's not used to anyone stopping his particularly terrible soliloquies. "That's not at all what I was going to say."

"Oh," he says, his forehead furrowing in that adorable way that makes him look like he's lost the plot, in the way that briefly sheds the bravado and makes him look so much more human. "Well, either way, I have to go, and I don't know when I'm going to be back."

I was all prepared to tell him that he had it wrong and that my hesitation wasn't about not liking him, but now *I'm* thrown off. "You don't know when you're going to be back?"

"My father said he's going to put her into a long-term-care rehab facility, because he doesn't have the time to take care of her at home." I wince, because as much as my parents fall short (and probably would hurt each other in trying to be helpful), they wouldn't ever just leave each other like that. "And I can't let that happen to her. She's too proud. She can't be in a strange place, taken care of by strangers, while she's in pain and recovering."

"What about your sister?" I ask.

"She has her kids to handle. It's not right for me to ask that of her."

"And so your mom wants you to come?"

He looks at me like I'm asking the wrong questions, as though I've missed an essential part of the plot. "Of course she does."

"So you've talked it over with her?"

He frowns, and I can't help but love all the ways he's so *Eli*. Overbearing, know-it-all steamroller Eli on the outside, who I now know—both through getting to know him in the past few months and now suddenly seeing the shades of J all over him—is soft and tender on the inside. Of course it wouldn't occur to him that he should ask his mother if she wants him to uproot his life. I can see him so clearly as that child standing so small in front of his mother, as the only bulwark against his father. I can see how projecting strength became the coping mechanism for a solitary boy who wanted to be wrapped up in love instead of having to be strong for a mother who let him.

I keep thinking how much talking to a therapist, rather than pushing away the only one he'd ever been forced into seeing, could've helped him. But that's an issue for another day, because I can already tell Eli is about to go back into the defensive mode I haven't seen from him in months.

"It's not about talking it over with her," he says calmly but surely. "She needs help. I'm not going to let my father turn her into some ignored patient. She's just turned seventy; she's not a geriatric who needs to get shipped off. I can be at home with her while she recovers."

All those shades of protective little boy are emanating from him.

And my heart sinks, because I know I can't tell him right now.

I can't add confusion to a man looking to take care of his mother. I can't make this harder on him than it already is. I can't throw this massive bombshell of intimacy and misunderstanding onto his day and confuse the hell out of him right before he gets onto a plane and enters into a circumstance I imagine his father isn't going to exactly welcome with open arms.

And while there's a piece of my heart that's already hoping that perhaps in a few weeks or months, he'll resolve things with his family and come back, there's a more logical voice reminding me that this current dilemma isn't the only problem. Whatever this thing is between us—and whatever I imagine it is between J and Eleonora—there's a part of him that *hasn't* been open. There's a part that was hesitant to meet right away, or he would have just come out and said he was in New York when I first texted him. And that lightly lonely man, searching for but scared of connection, needs to come to that realization in his own time.

Or maybe he isn't capable of it. And I need to not get deluded into forgetting all the reasons why that's probably the case. And why *I* certainly can't be the person to solve it for him. I *can't* parent another person. This thing with J/Eli has taken over so much of my mental space for so many months, and I've worked too damn hard to let someone else's inabilities overshadow my peace.

And while I want to believe that's the main reason, I also know there's another, uglier thought lurking at the edges. No one has ever chosen me for just me.

I don't think at this point I could handle being rejected by him, now knowing everything I know. I'm not sure my heart—which I've worked so hard to protect and keep safe, to the point where I've gone this long without ever getting it crushed—could survive that.

It's probably better this way, even if the realization hurts more than I would've expected.

"It's good you're going, then," I finally say, clearing my throat to stop whatever emotion is bubbling up in me from rushing out. I rub his arm to give him whatever physical reassurance I can, wanting to not have these last moments together be anything but comforting for him. "And just for the record . . . you didn't come on too strong."

Discernible relief washes over his face, and it makes me ache for him; even with one-hundredth the amount of confusing information, he's spiraling as much as I was.

"I'm a mess, Nora," he says quietly.

"Me too." I shrug, and he gives me one of those slightly curved, one-sided smiles that make him look so boyish and handsome.

"I'm sorry I'm just leaving," he whispers. "I didn't mean to."

"I know," I reply, and it's the truth. I hope at least whatever small part of him was homesick will get some relief when he gets back to London.

"It's probably for the best," he says sadly. "You're too good for me."

I'm about to protest, about to try and dispel his unwarranted acceptance of his own view of himself, but he pulls me in for a kiss so deep I can barely stand anymore. And it's sad how much it feels like a true goodbye. Not like a *See you in a few weeks* goodbye, but the kind of kiss

I'd imagine soldiers give to their sweethearts before saying goodbye. It's cataloging a moment and pulling the marrow out of it for safekeeping.

It's a kiss that turns into a hug, lingering long enough that I can't help but nuzzle into him, breathing him in and wishing today was somehow different.

So I can't stop myself from saying the one thing I know I shouldn't say. "Whatever pin there is in . . . whatever this is . . ."—the words stumble out—"we're still friends. You can call me or text me anytime, even if we're far away from each other, you know?"

He pulls back and looks at me, his gaze so intense it's almost like he's looking through me. "I'm not sure I could ever just be your friend," he says with the saddest version of that perfect crooked smile.

And then he squeezes my hand and walks out the door.

CHAPTER 27

"So the stupid fucker had to mansplain all over her instead of listening."

"Dane, that's an awfully judgmental way to view someone who's confused about their feelings *and* facing an elderly parent's health decline."

Dane and Tom are hard to take seriously in their beach chairs, but apparently they're having a conversation without me anyway. And somehow I've been conned into sitting on the roof, of all places.

After Eli left, I texted Dane to tell her what happened and then shut off my phone and crawled under the covers. The last time I cried, it was because J (. . . Eli. I have to keep reminding myself that he's Eli) had written about how words can speak louder than actions. But today, in this instance, the actions superseded the words.

Dane was right when she said written words were more measured— my words today weren't expressed as they should've been, so I let actions choose the course. And now I'm lonelier than I've been in a long time, because not only have I lost Eli but also there's no way to keep talking to him under the guise of J without being dishonest.

I was letting that realization sink me deeper into my crying jag when I heard a loud knocking.

"You're not the only one who can pound on a door, Nora Fischer!" Dane's voice called out. "Come out, I got you every quintessential New York food carb I can think of, and I'm not going to let you drown your-self in misery alone."

So somehow I find myself, at only ten in the morning after what's felt like an excruciatingly long day already, sitting on the roof in a canvas chair, with a picnic blanket and a smorgasbord of food laid out in front of me. All while Dane, Tom, and Kwan debate the merits of my dilemma—because of course on a Monday morning, Dane thought two retired men would be available, and she was correct.

Meryl had joined only long enough to bring us a giant bottle of vodka (which I am absolutely, in no way touching) and give me a wet kiss on the nose. "Congrats on the sex, condolences on the abandonment," she tutted as she scooted out the door.

So now I'm ripping off pieces of a chocolate-Nutella babka from one of my favorite bakeries, Breads, and trying to put myself in a sugar coma rather than listen to everyone debate the exact level of how sad my predicament is. But it's not working yet.

I eye the cardamom bun from Smør Bakery and grab that one too. I'm double fisting pillowy carbs, and I'm not particularly mad about this part of my day. The sun is shining, and I've got fluffy, airy breads at my disposal.

So at least that's one thing to be grateful for while a trifecta of busybodies dissects my life.

"When do you go to London?"

I snap out of my baked good trance at Tom's words.

"Well, that's what's sort of nuts," I say. "I'm going on Wednesday night. This event is on Thursday, and then I was going to stay for the weekend."

"What's happening to George?" Kwan asks, and Tom and Dane shoot him a look, as though he's missing the point. "What?" he says to them. "If you're stressed about your pet, you're not yourself! She doesn't need that extra layer."

"Thank you, Kwan," I say sincerely, tossing him a rugelach from the pile that he's eyeing. Dane really did go all out on the carbfest. He catches it impressively with one hand, and I'm now wondering how an octogenarian's reflexes can be better than mine. But that's not the problem to think about today. "He's going to a dog daycare that also does overnight boarding. He doesn't love it, but it's really nice, and he'll be okay."

"Why didn't you ask me?" Kwan says, incredulous. "You take Lucy all the time!"

"Oh, I just don't want you to feel obligated," I point out.

I'm shocked when he immediately stands up. He's not particularly tall, so whatever authoritative effect he's trying to have is sort of muted by his short stature and the long time it took him to get out of the low beach chair. But he's standing and looking disappointedly at me, nonetheless.

"Nora Fischer!"

"Why is everyone full-naming me today like I'm a child in trouble?" I muse.

But Kwan isn't stopping there. "You can't take care of everyone and then refuse to let others take care of you. This is getting ridiculous. I've talked to you about my issues with my daughter for *years*. You take care of my dog whenever I go to visit her. You introduced me to Dane when you heard I also loved pool. I'm not your patient, and I'm definitely not going to listen to some excuse about elders and whatnot. We are *friends*. And just because it took Dane ratting you out for you to start talking about some of your problems, doesn't make them any less important. You're not paying some strangers to take care of George when I'm right here and I'm happy to help."

Dane looks gleeful, and Tom is watching with intense trepidation to see what happens next. Kwan keeps staring me down, I guess hoping I'll eventually break.

I rustle off another piece of my babka, the chocolate-and-Nutella interior making my fingers sticky and forcing me to resist the urge to lick them like the toddler everyone's treating me like. I hand a piece over to Kwan, and he gladly takes it. But he doesn't break eye contact as he waits me out.

"Okay, okay," I finally say, and he sits back down, triumphantly taking a big bite of babka. "I just didn't want to bother you."

"I'm an old retired guy. You're not ever bothering me," he says matter-of-factly.

"And you can bother us!" Tom interjects. "It's okay to bother your friends. That's kind of the whole point!"

I'm about to fidget my way to a thank-you to both of them when my phone rings. Dane snatches it out of my hand before I can even look at it and scoffs. "Oh hell no."

"Who is it?" I ask, my sticky fingers now becoming more comical as I try to grab it back.

"It's your mother, and we do not need this today," she says, standing up and walking away from me. I try to get up, but it really *is* hard to get out of a canvas beach chair. I should've given Kwan more credit.

But Tom stands up first—far more elegantly than should be allowed—and motions to Dane to give him the phone. She hands it over without a second thought while I give her an elongated wave to indicate I'd prefer I get my own phone back.

They're both ignoring me, though, and Tom lifts the phone to his ear. "Hello, Nora's phone," he says crisply.

After a beat he responds, "Oh yes, this is her friend Tom. She had to step away for a moment, and I saw you were calling and wanted to take a message for her." He pauses and then laughs. "No, it's not chivalrous at all. We're just neighbors and I'm old fashioned."

I can hear my mother chattering away on the other end, probably flirting with Tom. He nods along as he listens, but his face morphs from amusement to confusion the more she talks.

"I'm afraid that's not going to be possible," he finally says, and now I have absolutely no idea what's going on. "Mrs. Fischer—"

I love that this man probably two decades her senior is calling her Mrs. Fischer. But his politeness doesn't seem to be an obstacle for her to keep talking.

"Mrs. Fischer, I'm really going to have to interrupt you there," he says, in a sterner voice than I've ever heard come out of Tom. "Nora is not your handyman. I know how much Nora does for you, because, well, my wife is a little bit of a gossip. And I've even heard how much Nora has had our own super do for you! But it's not her responsibility to house you in her studio apartment because you've made some errors in renovation judgment. And I'm fairly certain Nora's extensive psychiatric education does not equip her to come help you figure out your tiling errors. Really, Mrs. Fischer, you shouldn't be putting all of that on your daughter."

I'm frozen, with a piece of babka in my hand. It's raised to go into my mouth, but I'm unable to move it. I must look ridiculous, but I can't seem to force my body to do anything other than sit still, lest this upside-down conversation disappear. Is gentle Tom really scolding my mother right now? Using his most authoritative anchorman voice, which sounds like something out of a 1950s newsreel?

But he barely lets her speak before he continues. "I'm happy to relay your message, but I'm really going to insist on putting my foot down here. I'm under the impression that you and your husband are still in excellent health, correct?" He pauses, and I'm amused by the old-person-to-old-person way of discussing their ailments. "Well then, if you're not able to afford your life, you need to reconsider your lifestyle. That's just my two cents; obviously it's none of my business, really. But I think someone should be looking out for Nora, and it's disappointing that it isn't you. Good day, Mrs. Fischer."

He hangs up and looks over, as though he finally remembers there were three other people listening in on his conversation, all now standing stock still in response.

"What?" he says calmly.

"Tom, that was *brilliant*!" Dane shouts. "I *wish* I'd said that to Tina years ago. Truly badass."

"Quite right," Kwan says, nodding with immense approval.

I'm still standing here gaping. "Tom!" I finally blurt out, and he turns to me. He at least has the good sense to look a little sheepish. "What just got into you?"

But he keeps his ramrod posture intact. "We're stepping in, Nora. You can't go on like this. It's admirable that you want to be there for your parents, but they're taking advantage of your kind nature. This has to stop."

"Damn," Dane says quietly.

"Now *that*," Kwan emphasizes, "is being parental."

"Okay, this isn't a day to blow up every single piece of my life all in one go," I point out.

"No, that's true," Tom says, and I love that Dane's face looks like she was about to argue the point.

"So what am I supposed to do?"

I collapse back onto my beach chair, and on instinct all three of them pull theirs closer to me. Dane grabs the remaining babka and shoves it into my hand. A good first step, I suppose.

"You stand up for yourself," Tom says with authority.

I start laughing, because the thought is so ridiculous. I'm hungover, predumped by my neighbor who I shouldn't have slept with; my two major codependent relationships are with my dog and a person I only text; and I'm apparently being steamrolled by my parents way more than I thought.

"I think you did most of the standing there, Tom," I argue.

"So you needed a little help with your parents, big deal." He shrugs, like that telling off of my mom wasn't a watershed moment. "That's what friends are for."

"Exactly my point!" Kwan says, pleased.

"I appreciate that," I say, truly meaning it. Maybe there's something to having adults in your life who try and take care of *you*. Kwan insisting on taking George and Tom blocking me from my mother might be the most restful things anyone could do for me. And maybe that's my problem. I'm so loaded up with other people's nonsense, but no one is taking *my* loads off. There's only so much Dane can do—that I've ever *let* her do. It feels special to have other people gladly taking on that weight.

But it doesn't shift my impending dread about what to do about Eli.

"I can't bombard Eli right now," I say, thinking out loud. "He has to help his mom get better and deal with his dad, and that's a lot. I don't need to be complicating his life any more."

"Well, weren't you guys planning to meet up?" Tom asks. "I mean, J and Eleonora at any rate."

"We never confirmed a time," I say slowly. "He was being so cagey about the whole thing. Like, he kept insisting we *would* get coffee, but didn't want to pick an exact moment."

"Well, that makes sense now that you know he actually lived in New York," Dane points out.

"Yeah, but isn't that a sign that something was off to begin with?" I ask.

"It's not off. He's a complicated fellow," Tom sums up in just about the simplest diagnosis I've ever heard.

"Preach, Tom," Dane cuts in.

Tom continues. "His life is in disorder, with losing his grandmother and still fairly recently going through a breakup. I wouldn't hold it against him that he wasn't ready to divulge that particular piece. You need to *talk with him*. Don't make any more assumptions with half information."

Kwan is sitting and nodding but looking contemplative. I turn to him. "You're awfully quiet all of a sudden."

He looks at me with a shy grin. "I was just thinking about my wife, Lina," he says, and it makes my heart pang, realizing that even decades later, missing her can make him so wistful. "We met pretty late, all things considered. I was a little over forty, and she was a little under. We had so much activity in those years—we never wanted more than one child, so we were a happy little trio once our daughter arrived a few years later. I was always busy with my job. We were together twenty years when she got sick. I realized the other day that I've been living without her now longer than I had her. And she was only in a quarter of my life, total. Every year that percentage shrinks a little bit."

He looks up at the clouds and gets lost in thought. None of the rest of us speak, that sentiment lingering and spreading, like a dandelion's feathery seeds once they've been blown off the stem. It's somehow so beautiful and so sad at the same time.

When he looks back over to us, I can see his eyes are shining, the memories pushing emotion to the surface. "I'd give anything to have another day with Lina," he sighs.

And that there, that one sentiment, is all that matters, isn't it? There's no regret, no oversaccharine pretending that everything was once always perfect. But it's the fact that, when we are without someone we love, the big problems don't seem so big.

Dane reaches out and gives me a shove so hard I wobble the chair. "*Ow*," I hiss back at her.

"I don't think hitting is necessary to get the point across." Tom gives a look of amused exasperation to Dane.

"All right, but let's state the obvious," Dane says and then turns to me. "You've gotta tell Eli."

"You're seeing him in London anyway, even if he doesn't know yet that it's you," Tom points out.

"Yeah, but maybe I shouldn't . . . ," I venture, my mind a knot that seems impossible to untangle.

But Dane swats me again. "Stop being so self-sabotaging. He thinks he's doing you some favor by unburdening you with his complicated life. And you think you're doing him a favor by not complicating it even more with this bonkers secret. But that's all a pile of nonsense, especially when he realizes you've been having a pseudo-long-distance-friendship-relationship for years anyway. He needs to know."

"You have to give him the *chance* to know," Kwan says.

I grab the last cardamon bun.

Because I need all the sugar I can get. It's time to try and make a plan.

CHAPTER 28

But of course, the first wisps of a plan are quickly derailed by a text I wake up to early Tuesday morning.

> J: I'm so sorry, but I don't think I can meet up when you're in London. My mum fell and broke her hip, and it's been quite a crazy week dealing with that and also arguing with my father about her care (a long story for another time). I'm not sure I'm in a position right now to steal away even for a coffee. I hope that's okay, and I'm sorry to cancel on everything so last minute—I really am. Maybe someday soon there'll be another opportunity for us to meet in person.

I try not to deflate. After all, I probably should've guessed that Eli wouldn't have time for even the party when he's knee deep in arriving home to family drama. But I can't help but feel disappointed that the easiest avenue for me to tell him has been derailed.

I also notice I have a text from my mother asking me to call her "when I'm done hanging out with my less cute and much more judgmental neighbors."

I choose to ignore that particular drama for now.

I spend the day slogging through, trying to focus on my patients. But after the few days I've had, I'm grateful I'm seeing Ari in the evening.

It's a doozy catching her up on everything, and she listens intently as I tell my winding tale. When I'm done, she leans back in her chair, steepling her fingers and tapping her chin. She looks so deep in thought I don't want to bother her.

"One of the things I like most about having therapists as patients is that I don't have to explain too much when I get theoretical," she finally says, and I'm surprised that that's where she's going after so much information was dumped on her. But she keeps talking. "I've always liked Carl Rogers and the idea of self-concept. Who we *imagine* we are creates a kind of feedback loop into how we see ourselves, and that then influences who we actually are."

"You're into self-actualization?" I say with skepticism. I can't imagine opinionated Ari thinking anyone ever actually reaches their full potential. I'd have thought she and I were in that same sort of camp of believing that we're all always works in progress, muddling through the best we can.

"Oh god no," she says with a laugh. "But I like some parts of the self-concept idea. I take the more skeptical view that striving for that is often what makes us act how we act in front of various people. The role we're playing with a particular person can really influence our behavior. So this is such a fascinating concept to me—two versions of the same person being so different."

"Happy my misfortune is interesting for you," I crack, and she laughs, as though this is a delightful experiment she's getting to undertake.

"Are you familiar with Rogers's theory of unconditional positive regard?"

"Radical acceptance without judgment," I say, nodding. "I'm not sure I buy that that kind of therapy is actually helpful to anyone."

"I agree," she says, almost looking impressed, like she's the teacher and I'm the pupil. I wonder if Ari could've been a mentor to me if I didn't, ya know, need her as a therapist. "I've always sort of thought it was impossible outside of a clinical setting, but I kind of wonder if that's what you and Eli were giving each other when writing back and forth. You had an intimacy due to the columns that allowed a sort of unusual freedom. I think one of the many reasons he was so different in reality— besides, of course, the vastly different contexts of your interactions—is that that kind of perfect acceptance is impossible to maintain when faced with actual humanity."

"I never assumed he was perfect," I counter, a little annoyed at myself for feeling immediately defensive.

But Ari waves my statement away, like that wasn't even an option. "Of course not. I think the thing that I find interesting about this whole situation is that you almost were able to perform a kind of clinical test without even knowing it. You sort of disproved Rogers's theory, because that kind of environment can't stand up to a true two-sided relationship. It's why radical acceptance could work in a therapy session, but no one in the patient's actual life could ever live up to that—and then how disappointing, right? You don't want your therapist to be the person who accepts you the most."

"Glad I could be such an interesting case study in outdated therapy theories," I mumble, and at that she smirks again, like she's enjoying the volleys.

"I always liked Albert Ellis more," she says, and I snort. Of course she'd like the therapist most known for rationality. I guess this is why we get along so well. "Focus on the moment. Take immediate action," she says with a sly smile. "Do you know what my favorite quote of his is?" I shake my head. "He said, 'Neurosis is just a high-class word for whining.'"

I give a surprised chuckle, and she just smiles.

"Look," she says, "the point I'm making is people are capable of change. And I think Eli's been trying to, just as you have. But that unconditional positive regard has to be given to yourself, first. Work on accepting *yourself*. He's been searching for that, too, and I think you've probably helped him through your writing. By having this anonymous bubble, you've been able to give each other a kind of support that's incredibly healing and motivating. That's been good, but it can't ever be enough because it's not rooted in reality. So now it's time to get to the scarier bit. And you're ready. You've known for quite some time you needed to move your life forward and stop being so afraid of failure. Do what *you* want for a change."

"Yeah, but he doesn't have time right now," I say, throwing out the easiest excuse. "He's made that pretty clear."

She shakes her head, like I'm willfully ignoring her point. "He's scared of losing you—both versions of you, even if he doesn't realize yet they're the same person—and probably also of asking too much. Figure out how to not let him push you away. I know you can do it."

The conversation plays in my head on a loop. I think about it as I try to fall asleep on Tuesday; as I tiredly get ready the next morning; as the time ticks away on Wednesday with clients. Ari's words are churning through my mind and building me up.

I'm still thinking about it in the car on the way to the airport when I feel my phone buzzing in my pocket. I pull it out, irrationally hoping it's Eli.

But of course it's my mother. I should've known ignoring her wouldn't make her go away. I have to stop hiding from everything in my life and start being more deliberate. And I guess it needs to start here.

"I text you on a Tuesday and you can't bother to reply? It's Wednesday night!" she says, the pout coming through in her voice.

"I had patients and then I had to get ready for my trip."

"What trip?"

I sigh. I've told her at least fifteen times. "To London."

"Oh, for the blog."

"The column, Mom. In a paper."

"Well, your little friend was extremely rude to me," she says, changing the subject to the one thing I know she's been dying to say. I'd love to hear her call Tom my "little friend" to his face. I can only imagine what he'd have to say to that.

But I need to fight my own battles. I'm grateful to have friends flanking me, but I need to have this conversation myself.

"He wasn't wrong, Mom," I say, bracing for the argument I've been avoiding.

"Of course he's wrong. We're your parents. We raised you. It's not a big deal for you to help us."

"I'm happy to help you; of course I am," I say truthfully. "But you can't make messes with the explicit belief that I'll just clean them up. It's not fair to me."

"That's not—"

"It is, though." I barrel forward before I lose my nerve. "I told you not to pull out tiles on your own. I even suggested a few contractors who could help you. I've also handled all the financial-planning stuff. But you don't want my help; you just want to do whatever you want without having to deal with any consequences."

"But, sweetie, we appreciate everything you do to help," she coos, as though she can soften the issue at hand through flattery, like one of the Waldos coming to lick her face after they've torn apart a cushion.

"I love you, and I'm here for you, but you guys are also capable of thinking through some of your own issues. This isn't something I can help you with," I say definitively.

"Since you're not in your apartment this weekend, can your father and I stay there?" she asks. "And the Waldos, of course."

I sigh. She's not listening. She's probably never going to listen. But I can change my own behavior. I'm going to take Ari's advice and start right here with doing what *I* want. I have to stop ignoring and obfuscating. I need to set my own boundaries.

"No, Mom," I say. "I'm happy to send you the names of the contractors again so they can fix the tile properly. But I need to focus on my trip. I love you, okay?"

She's silent for a moment. This isn't ever the way our conversations go, and I'm wondering if she has to reorient some wiring in her brain that's used to being turned off while she hands things over to me.

"Okay, honey," she finally says, acquiescing in the face of an unknown variable. "If that's how you feel."

"It is. Thanks for understanding. I love you, and I'll see you when I'm back from London."

There's so much racing through my mind that I find it hard to even attempt to sleep on the flight. It's all churning in my gut as I deplane, jet lagged and loopy, Thursday morning into Heathrow.

I breeze through the airport, quickly moving through customs and then easily onto the Heathrow Express into central London. (Way to make New York and our terrible hour-long subway ride from the airport look extra janky. Thanks, London.) From the moment I land, every conversation around me reminds me of Eli, British voices and mannerisms surrounding my senses.

It makes me *miss* him.

I'd replied to Eli's WhatsApp message on Tuesday and said I totally understood. I didn't hear from him again—in either form of texting.

But it doesn't mean I should stay silent too. If I'm doing what's right for me, doesn't that include letting other people make their own choices instead of me burdening myself to make them preemptively? If I can say no to my mother, at the very least I can say hello to Eli. He doesn't have to respond, but I can give him the chance to know I'm thinking about him.

Fuck it, I'm going to text him. I don't have to say I'm in London, and I certainly don't have to mention Eleonora, but there's no reason to not simply check in and say I'm thinking of him.

Nora: Hope everything's been okay with your mom. Just wanted to say hi.

My phone pings so quickly it's almost startling.

Eli: You're up early.

Shit. My lack of sleep made me foggy enough that I didn't even think about that. It's ten in the morning here, but that makes it five at home. But before I can berate myself for being a weirdo, he texts again.

Eli: Scratch that.

Eli: I think the response a normal person would be going for is "thank you."

I smile as the train lurches to a stop.

Nora: Who said anything about normal?

Eli: Definitely not the guy who behaved like a total chump and has been mooning around wishing he could text you after dramatically declaring "no new friends."

Nora: Well, luckily I'd already declared us friends, so I'm fully ignoring that.

Eli: Never thought I'd be so grateful for a woman telling me I'm ignorable.

I step off the train, a grin on my face, and into the vaulted openness of Paddington Station, wrought iron arches beckoning me up escalators and spitting me out into the bustle of the street.

There's some sun poking through the clouds as I make my way and walk to my hotel. I've always loved the dramatic coexistence of central London—stucco and brick-fronted mews row houses from the eighteenth and nineteenth centuries are buttressed against glass office towers that have sprung up in recent decades. The hustle, diversity, languages, and verve remind me so much of New York, but the winding streets and low-rise historic features jutting out of every corner give it its own incomparable touch.

I'm grateful for the *Look Left* written on every crosswalk as small cars, curved black cabs, and red double-decker buses zip around, fighting traffic together.

I turn onto a small cobbled road and see the white-columned-portico row building that houses the hotel I've been booked in. The lobby is all polished marble and dark wood, velvet couches lining the bay windows. It's all somehow cozy and stuffy at the same time, that uniquely British brand of elegance. Although it does have the modern touch of letting me check in from my phone, so I instantly pad my way to my room and crash onto the fluffy bed, ready to get a nap in before this afternoon's lunch. But back to texting first.

Nora: I'm glad. And I really do hope everything's going okay.

Eli: Better now.

Eli: At least until I'm changing a bedpan again.

I send a heart emoji and leave it at that. I set an alarm for an hour and doze off, sleeping better knowing that Eli's not lost to me completely, even if I have no idea how to deal with whatever comes next.

Chapter 29

When I wake up, I immediately make myself an espresso in the over-wrought, fancy hotel coffee maker and throw cold water on my face. I have those jet-lagged sensations of too little sleep matched with my internal clock being thrown off, but they're nothing that caffeine and a walk can't fix.

I mosey along the Paddington Basin canal, letting the slim redeveloped waterway guide me. Soaring buildings, quirky bars, and converted warehouses line the water, a pedestrian cocoon amid a busy area.

I stop when I get to the location of the party—when Celia said it was at a place called the Cheese Barge, I didn't realize it was going to be a literally floating barge with wheels of cheese lining the expansive windows. As I walked along the canal, I noticed a number of barges that seemed to be homes or private boats, but quite a few were restaurants or bars as well, so this isn't an anomaly. They're all fairly thin, to accommodate the canal, but the bigger ones stretch out to around the length of a basketball court. It's charming in its own particularly London specificity.

I hear Celia shout "Nora!" and I look up to see her leaning off the upper deck, waving to me. I duck inside, the interior of the barge renovated in rustic wood and metal, with those large windows showcasing the canal.

"How do I get . . . up?" I ask a hostess at the front, and she points me to a small spiral staircase.

When I get up onto the deck, I see that the reception has already begun. A crowd of fashionable people is standing around (and everyone with a drink, so I guess we're still leaning into the British lunchtime-beverage stereotype). All the food appears to be cheese related, which I don't even have a moment to wonder about before a server comes over with a tray.

"Would you like to try our infamous Westcombe curried cheese curds? Or these Stilton grilled cheeses? On the table over there is some fondue, and our delightful half kilo of baked Baron Bigod Brie."

"Oh, when you guys say 'cheese barge,' you really take that literally," I muse.

The server laughs, "Oh yes, it's truly British cheese heaven over here."

Since most of the options are paired with carbs, I'm not going to complain. I grab one of the little triangles of grilled cheese as I notice Celia making a beeline to me.

"Nora! I'm so, so glad you're here. What a *treat* to have you!" She kisses both my cheeks and then holds me at length to look me up and down.

"You're looking gorgeous as ever; love this dress," she says, and I'm pleased she's noticed my shirtdress, because it's yellow and green and patterned with horses and riders and felt particularly apropos for a London jaunt.

"It's really nice to see you, Celia," I say, surprised at how true it is. As we catch up, I find myself enjoying the break from my everyday. Celia pulls in various members of the team to introduce me to and gushes over my column, gossips about people we used to know in college, and regales me with tales from the newspaper office. I meet the new boss, Donna, who immediately releases a barrage of compliments about my column in her thick Scottish brogue, and I blush with her enthusiasm.

"Your column, by the way, really does so well in digital," she says, not letting me ever change the subject. "Not just because of the traffic—although we do see an uptick around it—but the engagement as well in the comments. Are you checking in with the comments from time to time?"

"I can't say I do," I admit. "I always thought the important rule of thumb was to *not* see what others say about your writing."

Celia cackles and gives me a squeeze. But Donna continues. "Oh, well, you should, it's just about the most amiable comments section I've ever seen. I think the earnest tone of the column attracts a certain level of civility and kindness. It's really lovely."

Celia beams, and I appreciate her enthusiasm. (It was her goal, after all, to make a friendlier advice column.) I can't help but think about the safe space the column has given for Eli and me to discuss our lives, and it warms me to think about anyone else getting to share in secret when they need to.

But it's as though Celia can sense that I'm thinking about him, because she says, "It's really too bad your copyeditor, Eli, isn't here. He's *such* a fantastic editor, as I'm sure by now you well know. He's actually the person who manages the entire copyediting and fact-checking team, but he personally does all the columns and op-eds and also all the headlines. He's been working remotely for a few months, but I was actually hoping he'd make it to the party since he's back in London for a bit. But he has family troubles at the moment, so he's not here."

"Oh, is that so?" Donna says, their conversation light and breezy, while I now stand with my inconvenient knowledge weighing me down. It's amazing to think of all these versions of a single person—Eli, my cantankerous, surprisingly layered neighbor; my beloved secret pen pal; the defensive ex-boyfriend of a client; and now the dependable wordsmith for my friend and colleague Celia. All the shades in front of me and yet currently so, so far away. The discussion is like having a ghost standing in the middle of our conversation, and the mention of him makes me ache.

"I was hoping to meet him too," Donna continues.

"I'm trying to convince him to pop by the office at least so he can say hello to you," Celia says to Donna. "And he edits for other sections, too, obviously, so I think everyone is looking forward to a little catch-up."

"Yes, everyone speaks so highly of him." Donna turns to me. "I feel so lucky to have such a crackerjack team for your column—your writing combined with Eli's precision and Celia's encouragement and guidance. You make at least one part of my job incredibly easy."

I smile, trying to ignore the lurch that's settled in with the discussion of Eli. "I hope it's been a good transition so far," I say, trying to steer the conversation away.

"Oh, absolutely," Donna says, and she enthusiastically recounts the trials and tribulations of starting over at a new paper.

I can see why Celia likes her. They're two gears that rotate together, aligned and engaged, pushing each other and hyping each other up. It's a dynamic I've never really had in my work, since therapy is so solitary. It's understandable that Celia wanted me to meet her and get pulled into the team dynamic that I've apparently been a small piece of, but unknowingly, from across an ocean.

The day drifts into afternoon, and I'm stuffed with every possible British cheese imaginable. Our party overlooks the canal as the barge slowly churns even while we stay stationary, attached to the land next to us.

When it's time to go, I wave goodbye to Donna and Celia, with a promise that I'll come in for a tour of the office tomorrow, first thing in the morning.

I've started to make my way back to my hotel, ready for a low-key night of a pub dinner and a book, when I feel my phone vibrate in my pocket. I pull it out and have to sit down to take in the messages coming through now.

J: I hope the event went well—I can't believe I had to miss a party on a barge filled with cheese. That feels especially cruel.

J: Obviously my own doing, of course.

I see the dots pop up and go away as he stops and starts his texting. Clearly he's not just sending me a message to say hello and ask how the party was. But I wait until finally another text comes through.

J: And I've kept wanting to text you to say sorry that we're not able to meet up, but then that made me feel a bit guilty because there's actually something I've been keeping from you.

J: Or . . . that sounds a bit dramatic, since you don't even know me.

J: Ugh, I'm really doing great with this—that also came out wrong. You do know me. Probably better than most people. But I meant you probably don't care one way or the other about this since we're not real-life friends.

There's another slew of stopping and restarting, and my heart pounds, waiting for whatever is coming next.

J: Christ, I'm really putting my foot in it today. I think I'm not sleeping well lately.

J: Since I've bungled that completely and implied we're not friends even though you're probably my favorite person to talk to ("talk to"), I'll just come out with it.

J: You see, I live in New York now, actually. Which I know is where you live, obviously.

J: I mean, I *am* in London right now. My mum really is ill. That's not untrue.

J: But ever since we started texting about meeting up, I've been in New York. And I've felt strange about it, like I'm keeping something from you. But I didn't know how to tell you.

J: And this week, while I've been here and wondering why I cancelled on you when I could pop out and say hello (and I'm going to have to make time for work things anyway otherwise).

J: I think it's because . . . I wonder if maybe meeting in real life will ruin whatever this is. There's something safe in our conversations. And I worry that . . . I'm a better version of myself in writing. What if we meet and you realise I'm sort of a mess? What if I lose the one person I don't wreck things with?

J: I let my nan down. My ex-girlfriend tossed me to the side. And I suspect the woman I'm in love with thinks I'm ghosting her, when really I'm too scared to be honest.

J: So the thought of losing you too feels like too much.

J: Maybe I'm saying all of this and I'm already going to lose you because you're going to think I'm completely daft and in desperate need of a good therapist (know anyone? Ha). But I hope you understand why the thought of meeting in person seems too daunting. I hope we know each other well enough at this point that you understand why I might not be able to be brave when it comes to you right now.

J: But I hope you won't stop being my friend. Because you're really my favorite friend.

I reach up to wipe away the tears that have started pouring out of my eyes.

I have no idea what to say. The words have always come so easily when I'm writing to him, but now, with this—with *all* that he just wrote—I'm left wordless.

Figure out how to not let him push you away, Ari said. But he's pushing *everyone* away, even if I completely understand being scared to upset the precarious balances of your life. I've always been that way too—keeping people at arm's length, letting my parents keep behaving the way they always have. It's daunting to upset your status quo.

I know I have to find a way to get through to him. But it can't be over text. I can't just spring this entire scenario on him when he's not ready for it.

I need to sleep on it.

I'm going to stick with my original plan for tonight: I'm going to find a pub where I can get good and drunk. And I'm going to read a book where I already know the ending so at least one thing can feel contained and simple.

But first, I'm going to text Eli *something* back. Because I know there's one thing I can still say to reassure him, even if he has no idea it's all about to get upended either way.

Nora: We're still friends. I hope we'll always be friends.

Chapter 30

When my alarm goes off the next morning at ten, the world feels fuzzy.

Fuzzy because of jet lag. Fuzzy because of the three beers I had last night. Fuzzy because I can't stop spiraling over what Eli said, even in my sleepy first thoughts.

My favorite friend.

The one person I don't wreck things with.

The woman I'm in love with.

Is it possible for your heart to ache along with your head? Because that's how I'm feeling this morning. There's no amount of coffee in the world that's going to solve that.

I also look at my phone and see texts from a group chat inexplicably titled "The Noranators." I open it up to see Kwan, Tom, and Dane mostly debating the name and seeing it constantly changing within the chat.

Tom Rich named the conversation "Team Nora"

Dane: Tom, that's extremely boring

Tom: The goal of the chat is not to have an exciting name. The goal is to check in on our gal and see how she's faring.

Dane Jane named the conversation "Team Get Nora Laid Again"

Tom Rich named the conversation "Nora's A-Team"

Dane Jane named the conversation "Dream Team for Nora's Extremes"

Kwan: I feel a little left out that no one has taught me how to change the name of a group. I'm still picking up emoticons.

Dane: It's emojis

Kwan: No one told me that either.

Tom: This isn't the point of this conversation.

Tom: Dear Nora, please keep us updated on how it's all going. How was the party? Have you reached out to Eli? Do you need any moral support from us? The name is a work in progress, but the sentiment is still there. Love, Tom, Kwan and Dane.

Kwan: Even I know you don't need to write an introduction and a sign-off in a text message.

Tom: I just wanted to differentiate the portion that is merely us squabbling vs the part where we are actually addressing Nora. She's probably already asleep, so when she wakes up I don't want her to have to sift through this. She can just look for her name.

Dane: The logic is not logic-ing.

Kwan: Also don't know what that means.

Kwan: Also, Nora, since we're addressing you directly: George is doing great. He even licked Lucy's paw today, which was something I never thought would happen. It might be an accident. It might be some psychological way to assert his dominance. But I'm going to assume it's friendly until proven otherwise. He's a champ! Don't worry about him for even a second!

Tom Rich named the conversation "The Noranators"

I chuckle as I manage to sit up and swing my feet off the bed. It's a start.

There's something comforting about having this motley crew checking in on me. We're all certainly bumbling, but we're bumbling together.

I drag myself into the shower and manage to get dressed. The English breakfast I ordered myself, with greasy sausage and mushrooms smushed together with saucy beans and inch-thick toast, is helping immensely. It might also have something to do with the double espresso.

But I finally pull myself out the door and walk my way over to the *Sunday Tribune* office, silk black-and-raspberry eighties skirt swishing along and making me feel mildly put together.

When I arrive, the front desk buzzes and sends me upstairs, where Celia is waiting for me the second the elevator doors open.

"Oh, I'm just dying to introduce you around," she says, linking her arm through mine and immediately making me feel like a part of her orbit.

It's fun to trail after her for an hour, stopping into various cubicles and offices and seeing her gush over every single person on her team. Everyone is "an absolute wizard" or "completely ace" at their jobs. I'm not surprised she's convinced me to keep writing over the last seven years when I see her persuasiveness in person again.

And for an office setup without any razzle-dazzle—a newsroom bullpen is about as slapdash and filled with reams of paper as one might imagine—she seems to enjoy pointing all the various areas out. *Here's where the layout people work; here's where the researchers hole away; here's everyone's favorite conference room, because you can see that sliver of the river in the view.*

By the time she's walking me out, I'm energized and distracted far more than I thought I could be today.

That is, until we turn the corner heading back to the entrance and Eli steps out of the elevator.

It knocks the wind out of me. I've been thinking about him for days without reprieve, and suddenly without warning, he's movement and physicality right in front of me.

He's rolling his shirtsleeves up, so he doesn't immediately clock us. It's strange to see him like this, so out of context and yet so perfectly at ease. You'd never know this was a man in the middle of emotional crises on multiple fronts. There's no sign of wear from taking care of an ailing mother; there are no worry lines from distressing text conversations. There's just brash and bold Eli, coming into an office to check in on his colleagues, geared up and ready for whatever the day throws at him.

But then he looks up, and his face pales. His eyes dart from me to Celia and back again. His brow furrows, and I ache to kiss it better.

But I can't. Because this isn't how this was supposed to happen. This wasn't supposed to be how he found out this decidedly brain-melting information. He doesn't have a Dane to run to in his walk-of-shame clothes so that he can spiral out of sight. He doesn't have a therapist to overindulge with on psychological theory. He's the island of Eli, without anyone to process this with and standing in the middle of his *office*. I wonder if he can see the regret on my face.

"Oh, Eli!" Celia says, blissfully unaware of the mental detonations happening for the other two people in the conversation with her. "I'm so glad you could stop in and meet Donna today. I wasn't sure if you would! How's your mum?"

Her expression is so sincere that he can't keep glancing back at me, even though he clearly wants to. "Um . . . she's well. Well, not *well*. It's a hard recovery at her age, and it was a pretty major surgery. But she's doing better than we expected, so it feels on the right trajectory."

"I'm so glad to hear it," she says, reaching out and patting his arm. He seems scorched by the touch, as though he forgot for a moment that he's a person in a body.

And then her eyes light up as she realizes the introduction she gets to make. Or at least, what she thinks she's doing. "And oh my god, it's also such serendipity, because this is Nora! Or rather, Ask Eleonora, as it were. She came into town for the party yesterday. Isn't that so neat?"

He's totally stone silent for a moment, almost to the point of it being awkward. It's like he's a computer in the middle of a reboot. But he catches himself, clears his throat, and starts talking before it becomes too much. "'Neat' is definitely, most definitely, the word I would use here, yes. Definitely," he says, eyes boring into me, that placid mask he's so good at projecting now covering any hint of what he's thinking.

"I . . ." I have no idea what to say. I didn't know what his reaction was going to be even when I was expecting to get the chance to proactively explain it. Now I'm left looking to him like . . . like I lied? Like I knew? Like maybe I *didn't* know? Does he think I'm just realizing this in the moment as well? "Hi, Eli," I finally say.

"Oh, it's good you two are connecting now, because actually . . . !" Celia turns to me like she's realized something else delightful. "Nora— he lives in New York now, and he really doesn't know anyone. You should show him around! He's living downtown, too, so you'll have to show him all your favorite places."

"Yes," I say, trying to figure out how to telegraph what I'm thinking to Eli without making anything awkward in front of Celia. "I've only very, very recently put that together," I say pointedly.

"Did you?" he says now, still blank, still impossible to read.

"I . . ." I take a deep breath, not knowing how to salvage this. And then a light bulb turns on. "I'm actually really excited about the most recent Ask Eleonora letter I got," I say, hoping that I can somehow get enough wits about me to not scare him off but also not confuse Celia.

"Yeah, it's about a woman who accidentally reads a text on the guy's phone she just slept with. And she realizes they actually work together, but she didn't know it because they were always virtual. And um . . ."

I have no idea how to move this along. Our situation is too specific, too improbable. This was a bad idea.

"And did she keep it from the guy?" Eli asks, his mask slipping just enough to an expression aching as much as my head was this morning, and my heart sinks. I don't know what he's thinking right now. I don't know how to salvage this if he thinks I was texting him under some kind of false pretenses.

"No," I say emphatically, hoping he hears the desperation in my voice. "She doesn't know how to tell him. She doesn't want to confuse him, and he apparently has some of his own personal stuff going on, but she . . . she really cares about him and doesn't want to spring it on him when he's not ready to hear it. Or she didn't, anyway. It's . . . yeah, it's not what she expected."

"Why are you really excited about that?" Celia asks, clearly not following my sort of nonsensical tale. "I mean, she should just tell him what she knows, big whoop."

"True, true," I say, fidgeting now, wanting to scream out to make Eli realize that this is all a big misunderstanding.

"I mean, if he has personal stuff but still slept with her, doesn't sound like it's *that* big of a deal," Celia reiterates. I'm not sure whether to laugh or cry at the absurdity of this conversation.

"Well, I think it was before he had the personal stuff . . . ," I mumble.

"You're definitely going to have to edit that letter down—it sounds long and complicated."

"For sure," I reply, not able to look at Eli for fear that this is spiraling in the wrong direction.

But before I can either dig the hole deeper or somehow fix it, Donna comes waltzing in. "Oh good, Eli!" she says, pleased to see everyone gathered. "I'm Donna. Security buzzed me to let me know you're here. Want to come into my office so we can catch up? I'm so grateful you were able to make the time this morning to say hello. I heard about your family troubles, and I'm so sorry."

"No problem at all," he says.

"I'm glad I caught you at first glance. I had quite a tartle with one of the designers earlier. It's been so hard remembering so many new names!"

And I can't help but look at Eli when she says what I know is his favorite esoteric and normally unused word. And I see his eyes flick immediately to me.

But as she waves him forward, there's nothing to be done but for him to follow her. He walks slowly, like his joints have stiffened, but he's moving. As he walks past and away, he looks back to me, and I have to stop myself from grabbing for him. I want my expression to convey everything I'm feeling.

I'm sorry I didn't tell you the minute I figured it out.

And the thing that's the scariest, but the one that's been pulsing under the surface since the minute I saw him walk through the elevator door: *I love you. I love every version of you. Please let me have them all.*

CHAPTER 31

I'm staring at my phone.

Maybe if I stare at it long enough, it'll come up with the words that I need to say.

I waved goodbye to Celia and left the office in a stupor. And for the last hour, I've just been walking. Walking and staring. Letting London swirl around me while I can't take any of it in.

I wandered past the upscale houses and the shops standing at polished attention in Marylebone, past painted brick and through pedestrianized cobbled roads. I meandered through the open greenery of Regent's Park. Elegantly spaced-out trees shaded the joyful murmurs of picnickers; bikers and runners and groups of friends churned past me as I just kept walking.

I walked and walked, waiting for the movement to make my limbs feel again.

I'm waiting for the blood to come rushing back. I'm waiting to know what to do. But I don't know. So I stare at my phone, and I walk.

I walk across the patchy London park grass that never seems to fully fill in, perhaps because of too many cloudy days like this one. I walk past black lampposts and along carefully paved pathways. I give a wide berth to the zoo and go past a playground. And I find myself finally walking up an incline, just as a light drizzly mist hangs in the air.

I get to the top of Primrose Hill and look out on the city. I sit on a stone bench, etched with a William Blake poem. A small beagle runs around in front of me, collecting a ball over and over as his owner throws it. It adds a jolt of life into the view out onto the London skyscraper skyline that's now laid out before me, touching the clouds as the gray day continues unabated.

It matches how I'm feeling. A lot of awe and a lot of gray, all stretched out ahead.

The exhaustion of the walk is starting to kick in, and I stare at my phone again, for the umpteenth time, trying to decide what on earth I can possibly say.

I finally type out, Can we talk? Whenever you have time? And hit Send.

For the first time, writing to Eli seems harder than speaking. And maybe it's because now I know that to really understand him, I need to see all the parts of him that react to my words. I know the grooves in his smile when I say something amusing to him. I know the way his throat bobs when he nervously swallows. I know the way his forehead crinkles when he disagrees but doesn't want to admit it. I thought I knew him through just his words—and I did in a lot of ways; I knew so much about him—but I want it all. I want all the parts of him that he was afraid of showing—the messy, inept, unhideable pieces—along with the words.

So I kept my only message to him short. Because I can't just type and retype a message. I need him to react. When he reacts, he brings out *my* messy, inept, unhideable pieces. Eli gave me acceptance when he wrote as J, but it was his needling in person that pushed me to actually do what Ari's been trying to get me to do for years and accept that whole version of myself. And I never realized how much better I am when all those parts are on display.

As though I'm willing him to respond by still staring at the phone, I see a typing bubble pop up. It starts and stops and starts again. This should be considered a form of slow torture. Especially because now I know that I'm getting the measured Eli, the safe Eli. The Eli in writing is honest, but he's not raw.

And I just have to wait.

But after what feels like an hour (and is probably only about two minutes), a message comes through.

Eli: Can you meet at the botanic gardens at Kew?

Where even is that? I open my maps app and type it in. Directions to the Royal Botanic Gardens pop up. Two trains that'll take a while, but it's straightforward enough.

Nora: Of course. I'll be there in a little more than an hour.

He doesn't respond, just sends the location.

The mist has turned into a drizzle now, and I'm glad to be walking to the Tube, ferreting myself underground as quickly as my legs can take me. That numbness I was feeling has been overtaken by inertia and adrenaline.

Is he upset? Glad? Confused?

I hate that he's not writing. The person each of us would always write to about our problems has now turned into the person we need to see in person. I guess we were both left knowing that this wasn't a conversation to be had anywhere but face to face.

I unfortunately have a whole hour to stew in it. I sit on the out-dated cloth design of the train seat and fidget, picking at the hem of my skirt, unable to decide what I'm possibly going to say.

I'm relieved to get off the train and wander up to the grand Victoria Gate, the columned entrance with its intricate wrought iron gates leading me into the botanic gardens. I pay my entry fee and walk inside, having swapped one of London's leafy respites for another on the opposite side of town. I look more closely at the pinned location Eli sent. It's listed as the Temperate House, and so I meander my way there, past a columned temple and down a wide tree-lined path that—according to my map—has an old pagoda at the end of it.

But the glass-and-iron building rises out in front of me, and it's impossible to ignore. It's as long as an entire city block, with white filigreed metal encasing giant windows, large ornate columns topped with stone urns standing sentry. Greenery surrounds it, the fanciest greenhouse I've ever laid eyes on.

I walk inside, and the misty gray of London ceases to exist as I'm transported into an interior jungle. It's like if Paddington Station's vaulted ceilings held every tree imaginable instead of trains. Straight lines and curves surround leaves of every style. The sudden shift in humidity prickles my skin.

I look around, drinking it all in, and then my eyes land on the one thing I'm actually here to see.

Eli sits on a white bench, staring out at the visual in front of him, his elbows on his knees and his hands on his chin, like he's completely lost in thought. His body is taut like a rubber band, ready to move at any moment. His shirtsleeves are still rolled up, and his hair is mussed, as though he's run his hands through it over and over in anticipation. Without knowing anyone is watching him, he's dropped his mask, the vulnerability of waiting etched into him.

Seeing him like this gives me a sudden pang, a realization that I shouldn't always read the endings of my books. I don't want to be a person who always keeps everything safe. Life is meant to be lived. Books end—they have a trajectory and then a conclusion—but people go on. Messy, predictable, messing-up people. We fall down and get up with no guarantee we won't fall down all over again. Nothing is tidy, and there are no neat bows. Each of us is a hundred different versions of ourselves with different people, and they all converge into a single flawed human.

But when we have someone to share all the mess with, whether it's a group of friends texting us in the middle of the night or a lover curling around us sleepily, it makes the journey a bit more sheltered.

I want to share the mess with Eli.

So with that determination, I walk straight up to him. And when he sees me, he looks up and gives me a soft, sad smile.

"Hey there, Eleonora," he says.

"Hey there, Jarvis Eli, otherwise known in some writing applications as 'J,'" I explain, and he closes his eyes and nods, putting that particular piece of that puzzle to rest.

"When did you realize?" he asks, looking straight ahead again, as though he's not quite ready to look at me continuously yet.

"Monday morning," I say quietly, and at that he snaps his head in my direction, stunned.

"*This* Monday?"

"Yup."

"Like . . ." He trails off.

"Yup."

He slides a whistle, taking that in.

"I woke up before you and heard a phone beep, and I thought it was mine, but then I saw a text from Celia about Ask Eleonora, and it *wasn't* on my phone, and I started to wonder."

"You texted me Monday morning," he muses, almost as much to himself as to me, those puzzle pieces more fully turning into a shape.

"I wanted . . ."

I'm embarrassed, but he finishes for me. "You wanted to see if my phone lit up if you texted 'J'?"

"Yeah," I sigh.

"And it did."

"Yeah."

"And so you ran away?" he says with a smirk.

"I walked over to Dane," I reply, and he chuckles, I'm sure now able to picture the scene. "I needed to talk it out with someone. I was so shocked by the whole thing—I mean, what are the odds?"

"You didn't want to talk it out with me?" His voice is small.

"Well, I did actually, once I was coming back," I continue, taking a deep breath. "But then . . ." I trail off.

"Then I told you about my mum and said I was leaving," he says as he realizes.

I nod. He leans over and puts his head in his hands, running his fingers through his hair again, as though taking all of it in is hurting his brain.

I can't help but wonder what's going on in that swirling kaleidoscope of a mind of his. But before I can even theorize, he stands up.

"I want to show you something here," he says, grabbing my hand. His is warm in mine, and it makes my heart pound, like there's a string of hope now knotted between us. He drags me a few feet and then stops in front of a flower.

It's a showy one—lavender-lobed petals fan out, with spindly dark-purple tendrils above them, making a circle of dozens of the thinnest jazz hands you've ever seen. Rising out of the center is an elongated stalk, with ornamental and multipronged stamens pushing out on every side. I've never really seen a plant like it.

"It's called a passionflower," he says, and I snort.

"*Is it* now?" I smirk, and he shakes his head with a grin, as though he's disappointed in me but can't help but be amused.

"That's not the important part," he says pointedly. "This is the plant that makes passion fruit actually; it's a tendril climber."

"As a New York City kid, you're losing me with the plant knowledge, I have to admit," I say with a grimace.

"Eh, it just sort of means it's like a weed." He shrugs. We both stare at it for a moment, the whole plant beautiful and wild. But he continues, clearly having some point to get to, even if at the moment I can't quite fathom what it is. "This was my nan's favorite flower," he says, staring at it with a sad smile. "She said she loved it because it can be so many things. It has evergreen leaves all year, so a lot of the time it really does just look like a vine that can cover walls or a fence. Then it has the buds of the flower, which look like they'd just contain quite a normal flower. And then all of a sudden, they bloom, and you have this completely insane, vibrant, wiggly thing. When it goes away, you think that's it, but then a few weeks later you get these egg-shaped basic-green fruits, and *then* when you open them up, they're surprisingly practically neon-yellow, with black seeds."

I nod, starting to understand where he's going with this. "They have a lot of sides to them," I say.

"They have a lot of sides, yeah." He pauses and breathes in the humid air. "No one in the building seems to remember it, but Nan had a few of these plants on the roof when I was a kid. She had two chairs and two planters, and she'd sit upstairs with me, and we'd read books and she'd have a gin and tonic and I'd have a soda—which felt pretty exciting because my mother never let me have anything sugary. And because each flower only lives for about a day, there's only a couple weeks a year when they all come out on any given plant. So she would always get really excited about it. She once woke me up out of bed to say the first one bloomed, and we ran upstairs together to see. She told me the plants reminded her of me, because in the right conditions they open up and then once you think you've figured them out, they surprise you. After she died, I wondered if I'd lived up to that assessment."

He reaches out to touch the leaf of one of the flowers, tender, like the memory is right in front of him.

"I think she was absolutely right," I whisper.

"Yeah?" he says, turning back to me.

"You're full of surprises, Eli Whitman," I chuckle. "There's so many beautiful pieces of you that some people are lucky enough to see all of."

He gives me a small smile and turns back to the flowers.

"That's what I was building the planters for, by the way. Dane says there's only a few varietals that'll grow as far north as New York City, but I ordered the ones she recommended. I think they're the ones Nan used to have."

"There's so much Dane didn't tell me," I grumble, and I love the laugh that unintentionally hiccups out of him at that.

"But we have said quite a lot to each other over the years," he whispers. He turns to face me and gently tucks a strand of hair behind my ear, the small movement flint enough to practically set my whole body on fire. One finger lingers at my jaw.

"Apparently so," I respond, holding my breath in and wondering what comes next.

"I know . . ." He pauses and breathes deep, as though he's got to get ready. "I know you kind of already know what I've been thinking, because apparently I texted you all my internal thoughts," he says, his cheeks turning red in a way I've never seen before.

"I wasn't trying to deceive you or not tell you—" I try to explain, but he cuts me off.

"I know that," he says thoughtfully. "When I ran into you this morning, it really blew my mind."

"I know the feeling," I chuckle.

"My first thought was about those texts from yesterday."

I nod, knowing exactly all the lines he must be thinking about, because they're the ones I woke up with blazing through my mind.

My favorite friend.

The one person I don't wreck things with.

The woman I'm in love with.

I can see it written all over his face too. But he continues. "I was so embarrassed that you knew all my inner thoughts. It was like having your crush find your diary. Every insecurity, every fear . . . all the pieces I don't show anyone. I'd somehow already shown them to you. Only to you."

He blows out a steadying breath, like the realization is happening all over again. "But as I sat there, ignoring poor Donna—who, by the way, let me leave pretty quickly, because it was fairly obvious my mind was somewhere else, and thankfully she assumed I was distracted over my mother—I started to think about all the implications of you knowing everything you knew. I started to think about how over the last few months, I found myself opening up to *two* people. And one of them I'd suspected I was falling in love with, even if she probably still mostly despised me."

The words zip through me and steal the air from my lungs, because even though he'd written them yesterday, there really is something entirely different about hearing them said aloud. The words were speaking louder once again and making my heart pound.

He doesn't seem to notice the effect he's having on me, though, because he keeps going. "And all the while I'd been also wondering how this person I was writing to had unexpectedly become my best friend—this therapist, who I *also* spent a lot of time wondering about. The first person other than Nan I'd felt comfortable sharing pretty much everything with. And suddenly, what seemed like a total impossibility almost felt like an inevitability. I wasn't opening up to you in person because writing had made me more open; it was because you were *you*. You were always the person I wanted to talk to. So once I'd sort of mentally processed it, the first feeling was relief. But then the fear came back, because I remembered everything I'd said before, and . . ." His forehead wrinkles as he's lost in thought. "I guess I'm mostly wondering what you were going to say before I ruined everything by bolting on Monday?" he says finally.

And I laugh, because of all the things he could be wondering, that's absolutely the easiest.

"I was going to tell you about how a few months ago I told my therapist that I might be going insane because I was in love with someone I hadn't even met."

His eyes widen, and I adore watching that statement roll over him, like a tidal wave of information, the implications crashing and settling in.

And then he pulls me close.

Unlike our first kiss—frantic and reckless—this one is sure. It's full throttle, needy, but undoubting. It's hands in my hair, gripping like they're never letting go. It's deep sighs and hungry gasps and—a whistle from a bystander that makes us break apart with a sheepish grin.

"I think the botany lesson is over, yeah?" He smirks.

I grab his hand. And hastily pull us both back outside.

CHAPTER 32

I'm glad we're back in my room, because I was a little worried we were going to get thrown off the train. I'm not sure I've ever appreciated New York having express trains, but taking the Tube and having to stop at every single station while extremely turned on is just about the most torturous experience imaginable.

Especially when Eli wouldn't keep his hands off me, and I can't pretend I was doing a particularly good job keeping mine off him.

We stumble inside my little hotel room, and the hour of unintentional train foreplay means everything happens fast. The only thing he takes his time with is the button of my skirt, implicitly understanding that I might not want more clothes damaged. But otherwise it's shoes kicked off, shirts thrown to the side.

He traces my jaw and whispers, "I love every version of you," as though he can hear my thoughts from yesterday.

Desire takes over. Desire for each other; desire for closeness; desire to touch and feel and let go. He's on top of me and weighting me down, and I'm desperate to be nearer. It feels like nothing will ever be enough, even as we move together, touching, kissing, grasping on to each other like life depends on only this moment. I don't know how sex can feel feral and tender all at once; unbearably fast and exquisitely slow; undeniable yet still brand new.

But when it's over, we're both left gasping for breath, still hanging on, as though we both need to come down from the high of the earthquake we both unleashed.

I'm so sated I almost fall asleep, lost in the haze of delirium.

But after a few minutes he rolls onto his back, pulling me with him, and I squeal in delight. My head is on his chest, and I can hear his contented sigh echo through me.

"I have one question, just to make sure I've got this whole thing straight . . . ," he says eventually, and I roll over so I can look into his eyes. His hand lazily twirls a piece of my hair around his finger, and the whole scene feels like a perfection I couldn't have imagined even a day ago. "I told you to never surrender to your neighbor . . . who was me."

I burst out a laugh, and his eyes watch the movement, his mouth curving to one side in amusement at my reaction.

"Oh my *god*," I finally say when I can breathe again. "Yeah, actually. You did."

"Karma really always gets you in the end, apparently," he chuckles. "Couldn't just be a smug bastard, I also had to be committing the worst own goal of all time."

"It worked out okay," I say, reaching out to touch his chest, somehow needing to not let go of whatever is tactile between us. He nods and nuzzles into me, seeming to have had the same exact thought.

After another few minutes of just breathing together, he finally pulls back. "So, what happens now?" he says.

"Well, I told Celia and Donna I'd go for a drink with them once they were done with the day."

He shakes his head. "Much as I do want to trap you in this room for the remainder of your time in London," he says, miming a small bite to my shoulder before pulling back, "I meant . . . what happens now with you and me?"

His voice is casual, but his eyes are full of questions. This is the part that writing never could top (along with, obviously, the sex and nakedness). He's not a person who can be fully viewed without all the shades and layers on top of his words. He's *nervous*. Even after all this, after everything we've said, he's still waiting for a confirmation. On the surface, Eli would strike anyone as someone you'd have to be careful getting involved with. But below, it's clear that I'm going to have to be careful for *him*.

"Whatever it is, we'll make it work," I say calmly, taking his hand in mind, tangling us together. "You'll be here for however long you need, and I'll be in New York, and we'll talk and it'll be fine."

"That's it?" he says skeptically. "You're just fine with someone far away and distracted and probably stressed out? You don't think that's overly optimistic?"

I kiss the tip of his nose. "You love every version of me, yeah?" I ask, and I love seeing the way he blushes all the way from his cheeks to his chest. I love getting this vantage point.

"Yeah," he says softly.

"Okay, well I feel the same way. I loved you when I only got to talk to you once a week in different time zones through a work document. I think we can make London to New York work with texting, video calls, and regular phone calls. We'll talk it through, and we'll make it work."

"What about sexting?" he says with a smirk, nibbling on my earlobe again and making me sigh.

"Yeah, I think that can be arranged too," I say, as he rolls back on top of me and fully ends the conversation.

I stumble out of the hotel a few hours later to meet Donna and Celia for drinks. I don't think either I or Eli wanted to leave our little single-room sanctuary, but he needed to get back to his mom and I didn't want to cancel on the people who are the reason I'm on this trip in the first place. We make a plan to meet back up at the hotel after we're both done, and it already isn't soon enough.

But I'm also looking forward to seeing Donna and Celia again. It was invigorating to watch them work this morning. I'm really grateful to be a small piece of their success.

I spot them when I arrive, already nestled at a table in the sleek bar where we'd agreed to meet up. We all order a round of drinks and convivially chat about everything and nothing.

When the drinks are set on the table, Celia raises her glass. "To you, Nora," she says, and we all cheers. "I'm so happy you came out for the event yesterday. It was really special to introduce you to everyone and get to show you around."

"Aw, thanks, Celia," I say, touched. "It's been a real pleasure to get to see you both in action."

"I'm so glad you feel that way," Donna says, leaning forward. "Because actually, one of the reasons we wanted to take you out tonight is that I have a proposition for you. We're leaning heavily into adding additional forms of storytelling, and we want to start doing more podcasting that complements the pieces we already have. We'd really love for you to do more with us. We want you to not only have your column but also do weekly call-ins and advice podcasting. And then that in turn can become more content through transcripts and social posts. It wouldn't be anonymous in the way that your column is, but I think this is a huge opportunity to grow your brand and really expand what you're doing. What do you think?"

I'm completely thrown off. They're both looking at me so expectantly, as though they've just given me a huge present and they expect me to jump up with excitement. And of course, because I'm me, I can't say something disappointing.

"That's really a very cool idea," I reply, trying to say anything while the thought swirls in my mind.

"Oh, I'm *so* glad you think so!" Celia says, clapping her hands together. "When Donna mentioned it to me, I thought it was brilliant. So here's how it would work . . ."

I hear her launching into logistics and ideas. They all do sound like great concepts. If the column is doing well, why *not* expand it? Why *not* make the personality jump off the page with a real person? Why *not* create a live space for that kind comments section to come to life?

But all I feel while listening to them is the unique growing sense in my gut that this is just not for me. I love my life as it is. I love working with people one on one and seeing them grow and improve. I love my simple predictable schedule. My column is amazing, and I can't imagine my week without it. But it's a side project. It's the supplement to my work, not the piece I'm hoping to grow larger.

I expect the anxiety to set in—that specific people-pleasing fear of how to possibly make the people around you happy, even though your wants are diametrically opposed to theirs.

But for some reason, today I don't feel it. For some reason, this doesn't feel as hard for me as I suspect it would've at another time. All I can think of is Eli nudging me, telling me to *never surrender*, even though this time it's not accidentally advice against himself. I think of Tom calmly telling my mother no. And I think of myself, taking Ari's advice and making the kind of unimaginable leaps toward my own happiness I couldn't have fathomed a few months ago.

I know what I need to say. And while I hate disappointing these fantastic women, I have to do what's right for me.

"That's such an incredible plan, ladies," I say, steeling myself. "But I just don't have the bandwidth for that. I don't want to have to compromise for my patients. My schedule is quite full the way that it is, and if I was going to do this with you I wouldn't want to only be partially in. I really hope we can keep the column, because I adore doing it. And I of course wouldn't mind if you had another therapist doing the podcast and relating it back in some way—because it definitely could be a really great resource for people. I just don't think I'm the right person to execute it right now."

I can see the way they both deflate a little bit. I can't pretend that there isn't a small piece of me that wants to shout, *Just kidding! I'll do it!* But they're both incredibly gracious. They wave it off, and the night keeps going with ease. We chat about their work and their lives in London. They get my advice for where to go on their next jaunts to New York. I learn all about Donna's kids and what it's been like since the last one left the house for university.

The night is easy, and I squeeze them both extra tight when we leave a few hours later.

I walk back to my hotel, the mildly crisp air of a London summer evening glowing along with the lamps that dot the street. When I get back, I crawl into bed with my book.

A few hours later there's a knock on the door, and I open it to Eli, leaning against the doorframe and looking delectable.

"Hi," he says, coming in for a quick kiss that turns into something a bit longer.

"How was the hospital?" I ask, moving aside so he can come in and kick his shoes off. He immediately reclines on the bed and stares up at me. When he doesn't respond for a minute, I ask, "What?"

"I just was thinking how unbelievably surreal this is. You're just here, and you're *you*, and I get to waltz in here and tell you about my evening like that's completely normal and easy."

"It *is* normal." I shrug, plopping down on the bed next to him. "It's just in person instead of over text or while walking a dog."

"Okay, then maybe it's the easy part I'm not used to," he says quietly.

I give him another kiss, soft and simple, and then rest my head on his shoulder. "So how was it?" I ask.

He sighs, and it's weary, the happiness of our earlier revelations today having bled into reality as the afternoon went on.

"They're keeping her in the hospital for another couple of days because of her age and their worries about her stability. My dad is still trying to push her to look at facilities, and it feels like we're silently in a war with each other while we both pretend to be completely fine in front of my mother. It's exhausting."

"Sounds exhausting," I agree.

"I just need to get her home and take it from there," he says determinedly.

"I think one step at a time is a great plan."

"You're much more agreeable as a girlfriend than as a neighbor," he teases. And then his eyes go wide, and I can almost anticipate the meltdown that's incoming. "Not that we . . . not that you want . . . I just . . ."

I stop him from blabbering with a kiss. "One step at a time is a great plan," I repeat with a grin. "But that doesn't sound so bad."

His eyebrows rise, and I wonder if the goofy grin on his face is what mine looks like too. "Yeah?"

"Yeah," I agree, as he rolls me over to give me another kiss.

"I can't believe you're only here for another day," he groans. "This *timing*."

"It'll be okay," I say. And then, testing our new in-person honesty limits, I venture out on a limb with the one question I really want to know. "Do you have a sense of how long you think you'll stay once you get your mom home?"

He's silent for a minute, distracting both of us easily with light kisses across my shoulder. But then he looks back up. "I don't know," he says. "I can't let my dad just put her somewhere. As long as he's unwilling to oversee her care, I don't really know how I can be anywhere but here until she's fully back on her feet. It's such a slippery slope—once someone goes in one of those places, it's hard to get out, you know?"

I nod, wanting to be supportive. "Well, maybe it's a silver lining if you were homesick for London anyway."

He tilts his head at me, like he's not computing. "I'm not homesick for London," he says.

"You're not?" I ask, one of my last niggling questions now weaseling its way to the surface.

"No, I actually love New York."

"All the baking and . . . I don't know, sometimes you just seemed a little sad to be there," I point out.

A wistful look of understanding washes over him. "No," he says with another kiss to my shoulder, like if he doesn't touch me every so often, he'll stop believing I'm real. "I'm homesick for Nan." He takes a deep breath. "The last few months, I've been missing her terribly, so I've been trying to do the things we used to do together, like the baking and the planters. I just miss her. But New York makes it better, strange as it sounds. It's comforting to be in her space, even if it's hard sometimes."

I wrap my arms around him, grateful to now know. Grateful that my biggest fear—that he'll want to stay here, in London—is unfounded.

"Well then, you've got to focus on getting your mom home, settled and healthy. And then you need to actually have a real conversation with your dad about your feelings. No more silent wars."

"Do I get free therapy now if we're dating?" he says, and I can hear the smirk in his tone. I sit up and give him an exasperated look.

"Okay, for my mental and ethical ease of mind, we are making it *extremely* clear that I was not your therapist for quite a long time before any of this started and even then it was only a few sessions. So no, never your therapist again. Besides, it's not *therapy* if it's just advice. I can't help that I'm trained to communicate."

He narrows his eyes gleefully. "Trained to communicate—*except* when it comes to parents! I'll have a heart-to-heart with my dad when you finally sit your mother down and set some boundaries."

I know he thinks he's got me pegged, but I'm thrilled that—even if it wasn't my own doing—I have him beat. "Actually, you'll *never* believe what Tom said to my mom . . ."

It's amazing how much we laugh all night. It's surreal how much we have to say to each other, as though in person we just get to be exactly the same as we always were, but now with truly nothing between us anymore.

And when we fall asleep together that night, I know that even if the next few months look unconventional, we'll be able to handle whatever comes our way.

CHAPTER 33

I love New York in early September. Everyone is running around in back-to-school mode while ignoring the fact that it's still hot and summery outside. The college students are back and wandering around the neighborhood, overtaking the streets around Washington Square Park by walking in nervous packs, afraid to strike out on their own yet.

Mostly I love that the farmers' market is still in a full vibrant color explosion. The line for tomatoes at the Eckerton Hill stand snakes around as people choose between the peak heirlooms and Sungolds. You can smell the peaches as you walk by the northwest corner of the market. And the late-August lull of having everyone away is replaced by dogs circling children, even as a musician still sings about summer loftily at the entrance.

And on this late afternoon, everyone is lingering, as though they know the good times aren't going to last and we need to soak it up while we can. It's even making Kwan seem to walk more slowly. But it's been a lovely afternoon meandering together, and we're both enjoying stopping at every stall and observing and chatting. Lucy is sniffing every dog she can find. George, of course, hates it. He hates the conflation of heat and crowds, so this particular moment is his actual worst combination. He gives everyone a side eye as he trots past, as though he's personally offended by their reappearance back after their beach trips and summer sojourns.

"Did you know that Gladys actually knows quite a bit about plants?" Kwan is saying, and I snap back to attention.

"Gladys in our building?"

"Yeah, I mentioned I was keeping up Eli's planters, and she gave me some pointers. Honestly, I could've used her advice a few weeks ago in the heat wave, but I'm definitely in the learning curve! Dane may have gotten me started, but I'm doing pretty well now."

"That's really great," I reply, happy to know that Eli's original project is still proving me wrong so many months later.

"I think next spring I might put a few planters up there for myself. I may actually set some up in the next couple of weeks, because Gladys says this is really the time to plant bulbs. I know we did Eli's bulbs for next summer, but I hadn't really considered it for myself."

I don't have to respond, because he's delightedly distracted by some buffalo mozzarella from Riverine Ranch, even though it's the same mozzarella he's purchased every week for the better part of a decade.

The truth is, every mention of Eli feels like another poke in the ribs, and it's all making me sore. I miss him. We've chatted every day, but it feels like we're living in some suspended animation, waiting for our life to begin. We had New York as friends, and we've had writing from a distance, but we've yet to get the whole package in one place—save for our dreamy weekend in London. I want it.

But I can't *say* that I want it, because I already know we both do. He has to figure his family things out in his own time. And I know he's made leeway. His mom has come home, and his dad has started to soften ever so slightly. He keeps saying the right opportunity for a real conversation about the future hasn't come yet, and I'm definitely not going to push him. Aging parents aren't something we can handle like bulldozers, and I'm glad Eli, of all people, sees that.

So we catch up on FaceTime and send each other notes throughout the days. We compare what we're baking and watch movies at the same time. Slowly but surely, I think Eli's starting to settle in to the idea that I'm not going anywhere.

And I've leaned on my expanded friend group to keep me sane while I wait for his return. Case in point, before coming to the market, Kwan wandered with me down to Librae Bakery to get scones before we swung back up here, because I wanted to do some research on flavors so I can work on my own recipe. He might've ribbed me for shifting my carb allegiance to a British baked good, but I enjoy the teasing. And he's not wrong—the scones *are* for Eli. It gives me something to work toward for when he comes back.

I finally drag Kwan away from the cheese, and we make our way home.

"Can I come upstairs with you and have a coffee?" Kwan asks.

I'm tired, and my introvert social meter might be ready for a break even if I don't want to disappoint him. But on the other hand, a coffee does sound good. I start to say "Sure," but he cuts me off.

"Don't tell me to come up if you don't want me to," Kwan chides. "I'm a big boy; I can make my own coffee."

I laugh but shake my head. "I appreciate it, but now you've sold me on the idea. Come up for a few minutes, and then I'm going to kick you out when I want to curl up and read alone."

"Sold," he says with a grin.

But when I open my door, I'm stopped in my tracks. The whole apartment smells like something delectable is baking, and Dane and Tom are sitting at my kitchen table, already drinking cups of coffee.

And Eli is here.

Eli's adorably, haphazardly wearing one of my aprons, folded so it's just around his waist, and he's cleaning up what looks like the remnants of a dough. A rack with scones is sitting to the side, cooling.

He barely has time for his crooked smile to form before I'm barreling into him, flinging myself fully around him, arms around his neck and legs around his waist, and he quickly grabs hold tight, not giving any signs of letting go.

I kiss him like he's a mirage in a desert. He tastes like coffee and scones and smells like my shampoo.

"How are you *here*?" I say, burying my face in his neck.

He carries me over to the counter and sets me down, stepping back to look me up and down. "So, incredibly, there are these things called 'airplanes,' and they carry you across an ocean."

I swat at him, but I'm so distracted I pull him back into a hug. "You're hilarious. Seriously, why didn't you tell me you were coming back?"

"I wanted to surprise you," he said. "And I settled everything yesterday and couldn't wait another minute."

"So how did you . . ." I trail off, remembering that we aren't exactly alone. I turn to look at Dane, Tom, and Kwan, all watching delightedly. Dane's smirking a little more than Tom and Kwan, but even she doesn't seem to be immune to this sappy gushing session they've just witnessed.

"The man wanted you to come home to scones, and who am I to stop him?" Dane shrugs.

"I promised her I'd give her a scone if she let me in," Eli whispers in my ear, and I snort.

"And *I* was the distracter!" Kwan says proudly. "I don't know if you noticed how slowly we walked to Librae—"

"Oh, I noticed."

"Well, it was a great suggestion because it took a lot of time. Although I almost ruined the surprise when you said you wanted to buy scones, because that just felt too kismet."

Eli turns back to me. "You bought scones?"

I grab the filled bag and hold it up. "They have feta dill, and fig and fennel. I've been practicing making them, and no one ever said research hurt."

"You've been practicing?" he singsongs, knowing it's clearly for him.

"I thought maybe you'd miss them whenever you got back," I admit.

He scoops me up again and kisses me, tilting me back. I hear Tom say, "Ahem," and Dane gives a low wolf whistle.

We begrudgingly break apart to the good-natured teasing of our friends, and Eli sets me down in a chair at the kitchen table. He darts over to grab the scones, and then we all settle down at the table.

Everyone catches up with Eli for a bit while I just sit back, happily munching on a scone and watching the whole scene unfold.

Eli is *here*. He's here, making scones, in my apartment, enveloped by my friends. Friends that I've let into my life. Friends that conspire with my boyfriend to surprise me. With my beloved carbs.

I'm not sure life could get any better.

After half an hour, Tom nudges Dane and Kwan to leave, and they all grab some scones to go and make their exit.

When the door closes behind them, I take Eli's hand, still beaming from his unexpected immediacy.

"I previously would've said we've had enough surprises for a lifetime, but I think this one was pretty great."

He kisses my hand and holds on to it. "I can't help wanting to get a reaction out of you." He pulls my chair closer and lifts my knees up so he can drape my legs over his lap. "I'm really, really happy to be back."

"Are you here just for a visit?" I ask, not wanting to get too excited too fast.

He grins and shakes his head. "I had a long conversation with my dad last night, and I've got to say, you might be onto something with that communication and listening stuff you're always talking about."

I roll my eyes, and he cackles, enjoying goading me as always. But then his expression softens a bit. "No, actually, before you nudged me, I'd never really considered just . . . asking him? Just saying 'Why is this what you want' and being willing to listen. I never quite realized how *scared* he was. Scared of aging; scared of not being able to keep up; scared of failing and not having anyone to ask for help. I think he thought if he was responsible for my mother at home and he got frustrated or tired and needed help, he'd be stuck. And that fed into everything else that's looming for him about not wanting to retire and feeling like he isn't sure what to do in the next stage of his life."

"That's . . . wow, I'm so glad you talked to him about it," I say, wanting to just wrap him up in a hug but trying to take my own advice about listening first.

"I also don't think he quite realized that we *could* have those kinds of conversations. That combativeness is a well-honed skill, you know?" he laughs, an edge to the thought. "We've always communicated like that, and so we each gave it back to the other. Telling him I wanted to listen I think shocked him, actually."

I smile. "I can only imagine."

"But it shocked me too. It was . . . it was really good. And we cleared the air, and he agreed to keep up the system I've put in place with the home nurses and the check-ins. And my sister says she's going to come down more often. I'm going to go back every four or six weeks or so over the coming year so she has support and he has some down-time. But yeah. It's all worked out. I'm home."

"'Home,'" I repeat—a word so joyous I can feel the stretch in my cheeks.

"*You* feel like home," he says quietly, running his fingers along my smile, tracing the happiness he's unleashed. "These last few weeks away . . . I thought writing to you or calling you would be enough, since we'd done it for so long with so much less. But that wasn't enough anymore; I want it all now. I meant what I said before—I love London, but this is where I belong. I love you, Nora."

"I love you too," I whisper.

He gives me a quick kiss and then pulls back to look at me, his fingers tangling further into mine as though he needs to keep some physical tether.

"What happens now? Now that you're home?"

"Yeah, I'm thinking we start a new construction project," he says. "What do you think? Duplex? I'll just bang a hole between our apartments and build a staircase?"

I snort a laugh, because the mischief in his eyes tells me everything I need to know. "Didn't this all start with you getting a little overzealous with construction tools?"

"I think you know we started well before I moved into the building."

"Fair enough." I squeeze his hand back. "For now, though, I think I'm just going to relish having you one floor away instead of across an ocean."

"On that we can definitely agree," he says, pulling me to him and wrapping his arms around me.

"Welcome home, neighbor," I whisper, and then there are no words left to say for tonight.

EPILOGUE

"We have an announcement to make. We're getting married!"

After a moment of shock, I shriek and throw my arms around Kwan.

It's a glorious sunset on our roof tonight. The clouds contain those painterly sherbet shades, pinks and oranges dancing across the New York City skyline. The July mugginess hasn't set in yet, so it's still that perfect level of warm without hot. And now that Eli's had a year to really build out his rooftop dreams, I have to admit that there are very few places I'd rather be on a night in the city.

His planters are in full bloom, his evergreens overtaken by colors, and finally today the passion fruit flowers started blossoming. I was a little worried he might get emotional about it after how long he's built it up, but the only over-the-top thing he did was insist on carrying Paws and Whiskers upstairs because he thought they'd appreciate seeing them again, since his grandmother *must've* shown the original flowers to them. I didn't want to point out that it's fairly impossible to think these cats were alive the last time she'd had flowers up here, so I dutifully carried one cat while George begrudgingly walked behind us.

I've spent most of tonight trying to stop Eli from burning everything on the grill to a crisp. I distracted him with his favorite Strongbow cider, which he was completely delighted to find could be purchased outside of the UK.

And it's mostly been pretty light and convivial. Dane, Tom, and Meryl enthusiastically agreed to join our Fourth of July barbecue and bring other dishes so we wouldn't just be stuck with Eli's grilled meats. ("Although," Meryl said to me when I invited her, "I'd probably agree to anything that man asked me for." She wiggled her eyebrows in a way I'm not sure I wanted to see.) Every other neighbor we mentioned it to promptly said yes as well, so we've got Aretha's cookies, Hearn's eclectic craft beer selection, and a few other bottles of wine from the residents of the second and fourth floors.

I was surprised that Kwan and Gladys were late. In recent months it was heartwarming to see how much time they'd been spending together. What started as Kwan's plant project to supplement Eli's quickly became an obvious ploy to hang out with Gladys. And when Gladys started claiming a real interest in walking Lucy in the hopes of seeing if she wanted a dog, it started to be fairly clear that they both were looking for excuses to keep seeing each other. I don't think I'll ever get tired of hearing Kwan proudly and bashfully say "my girlfriend."

Although apparently we're all going to have to change that word.

"He asked me a few hours ago, and of course I said yes." Gladys beams, looking up at Kwan like he's the most romantic man who ever lived. "We're thinking of eloping later in the summer, because there's no time to waste. What's the point at our age?"

"No more lonely hearts in this building, that's for sure!" Meryl whoops.

Someone turns on Ray LaMontagne's "You Are the Best Thing" and turns the volume up on the little portable speaker Dane brought.

I feel someone wrap their arms around my hips, and I turn around to see Eli.

"I was really hoping that was you."

"I wouldn't put it past Hearn," he laughs with a wink. We start swaying to the music, and I loop my arms around his neck. "No more lonely hearts, eh?" he says. "Do you think Meryl meant us, too, or is it just reserved for the elderly crowd?"

I bury my face in his neck and breathe him in. I want to bottle this moment, because while nothing in life is foolproof, the journey feels so much easier right now. The loneliness I felt last year, trapped up on this roof with Eli, seems like an entire world away. All those versions of myself that were sometimes at odds and contributed to that lonely feeling—daughter, friend, reader, therapist, patient, girlfriend—are becoming more honest and closely related. I can give different things to different people, but I'm working on obfuscating less. I'm learning to stop adjusting for others.

Ari would say it's because, outside of work, I've stopped always trying to solve everyone else's life and have started enjoying my own. Dane would say (and has, too many times to count) that it's because I'm getting laid on a regular basis. But I'd probably embarrass her by pointing out a lot of it actually has to do with being supported by her. It's not only true but it would also shut her up. Kwan and Tom would get a big portion of that friendship pie at this point too.

But if there was ever a metaphor for letting people in, of course Eli would've been the wordsmith to inadvertently come up with the perfect one: we're actually moving ahead with his duplex plan. What started as his favorite joke—about playing telephone between our apartments or adding in a fireman's pole—soon became an idea he was casually looking into. It started with a few articles about apartment combinations ("Hey, Nora, look at the photos of what these people did! That spiral staircase really doesn't reduce the square footage almost at all!"), and eventually ended with a dinner party where a friend who was an architect pulled out a measuring tape. When I asked him if he was serious, he looked at me with shining eyes and said, "Only if you really want me to be."

And in that moment, I knew I truly did. I've spent my whole life bending to fit other people, making myself smaller when someone needs me to be, or picking up their slack when they don't want to carry it anymore. And I like being reliable. I like being a steady hand for people who live their lives a little wilder. But I want to be an equal. I want to build a spiral staircase between two identical apartments and let combining two lives double our capacity—neither person taking any more or accepting any less.

Our life isn't perfect—I can't control my parents, I can't make my brother step up more, and I can't solve everything for my clients the way I would like. Eli's mom's health is still a concern, and he and his dad haven't magically resolved all their issues. And the thought of making George permanently share space with Paws and Whiskers is truly keeping me up at night.

But I've stopped reading the ends of my books first. I finally feel like, for the first time in my life, it's okay to not know what the ending looks like.

So tonight I'm going to dance on my roof with all my best friends, toast to our futures, and go home with the man I love. And those sound like the best words imaginable.

UNLIKELY STORY–INSPIRED RECIPES

I always love writing about my home of New York City, and I'm equally grateful to also be able to travel in this book to London. I lived in the UK for four years in college and now continue to visit as much as possible to see beloved friends, so it holds a special place for me.

I adore including recipes in the back of my novels because it allows you to continue experiencing the story on a sensory level long after you've finished reading. There's so much of New York and London coursing through Nora and Eli, and their food is a big part of it. We see Eli embrace the cornbread Nora makes with her seasonal Union Square farmers' market ingredients, and we see Nora trying to make a shepherd's pie after Eli mentions it. Food brings them together throughout the story and then so perfectly when they reunite over scones.

So I hope you enjoy cooking these recipes that are so close to Nora's and Eli's hearts. Maybe trying the recipes will make you want to take a trip to New York or London. But if you can't get to the market or onto the Cheese Barge, then these are the next best options.

STRAWBERRY-RHUBARB CORNBREAD

Besides my beloved scones, my favorite simple baked good to make is cornbread. And this version, with spring's best gift, is tangy perfection. If you can't find rhubarb, you can swap it for almost any fruit you enjoy—there's something about the nuttiness of cornbread and a tart bright flavor that sings. Just don't let everyone steal it from you the way Dane and Eli do to Nora.

Makes 8 servings.

Ingredients

1 cup coarse yellow cornmeal
1 cup all-purpose flour
1 teaspoon baking soda
1 teaspoon coarse salt, plus additional
1 large egg
1 cup milk
1/2 cup plain yogurt
1 tablespoon honey
1/2 cup chopped strawberries

4 tablespoons butter
4 to 6 large stalks of rhubarb

Preheat the oven to 400 degrees Fahrenheit and put a cast-iron skillet into the oven. Combine the dry ingredients in a bowl. Add the egg, milk, yogurt, and honey to the bowl and carefully combine, then add the strawberries last and gently mix them in.

Remove the skillet from the oven and put the butter in—make sure to coat the bottom and the sides. If your skillet doesn't appear to have a significant layer of melted butter, you can always add more. Lay the rhubarb down at the bottom—if it is long, you can trim it and lay the extra pieces in. If your rhubarb is particularly large, you can also cut the stalks in half. Pour the cornbread mixture on top and place in the oven for 20 minutes or until the cornbread is ready. Allow it to cool for 5 minutes and then flip it so the rhubarb is on top. Serve warm.

SHEPHERD'S PIE

Shepherd's pie is a classic British dish that I gave all the warmth of Eli's beloved mother, because that's how it always has made me feel. It reminds me of the time I spent living in the UK and how warmly I was accepted into my friends' homes. Unlike the crust an American potpie has, shepherd's pie has fluffy, delightful mashed potatoes on top. It makes it one of those foolproof dishes that someone *would* pine over if they were living away from home. Eli's lucky that Nora figured it out, and now you can make it too.

Makes 4 to 6 servings.

Ingredients

Topping
1 1/2 pounds russet potatoes (2 large), peeled and cut into chunks
3 tablespoons unsalted butter
1/4 cup milk
1 egg yolk
Dash of salt

Filling
2 tablespoons butter

1 chopped yellow onion
1 cup chopped carrot
4 garlic cloves, minced
1 pound ground lamb (or beef if you would prefer)
2 tablespoons flour
1 cup beef broth
1 tablespoon Worcestershire sauce
1/4 teaspoon ground cloves
Dash of salt and pepper
3/4 cup peas (fresh or frozen)
1/2 cup corn kernels (fresh or frozen)
2 tablespoons chopped fresh parsley
2 tablespoons chopped fresh rosemary

For the topping, preheat the oven to 400 degrees Fahrenheit. Bring a large salted pot of water to a boil. Add the potatoes and cook for 10 to 15 minutes until the potatoes are mashable. Drain the potatoes and then add them back into the empty pot, along with the butter, milk, egg yolk, and salt. Mash the potatoes until everything has combined—they won't be as creamy as your typical mashed potatoes, but don't worry: that's how they get browned on top. Set the potatoes aside.

For the filling, place a large oven-safe pot on medium-high heat and add the butter. Once it melts, add the onion and carrots and cook them until they start to brown slightly, approximately 3 to 4 minutes. Add the garlic cloves and lamb and allow them to brown another 3 to 4 minutes without stirring too much. Add the flour, broth, Worcestershire sauce, cloves, salt, and pepper and bring to a boil. Reduce the heat to low (so that the boil will turn into a simmer) and cook for 10 more minutes. Turn the heat off and stir in the peas, corn, parsley, and rosemary. Place the mixture in a glass baking dish and then top with the mashed potatoes, ensuring that they are spread evenly.

Place in the oven on the middle rack and bake for 20 to 25 minutes or until you see the mashed potatoes start to brown on top. If your oven is the kind that doesn't brown things effectively, you can turn the broiler on for the last minute to get a bit of that browning. Remove from the oven and allow to cool at least 10 minutes before serving.

Stilton-and-Fig Grilled Cheese

The Cheese Barge is a real place that a friend took me to, and it has remained a restaurant of my dreams ever after. Its menu has a few variations on the classic grilled cheese, so I wanted to include one of my own in an homage to the Cheese Barge's brilliance—using a British cheese, of course. I love a creamy strong cheese paired with a fruit, and figs give the perfect edge of sweetness to this combo.

Makes 2 grilled-cheese sandwiches.

Ingredients

4 fresh figs (or 1/4 cup fig jam)
2 tablespoons salted room temperature butter
4 slices bread of your choice (around 1/2 inch thick)
3 ounces Stilton (a little less than 1/3 cup, but it doesn't need to be exact)

Heat a large skillet on medium-low heat. If you're using fresh figs, mash them up in a bowl. Spread butter on one side of all the bread slices, then flip them over and spread the Stilton evenly across two of the slices. Add the figs and then top with the remaining bread slices.

Cook the sandwiches for around 3 minutes on each side, or until the bread has browned and the cheese has melted.

BLACK-AND-WHITE COOKIES

I love how we see so much of Eli's love of New York through his adoration of the classic black-and-white cookie, so I thought it was imperative that anyone who wants to travel via cooking have this recipe. Black and whites have always held a sort of bizarre place in cookie iconography. Considering their texture and icing, surely you'd be forgiven for believing they might veer more toward mini cakes than cookies—but that's what makes them seem so uniquely New York. A little odd, a lot delicious; distinctive but beloved. This is my take on one of the city's best treats.

Makes 12 to 16 cookies.

Ingredients

Cookies
3 cups all-purpose flour
1/2 teaspoon baking soda
1/2 teaspoon baking powder
1/2 teaspoon kosher salt
14 tablespoons unsalted butter, refrigerated

1 cup granulated sugar

2 large eggs

1 large egg yolk

3/4 cup buttermilk

1 tablespoon vanilla (preferably paste, but extract is fine)

Icing

1/2 cup heavy cream

2 teaspoons vanilla (preferably paste, but extract is fine)

3 1/2 cups powdered sugar

1/2 cup dark cocoa powder

Preheat the oven to 350 degrees Fahrenheit and line two baking sheets with parchment paper.

Whisk the flour, baking soda, baking powder, and salt together in a large bowl. In the bowl of a stand mixer (or a large bowl with an electric mixer), beat together the butter and sugar for 2 minutes until it looks fluffy. Add the eggs and extra yolk slowly, mixing as you go, and then mix in the buttermilk and vanilla. Add the flour mixture slowly to the bowl, a quarter of it at a time. You should scrape the sides down between each batch of flour. Only mix until just combined (you don't want to overmix here).

Using an ice cream scoop (1/4-cup size is best), scoop the batter onto the baking sheet. Keep in mind the cookies will spread, so leave room between them. Place the cookies in the oven and then cook for 16 to 18 minutes or until just cooked through. Remove from the oven and allow the cookies to cool.

While the cookies are cooling, make the icing. In a bowl, mix the cream, vanilla, and sugar until fully combined. Put half the icing into a different bowl and add the cocoa powder to this bowl, along with a few teaspoons of water. Mix together, adding more water as you go until it's the consistency of the other icing.

To ice the cookies, use an offset spatula (or carefully use a butter knife and a ruler) to cover each half of the cookie, one side black and one side white. Let the icing set for at least an hour.

Passion Fruit Mousse

Come on, you knew there had to be some passion fruit in here, right? Some people find Eli's favorite fruit intimidating, but this recipe makes it easy by using store-bought pulp—although you could certainly buy the fruit fresh and make it that way; just be sure to strain the seeds. Otherwise, this is one of those delightfully simple make-ahead desserts that seem fancier than they are.

Serves 6 to 8.

Ingredients

2 cups passion fruit pulp (you can use passion fruit concentrate if you can't find the pulp)

1 14-ounce can coconut milk

1 tablespoon honey

1/2 cup room temperature water

1 envelope unflavored gelatin (approximately 1 tablespoon)

1 cup Cool Whip (or whipping cream)

Mint leaves to garnish

Combine the passion fruit pulp, the coconut milk, and the honey until smooth. Set aside. Boil 1/4 cup of the room temperature water. While the water is coming to a boil, combine the remaining 1/4 cup of room temperature water with the gelatin. Let it stand for 1 minute to rest, and then add the boiling water. Stir constantly until it is completely dissolved. Combine the gelatin with the passion fruit mixture until fully incorporated. Then fold in the Cool Whip to the mixture. Pour into ramekins (or small cups if you don't have ramekins). Top with a sprig of mint (or chopped mint if you prefer). Cover with Saran Wrap and refrigerate for at least 2 hours before serving.

ACKNOWLEDGMENTS

I'm going to start with my mother again, since I want to keep making it easy for her to find herself: Hi, Mom! Love you. Thank you for being my biggest cheerleader.

I have two other extremely important cheerleaders who did not give birth to me but definitely gave birth to this book (that phrase sounded less gross in my head, but I'm going to run with it). Lauren Plude: All the babkas for you! Thank you for being so firmly in my corner, for not being scared off when I text you anxious questions, and for your perfect insights that make my books soar. I'm so grateful you're my editor. And to Wendy Sherman: You're the guide I would trust blindfolded. You're the agent with the best professional advice but also the friend who listens. Thank you for being the powerhouse you are.

Thank you to Lindsey Faber, the developmental editor of my dreams. I truly feel like getting to work on three books with you has given me more of a master class than any writing program ever could. You make me better, and I just could not be more appreciative of how much you pull out of me (in also the gentlest, kindest of ways!). Thank you so much to Anna Barnes for so brilliantly copyediting this ode to copyeditors. And to Bill Siever, for being my original copyediting friend, even if you gamely took on proofreading duties here. Thank you, Karah Nichols and Nicole Burns-Ascue, for ensuring that the edits ran so smoothly.

Because a book comes out so long after these acknowledgments are written, I want to also say thank you to the team who shepherded *Alternate Endings* into the world. Jessica Brock, Allyson Cullinan, Courtney Greenhalgh, Kristin Dwyer, and Stef Sloma—thanks for your championing of my words. Thanks also to Katrina Escudero for taking my stories to the next level—I feel so lucky for your support and patience with me.

For fiction to shine, it has to be rooted in some realities, and I am forever in debt to the people who took the time out to make sure my writing reflected some important realities where my knowledge base could only take me so far. Camilla Hammer, thank you for making Dane's urban gardening as accurate as could be. I'm sorry my black thumb will never get to put your brilliance and expertise to use. Chana Sacks, I've always been lucky that you've tolerated my medical questions in everyday life, but I'm extra lucky you took the time to noodle through Eli's illness with me (when I know you have many more-important patients to be concerned with). Abbey, thank you so much for the therapy insights and making sure I didn't go off course with all the therapy speak I am absolutely not qualified for! Thank you, Hannah Campbell, for ensuring that Eli sounded properly British and that I didn't humiliate those who dutifully taught me during my years in the UK. I hope you and the rest of the Team enjoy my *Love Actually* defense, even if you'll roll your eyes at the Strongbow.

I am forever indebted to friends who double as early readers and pull no punches. Juliet Izon: Where do I even begin for this book? You not only read it and then spent an inordinate amount of time indulging me talking through changes, but you also propped me up when things outside my writing began fraying. Thank you, and I can't wait for people to get their hands on *yours*. Nicole Campoy Jackson, you have patiently read everything I've written over the last few years and never once batted an eye. Thank you for your insights and your friendship. And thank you to Maya Rodale, who let me go from a fangirl to a friend and so kindly didn't blink when I handed her an entire book. How lucky am I to have had your perfect, precise feedback on this story?

I might get a bit maudlin here, but one of the best parts about having books come out has been seeing authors I admire read them and share them. Holy smokes, I can't believe I've had writers like Tia Williams, Lynn Painter, Kate Clayborn, Fern Michaels, Emma Barry, Jenn Comfort, Elizabeth Bard, and Tarah DeWitt write blurbs for my writing. I'll keep thanking them forever. And I want to give an extra-giant thanks to Tarah and Emma and also Olivia Dade for letting me vent and share and for being (dare I even believe it?!) my friends. What a truly incredible bonus for this writer who is an unapologetically devoted reader first.

This book has two character names that were chosen by people who donated to an auction for an amazing organization—Artists Against Antisemitism. Thank you, Mimi and Lauren, for your donation and for bestowing Meryl with such a perfect name. I hope your book club enjoys reading about her. I'd say thank you to my brother, Will, for winning the bid on the item where you got to name an annoying character, but really I have to mostly acknowledge Will O'Hearn, who was a good sport about having a friend like my brother, who enjoys pranks. You're always invited to my house, Hearn!

Speaking of character names, this book is in part a twenty-first-century nod to one of my favorite films—*You've Got Mail*—and as such, the Nora in the book is an ode to Nora Ephron. I'd give anything to get more of her words, but I'm so grateful for the ones we have.

Thanks always to my family for all their support—my mom and dad; my sister, Annie, and my brother, Will, and their spouses, Jon and Skye. And Yehuda, Natalie, and Aaron (and always with Rachel on our minds). I'm the luckiest.

So much of this book is about what makes up a home, and that answer is luckily easy for me. Early-morning sleepy snuggles, dancing in the kitchen, New York adventures, dogs on laps, and even the chaos of arguing kids make up the busy tornado of my homelife, and I couldn't be more grateful for it all. Guy, Rae, and Joy, you're my center. And Daniel—over twenty years in, and you're still my favorite person. I can write imperfect people having their love stories because we've proven it's real. Love you.

ABOUT THE AUTHOR

Photo © 2022 Melanie Dunea

Ali Rosen is the bestselling author of *Recipe for Second Chances*, a novel about which *New York Times* bestselling author Fern Michaels said she "couldn't turn the pages fast enough." Her second novel, *Alternate Endings*, was named an Amazon Editors' Pick.

Aside from loving to escape into fictional worlds, Rosen is also the Emmy- and James Beard Award–nominated host of *Potluck with Ali Rosen* on NYC Life, as well as the author of cookbooks like the best-selling *Modern Freezer Meals*, *15 Minute Meals*, and *Bring It!* Rosen has been featured everywhere from the *Today* show to the *New York Times*, and she has written for *Bon Appétit*, the *Washington Post*, and *New York Magazine*.

Originally from Charleston, South Carolina, Rosen lives in New York City with her husband, three kids, and rescue dog. She can usually be found wandering the Union Square Greenmarket or curled up in a chair reading a romance novel.

Connect with Ali online via her website (http://ali-rosen.com), Instagram (@ali_rosen), or X (@Ali_Rosen).